# LANDED GENTRY

## THE MEDICI SQUADRON

Jacquelyne Morison

Medici Publishing
Cheltenham

ISBN 978-0-9929973-9-7

Published by Medici Publishing in 2023

Cover design by GermanCreative

# CONTENTS

# PART I
## DISTANT THUNDER

*Win by persuasion not by force.*
**Greek proverb**

### INGRID'S ARRIVAL

Ingrid Durbine drove through the wrought-iron gates into the Havercoyne Stanley estate owned by Cuthbert Gansville-Stubbs. She wished that she had, at least, run a wet cloth over her clapped out mini but it was too late now. Tentatively she approached the enormous front door of Havercoyne Grange but, in doing so, she assumed an air of confidence and composure. She reached up to grasp the heavy brass knocker and she banged loudly on the oak door so that the noise seemed to reverberate on the outbuildings in the distance.

"Ah, you must be Ingrid," declared a heavily pregnant woman as she struggled to haul the heavy door open.

Ingrid hastened to assist her fellow woman by pushing the door open herself as she replied in the affirmative.

"His Lordship will be ready for you shortly but do take a seat in my office please while I just take a few details."

The present incumbent in the secretarial post then led Ingrid into the main office to the right of the front door and just off the entrance hall. Ingrid sat down on a black velveteen-covered hard-backed chair which was indicated by Cuthbert's secretary while the woman laboriously returned to her own seat behind her desk. Ingrid observed that it would not be long before a new member of the human race would be inhabiting the planet.

"I'm Louise Fulham-Price," obliged the woman behind the desk, "and, of course, as you see, I shall be off on maternity leave soon for six months. And so, we're looking for my temporary replacement while I'm away."

Ingrid nodded her acknowledgement of Louise's statement.

"Your credentials look very much as if you'd fit in here well. And you come highly recommended. I've discussed your career resumé with Lord Gansville-Stubbs and he seems quite keen to meet you."

Ingrid now felt that she ought to take charge of the conversation and so she made her own contribution to the discussion.

"Well, I've worked on several large estates up north as you'll have seen and I'm not unfamiliar with working for the landed gentry. I also grew up on a large farm myself."

"Yes, that's why you were called for interview, Ingrid. Your experience should prove very valuable to His Lordship."

Louise was, in fact, lying through her teeth because there had been very few applicants for the post and so far all had turned the job down when it had been offered once they had met the peer of the realm himself.

"And when is baby actually due?" asked Ingrid who wanted to turn the conversation towards a topic which she knew Louise would relish.

Louise blossomed by stating that baby Harrison would be due in late March but that she would want to leave as soon as her replacement could be recruited.

"A spring baby. How wonderful!"

"Yes, I'm looking forward to unloading this little fellow," stated Louise as she patted her bump and smiled wistfully.

"Your first?"

"Yes. But I think he may be premature if what I feel like just now is anything to go by."

Ingrid emitted a warm and womanly smile.

"Would you be ready to start soon?" asked Louise.

"Certainly. I left the Foxfield estate in November and I've been travelling since then. I've always wanted to do a bit of globetrotting and the opportunity arose for me to work in Paris for a while. But now I'm back and raring to go again."

"I understand," said Louise who realised that Ingrid had actually answered some of her outstanding questions about why she had left her previous employment at Foxfield estate and why she had not gone directly into another job. Louise also suspected that Ingrid Durbine had private means and so a gap in her career history would not be at all unusual.

"You also come highly recommended from Dunbar Appointments plc and so that will certainly act in your favour should you wish to join us."

"Can you perhaps outline the work of the estate for me, Louise?" asked Ingrid who did not want to hang around chatting inconsequentially for too long.

Louise then explained that most of the vast twenty-acre estate was devoted to rearing cattle and sheep. There was also a vineyard, an orchard and a kitchen garden together with a number of fields for crops. The stables housed His Lordship's racehorses but there was ample space for these animals to wander and to graze freely. A part of the house in the west wing was also open to the public as a museum but His Lordship's quarters and the administrative offices were quite safe from public invasion.

"And is your trainer employed here full-time or does someone come in from outside?" interposed Ingrid.

"Oh, we have a full-time trainer who owns the Braxwood Yard in Grayling Wood about five kilometres from here. The horses train on the surrounding hills. The horses are taken to Ian Manningbury's every morning where he or one of his staff to do the runs and the gallops."

"So you employ farmworkers and stabling staff? Am I right?"

"Yes, and, of course, there is Byron Travers our live-in estate manager who runs the place generally. And we also have a housekeeper, Elizabeth Garrick, who has her own complement of workers."

"I see. Just wanted to get a picture of who's here and what they do," stated Ingrid.

"I understand. Of course, your work would be as secretary to His Lordship who needs secretarial assistance for his personal correspondence and private business affairs."

Any further chat between the women was interrupted by the arrival of the man himself. Talk of the devil and all that.

His Lordship was tallish with steel-grey hair, a fetching moustache and a permanently mystified expression. Cuthbert was an aristocrat and no mistake. He had obviously seen better days in his youth but now he had the tedious job of running the family estate in order to upkeep it to an acceptable standard and to earn a crust for himself and his family. All this weighed heavily on Cuthbert's shoulders.

"Good morning, Miss . . ." began Cuthbert.

"Ingrid Durbine, your Lordship," supplied the newcomer to the establishment.

"Yes, of course. Please come into my office. Louise, can you please see that we're not disturbed for a while?"

"Certainly," replied his pregnant secretary who obviously comprehended the routine.

Cuthbert led Ingrid up the stairs to an office-cum-library on the first floor. He asked her to take a seat which Ingrid was relieved to do after her long climb upstairs. I don't suppose Louise relishes this ascent too often just now.

Cuthbert immediately moved towards the drinks cabinet but then he thought better of it. I'd better not advertise my need for alcohol so early in the morning.

"Can I get you some coffee, er . . . Ingrid? That's right, isn't it?"

Cuthbert was presumably not a great one for names. Ingrid ignored his forgetfulness as she agreed to take some black coffee which the peer poured from a coffee machine on a table near to his desk. The coffee was hot but tasted putrid and so Ingrid simply let it get cold and left it on Cuthbert's desk. I shall have to teach his nibs how to make coffee obviously.

The office was very untidy and the furniture had seen better days. The chattels had probably been in the family since the time of King Arthur.

Ingrid noted that the contents of the room would doubtless have had some value once but now it would only be best used as firewood. No respectable auction house would touch such dilapidated lots if given the choice. But then Cuthbert might as well use the assets in the room for himself as the cost of replacing this furniture would probably be prohibitive.

"So, you have worked for old Johnny Gatesbull at Foxfield's then?" began Cuthbert.

"Yes. I worked for John for about two years before I went travelling in Europe."

"You did the grand tour then?" he chuckled.

"No, I just did some travelling and then took up an office job in Paris for a couple of months. I returned recently to settle here."

Cuthbert was not really listening because he was locked in his own reverie.

"Met old Johnny several times at race meetings up and down the country, you know. He had some splendid winners. Excellent thoroughbreds. Pretty Picture and Firebrand were his best stallions. Pretty Picture died at Epsom – terrible, terrible business. Firebrand is now out to stud, of course. And Bricking Over and Gallant Knight were wonderful too. Saw them race many times. Beat my best every time."

Ingrid switched off. Oh, my God, will I have to endure all this horsey stuff if I get the job?

At last Cuthbert came back down to earth and he began to interview Ingrid in earnest. He asked no further questions about Ingrid's background, much to her relief. But he spoke in very general terms about the role which his secretary would undertake. Apparently Cuthbert's new secretary would be responsible for handling his correspondence, organising his diary, keeping an account of his spending, liaising with staff on the estate and making travel arrangements. So what's new? Ingrid also wondered what else she might be asked to do which had not been listed. Keeping his wife amused? Collecting his dry cleaning? Mucking out the stables? But she decided to cross that bridge when she came to it because she needed the job very much.

Cuthbert's business interests ranged from running the farm, investing in property deals, hoping to get a grand national winner one day and playing the stock market to acting as a non-executive director for a number of companies who sought to acquire his prestigious name for their headed stationery. Although, as a hereditary peer, Lord Gansville-Stubbs was entitled to sit in the House of Lords, he seldom bothered his ugly big head with this obligation.

Cuthbert eventually stopped talking about himself and he asked his interviewee how soon she could start. Ingrid noticed, however, that Cuthbert had not actually asked her if she wanted to work in this dishevelled and threadbare environment. Does this mean that I've got the job then?

"Are you offering me the job then?"

Cuthbert merely murmured agreement and frowned. What a stupid question. I'm desperate to replace Louise.

"I could start almost immediately, if you wish," Ingrid confirmed, eager not to lose the moment. "I'm just staying at a B and B locally and so could start at any time to suit you. I'm sure I can get permanent accommodation in the village easily."

"Well, you see it's very difficult right now with Louise just about to drop a colt. And so I'd appreciate it if you could start as soon as possible."

"When would you like me to start then?"

"Next week if you can. Louise will show you the ropes and then she can leave to have the sprog."

If Cuthbert had actually made a joke, it was lost on Ingrid.

"I'd like to think about it," lied Ingrid, "but I'll let you know later today."

"Very well, then. Good. That's all settled."

Ingrid found the walk downstairs easier than the climb up. Cuthbert told Louise that Ingrid was going to think about joining the firm and then come back with an answer later that day. Ingrid hence shook hands with Cuthbert and she besought Louise to take care.

"So what did you think of Ingrid?" enquired Louise after the interviewee had departed.

Cuthbert looked a bit puzzled by this question.

"Damn fine filly, I would think. Worked for old Johnny Gatesbull, you know."

Well, yes, Louise did know but that did not count for much as far as she was concerned. Because Cuthbert had made very few enquiries of his secretarial candidate, he was not really able to answer Louise's question satisfactorily. But Louise had already made her own assessment of Ingrid using her feminine intuition and she had been favourably impressed. And besides she wanted to get out of the place and to focus on maternal responsibilities and so virtually anyone would foot the bill from her standpoint.

Meanwhile, as she drove away from the estate, Ingrid vowed that she would update her old mini once the paycheques had started landing. But the old jalopy went tolerably well for now. At least she didn't have to crank a starting handle. Next Ingrid sought some low-priced accommodation in Havercoyne Stanley and she soon found a bedsit which would suit her admirably. Her future landlady was most obliging and friendly and hence Ingrid believed that she would be very comfortable. Ingrid also felt that her landlady, Mrs Jones, might be a useful source of information about the demesne and the village.

Later that day Ingrid rang Louise in order to accept the post with an agreement to start the following week.

"That's really good news," announced Louise who promptly telephoned the glad tidings through to her employer. She could not face the stairs just now.

So all was turning out well. Louise felt relieved that someone would be relieving her almost immediately. Cuthbert considered that all had been settled satisfactorily. And Ingrid believed that it would just be a matter of time before she got to grips with having to work for that crazy old relic known as Cuthbert Gansville-Stubbs.

## VANESSA'S TEDIUM

"This is the main dining room used by the Gansville-Stubbs family dating back to the nineteenth century. Lord George Gansville-Stubbs was the uncle of the present owner, Cuthbert Gansville-Stubbs, who inherited the estate from his forebears."

"Oh, and is His Lordship still around?" asked an eager American visitor.

"Certainly he is. He and his family reside in the east wing in their private quarters," replied the tour guide.

"And will we see him while we're here?" persisted the visitor.

"He does appear very occasionally but he's obviously a very busy man."

There were groans of disappointment from the floor but the tour guide, Vanessa Maunders by name, hastened to move on in order to avoid any further interruptions to her monotone spiel. Once she had been wound up like clockwork, it was dangerous to stop Vanessa midstream. But all listeners present still showed, or, at least, feigned, interest in what the tour guide was saying because they had paid their entrance fee and they wanted to get their money's worth.

"You will observe the inglenook fireplace here. It is estimated that this room was used as the main family room during the winter months. The dining table and chairs date from Queen Anne's day in the eighteenth century which is determined by the decorative shaping of the cabriole legs and the shell carvings. Note also the s-curve scrolls on the chairs and sides of the table. Several of the occasional tables also show Queen Anne legs."

The audience tittered and murmured their appreciation of the droll joke but Queen Anne, no doubt, would have turned in her grave at the gag had she been alive today. The tour guide effected not to have even noticed the reaction which she was used to and bored with by now. She had seen and heard it all before.

"You will note several Queen Anne japanned highboys – or tall chests – throughout Havercoyne Grange and, indeed, you will see several examples in the next room which I'll point out to you when we reach it. When you descend to the upper floors you'll also see more fine examples, particularly in the bedrooms."

"Does that mean that we'll have to do upstairs before we can have lunch?" whispered one woman to her friend.

"Quiet, dear," replied her slightly embarrassed companion.

But the museum guide felt obliged to continue relentlessly.

"There are also several examples in this room of the work of Thomas Chippendale from the latter part of the eighteenth century and I would draw your attention to the mahogany dresser and the walnut card table with its ball-and-claw feet."

Just as the punters were beginning to look interested by this change of emphasis, however, Vanessa ushered the party forward into what was once the family's living quarters. One or two of the viewers even felt inclined to inspect the furniture detail with binoculars but these devices were obliged to simply dangle when the party moved into the next room.

"This room was considered to be the family's main withdrawing room, especially during the summer months, in which you'll see a number of Victorian upright chairs of the French restoration period dating from the nineteenth century. Note here the distinctive motifs on the chairbacks which reflect the classical Greek and Egyptian influence. There is a particularly fine specimen of an Elizabethan sofa and chairs which have been restored as part of the house's collection."

Some of the chairs actually looked a bit moth-eaten to most of the onlookers but their thoughts remained unspoken. What would the chairs have looked like had they not been restored?

The guide's audience was beginning to flag and, indeed, tour guide Vanessa was herself looking forward to her forthcoming break for lunch and a cup of tea. And thus she moved the party into the baronial hall so that the visitors could admire the tapestries and the portraits of Cuthbert's ancestors.

"The baronial hall was used for the family's twice-yearly balls and other state ceremonial functions which occupied the time of Lord George and his son Lord William. As you will see from your guidebook, several famous statesmen are known to have stayed at Havercoyne Grange throughout the time when the previous family resided here. Both Lord George and Lord William were senior statesmen."

"But what about the current Lord Gansville-Stubbs? He's not a politician, is he?" asked one of the more attentive members of the audience.

"He's not involved himself in politics, no. Cuthbert Gansville-Stubbs is a member of the House of Lords, of course, but he seldom sits in the house. His interests lay more in business affairs. His Lordship only inherited the estate by default when his uncle George died without any surviving male issue. Lord George's only son, William, had died prematurely in his youth."

"What sort of business is Cuthbert Gansville-Stubbs involved in then?"

"Various company directorships, I believe," replied Vanessa who really did not want to go down that avenue.

"Can you give me an example of his business activity?" asked the avid questioner.

Vanessa hastened to ignore this persistent line of enquiry by steering the troops up the staircase so that they could torment one of her colleagues.

"Now if you would like to make your way up the back staircase, my colleague there will conduct you through the upper rooms."

Vanessa now made a beeline for the staff kitchen for some much-needed sustenance. The tour guide, however, was buttonholed by two eager beavers who wanted to engage her in more conversation.

"I very much enjoyed your interesting talk," stated the charming man who had accosted Vanessa and who had forsaken the rest of the party.

"Thank you, sir. I'm glad you enjoyed it."

"And my wife was most interested in what you were saying about the Queen Anne collection and the Chippendale. Weren't you, dear?"

"Indeed, yes. I think you've some very fine specimens here," his wife declared.

"Yes, we certainly have."

"How long have you worked here?" asked the woman.

"Oh, for several years now. I came here from a small museum on the outskirts of London," replied Vanessa who was beginning to wonder how she might escape from the clutches of these visitors because lunch and some liquid refreshment were beckoning.

"And you obviously enjoy your work?" asked the enquiring female more as a statement than a question.

"May we show our appreciation by offering you lunch?" asked the man.

Vanessa began to weaken but she felt it might be over and above the call of duty for her to fraternise with the troops.

"How kind of you. But, no, I can't spare the time just now. I've a heavy schedule this afternoon. But thank you, all the same, for your generous offer."

"OK. Well, we'll not detain you further then. Come, dear. Thank you and good bye," concluded the man, much to the relief of Vanessa who scurried away immediately.

On the upper floors the weary visitors were shown the bedrooms, the Victorian water closets, the nursery which doubled as a schoolroom, the storage facilities for household linen, the servant's robes and finally the rooftop quarters for the valets and maids. And, of course, the company continued to ask more tiresome questions despite their boredom and their rumbling stomachs.

A quick look at the cramped and spartan servants' quarters in the basement finally disgorged the party through into the café for lunch or tea and cakes according to preference.

A gift shop completed the tour, a port of call at which the American contingent spent copious sums of money while the British among the party balked at the inflated prices and the unnecessary tat.

The two visitors who had previously waylaid Vanessa also stopped for lunch because they had found the whole experience very enlightening.

"So what do you think, angel wings?"

"Well, this chicken and mushroom pie is not up to much. Not up to your standards. But how's your lasagne?" she replied.

"Ha, ha! But what about Havercoyne Grange and its antiquated museum?"

"Well, it's quite a place, I agree, honey bee. Wouldn't want to live here myself though. Bit draughty."

The questioner continued to ignore his partner's uncalled for repartee.

"And what about our illustrious tour guide?" the man asked.

"Well, I don't really think our Vanessa was that enthusiastic for the job. Do you, lion cub?"

"No, I don't but I wonder why, buttercup?"

"Well, we'll soon find out, won't we?" concluded his partner.

"Hm," agreed the man.

"We've got the ball rolling now and so only time will tell whether this project has any clout," came the woman's final pronouncement. But she too was consumed by deep thought.

The pair, nevertheless, had mounted more exacting projects than this and all had turned out well in the end. And so the couple was not too downhearted at any initial slow movement on the information-gathering front. Both thus concluded that the tedious tour had been necessary and informative for their specific purposes.

"OK, let's get back to the hotel now," suggested the woman.

"Right!"


## BYRON'S DECEPTION

Byron Travers had been the estate manager for the Havercoyne Stanley estate for several years now and he was a vital member of the team which ran the enterprise.

Byron had worked in private estate management all his life. Having grown up as the son of an estate manager himself, Byron had early on decided to follow in his father's footsteps. He thus firstly took a degree in land management as a precautionary measure but, in essence, his real market value was the experience which he had gained when helping his father voluntarily as a child and later as a paid teenager.

Byron's first appointment had been as the manager of a small holding in Bagshot Wagstool but, as he soon outgrew this position, he looked around for pastures new. A word-of-mouth recommendation then, by a somewhat circuitous route, landed Byron his current post at Havercoyne Stanley. Byron's work on the estate entailed supervising the administrative operation, overseeing the upkeep of Havercoyne Grange itself along with its numerous farm outbuildings and ensuring that the farmland returned a handsome profit because it was being cultivated wisely.

The farm particularly posed a number of trials and tribulations for Byron because of the fact that it was run as a mixed farming culture which consisted of both arable land for crops and grazing land for animal husbandry. The animal husbandry business sector was something of a headache for Byron both in terms of his time and the calls on his budget because the livestock constantly required a high investment in nutritious sustenance, veterinary fees and medicines. Byron was also responsible for supervising the staff on the estate which included the gamekeepers, farmworkers and gardeners as well as his own administrative personnel. Fortunately, the housekeeper, Elizabeth Garrick, organised and employed her own staff, even though notionally she reported to Byron as her immediate line manager.

While Byron came to work mostly in country gent's clobber, he was not at all averse to donning his overalls and wellies in order to pitch in with the farmworkers if a crisis occurred when all hands to the pump were required. Byron's willingness to dirty his hands and to exert his strength actually elevated him in the eyes of his employees who respected him all the more for his consideration and understanding of their needs.

Currently Byron was engaged in reviewing the performance of his budget for the previous year and for forecasting spending requirements for the forthcoming year. Forward planning was vital in Byron's work because it presented the most challenge both to his mental faculties and to his financial management skills.

But generally Byron was happy in his work. Byron valued his ability to work both indoors and outdoors as this unusual mix gave him the stimulation which had attracted him to the occupation in the first place. He also liked his eccentric employer who gave him a free hand in order to get on with the job for which he was paid. Byron was well remunerated for his more-than-full-time occupation and he was also fortunate enough to have acquired rent-free accommodation in Havercoyne Lodge as a perquisite of his job. Very wisely Byron had also purchased a house locally in nearby Aberville in which his ex-wife and their two children resided. And, therefore, Byron had a nest-egg apart from his domain on the Gansville-Stubbs estate.

Byron was on reasonably good terms with his ex-wife, Matilda. They sometimes sniped and snapped at each other but they never actually barked, bit into flesh or drew blood. Byron saw his two children, Leone and Constantine, regularly at the weekends but he realised that soon the fledglings would flee the nest in favour of university and freedom from the shackles of childhood. Byron's marriage had foundered because, unfortunately for Matilda, her husband had a roving eye which had led to trouble and strife between Byron and his wife on several occasions. Indeed Byron had also caused troubled on the Bagshot Wagstool estate when he had taken a fancy to some of the riding-school's employees.

Byron had, moreover, had a slight ding-dong with one of the former housemaids at Havercoyne Grange but trouble had been averted because she had promptly left when he refused to make the affair a more permanent arrangement. The sex was an infinite pleasure but a long-term commitment would have been sheer agony for the carefree estate manager. Only a limited few on the estate had been party to this erstwhile liaison and so Byron had not really risked any serious reprimand from his employer. Some of the female farmworkers had also casually obliged Byron in the past but he had soon tired of them.

But Byron now wondered where his next sexual conquest could be found and his thoughts roamed over the female employees on the estate.

Housekeeper Elizabeth Garrick had never really been a contender because she was so unbending and unattractive that Byron had seldom actually given her a second's thought. Cuthbert's secretary, Louise Fulham-Price, furthermore, had been given only a cursory glance because someone else had obviously had the pleasure first and the evidence was now apparent. But what about Louise's replacement? I must check her out for size. I believe she starts next week. There is also that new girl in the kitchen who arrived recently. Quite a sweetmeat. Nancy might be worth a shifty. But I cannot seem to catch her on her own. And I'm sure that Joyce the cook would stand guard and protect her like a mother hen.

Byron had also made a point of habitually seducing his secretarial staff on a regular basis but this tendency was beginning to adversely affect his budget figures because there was a high turnover of such personnel. So currently his secretary, Delia Perkins, had been recruited for her efficiency and brusqueness rather than for her sex appeal which was virtually non-existent as far as her manager was concerned.

As part of his budgeting review, Byron wondered about having to employ some more staff in the office and in the stables. Another typist who could assist Delia in the office might be needed, for instance. This might offer some more opportunity for me perhaps?

Byron soon wearied by being indoors and stuck at his computer as the fields and the grounds were beckoning. Byron liked the exactness, precision and fulfilment of administrative work in small doses but he also relished the outdoor life. And so he put his budgetary decisions aside and grabbed an overcoat and gumboots.

Byron tramped around the fields and patted the horses. He checked that the stable grooms were keeping everything clean and tidy and that the animals had been properly fed and watered. Apparently Angel Prancer, soon due to foal, was ailing and so Byron put in a call to Albert Fotheringay, the local veterinary surgeon, who regularly attended to the horses.

Byron then went to see how the cattle, the pigs and the sheep were doing and he learned that all was well in that quarter and that Albert Fotheringay could rest on his laurels just now as far as the farmyard stock were concerned.

Before Albert had reached the gates of the Havercoyne Stanley estate, Byron took a quick tour of the vineyards and the orchards just for the hell of it. Despite the expense, Byron looked forward to seeing Albert because it usually meant that he would be able to indulge in a late breakfast at the house with the vet. Cuthbert's cook, Joyce Glemtree, did a rare line in sausage, bacon and eggs from the farm.

Albert soon arrived and he promptly pronounced that Angel Prancer merely needed to rest and to take some harmless herbal medicine. Albert's inflated bill, however, would still be rendered even though he did little to earn it on this occasion. But breakfast was still granted to Byron and Albert by tradition.

Byron liked the farmhouse kitchen and he made an effort to cultivate Joyce because he had no taste for cooking himself, despite having a great appetite for eating. Joyce was not by any means on his list of suitable bedfellows and so their relationship was natural and easy. Joyce, indeed, regarded Byron as a surrogate son whom she could cater for with warmth and affection which was always appreciated by the estate manager. Byron, in turn, needed a mother-substitute too and so the relationship worked well.

"So how's the family?" asked Byron once he and Albert had settled down at the scrubbed-pine kitchen table.

Byron always employed small talk as his means of buttering up the vet and keeping him on good terms so that he could pull a few favours here and there when necessary, even though Albert's invoice would be just as crippling.

"Suzie's well but the boys are a handful as always."

Albert neglected to ask about Byron's family in case his relationship with Matilda had degenerated in any way.

The pair then went on to discuss schooling for Albert's two boys, whether they were bullied at school – or accused of being the bullies themselves – and what their prospects were for learning anything at all in private education. Byron knew that Albert's boys were sent to a reputable private school because their education had been financed from the proceeds of Albert's work for the Havercoyne estate. But, as a consolation, Byron did entertain the hope that maybe one of the boys would like to come and work on the farm at some stage temporarily as free or, at least, cheap labour. And Byron definitely intended to sow that seed in a year or two.

Albert took his leave after their hearty breakfast and Byron then returned to his budgeting. Joyce, of course, was thanked profusely by both men on their departure coupled with a platonic hug from her quasi son Byron.


## Cuthbert's inheritance

Cuthbert Gansville-Stubbs had led a sheltered life where money, and the privileges which it can afford, was a commodity which was not by any means in short supply. Cuthbert was thus generally impervious to the perils of destructive hurricanes, spiralling inflation and global warming as well as the threat of an impending world war or an outbreak of the latest killer virus.

Cuthbert was the younger son of Wilhelmina and Quincey Gansville-Stubbs. Quincey's elder brother George had originally been the heir apparent to the Havercoyne Stanley estate, including Havercoyne Grange, which, on his death, had been due to be passed on to his only son William.

Cuthbert had often visited the Havercoyne Stanley estate with his parents together with his sister Carlotta and his younger brother Damian during his childhood years. Cuthbert, Damian, Carlotta and cousin William had regularly played as children in the extensive grounds surrounding Havercoyne Grange. But all Cuthbert's immediate family accepted that the Havercoyne inheritance was assured by William Gansville-Stubbs and his own male issue. Wilhelmina and Quincey were not too happy about this situation but Cuthbert and his siblings were unconcerned in their youth.

Cuthbert and cousin William were particularly good friends in adulthood and there was no animosity between them. Cuthbert and William, who were roughly the same age, had gone to university at the same time and so they had frequently bunked off lectures in tandem, got blind drunk together and shared a bed with sundry obliging female undergraduates – but not always at the same time.

Then fate stepped in and upset the hereditary apple cart. Before father George had reached the final checkout, son and heir William was killed following a fall from his horse while out foxhunting one morning. The result was that the Havercoyne millions passed into Cuthbert's hands by default on the demise of his brother George who almost immediately died because he had never fully recovered from his son's untimely death. Cuthbert had then moved into Havercoyne Grange where he had officially, albeit reluctantly, taken over the reins of running the estate.

Cuthbert's father had soon followed his brother George into the family vault at St Mary's church in Havercoyne Stanley. But Quincey died a happy man knowing that his eldest son and his progeny would inherit the Havercoyne Stanley estate.

Wilhelmina Gansville-Stubbs had lived briefly at Havercoyne Grange after her husband's demise but she soon followed him into the family grave. Here Wilhelmina could keep her husband Quincey, her brother-in-law George and her nephew William company. Wilhelmina had, it seems, died of a broken heart because of the loss of her husband. But she too died happy, safe in the knowledge that her son Cuthbert had now officially become one of the landed gentry.

Cuthbert's cranky aunt Prudence, George's widow, conversely, remained doggedly determined to retain a zealous hold on life. As Prudence probably would never die naturally, it was a family joke that they would almost certainly need to shoot her like a lame racehorse once she had reached 150 years of age. And then she could be sold off as horse meat. When Prudence heard this unsavoury jest she gave a wan smile but she was, in consequence, determined even more vociferously to stay alive in order to exact her revenge on the jokers.

Prudence, of course, lived in Havercoyne Grange – not because she had been invited to do so but because she had asserted the privilege as her exclusive right. Cuthbert accepted this diktat without question whether he liked it or not. Aunt Prudence was assigned her own suite at the top of the house from whence she still managed to rule the household with a rod of iron. She seldom left her room but somehow she managed to make an uncannily impromptu appearance whenever it suited her.

Cuthbert's sister Carlotta, after a reckless spending spree and a leviathan world tour, elected to join forces with her elder brother and to work towards building up the business and thereby to remain at Havercoyne Grange. It is sometimes a good thing to sow a few wild oats before settling down.

Carlotta worked on the farm occasionally but she was mostly mistress of the stables because of her love of horses and her ambition to breed a winning racehorse one day. Carlotta was a typical horsey-type who was not in any way a candidate who could possibly capture the interest of Byron Travers, although he appreciated her dedicated to her work as the stable manager.

The residents of Havercoyne Grange also included Cuthbert's wife Lady Agatha Gansville-Stubbs and his younger brother Damian. Cuthbert's son and heir, Nathaniel, was an absentee member of the family home.

The easy-going Agatha was obliged to suffer the demands placed on her by the devilish aunt Prudence without demur. But she drew the line at taking any active part in the running of the estate. She left that task to Cuthbert and his minions. Lady Gansville-Stubbs did, however, enjoy an active life by organising coffee mornings in order to raise funds for various local charities, by supporting the local women's institute and by becoming a prominent member in the local amateur dramatic society. Agatha, by this means, could studiously avoid the rigours of life, circumvent the vexation of running the estate and bury her head in the sand with regard to the conduct of her absentee son.

Nathaniel, who would eventually inherit the estate and the peerage, was essentially a society drop-out. He had no interest in running, or even visiting, his ancestral home. Nathan was currently living in Spain with a señorita and he was trying desperately to make ends meet by working in a bar in Malaga. Nathan and señorita Luciana had, unknown to Cuthbert and the rest of the family, produced a son and heir. Nathan realised what an uproar this knowledge would cause and so he endeavoured to keep his son a secret for as long as possible. And, if necessary, he would be prepared to marry Luciana in order to legitimise master Sebastian. But that was looking too much into the future which Nathan by nature was disinclined to do. Nathan, therefore, was constantly ducking and diving, skimping and skiving as a way of life.

Cuthbert was, in fact, regularly asked to fork out cash in order to keep Nathan afloat – a vocation to which Cuthbert was reluctantly resigned. Despite much feigned bluster when Nathan made his demands, Cuthbert knew that, because Nathan would eventually inherit the pile once he was dead and gone, wife Agatha's position would be a parlous one if he did not agree to his son's requests. Agatha and Prudence, of course, were not party to this arrangement and Cuthbert hoped that the situation would stay that way indefinitely.

Damian, Cuthbert's younger brother, on the other hand, loved organising the guided tours in the museum and generally running that aspect of the business as if he were the lord of the manor. He had styled himself as the self-appointed curator of the museum and no one had appeared to object. Damian had hoped to marry tour guide Vanessa Maunders but she apparently was playing hard to get.

So, in the village of Havercoyne Stanley, George and William, together with Quincey and Wilhelmina, rested in the churchyard while Cuthbert, Agatha, Prudence, Carlotta and Damian inhabited Havercoyne Grange. And, all the while, Nathaniel wisely enjoyed his relative freedom in Spain with Luciana and Sebastian.

While Cuthbert disapproved of his eldest son's neglect of the family escutcheon, he could see himself reflected in Nathan when he thought back to his youth and the time he had spent with his late cousin William.

On the top floor of Havercoyne Grange was a room whose only resident was the Overland Shuttle, an ancient mechanical trainset. And, despite the fact that the garret room was close to the dreaded Prudence's quarters, Cuthbert often took the opportunity to sneak up there with a hip flask in order to contemplate life while he watched the train idly perambulate around the track.

When Cuthbert watched the Overland Shuttle whistle past the signal box and under the railway bridge, he remembered those heady university days and the fun which he had relished while supposedly studying ancient history. He chuckled as he remembered the succession of women who had trooped through his room, trying desperately to evade the notice of the concierge.

Cuthbert also recalled his days after university when he had, like Nathaniel, drifted around Europe in search of more bedfellows, cheap booze and a hectic nightlife. The Overland Shuttle trundled past the church, the farm, the factory and the town in sympathy.

Then the Overland Shuttle reached and stopped at the little station at Homeland Village. Cuthbert now recalled returning home and being obliged to find himself a wife as a means of fulfilling his destiny as a procreator of humankind. So, all in all, Cuthbert could not get too excited about the fact that Nathaniel was rather wayward. He was sure that Nathan would in time grow up and settle down so that he could take possession of the family inheritance.

The Overland Shuttle, however, entered a long dark tunnel which prompted Cuthbert's thoughts to move into murky waters. He remembered a time when, like Byron Travers, he had admired the stable girls and he had frequently indulged in a bit of harmless fun behind Agatha's back. This was a heart-piercing memory for Cuthbert because he was revisiting a time when he had done many reprehensible things and, so far, he had got away with all of them. The recollection, however, left a pretty dark cloud in Cuthbert's mind from which he could not possibly escape. But in the last ten years he had managed to evade detection. Only his conscience was party to the secret. Although Cuthbert had, in fact, only just reached his half century, he now appeared to be old before his time – perhaps as a result of his shadowy past.

The Overland Shuttle next sidled into the sidings for a rest after its exciting yet taxing journey and, of course, Cuthbert was brought back down to earth when he realised that he had business responsibilities to which he should attend sooner rather than later. Cuthbert was then startled back to reality by a loud voice from the corridor and a decisive bang on the door of his attic sanctuary.

"Cuthbert, is that you?" boomed a forceful and stentorian voice.

"Coming, Aunt Prudence," replied a despondent Cuthbert.

He quickly gulped down his brandy and hid his hipflask beneath the table on which the Overland Shuttle resided. Cuthbert now ventured forth to see what the hell she wanted and he wondered what trouble would now be in store for him. Bloody woman!

# HARRY'S REVELATION

The pub sign swayed gently in the breeze during a few of the summer months but, for the rest of the year, it banged and flapped around in the howling gales. The sign depicted a man clad in a smart red coat mounted on an impressive stallion. The hunter was blowing a long and spiralling hunting horn while the hounds looked frisky with their tails erect in the foreground against a grey sky in the background. The sign advertised the services of, would you believe it, the Hunting Horn hostelry.

The Hunting Horn was a typical English country pub lovingly restored by the current owner-occupiers in order to attract customers from further afield than the local village of Havercoyne Stanley. It was nicely turned out with inviting décor and hordes of trinkets and other useless paraphernalia which the locals had ignored for years. A few tankards hung from the rafters, the obligatory stag's horns and a few actual hunting horns adorned the walls.

The Hunting Horn had a single main bar into which the front door opened with a restaurant at the back. Several cosy rooms upstairs could also be had for a princely sum for those who wanted to stay overnight. The serving area sat in the centre of the building where a friendly landlord and an attractive barmaid were attentive to regular customers and welcoming to casual visitors.

Two newcomers entered the establishment one afternoon following a spell of being subjected to tour guide Vanessa's monologue and a rather unexciting lunch in Havercoyne Grange's underground restaurant.

The landlord of the Hunting Horn beamed a welcoming smile and then, with income uppermost in his mind, asked what the couple would like to drink. The man ordered a scotch and soda while his wife opted for a glass of rosé.

"New to the district, are you?" enquired the landlord who was perfectly well aware that the duo were strangers to the area.

"Yes. We've just been visiting Havercoyne Grange," explained the man.

"Oh, yes. Very interesting place, Havercoyne Grange. Did you do the official guided tour?"

"We certainly did," came the man's reply. "My wife and I are historians and we wish to study old houses, such as Havercoyne Grange, for our scholastic research."

Oh, blimey. A couple of bloody eggheads. But the landlord feigned interest all the same.

"I'm Professor Lyall Vanburgh and this is my wife Dr Katherina Vanburgh," announced the stranger.

"Pleased to meet you, folks. I'm Dave and this is my wife, Nellie," replied the hostelry owner-manager.

The two academics then shook hands with the landlord and the buxom barmaid.

"Do you know of anyone who could tell us more about the history of Havercoyne Grange?" asked Katherina who wanted to get to the heart of their reason for entering the establishment.

"The guided tour only gave us a cursory introduction," added Lyall Vanburgh.

"Well, there's old Harry. He knows quite a bit about the place because he used to work in the stables in days gone by," chimed in Nellie who wanted to join in the conversation because there was not a lot to do mid-afternoon and she was bored with inactivity.

"Yes. And he should be here sometime soon," confirmed Dave who was anxious to please the visitors.

The two academics then retired to a window seat in order to await old Harry's arrival in the hope of learning something to their advantage. When Harry entered the pub he was introduced to the newcomers by Dave. And Lyall, right on cue, immediately offered to stand him a drink. Old Harry was delighted to accept.

Katherina and Lyall then spoke of their interest in Havercoyne Grange and its estate and they invited old Harry to take a trip down memory lane. Old Harry willingly obliged with another monologue as a Vanessa lookalike after a couple of stiff whiskeys and a few cigars. Harry's soliloquy, however, was not quite as dry as that of Vanessa's which the couple had just sampled.

"I used to work in the stables back in them days. Worked there for many years, I did. Mucking out the horses and doing the gallops. Did some work on the farm too."

Katherina hoped that they had plied old Harry with sufficient drink in order to loosen his tongue but not enough to send him to sleep. Old Harry, however, rambled on for a while in order to please his benefactors.

"Used to sleep up in the 'ayloft, I did. Some of the stable gals did the same too," continued old Harry with a chuckle and a wicked grin.

The two researchers chortled obediently at old Harry's insinuation. But they did not want to interrupt his downstream flow.

"Are any of the former stable girls still around in the district?" asked Lyall who found this topic of some interest.

"Most of 'em left 'ere and got married, they did. Some died off last winter when we 'ad that sharp frost. And one disappeared without trace."

The stable lasses sounded like a crop of potatoes to Lyall's ears but Katherina brightened at old Harry's words. This was the news which she wanted to probe before old Harry actually fell asleep.

"Disappeared without trace?" repeated Katherina who moved closer to old Harry as her means of inviting him to reveal more information.

"Oh, ah. Disappeared wi'out trace, her did. No one's seen her since the day she disappeared. She just upped and offed, she did."

"But surely someone has been in touch with her since? Would there be anyone in the village who might know where she went?" asked Lyall.

"No one knows. There were rumours, of course."

"Rumours?" encouraged Katherina with her most engaging smile.

"Well, I don't listens to rumours meself."

"But what were the rumours?" persisted Katherina who did not want to let this fish escape.

"Well, some say she was with child and 'ad to do a moonlight, if you knows what I mean."

"Pregnant? By whom?" urged Katherina who had realised that this was the nub of the information which they sought.

"Well, there's some as say that the big 'ouse had had a bit of fun with 'er, you know. But it's only a rumour. And I don't listens to rumours meself."

No, I'm sure you don't, thought Katherina. But there's gold in them there hills.

Lyall felt that it was time to offer old Harry another drink, although Katherina questioned the wisdom of this course of action just now. Old Harry accepted Lyall's kind offer naturally.

While Lyall was at the bar, Katherina prodded further by asking the name of the stable girl who had disappeared. Apparently old Harry himself had been a bit sweet on Betsy Drury but her head had been turned by one or two of the young bucks from the stable yard at about that time. But when Cuthbert had taken over the estate, Betsy's interest in the smelly stable boys had evaporated instantly. This news was worth all the money which they had spent on drinks for old Harry who didn't listen to rumours.

Old Harry soon looked too sleepy to continue and so the pair of scholars retired from the establishment with thanks to old Harry, Dave and Nellie. And with a promise to reappear like a couple of homing pigeons in the near future.

Katherina and Lyall then returned to High Woodfield Hotel in Grayling Wood in order to sift through their discoveries. The duo deduced that Cuthbert had probably entertained Betsy Drury and that he was possibly the culprit who had instigated her rapid departure.

"But we must find out more, poppy poppet," stated Lyall emphatically.

"Yes, and we must work out how that can be achieved," replied his ever-practical partner.

"Vivien will be a good ally," remarked the professor.

"When does Vivien start then?"

"Next week."

"Excellent."

# INGRID'S LANDING

Ingrid drove her ancient mini through a car wash as a precursor to starting her secretarial post with Cuthbert Gansville-Stubbs. She told the mini, however, that this was a special treat to which it should not endeavour to become accustomed. This was definitely a one-off performed in a fit of madness by Ingrid. The timeworn mini groaned appropriately at this news.

On arrival at the Havercoyne Stanley estate, Ingrid parked in an unobtrusive place in the staff car park in the hope that her lack of funds would not be obvious to the rest of the inhabitants on the premises.

Today her knock on the front door of Havercoyne Grange was answered by housekeeper Elizabeth Garrick who explained that Louise was indisposed today but that the mother-to-be hoped to return tomorrow. Her apologies were profuse. Also Cuthbert was in London today. More apologies were forthcoming from Elizabeth.

That's a good start, thought Ingrid. What the hell shall I do all day now? But, on the other hand, I shall have the place to myself. Quite an advantage actually.

"I understand that Delia Perkins, the estate manager's secretary, will be here shortly in order to welcome you to the Grange's administrative side," stated Elizabeth.

"Thank you, Elizabeth," replied Ingrid politely.

"Perhaps you'd like to familiarise yourself with Louise's office while you're waiting?"

"Of course. Thank you."

"Can I get you a coffee?" asked Elizabeth.

Ingrid thought back to the time when she had been offered coffee in Cuthbert's office and so she decided that it would be better to decline the offer and to make her own beverage.

"Please don't trouble. I'll make coffee in the office here. I'm sure there's a kettle somewhere."

"Indeed, we have a coffee machine," remarked Elizabeth who proceeded to show Ingrid where the drinks-making machine was located and where the tea and coffee supplies were stored. More intricate details of the coffee machine's mechanism could obviously be deduced by Ingrid herself.

"I can easily make myself at home here, Elizabeth. Thank you."

"Good. Lunch will be ready from about noon onwards if you would like to make your way into the kitchen just along the corridor behind this room. Through that door is the quickest way to get there," announced Elizabeth who pointed to a door at the back of the secretarial bureau.

"I see. Thank you," replied Ingrid who was interested to note that lunch would be provided. But will I have to pay for it? And how much will it set me back? No one stated that it would be a perquisite of the job. It was not that Ingrid was mean but that she was seriously strapped for cash just now.

Ingrid was keen to dismiss the housekeeper because she wanted to use this heaven-sent opportunity of being alone in the office and hopefully to avoid any interruptions. Thus, when Elizabeth had departed, Ingrid set about making herself some decent coffee and familiarising herself with the computer equipment, the filing system, her new desk and the cloakroom facilities. She had a good look through the files on the computer in order to discover the contents of the recent letters which Cuthbert had written and to check on the state of the accounts.

Cuthbert, it seemed, had lately attended some boring board meetings and he had invested in some machinery for the farm in order to streamline the crop harvest. Ingrid also noted Cuthbert's share dealings as well as the huge sums which were paid out to trainer Ian Manningbury and to vet Albert Fotheringay. The care of Cuthbert's racehorses was clearly an expensive hobby.

A gentle tap on the office door shortly announced the arrival of Delia Perkins who entered the office with a welcoming smile and a kindly manner.

"Ingrid, I presume. I'm Delia, secretary to Byron Travers. I work over in the estate office."

The two secretarial staff shook hands formally.

"Pleased to meet you," stated Ingrid.

"Louise is absent today I gather and so I came to see if you're settling in OK."

"Indeed."

"I can show you the estate office and give you a tour of the estate, if you wish."

"That would be very kind. Yes. Thank you."

Delia then led Ingrid over the estate so that she could see the farm at work, the stables where the racehorses were recovering from their morning gallops and the sheds where Cuthbert's newly purchased agricultural machinery was housed in readiness for the autumn harvest. Ingrid also saw some of the pigs, sheep and cattle which were idly grazing in the fields but she was not at all inclined to trample in the mud so early in the year in order to inspect these animals more closely.

Next the pair returned to the estate office where Ingrid met the charming Byron Travers and she liked what she saw. Byron, moreover, obviously had an appreciative eye when he clapped eyes on Ingrid. More coffee was offered for Ingrid and this time she risked acceptance. She wanted to see how other people made coffee and to remain in Byron's company for as long as would be thought appropriate.

"This is where it all happens, of course," boasted Byron.

"Really?"

Byron was taking a break from perusing his completed budgets before finally submitting them to the big white chief and so an idea stuck him as he consulted the computer clock.

"Would you like to join me for lunch, Ingrid?"

Ingrid felt that Delia was considering asking the same question and so she looked uncertain about whether to accept Byron's offer. I may not have to pay for lunch if I go with Byron. But I don't want to disappoint Delia.

"Will Delia be joining us?" asked Ingrid as a compromise.

"No, I'll stay here and hold the fort while Byron's away. We can have lunch together some time later in the week," suggested Byron's secretary who was used to accommodating her employer's erotic whims.

"OK, then. Thank you, Byron."

"I'll ring through to you in a couple of days and we can make a date when the office here is less busy," added Delia helpfully.

Byron looked keen to make a start towards the kitchen and he obviously did not relish all this idle chatter between the girls. Hence he moved towards the door and Ingrid felt obliged to follow. They made their way across the driveway and into the house via the back entrance which led directly into the kitchen.

Joyce Glemtree greeted Byron warmly as her surrogate son and Ingrid noted this affectionate relationship.

"Pleased to meet you, Ingrid. This your first day?" asked Joyce.

"Yes, and I'm being made most welcome, thank you."

"Quite right too! I hope Byron's looking after you properly."

Ingrid declined to reply. She suspected that Byron would want to look after her quite improperly if he were given half the chance.

"What's for lunch today, Joyce?" asked Byron quickly changing the topic of conversation.

Lunch turned out to be a hearty beef and mushroom pie in which there was evidence of the farm's produce which Ingrid appreciated. As Ingrid did not see a menu anywhere in evidence, she continued to wonder whether she would have to pay for her meal. And whether she could really afford it! She also indeed considered whether Byron would offer to pay if a charge were levied. A series of expensive lunches would certainly not suit her pocket just now.

"What do you think of the estate? Have you had a guided tour of the estate yet?" enquired Joyce.

"Yes. And as far as I can see the emphasis is on racehorses. Am I right?"

"Quite right. Old Cuthbert likes his racehorses. Did you meet his sister Carlotta on your travels? She manages the stables."

"Not that I was aware. But, in any case, my tour was only rudimentary."

"We must rectify that omission soon," admitted Byron who hoped that he would have the pleasure of showing her the hayloft in due season.

Again Ingrid did not volunteer an answer to Byron's hopeful and loaded question.

The diners then turned to discussing Byron's work. He offered some detail about the way in which he managed the estate together with a run-down of the Grange's history. Ingrid attempted to probe more about Cuthbert but Byron did not seem to be interested in talking about the family. Ingrid, of course, trusted that Byron would loosen up on this topic when she got to know him better.

Eventually it transpired that lunch was on the house for staff by tradition and Ingrid was ecstatic and relieved by this news.

"Of course, we always give Joyce a good present at Christmas for her services. But it's traditional for big farms to feed their workers and I made sure that the admin staff fell into this category too," Byron whispered.

"I'm glad to hear it."

No doubt my salary would have been adjusted accordingly, pondered Ingrid. Byron had carefully neglected to mention that feeding the workers was not false economy because the staff could be paid less and then think they were getting something for nothing as a result. But not everyone was deceived by this ploy. The prestige of working for the landed gentry, however, still counted for something in the employment field.

Byron flirted mildly with Ingrid throughout the meal while Ingrid noted his restraint. After all they had plenty of time to get to know each other now that she was officially working on the team. Perhaps Joyce's hovering presence was having a damping effect too.

After lunch Byron escorted Ingrid back to her office and, when she did not offer him any post-prandial coffee, he returned to his own domain in order to relieve Delia and to contemplate what he thought would be a solution to his latest problem of where to find his next bedfellow.

Ingrid then got down to opening the day's post because not only did it normally arrive late in the day but also because she wanted to appear as if she were working industriously. Ingrid assembled the letters which were addressed to Cuthbert and she took them up the Mount Everest staircase to his office. She placed the consignment of post on the desk for his attention when he returned. It's clear I'll be getting plenty of exercise in this job!

Ingrid took the opportunity to do a bit of investigative work in Cuthbert's office now that she was alone. Accordingly she snooped around in his desk, found a wall-safe behind a picture and generally took stock of her surroundings. She discovered a couple of interesting photographs in Cuthbert's desk together with a plentiful supply of whiskey in the drinks cabinet. Cuthbert's desk diary revealed very little but a sheaf of papers on a side table looked as if it could contain some extremely valuable information.

Ingrid soon felt that she had spent a sufficient amount of time here in order to get a feel for the place and so she made her way downstairs again. She now looked for a way of wasting more time until the end of the day but an idea did not really strike her. And so she twiddled her thumbs for a while until it was time to leave for the day.

## CARLOTTA'S RESCUE

Carlotta had spent a most enjoyable interlude earlier that morning participating in the runs over the hills and dales surrounding Grayling Wood during that morning's training exercise organised by Ian Manningbury of Braxwood Yard. She had taken her own horse, Jonquil, in order to give her some refreshing exercise. After this session, Carlotta had taken Jonquil for an extra jaunt locally and, consequently, she had yet to meet the new secretary who had recently joined the family firm. But Carlotta found people somewhat difficult – horses being more in her line as friends. And so she was not particularly interested in meeting any new employee, although she did not deliberately avoid anyone.

Carlotta took Jonquil for a gentle stroll and a brief canter. The mare was not part of the racing stables but she was Carlotta's own horse whom she loved more than any of the estate's steeplechasers or flat-race champions. Jonquil had engaged half-heartedly in the morning's exercise as she was not in training for a race but, nevertheless, the mare was a little tired from the workout. While on her outing, unfortunately, Jonquil showed signs of fatigue and, when Carlotta examined her mare's foreleg, she detected a slight strain around the knee which was obviously upsetting her ride.

Carlotta, regrettably, was far from anywhere but she had no option but to remain dismounted. So Carlotta began to mull over what could be done. Perhaps I could ring the stables and ask one of the lads to bring the wagon? But I may have to wait a long time for this favour. And the staff wouldn't be happy to do this errand, I'm sure. Or I could just rest here awhile and then perhaps walk Jonquil home slowly. But it's a long way for a lame horse.

"Good morning to you!" called a voice from the middle distance.

Carlotta looked up in surprise.

"Your mare lame then, dear lady?" enquired the perceptive man.

"Yes. She's probably a bit weak at the knee," replied Carlotta who had by now noticed two riders heading swiftly towards her.

"Pity. Bad luck," the man continued while his female partner took a more practical approach by dismounting and examining Jonquil.

"But I'm sure we can assist," stated the woman, "as we can get our horsebox here quite easily and give you both a lift home too."

Carlotta was overcome with the generosity of this woman and she thanked the skies for this fortuitous and timely intervention.

"Oh, that would be extremely kind but I don't want . . ."

"Think nothing of it, dear lady," interjected the man, "we could get the horsebox here in minutes. We live very near."

As good as his word and heedless of Carlotta's protests, the male rider phoned through to his stables and promptly summoned the horsebox for Jonquil. Carlotta could have wept with relief.

"The box will soon be here. Fret not, dearest lady. I'm Aubrey Bankover, by the way, and this is my sister Florence. Pleased to meet you, my dear lady."

Carlotta introduced herself to the siblings. She thought that she knew everyone locally but obviously she had been mistaken. Although Florence soon supplied the answer to Carlotta's wondering.

"We have just moved into the area in order to be near the Braxwood Yard owned by Ian Manningbury at Grayling Wood. Do you know it at all?" asked Florence.

Carlotta admitted that she knew it very well and that she had just been out at the crack of dawn on the horse-training routine.

"I thought I recognised you," remarked Florence while Aubrey nodded his acquiescence.

The horsebox appeared in the distance and the three new friends greeted its arrival with a mixture of pleasure and relief. The box trundled its way towards them and Jonquil was duly installed and secured. Florence and Aubrey remained on their mounts while Carlotta elected to stay with Jonquil inside the box in order to reassure her beloved horse that help would soon be here at hand.

Back at Havercoyne Grange, one of the lads took the hapless Jonquil back to the stables and he also agreed to phone Albert Fotheringay. Carlotta enjoyed working on the estate because her veterinary fees were automatically paid for her out of Byron's administrative budget. Good deal, eh?

"Will you stay for lunch as my guest? It'll only be very modest, I'm afraid, but you'd be very welcome," offered Carlotta.

Florence gladly accepted the invitation on behalf of herself and her brother. Aubrey's horsebox then returned to its own residence while the horses belonging to Florence and Aubrey were taken to Carlotta's stables for their own brand of refreshment.

"We can have a drink first," decided Carlotta as she steered Florence and Aubrey into the house and guided them in the direction of the drinks cabinet in the drawing room. Once the drinks had been dispensed to her guests, Carlotta popped into the kitchen in order to inform Joyce that two extra lunches would be required for her guests in the dining room.

Nancy Emery, the kitchen assistant who also acted as a waitress for the establishment, was detailed by Joyce to set three places at one end of the long dining table. Barraclough, Havercoyne Grange's poor excuse for a butler, selected some wine from the cellar in order to celebrate the occasion.

"Lunch is served ma'am," announced Barraclough soon after noon and the trio then made their way expectantly into the dining room.

Nancy wheeled in three portions of shepherd's pie on a trolley together with numerous serving dishes containing home-grown vegetables. Barraclough offered and poured a specially selected red burgundy for Carlotta and her guests.

"Whereabouts are you based then?" enquired Carlotta.

"We've just taken a place not far from Grayling Wood. The Old Foundry – about two kilometres north of the village," stated Aubrey.

"I know it. By the stream and the old watermill," proclaimed Carlotta.

"That's right," replied Florence.

"Nice run on the downs there. I've taken Jonquil there a few times."

The door to the dining room was suddenly and loudly flung open and aunt Prudence invaded the sacred territory, claiming it as her own.

"I've told Barraclough that I'd be joining you for lunch," asserted Prudence who did not seem to believe that she warranted an official invitation to the party.

Carlotta made the introductions briefly but she felt seriously aggrieved at being unable to banish Prudence from the room and at her aunt's audacity and meddlesome curiosity. Prudence obviously wanted to know who these invaders were and she assumed that she had a right to know.

Barraclough next appeared with Prudence's portion of shepherd's pie but the plate was received with little thanks, other than a condescending nod, when the butler placed her meal in front of her.

"That will be all, thank you, Barraclough," said Prudence imperiously as if she owned the house and grounds.

"And where did you meet these people then?" demanded Prudence as she inspected Florence and Aubrey over the top of her pince-nez.

"Florence and Aubrey very kindly rescued me when Jonquil went lame," explained Carlotta.

Prudence grunted.

"We have taken the Old Foundry at Grayling Wood so we can exercise our racehorses at Ian Manningbury's stable yard with a view to settling here permanently," explained Florence who could see that the old harridan was sizing them up as interlopers into Havercoyne Grange.

A rather stilted and uncomfortable lunch then ensued at the table with only the occasional embarrassed comment from Florence or Aubrey and a few snidey remarks from Carlotta. Prudence asked very few additional questions because she had by now made her assessment of Florence and Aubrey and the pair were obviously found to be wanting in her estimation.

Prudence, it seemed, did not approve of newcomers and unknown upstarts in general terms.

Eventually Florence and Aubrey made their excuses by way of taking their leave of Havercoyne Grange post haste – more in order to escape the scrutiny and disapproving glances from Prudence than because of pressure of work which had been their pretext for a premature departure.

"I do apologise for my aunt. She is a meddlesome, prying creature. Perhaps we can meet some other time in more relaxed circumstances?" suggested Carlotta who was covered with embarrassment as her guests departed.

"Indeed, yes. Perhaps you can dine with us at the Foundry soon?" contributed Aubrey.

Carlotta readily acquiesced with this suggestion and the party exchanged contact details. Once she had closed the main door, Carlotta stormed back into the dining room with a fury which threatened to rock the foundations of the house. Any restraint which Carlotta had exercised during lunch was now thrown to the wind.

"How dare you waltz in here and just assume you can join me and my guests for lunch! You're nothing but a nosey, interfering bitch."

"I live here and I've a right to have lunch where I please," retaliated Prudence defiantly.

"You have no right to live here. And you normally take lunch in your room. You just came down here to check them out. And all you've done is embarrass me with your outrageous nosey-parker tactics when I have guests. Don't do it again or I will create a scene you really wouldn't like."

"I don't know where you get your temper from or your new-fangled language. You wouldn't have learned it from this household. And I'll lunch where I like and when I like. Thank you very much, young lady."

Prudence was adept as deflecting the subject by a non sequitur but her tactic only inflamed Carlotta even more.

"In future, you keep out of the way when I'm entertaining guests or I'll get Cuthbert to evict you! You've no right to live here and I'll be glad when you leave . . . preferably in a coffin."

"When your mother died I took it on as my responsibility, as the head of the family, to take care of you and see you don't come to any harm by entering into relations with unsuitable people."

"Well, what I do is none of your business. I'm an adult and I've been one now for a couple of decades in case you haven't noticed. And so I'll thank you to mind your own bloody business in future."

"Language, child."

"I'm not a child!" screamed Carlotta, "And if you want language, I'll give it to you. Mind your own fucking business!"

Prudence, though rooted to the spot with shock by such words, remained impervious to Carlotta's insults which gave Carlotta her cue to leave the dining room abruptly.

The door concluded the contretemps by merely saying "slam" loudly as Carlotta disappeared in a cloud of wrath.

Prudence continued to enjoy her wine and to be totally unaffected by her niece's rude remarks. Wayward child! I shall have to have a word with young Cuthbert about her.

Carlotta's immediate response was to leave the Grange. And she resolved to have a word with Cuthbert in order to see if she could master the Prudence problem permanently. Some hope!

## Nancy's astonishment

Back in the kitchen, Nancy was busy stacking the dishwasher while Joyce was making some pastry in readiness for the evening meal. Barraclough, meanwhile, was helping himself to the remains of the red burgundy in the butler's pantry.

When Carlotta's outburst shook the house, the butler, the cook and the kitchen maid could not avoid overhearing the kerfuffle. All three employees had stood stock-still in order to listen with avid curiosity.

"What a to-do, eh?" Nancy commented after Carlotta had stormed off the premises.

"Prudence causes a lot of trouble here. She thinks she owns the place," remarked Joyce.

"She claims the place as hers by right," contributed Barraclough who had emerged suddenly from the butler's pantry slightly worse for wear. "The house would be a much happier place without her."

Maybe we shall not have to wait more than about a decade, thought Joyce to herself.

Nancy, who had only just joined the staff a few weeks ago, had soon learned about Prudence's ironclad fist but she had not discussed the subject before with either Joyce or Barraclough. She had chatted to the stable lads and some of the farmworkers about Prudence's all-demanding nature but she had not so far realised that the opinion voiced in the estate grounds was actually also shared by the household cavalry. Food for thought.

"What was the fuss all about this time?" asked Joyce.

"Apparently old Pru was inspecting Carlotta's guests to see if she approved. And Carlotta took exception," responded Barraclough.

"And used some very choice language," remarked Nancy as an aside.

All agreed that aunt Prudence was a menace and that there was a regular rumpus in the household because of her assumption that she was the matriarch of the family and that she could act as she pleased. Cuthbert, Carlotta and Damian did not want or need their lives run for them, thank you very much.

As the conversation proceeded, Nancy learned something of the history of the family from the slightly inebriated Barraclough who had served the Gansville-Stubbs clan for many years. And he had even been around in the reign of Cuthbert's late brother George. Nancy also discovered that old Cuthbert had always had a roving eye in his young days and that some scandal had been attached to him when one of the stable girls had unexpectedly disappeared without trace. An interesting piece of juicy gossip. Who'd have thought it of old Cuthbert?

"Can you take the tea out to the lads now please, Nancy?" asked Joyce who had assembled some flasks of tea and homemade cakes in a basket. This was Nancy's regular afternoon duty.

"Of course," replied Nancy who closed the door of the dishwasher in order to set it in motion.

"And I'll put together some tea and cakes for the farmworkers. You can take that out when you return."

"Yes, of course."

Nancy made her way to the stables where Ned greeted her with almost as much enthusiasm as he did his afternoon tea.

"Have you got time for a chat?" asked Ned.

"I can only stay a second."

"I got some scandal for you," Ned tempted.

Nancy hesitated but she was eager to hear what Ned might have to say on the latest subject of Prudence's imprudence.

"Carlotta stormed out of here in a fury just after lunch. She took one of the prize stallions with her too."

"I know," said Nancy and she proceeded to flesh out the details about the showdown in the dining room.

Nancy and Ned naturally relished a bit of gossip.

"She's a right old cow, that one," announced Ned.

"So it seems."

Again Nancy learned more about the history of the family and about the way in which Prudence interfered in the lives of the inhabitants of Havercoyne Grange. Nancy was beginning to get a very clear picture of the state of the empire in the household, a subject which was sure to arise when there was a row in the household.

"And what's this I hear about old Cuthbert being a randy bugger?" enquired Nancy.

"Oh, yes, that's a well-known fact. When he was younger, of course."

"I'd love to hear more but I must get back," reported Nancy.

"Perhaps we could meet one night and have a drink in the Hunting Horn?" suggested Ned who had wanted an excuse to ask Nancy out ever since her arrival.

"Perhaps."

Nancy did not feel inclined to commit herself but she did want to garner some more information about the family and she believed that Ned could supply a goodly portion of it.

"What about a jar on Friday night then?" persisted Ned who wanted to press home his advantage.

"I'll let you know when I've sorted out my hours this week."

Nancy left promptly then but with a feeling that she only had to say the word for Ned to spill the beans about the family. Ned also felt optimistic that the coquettish Nancy would eventually come around to his way of thinking.

Nancy next took the tea and cakes out the farmworkers who usually assembled in the barn at this time of the day in expectation of refreshment – rather as the cows did at milking time. Nancy exchanged a few words with some of the farmworkers and she learned some more about the sexual proclivities of Cuthbert, although she tried to hide her enthusiasm for the news which was imparted.

On Friday afternoon when Nancy delivered the tea basket to the stables, Ned was patiently waiting for her in the hope that she may have made a decision about his proposed evening drink.

"You still up for a drink tonight, lass?" asked Ned.

Nancy failed to mentioned that she had not, in fact, agreed to anything but she ignored Ned's distortion of the truth. By now she had decided that it might be worth going for a drink with Ned simply because of what she might learn in the way of interesting blether.

"Tonight?"

"Yes. You said you might come for a drink at the Hunting Horn."

"Well, yes, all right then. I'll meet you at the pub when I've finished my shift at about 8 pm," she declared.

As a teaser, Nancy abruptly turned away and made her way back to the house without a backward glance. Ned noticed Nancy's evasiveness but he interpreted this tactic as a good sign. I'll have a shower before we leave and put on a clean shirt perhaps? Must impress the lady.

Nancy arrived at the Hunting Horn well after 8 pm. She decided that it would be politic for her to arrive deliberately late for her date. Ned instantly rose when Nancy entered the pub and he waved pointedly in order to attract her attention.

"Can we sit by the fire?" asked Nancy who noticed that Ned had already secured a table by the window.

Ned obediently collected his drink and obligingly moved to the table of Nancy's choice. Must accommodate the lady.

"What can I get you Nancy?"

Nancy ordered an orange juice, although Ned was slightly disappointed that she could not be tempted with anything stronger. He resigned himself to the fact that he was obviously not going to further his cause by getting Nancy drunk tonight. Nancy, meanwhile, was wondering how she could extract the maximum amount of information from Ned while keeping him at arm's length.

"So tell me more about old Cuthbert and the vanishing stable girl?" enquired Nancy as her conversation opener. Why waste time on incidentals?

Ned explained that Betsy Drury had suddenly disappeared. She just didn't turn up for work one day and she was never seen or heard of again. Nancy found this fact most interesting. This is the kind of detail I want.

"How long ago was that then?" asked Nancy.

"About ten years ago. She'd disappeared just before I first started work here."

"And she was having an affair with Cuthbert? The old rogue."

"Apparently. I heard juicy reports from several of the stable lads just after I arrived and they seemed to think she'd had regular assignations in the hayloft. But, of course, I didn't witness anything personally. Maybe it was just talk."

"Maybe. And did I hear she was up the duff?"

"Well, that was the rumour but it may have been just guesswork."

Nancy realised that Ned might only be reporting hearsay gossip but she still felt that the topic was worth probing.

"Do you think she went away to have the kid or get rid of it?" Nancy persisted.

"Don't know."

Had they reached a dead end? Nancy contemplated her next move.

"Did she not have any relatives or friends locally?"

"I think her parents live up north somewhere. Newcastle way, I reckon. But I don't think anyone contacted them when Betsy left cos I heard nothing about it."

Was this another cul-de-sac?

"Who else was around at the time?"

"Well Barraclough, of course."

"But no stable lads or farmworkers then?"

Ned was beginning to get irritated because this topic was not what he wanted to talk about.

"Tell me about yourself Nancy," Ned invited in his quest to turn the conversation towards more important chat-up matters.

Nancy explained that she had worked in several places but always in the catering trade. And that she had wanted this job because accommodation was included in the package. But she was, of course, concerned to get back to her favourite topic.

"So who else was around at the time when Betsy left and when she was having her fling with old Cuthbert?"

Ned now realised that Nancy was more interested in learning about Betsy than turning her mind to matters which interested him and so he decided that he would not be forthcoming any longer.

"Not sure," Ned said in the hope of concluding the conversation.

Nancy also appreciated that Ned was not going to play ball anymore and so she resigned herself to ridiculous chit-chat while, simultaneously, thinking of an excuse to go home early. She decided, however, that she could approach some of the other stable lads who looked at if they had worked on the estate since god was a boy. And so she concluded that Ned had served his purpose for the present.

Nancy now made the excuse that she needed an early night because of an incipient migraine and an early start in the morning. She then returned to Havercoyne Grange as swiftly as she could after downing her orange juice.

Ned conceded defeat and he bade her farewell without any hope of persuading the kitchen maid to come out with him again. Poor sod!

## CARLOTTA'S DECISION

Carlotta had taken Morning Mist for a brisk canter across the downs after her run-in with Prudence in an attempt to discharge her anger. She knew that Cuthbert would disapprove of her riding any of the racehorses but she chose to ignore this unwritten law for once.

Morning Mist was surprised to be getting a second bout of exercise that day and he was not too keen on having his munching interrupted for the purpose. What's the matter with my mistress? She's normally only interested in riding Jonquil. Why have I suddenly come into favour? Oh, well, at least, I can get out of those dreary stables.

Carlotta found that physical exercise often calmed her when she was in a rage. Most of Carlotta's anger these days stemmed from the arrogance of aunt Pru who seemed to think that she had a god-given right to rule the household like an omnipotent being. Carlotta knew, moreover, that Cuthbert felt the same way about his obnoxious relative. And, of course, Carlotta wanted to decide what could be done to shut Prudence's mouth up for good. During her frolic, therefore, Carlotta reviewed her options.

She could move out of Havercoyne Grange but then she would lose her home, her livelihood and her beloved horses. So that was not really the answer. Option one discounted.

Carlotta could insist that Cuthbert ask aunt Pru to leave because she was causing so much trouble. But Prudence would probably refuse to budge and it was unlikely that she would keep her mouth shut even after numerous fire-and-brimstone warnings. And Cuthbert could probably not forcibly evict Pru against her will, even if he had the guts to try. Carlotta knew that Cuthbert had probably reached the same conclusion about Pru. So this route was not an option either. Option two discounted.

Carlotta next recalled the many occasions when Prudence had caused an upheaval in her family home. When Carlotta had become interested in one of the stable lads, for instance, Prudence had managed to coax him into leaving his employment with a hefty bribe because he was regarded as an unsuitable match. A similar pattern had been repeated when Carlotta had indulged in a liaison with one of Cuthbert's jockeys. She fumed at this disappointment. Perhaps if I had got married, then I would have been able to get out of this place and still keep Jonquil in the stables? Oh, what might have been!

And now that Carlotta was interested in striking up a friendship with Florence and Aubrey, she did not want Pru to stand in her way. Carlotta valued Florence as a friend and Aubrey maybe as a potential lover. So Prudence has got to be muzzled and forcibly restrained.

Carlotta also considered all the times when Cuthbert himself had been brought to heel when he had been inclined to stray from the straight and narrow as was his wont in the romantic liaison department. Finally, of course, Cuthbert had kerbed his amorous tendencies – perhaps as a result of advancing age – but the upshot was an aggrieved and discontented brother unlike the Cuthie she knew of old. Cuthbert's unhappiness was all the result of aunt Pru's interference. He had really only married Agatha in order to appease Prudence and the marriage now just hung together by a thread of convention.

Carlotta knew, for instance, that Cuthbert had been friendly with a stable girl some years ago and that they had amused each other splendidly in the hayloft for a while. But what had happened to her, I wonder? Betsy she was called, I remember. She disappeared rather suddenly and without a backward glance. And Cuthie had taken some rather drastic steps, if I remember. Was that more of Prudence's meddling? However, that's all in the past now. It's the present and the future I'm more concerned with. But what can be done about the old dragon? I can't gag her. I can't throttle her? We can't evict her? No options left.

With these recollections and her contemplation, Carlotta burst into tears and so she was forced to dismount and to tether Morning Mist to a tree while she outpoured her grief. The tears flowed strong and hard for some while as Carlotta unburdened her soul to the hills. Morning Mist nuzzled close in order to comfort Carlotta and this expression of kindness in time did the magic. Poor lass, Morning Mist was thinking. I see now why I had to go for a ride with Carlotta so that she could get away from it all. It's probably that cantankerous old mare they call aunt Prudence.

Then a brilliant idea struck Carlotta which might prove to be a lasting solution. It would be a drastic measure – true. But then the situation calls for it. And it would be one hundred per cent watertight most definitely. Carlotta brightened at the prospect of an answer to her prayers. And so she set about scheming in order to bring her burgeoning idea to fruition. After some more serious cogitation, therefore, Carlotta remounted Morning Mist and she rode him home in a new uplifted frame of mind. Carlotta now had an idea and she would make sure that it worked to her advantage.

When she arrived back at Havercoyne Grange, a few employees noticed that Carlotta looked a lot brighter and more resolute. She was in quite a different mood from her departure and it was observed by all.

After checking on the horses and returning Morning Mist to one of the girls, Carlotta wandered towards the orchard still deep in thought. She then made her way to the potting shed in the kitchen garden where she noted its contents and she was pleased with what she beheld. Carlotta then returned to the house and made straight for Ingrid's office where she kept her computer. Carlotta had now met the new secretary and so she felt justified in invading the administrative office unannounced.

The internet was often temperamental at Havercoyne Grange but today it delivered the goods supremely to Carlotta's satisfaction. Carlotta undertook searches for "poison" and "weedkiller" and she avidly read the results of her researches. She felt very pleased with her efforts and she began to formulate a plan in her mind. Carlotta concocted a recipe which could slowly be used to exterminate aunt Prudence and she realised that her task would be easier than she had expected. And so she smiled a smile of self-congratulation over her ingeniously hatched plan which would achieve her aim with slickness and efficiency.

But I shall need an accomplice. Who can I trust? It will have to be one of the family and there's only one possible candidate. So Carlotta shinned up the stairs to the attic room where Cuthbert was busy playing with his adored Overland Shuttle.

"I need an urgent word with you in private," she demanded of her brother.

Cuthbert was feverishly engaged in hiding his hipflask under a cushion when he heard a footfall outside the door but he was enormously relieved when he realised that it was not aunt Pru who had invaded his sanctuary.

"We must talk. But not here. Come for a walk in the grounds with me."

"What now?"

"Right now!"

Cuthbert retrieved his hipflask and returned it to his office desk on the way down the staircase.

"What the hell's so urgent, sis?" enquired Cuthbert, once the siblings were out in the open air and out of earshot of the remainder of the inhabitants of the Grange.

"I have a plan to rid us of all our troubles but I need your co-operation."

Carlotta was not the one to beat about the bush.

"What troubles?" asked Cuthbert.

"Aunt Prudence."

"She's certainly one of our most awful troubles, I agree. But I can't see how she could be ousted from the place."

"In a coffin," proclaimed Carlotta.

"But she could last for years," protested her brother gloomily.

"Yes, I know. But we could give her a nudge."

"What have you in mind then? Shove her under a train? She never travels by train. Get the horses to trample on her? They wouldn't soil their hooves. Sell her into slavery? No one would want her. Kick her down the stairs?"

"Shut up. No better than that. Weedkiller!" announced Carlotta with pride.

"What kill her? But that could land us both in jail!" cautioned her astonished brother.

"Not if we're clever."

Carlotta's enigmatic remark stimulated Cuthbert's interest yet halted his pathetic jokes.

"You're not serious, surely?"

Carlotta remained impassive.

"OK. How then?" he demanded with scepticism.

Carlotta noticed with amusement that Cuthbert was not averse to the idea in principle but that he was cynical about the effectiveness of her proposal and their ability to get away with it. So she outlined her plan in more detail. Cuthbert still wavered but he did not dismiss the idea out of hand.

"We could still be caught red-handed. Particularly if there's an autopsy or, worse still, a police investigation."

"So you're interested then?"

"Oh, I don't really think I'd want to be part of it," asserted Cuthbert.

"But I need you to help me."

"No chance!"

Cuthbert had obviously made his decision but Carlotta found a way of twisting his arm so that he came around to her way of thinking very decisively.

"Betsy Drury disappeared without trace but, if the police, started investigating that episode, you might not like it."

There was a stunned silence while Cuthbert contemplated the significance of Carlotta's last statement of fact.

"But you can't hold that against me. That was years ago," Cuthbert protested in a desperate voice. "Are you blackmailing me?"

"If you like to put it like that, yes."

"You wouldn't?"

"Wouldn't I? Help me out here Cuthie and solve all our problems in one hit," beseeched Carlotta.

"I must admit, I'm tempted."

"Well, sleep on it then and I'll do some more thinking."

Cuthbert realised that life would be considerably better without Prudence around the place but he was not sure that he wanted to join forces with his sister for such a dangerous venture. He agreed, however, to give the proposal some further consideration.

Carlotta felt content with her progress so far because she was sure that her brother would eventually come on board and join the party. She, therefore, decided to do some further research and planning with a view to bringing Cuthbert in on the scheme. Carlotta was determined to suborn Cuthbert with her blackmail scheme because he would make life much easier for her with regard to her brilliant project.

The two siblings then went their separate ways with their minds full of buzzing bees and scratching rats with only minimal reservation about the proposal. But with no qualms at all about putting the old bitch down. And, of course, both were very excited at the prospect of freedom from the venom-breathing snake. Needs must when the devil drives and this sentiment was felt by both siblings. Prudence was obviously asking for it and she had been for some time. Option three in motion.

## LOUISE'S DEPARTURE

Louise's departure was an occasion for celebration at Havercoyne Grange not only because she was leaving, albeit temporarily, but also because she would soon be bringing baby Harrison into the world. And the household was also greeting the arrival of the newcomer.

The family, household servants and estate workers, consequently, were assembled for drinks in the dining room of Havercoyne Grange in order to toast Louise Fulham-Price's exodus and to welcome Ingrid Durbine into the tribe. Byron, of course, was more inclined to toast the new arrival than to celebrate Louise's departure.

Joyce had made some sausage rolls and sandwiches for the occasion and Nancy was arranging plates of this rather uninteresting nosh on the dining table.

Agatha and Cuthbert arrived early for the event and Cuthbert took the opportunity to get stuck into the drink. Red and white wine had been provided and this was a good follow-up to the whiskey which Cuthbert had already consumed in the attic room while watching his trainset do its daily rounds.

The rest of the party arrived in dribs and drabs and the wine was poured by Barraclough as the company gradually assembled. Nancy offered the plates of food around as the guests entered.

The two guests of honour soon arrived. Louise obviously declined the alcohol but she was given fruit juice to drink instead. Barraclough had thought this one through satisfactorily with only minimal prompting from

Joyce who was more concerned to ensure that the butler arrived sober for the occasion. Ingrid confined herself to a glass of white wine and she approved of this beverage as a vast improvement on Cuthbert's coffee – once sampled never to be imbibed again.

Once the entire company were well catered for, Agatha gave Cuthbert a nudge as her means of prompting him to make a speech for the occasion. Cuthbert had not expected to be asked to make a speech and he was thus unprepared. Cuthbert, in desperation, wandered towards the dinner gong and he banged it loudly as his means of stalling for time while he thought about what he might say. The room fell silent.

"Ladies and gentlemen, may I have your attention please?" Anyway that's a good start, thought Cuthbert. "We're gathered here today to celebrate the passing of Louise and to introduce er . . . Ingrid to our happy company."

Not original but it would do. Fortunately Cuthbert had at the last second remembered Ingrid's name. Agatha wondered whether he would be making the father-of-the-bride's speech at a wedding and so she gave him a warning look which Cuthbert did not even notice.

"Louise will be leaving to have her baby and we wish her well."

Again not original but a pretty fair attempt for an unrehearsed speech. Also Cuthbert knew very little about Louise because he really was not able to engage with people. He would, in fact, have made a better spontaneous attempt at a farewell speech if he were talking about one of his racehorses. Cuthbert regarded both Louise and Ingrid merely as people who came into his office every morning, filtered telephone calls, typed his letters and arranged a few appointments. What else was there to know?

"Louise has been with us for some time and now we see her life will be moving in a different direction and we wish her well in dealing with sleepless nights and washing nappies."

A bit tactless but it caused a polite titter in the room and Cuthbert believed that he had succeeded. Louise simply felt that Cuthbert was doing the best he could in the circumstances and so his joke did not upset her too much. Agatha was, moreover, relieved that Cuthbert had not dried up after his first sentence.

"We also welcome our newcomer, er . . . Ingrid, to the estate and we hope that she will work here for some time to come."

Cuthbert had obviously forgotten that Louise would be returning after her maternity leave and that Ingrid was only a temporary replacement in the interim. Ingrid too was unfazed by Cuthbert's oversight. Ingrid had soon got the measure of Cuthbert and so she did not react to his inept effort at a speech. He will find out soon enough that I'm leaving when I walk out of this place.

The day was saved, however, because Cuthbert's thoughts evaporated and so he was forced to bring his speech to an abrupt conclusion by inviting the drinkers to toast Louise and er . . . Ingrid.

Agatha scowled at Cuthbert but she decided not to reprimand him for his incompetence or his tactlessness. She felt that the subject was best left alone and, in any case, she was sure that the two secretaries would have, by now, understood that Cuthbert was a bloody fool.

With the formality out of the way, Byron decided to make a move before the opportunity escaped him. He, therefore, sidled up to Ingrid in order to enquire whether she was enjoying her new job.

"How are you settling in your new job as old Cuthbert's secretary then?" began Byron.

Byron was obviously not original in his chat-up line any more than Cuthbert was when delivering a farewell speech.

"Very much," Ingrid lied.

Ingrid was becoming accustomed to the routine of her work for Cuthbert at Havercoyne Grange. The morning's post generated letters to type, meetings to arrange and telephone calls to make. Ingrid found the job very uninteresting on the surface but she liked the atmosphere on the Havercoyne Stanley estate and she got on well with all the staff. Ingrid's job was not very exciting but it did, at least, bring in some money. Her antequated mini could already see its name written on its own death warrant because Ingrid was planning to replace it in the near future with a more up-to-date model.

"He's a bit of an old fossil, I know," continued Byron who wanted to ensure that Ingrid knew his true opinion of Cuthbert.

"Most of this place is," she remarked.

Wise lady, thought Byron with a smile.

"Are you doing anything this evening, Ingrid? Do you fancy a follow-up drink in the Hunting Horn after this bash?"

Ingrid was a little taken aback by Byron's invitation and for a second she could not decide how best to reply.

"Well, I really should be off soon."

"We could have a quick bite to eat there too, if you wish," suggested the persistent estate manager.

Ingrid realised that she had not actually stated that she had any prior engagement that evening and so she was still in a quandary about whether to accept Byron's invitation.

"I have some urgent things to do this evening which I cannot really shelve," she finally admitted, "But thank you anyway."

Ingrid felt that she needed time to consider whether she actually wanted to see Byron out of hours. Ingrid had got some inkling of Byron's intentions when they had lunched together on her first day but she had not been expecting him to make such a decisive move quite so soon.

"Another time perhaps?" said Byron who thought he might have a crack at Nancy instead.

"Yes," replied Ingrid rather unenthusiastically.

As the party began to wind up, Ingrid saw an opportunity to leave as her means of escaping from Byron as well as making it look as if she had urgent business for that evening. She, therefore, said farewell to Louise and she wished her a trouble-free delivery of baby Harrison.

The rest of the party were now leaving while Nancy, Joyce and Barraclough were engaged in mopping up the debris. Byron took the opportunity to help Nancy out as his means of approaching her with evil intent. Byron, therefore, helped carry plates out to the kitchen but he balked at stacking the dishwasher.

"Fancy a quick drink down at the Hunting Horn, Nancy?" whispered Byron as he feebly handed her some empty plates for the dishwasher.

Nancy was beginning to think that the entire male contingent on the Havercoyne Stanley estate would eventually get around to asking her out for a drink at the pub. But she felt that this fish would definitely need to be stalled for as long as possible. She had already heard something of Byron's reputation and she did not want to become another notch on his bedpost quite yet.

"A bit late for me now, thanks. And I think I've had enough wine already," claimed Nancy.

Byron went through the same routine of offering Nancy a meal which could act as blotting paper for the wine but it seemed that the kitchen maid could not be tempted. Nancy then tracked down Joyce and beseeched her to act as her protector. Joyce rose to her task admirably by loudly instructing Nancy to set the dining table for dinner later that evening. Byron had been thus sent away with a flea in his ear by two women that evening but he resolved more earnestly to reel in the fish at some other time. Playing hard to get can sometimes make the desire to succeed grow stronger.

Ned, of course, was pleased to note that Byron had been given the old heave-ho by Nancy and so he optimistically believed that he might have a chance with her. Ned, nevertheless, went along to the Hunting Horn by himself in order to celebrate alone.

## FLORENCE'S INVITATION

About a week later Carlotta received a written invitation from one of her neighbours in the form of a semi-informal note. Carlotta was glad to hear from her new friends and so she shelved her contemplation about despatching Prudence temporarily in favour of thinking about the attractive Aubrey who had stirred up some interesting thoughts within her soul.

---

*Dear Carlotta*

*Just a quick note to thank you for kindly giving us lunch the other day.*

*I do hope Jonquil has recovered well. Such a lovely mare.*

*I was wondering if you would like to join us for dinner on Saturday. Please bring your brother Cuthbert and his wife and your brother Damian so that we can have even numbers at the table.*

*I have also invited a couple of academics who are visiting the area and doing some research into country estates. I'm sure you'll find them interesting company.*

*Do say you'll come, my dear friend. Aubrey and I want very much to see you again and to meet your family.*

*Sincerely*

*Florence Bankover*

---

Carlotta was pleased to receive this invitation and even more ecstatic to discover that the odious Prudence had been omitted from the guest list. Since Carlotta's outburst and her attack on Prudence, she had spent most of her time pointedly avoiding her aunt and she hoped to continue the practice indefinitely.

Carlotta had also spend many hours and days planning the way in which she and her brother could rid the planet of the abominable Prudence. Carlotta and Cuthbert had now become closer because they were united by their hatred of aunt Pru. And Carlotta was sure that Cuthbert would readily fall in with her plans once they had finally been successfully formulated. Lady Macbeth was good at recruiting weaker vessels to her cause.

Carlotta was eager to meet Florence and Aubrey again. And so she planned to smarten herself up for the occasion. Carlotta also looked forward to introducing the rest of her family to her new acquaintances.

Damian was especially eager to meet the academic researchers whom Florence had mentioned because he felt that he would come into his own as the curator of the museum at Havercoyne Grange. And so Damian too donned his best bib and tucker for the occasion.

Cuthbert and Agatha dressed formally for the dinner but they both hoped that they would not have to sit next to each other at the meal table. Their frosty relationship did not, of course, stop them from accepting the invitation jointly from Carlotta's new companions. But keeping up the pretence that they were happily married for too long was a considerable strain which both parties wished to avoid if possible.

Florence and Aubrey heartily welcomed the Gansville-Stubbs family as they ushered the party into the hall at the Old Foundry. Carlotta made the appropriate introductions.

"Our other guests have not arrived yet but I'm sure they'll be here soon."

"Yes, we're slightly early. Sorry," responded Agatha.

"Not at all. Come and have a drink," invited Aubrey as he indicated the direction of the lounge.

The pre-prandial drinks were dispensed by Aubrey who was thrilled that such distinguished guests had accepted his invitation to an evening party. Florence ensured that all were seated comfortably before she handed out some canapés which her cook-housekeeper had prepared to perfection.

The academics shortly arrived in order to complete the party and the introductions were speedily effected.

Lyall Vanburgh described himself as an Emeritus Professor of Architectural History who was currently working for an unspecified university in Japan in a consultancy capacity. Dr Katherina Vanburgh was apparently undertaking research for a series of articles which she proposed to have published in a number of scholarly journals.

"What sort of research are you engaged in then?" asked Damian who seemed the only one interested enough to know more about Katherina's work.

"I have been looking into the state of ancient country estates and the extent to which they have been preserved."

Damian, who believed that he would at last make his mark on the world, blossomed like a spring tulip which was opening at dawn and was captured on a fast film. The rest of the Gansville-Stubbs family merely smiled politely. Most of them were wondering whether any more canapés would be circulating soon.

"Well, Havercoyne Grange was built in the nineteenth century. We estimate the date to be around 1860," declared Damian.

"Victoria's reign is exactly the period in which I'm most interested," replied Florence.

"Have you visited the Grange?" asked Damian.

"Oh, yes. We've both done the guided tour," interposed Lyall.

"Well, the guided tour is rather rudimentary, of course. But why not come one day and I'll give you a more detailed tour and commentary."

"How very kind. I'd certainly like to take you up on that," enthused Katherina emphatically as Damian proffered his business card.

Aubrey offered some more canapés to those in the room who, apart from Damian, seemed to be regretting having accepted the dinner invitation if the chatter were to be confined to the Grange's history.

"I can show you some of our archives and the rooms which are not open to the public," continued Damian.

"Splendid. That would be splendid. I'd be so grateful," stated Katherina as she inspected and pocketed Damian's card.

Light relief was soon afforded by the cook-housekeeper who entered the lounge in order to announce the arrival of dinner.

The party decanted to the dining room and, of course, Damian ensured that he sat next to Katherina at the table so that they could continue their conversation which was beginning to bore the pants off the rest of the assembled company.

Aubrey then managed to grab a seat next to Carlotta while Agatha engineered the situation in order to sit beside Lyall. Cuthbert thus was left with the only remaining seat at the table next to Florence but he was not at all displeased with this arrangement.

Damian and Katherina talked avidly about the history of Havercoyne Grange, even though Katherina did not want to burn her boats by over-egging the pudding at this stage. Damian, however, visualised his name in academic lights when Dr Vanburgh published her articles and gave him due acknowledgement for his contribution to her research.

Aubrey meanwhile was chatting up Carlotta with a new spin on the usual routine.

"Tell me about the racehorses in your charge, Carlotta."

"Well, Jonquil is my own horse but she, of course, doesn't do any racing."

"But you do have racehorses in the stables?"

"Oh, yes. There's Morning Mist who's won several times at Newbury and Epsom. Gathering Thunder won Epsom last year on the flat. And Balleytree we're hoping to start next year as a steeplechaser."

"Really. You must come and see our stables sometime. We only have Pink Dust and Magic Fury here as yet. We hope they will do steeplechasing when Ian Manningbury thinks they're ready. My own horse is Honey Nectar but he, of course, is no racer either."

"I'd love to come," replied the horsey Carlotta who was keen to see any horses which might be in the area.

"Well, when will you next be at Ian's jumps?"

Carlotta outlined her schedule for the forthcoming week and so Aubrey agreed to meet her one morning for a casual jaunt over the downs after the matutinal exercise of their respective horses. Carlotta said she would bring Jonquil and Aubrey added that Honey Nectar would suffice for the occasion. The racehorses could then make their own way home with the grooms.

Agatha found Lyall's company most uplifting and she wondered whether she could entice him into seeing her more often away from the family enclave. Agatha thus broached the subject of the latest production which the Havercoyne Stanley Players would soon be inflicting on the local residents. And she suggested that Lyall and Katherina might wish to purchase a couple of tickets perhaps.

"I would certainly like to see the play if at all possible," affirmed Lyall.

Agatha was delighted to hear this news from Lyall because she had secured for herself the starring role of Helen Lancaster in Norman Charles Hunter's play *Waters of the Moon* for this production. And she naturally wanted to display her talents to all the world and, most particularly, to the attentive professor.

Cuthbert and Florence on their corner of the table did not hit it off quite as successfully as the rest of the diners, although they were not in any way averse to sitting next to each other. Cuthbert could acknowledge that Florence was quite a good looking woman but regretfully he realised that the lovely lady would these days probably be beyond his grasp. And she was a bit near to home anyway.

"So what occupies your time at Havercoyne Grange?" asked Florence politely.

Cuthbert explained that he oversaw the running of the business but that he had other business interests elsewhere.

"What are your other outside interests then, Cuthbert?" persisted Florence.

"Oh, I do a bit of share dealing and I sit on a few boards. A bit of investment in property. I back a few projects, that sort of thing, you know. All very boring really."

Florence's silence indicated her agreement with Cuthbert's assertion.

By the end of the evening, however, progress had been made overall. Carlotta and Aubrey had made a date on the downs scheduled for next week, Katherina and Damian would soon be touring Havercoyne Grange and Lyall had agreed to attend Agatha's star performance. Florence and Cuthbert, on the other hand, had merely parted with a see-you-around-sometime-soon farewell.

The Gansville-Stubbs contingent, consequently, returned home to Havercoyne Grange each with an array of thoughts about the new friends whom they had met and got to know better during the course of the delicious evening meal.

Florence and Aubrey afterwards declared that the evening had been a great success and so they retired to bed content with their evening's work.


## BARRINGTON'S RESEARCH

Calendula Fortescue-Bligh and Barrington Flint of the Medici Squadron were having a drink in the High Woodfield Hotel in which they were staying in Grayling Wood.

"I thought last night's party was a great success," proclaimed Calendula.

"Absolutely!"

"And the information is filtering through nicely. Don't you think?"

"Certainly," replied Barrington.

"So where are we now?"

"Well, we know that Cuthbert has some letters and things in his desk as keepsakes from his affair with Betsy but we don't know why she disappeared. But there's an office safe behind a picture."

"But we need to do some more research," announced Calendula who was adopting a pragmatic approach.

"Yes," agreed her partner, "we need to find out whether she's still alive and where she's living. I've already ordered a copy of her birth certificate which should arrive any day now. But I can't find any trace of a death certificate."

"But that doesn't mean that she's still alive, of course."

"I agree. We need more troops on the ground perhaps."

A meeting of the Medici Squadron then ensued as both parties gave the dilemma some thought. They soon came to some decisions about how best to play their next card.

"I think we still need to keep digging and discovering," said Calendula who was the creative brains of the team.

"Do you think we need any more groundworkers?" mused Barrington.

"Not yet awhile. We shall, of course, need Foxy at some point in the future but let Vivian see if she can identify any more evidence first before we send him in. And Maisie may uncover some treasures soon too."

"And Jules?" enquired Barrington.

"Not just yet, I think. But we shall need him eventually."

"I don't think Cuthbert's very computer literate so that may give us an opening."

The two had now reached an impasse in reviewing the project and so they just sipped their drinks and contemplated dinner.

"Shall we stay here for dinner or go out on the town?" asked Barrington.

"We could try the Hunting Horn again to see if old Harry can cough up anything else perhaps," pondered Calendula.

"Oh, I think we've blood-sucked him dry but there may be others we could approach."

"Maybe."

Calendula was still lost in thought but it seemed that her creative juices were not flowing abundantly that evening.

"Let's just have dinner here tonight and then we can sleep on the problem."

Dinner was a succulent roast for Calendula and Barrington who then retired early to bed after a luxurious romp in the ensuite jacuzzi in their room.

The next day brought a copy of Betsy Drury's birth certificate which proved that she had been born but, more importantly, it revealed the names of her parents. Barrington instantly jumped on the internet in order to find out whether there was anyone by the name of Drury in the Newcastle area. An online telephone directory exposed about a dozen names and he proceeded to make his way down the list.

"Hello, this is the census office in London, could I please speak to Mr or Mrs Drury? I'm trying to trace the whereabouts of their daughter Elizabeth, known as Betsy."

This patter uncovered a series of responses to Barrington's request to which his ears were assailed.

"I'm not married, sir. And I resent your implication!"

"Not today, thank you."

"I never speak to government officials, sir. Please put your request in writing."

"Fuck off!" said an angry female voice and "slam" said the telephone receiver.

"Sorry this line is very bad. Can't hear you. Don't know no Betsy. Can you ring back next week?"

"Sorry, wrong number."

"I only 'ave a son and 'is name's not Betsy."

"Betsy Drury, you say. Never heard of anyone called Betsy Drury. I do know a Betty Mason but she moved away many years ago now."

"I think there's a Betsy who lives at number 6. But her name's Brown."

This routine seemed to go on for hours until, at last, Barrington struck oil.

"I'm Mrs Drury – Betsy's mum. But we ain't seen her for years, Mister. Sorry," said a sad female voice.

Had Barrington discovered the key to the treasure chest?

"I'm sorry to hear that," Barrington assumed his most encouraging and empathetic tones. "Do you know where she's living now?"

"Last we heard she was working on a farm in Devon or Somerset somewhere. Some country estate or something for some lords and ladies. But, as I say, she ain't been in contact these last ten years at least."

Barrington continued to probe in order to see if Mrs Drury could provide any more clues as to ways in which he could track down Betsy but he drew a blank every time. Finally Barrington concluded the conversation with warmth, sympathy and best wishes to Mrs Drury. Her husband, Barrington also discovered, had been in decline for many years and he was now just simply sitting in god's waiting room. Barrington offered what comfort he could in the circumstances and he terminated his call to Mrs Drury with sorrow and regret.

Maybe our researches will bring more bad news for Mrs Drury, poor soul? I wonder whether we could make her life more tolerable perhaps? Barrington seemed lost in sad thought about the situation for some time before he reported his findings to Calendula who felt a similar degree of pity for Betsy Drury's parents.

"Well, if she's not contacted her parents for years, where the hell can she be then?" pondered Calendula.

"Under the patio? Or beneath the haystack?"

"I reckon Cuthbert must be the key to this whole equation," Calendula decided emphatically.

"I agree. We must keep probing in that quarter. Could we send him a lover, do you think?" asked Calendula.

"He's a bit of a prune and might no longer be susceptible."

"Oh, you're never too old for that! Who can we think of? Someone young but not too young."

"Let's give the matter some thought. I'll look on the database," concluded Barrington.

"Well, if you take me out to lunch, then I might be able to do some creative thinking," replied his partner in love and crime.

The Hunting Horn, therefore, received two customers for the lunchtime special and the landlord, Dave, was delighted to welcome the return of Professor Lyall Vanburgh and Dr Katherina Vanburgh who elected to eat in the restaurant and they decided to order the most expensive dishes on the menu. By lunching at the Hunting Horn, Calendula and Barrington believed that they could kill two birds with one stone.

"Are you still doing your research at Havercoyne Grange then professor?" asked Dave who was eager to cultivate these two new and valuable customers.

"Yes, indeed, we met the family the other night through a mutual acquaintance and Katherina will be visiting the museum shortly," replied the professor.

"Only I thought you could also ask Jessie Braithwaite who used to work there as cook and still lives just outside Grayling Wood."

Things were certainly looking up for the Medici Squadron who were anxious to follow up this lead.

"Do you have her address by any chance, Dave?" asked an eager Calendula.

"Don't know it but I'm sure if you asked anyone in Grayling Wood you'd soon find out," answered Dave obligingly.

"We'll do that, Dave. Thank you," said Calendula with a winning smile.

Lunch consisted of a starter of Stilton-stuffed mushrooms for Calendula and some bruschetta for Barrington. This repast was followed by braised tenderloin pork with sauerkraut and creamy mash for Barrington and monkfish tails with a prawn and shrimp sauce for his beloved.

When Nellie brought in their starters, she was able to supply further information about Havercoyne Grange's former cook, Jessie Braithwaite.

"I think she lives in a cottage in Grayling Wood just up the hill from the main street. Ivy Cottage or something like that," asserted Nellie.

"Does she live alone?" asked Calendula.

"With her sister, Elsie, I think. She used to work at the house too, I think."

It was obvious to both Calendula and Barrington that Nellie did a lot of thinking but her thoughts were quite useful for their purposes. They both exchanged glances which contained a hint of satisfaction as Nellie returned to the bar in order to serve the next customer.

Calendula and Barrington drove back to their hotel after lunch and they plunged into the jacuzzi in celebration of their discoveries.

"We can easily pump Jessie and Elsie for information now that we know where they live," stated Calendula.

"Yes. And I know just the cookie to do the job!" announced Barrington proudly.

So watch this space.


## CALENDULA'S INQUISITION

Damian Gansville-Stubbs was up early because for him it was a special day and he dressed in his smartest country casuals for the occasion. Damian first gave a kit-inspection to that part of Havercoyne Grange which was open to the public in order to assure himself that everything was hunky-dory and that the place generally looked impressive.

Damian then wandered into the main staff office in the hope of bumping into Vanessa for whom he had carried a torch for many years. Vanessa, who had repeatedly made it clear to Damian that she was not about to accept any of his repeated proposals of marriage, was making coffee in the small staff kitchen.

"Morning Vanessa," began Damian with much enthusiasm.

"Morning," returned Vanessa with no enthusiasm at all.

"How are you this fine morning?"

"OK. And if you have come to pledge your love to me yet again then the answer is still "no". Go away!"

Damian ignored Vanessa's sneer.

"I came to say that I shall be receiving a special guest today. I'll be showing her the museum."

Vanessa made no comment while she continued to stir her instant coffee and she delicately selected a biscuit from the tin. She failed to asked Damian, however, if he wanted a cup. Why not marry your special guest instead then?

"Doctor Vanburgh will be here at 9.30 am and I've agreed to show her the place. Would you like to join us?" continued Damian hopefully.

"I have a couple of tours to do this morning," stated Vanessa blandly. Her clipped speech was obviously a rehearsal for her imminent tours that morning.

"Well, perhaps you could join us for lunch at about noon then?" volunteered Damian expectantly.

But Damian was flogging a dead horse in his quest to interest the icy-cold tour guide. Vanessa was noncommittal about whether she could join Damian and his guest for lunch. And so Damian decided that he would simply ask her again at midday but he did not press her for a decision right now. Damian should have, by now, become accustomed to the fact that Vanessa was extremely reluctant to commit herself. After all she had been rebuffing his overtures for several years. Poor sod! But some men never learn.

Damian then wandered into Joyce's kitchen in the main part of the house where Nancy was glad to make him a coffee and offer him a biscuit which he took back to his small office behind the museum. Breakfast seemed a long way off as far as Damian was concerned.

The museum's receptionist, who received visitors and who arranged the tour bookings, soon rang through to Damian's office in order to announce the arrival of his esteemed guest – Dr Katherina Vanburgh. Damian instantly jumped up at the news and he hastily made his way to the reception area in order to greet his visitor with gushing acclaim.

Calendula, who had the other evening been clad in a becoming silver-grey dress with a splash of scarlet at the plunging neckline, had elected to dress more soberly in a navy trouser suit with a white turtle-necked silk top. She had decided that she now needed to play the part of the successful academic.

"Katherina. How nice to see you again," proclaimed Damian who tried hard not to grovel too much in the presence of his important guest.

"Thank you for inviting me, Damian," replied Calendula with the best impression she could muster of sincerity and eagerness.

"Would you like to have tea or coffee first? Or would you like to go straight through to the museum?"

"Well, let's make a start on the museum first, Damian. Just so that you can refresh my memory and then we can have a break when I have some more questions."

Calendula drew a clipboard and pen from her briefcase in her effort to look businesslike.

Damian escorted his guest through the principal rooms which she had already seen under the watchful eye of Vanessa a couple of weeks ago. Calendula was careful to ask as many questions as she could dream up. She hoped that her scanty and hurriedly mugged up knowledge of the history of architecture and antique furniture would not display too many gaping holes. Calendula, of course, took copious notes because she felt that this action would impress her host.

When the pair retired for refreshment in the museum's below-stairs restaurant, Calendula decided that her line of questioning should, however, take a different turn.

"But, Damian, can you tell me more about the people who have lived here and what they did please?"

Damian now began a long rigmarole about his ancestors and what they got up to. Calendula felt that she was cantering on to the right track and so she murmured her encouragement of Damian's account while constantly taking notes and smiling at him beatifically.

"And you've been here since your brother took over about a decade ago?"

"Oh, yes. And I've run the museum side of things since it opened. Shortly after Cuthbert took over," Damian boasted.

"And what about the staff here then? Who were they?"

Calendula was determined that her tedious morning spent in Damian's company would somehow bear fruit for her purpose. Damian then explained that Barraclough had been in residence from the start and that the butler had been inherited from the time when George had briefly run the show.

"And the other household staff?" persisted Calendula.

"They've all left now. But our former cook still lives locally, I believe."

Calendula already knew this relevant piece of data because she and Barrington had made plans to contact her anyway.

"I see. What about the stable staff and the farmworkers then? I would be interested to talk to anyone who has worked on the estate within living memory."

"Well, there's Ned in the stables, I believe. And, of course, our estate manager, Byron Travers. I could arrange for you to meet them later if you like? They've been here a goodly while. As long as I have at any rate."

Damian was beginning to feel that Katherina's interest was turning away from his neck of the woods but he decided to endeavour to appease the scholar as much as he could because it would reflect well on him.

"I would be glad to meet anyone who could perhaps tell me more about life in the house and on the estate. It is often the best way for a historian to discover bits of very useful information."

"I see," said Damian who really didn't see anything at all but he agreed to play the game.

After their mid-morning refreshment, Damian showed Calendula into some of the rooms which were not part of the museum and which were still retained by the family. He kept up a running commentary throughout this part of the tour. Calendula continued to scribble avidly on her notepad. And she hoped that she would not inhale too much of the dust which was liberally strewn about the place in the unused rooms.

"Our housekeeper, Elizabeth Garrick, has instructions to only really clean this part of the house once or twice a year, I'm afraid," explained Calendula's host by way of an apology.

That much is obvious thought Calendula but, out of politeness, she smiled her acknowledgement of this unsavoury fact. From this part of the tour, however, Calendula learned of the whereabouts of the main living rooms in Havercoyne Grange, Cuthbert's office, the Overland Shuttle's residence and Prudence's headquarters. Calendula drew a plan of the layout of the house and she took a few discreet snaps because she believed that this information could prove useful in time. The pair, however, did not actually venture up to the attic rooms for fear of an assault from Prudence.

"Can you stay for lunch, Katherina?" asked Damian at the appropriate hour and Calendula gladly accepted.

Damian telephoned through to Vanessa but she was still being obstinately evasive by vaguely citing pressure of work as her excuse for not joining the party. Damian, however, felt that, on this occasion, he was glad to have his academic visitor all to himself.

After lunch Calendula was taken to meet Ned in the stables from whom she learned that Cuthbert had been more active when it came to riding the bloodstock back in the day.

"Why did he stop riding, do you think?" asked Calendula.

"I suppose he just got too tied up with the business and running the estate to have much leisure for riding," replied Ned.

"Do you ride yourself Katherina?" interjected Damian.

Damian was hoping that he could find an excuse for luring Katherina back to the house where he could show off more of his intimate knowledge of the Grange and its artefacts but he soon realised that he had obviously drawn a blank here.

"No. I did briefly as a child. But now I'm far too busy with my academic work," lied Calendula. What the hell would I ever want to get on a bloody horse for?

Calendula was next taken to the estate office where she met Byron and Delia. Delia, a relative newcomer, had no useful information to offer Calendula but Byron was more obliging to Damian's guest.

Byron visibly swelled at the sight of Calendula. Caw, she could ask me any questions she liked any time! Byron began to believe that his harem might grow considerably if Ingrid, Nancy and Katherina were all willing to come on board. He, therefore, proffered his business card and he suggested that they might meet for a drink one evening so that Katherina could ask him further questions when he was not as busy on the estate as he was today. Byron pretended that he was overworked during the day so that he could manipulate the situation in his own favour. Delia raised an eyebrow because she was not deceived and she knew Byron of old.

Calendula accepted Byron's business card with a promise to contact him shortly. Calendula now felt that she should take her leave of the Havercoyne Stanley estate and its inhabitants in order to mull over her findings.

"Thank you very much for your patience and co-operation," she said as she shook hands with Byron and Damian and then made her way back to her car escorted by an obsequious Damian.

Damian dreamed of the notoriety which he would acquire from Dr Vanburgh's research while Byron savoured the hope that, if he could reel in this fish, he would be a very contented man. *I could keep her amused for hours. And I might not be too tempted to look elsewhere. Well, not for some while, at least, that is.*

Calendula's thoughts, however, were taking a very different turn. She had now identified those residents and employees at Havercoyne Grange whom she could tackle for her own purposes. Byron would be a pushover. Ned could easily be tapped for more information no doubt. Barraclough could possibly be approached and persuaded to talk after being plied with some house claret. Carlotta and Agatha would soon come across may be. But Damian was a fool and thus he was hardly worth the effort.

Barrington was delighted when he heard of Calendula's fruitful research mission and the way in which their project could be accelerated. Together they compiled a list of what needed to be done, who needed to be contacted and who could be cracked together with the easiest route in order to achieve this objective.


## PRUDENCE'S IMPUDENCE

Nancy climbed the many stairs up to the top floor with Prudence's lunch for that day as usual. She tapped lightly on the door in order to announce her arrival.

"Who is it?"

"Your lunch, madam."

"Come in."

Nancy obeyed Prudence's command and entered the top-floor rooms. Prudence's suite consisted of a decent-sized sitting room with a dining table and chairs, several bookcases and two sofas, although Prudence seemed to favour sitting on hard upright chairs because her back was not what it used to be. Nancy swiftly arranged the plates and dishes on the dining table and she hastened to make an exit with the empty silver salver because Prudence was not particularly good company.

"Who was that who came to see Damian yesterday?" demanded Prudence.

"Not sure, madam."

"Come, child. Surely you must know? A woman came into the Grange and Damian showed her over the place. She didn't come up here naturally but I heard them talking downstairs. Who was she?"

"Don't know, I'm sure, madam."

Nancy had heard of the visit of Dr Vanburgh to the museum and the house because Damian had been in his element about it but she was damned if she would spread gossip in the direction of old Prudence's ears.

"Then go and enquire and report back to me immediately. Is that understood, child?"

Nancy now really had no option but to accede to the old martinet's wishes. And so she nodded politely and left the room with a promise to return in order to collect the remains of lunch and to deliver a news update in due course.

Prudence always wanted to know who came into the Grange and, if she could not actually observe visitors herself, she had other methods of finding out from the servants who could not refuse her request. Prudence, therefore, contentedly settled down to her honey-glazed gammon steak with pineapple while she contemplated her next move.

Back in the kitchen Nancy reported on the task which had been assigned to her by old Pru.

"The old bitch is demanding to know who visited Damian yesterday," advised Nancy.

"Well, I hope you didn't tell her," replied Joyce.

"No, of course, I didn't. But she won't stop nagging me until I spill the beans."

"Barraclough!" called Joyce loudly in the direction of the butler's pantry.

Barraclough, who had been doing some stocktaking on the wine and larder provisions, eventually emerged with notebook and pen in hand. He was trying to look busy and efficient obviously.

"Yes?" responded Barraclough without much curiosity.

Joyce couldn't tell whether Barraclough had been at the cooking sherry that morning but he did appear to be fairly sober for once.

"Barraclough! Old Prudence has been questioning Nancy here about Damian's visitor to the museum yesterday."

"Apparently she heard them talking in the house," added Nancy.

"I see," mumbled Barraclough.

"What are you going to do about it then, Barraclough?" asked Joyce who was determined that her kitchen maid would not be recruited as an unpaid spy for Prudence.

"What the hell can I do about it?" protested Barraclough vehemently.

"Go and tell her the bare facts and shut her up!"

"Easier said than done, Joyce," proclaimed Barraclough who was not interested at all in becoming involved.

"Well, go and see her anyway," insisted the cook.

"And what shall I tell her? I've no idea who comes and goes around here."

Joyce noted Barraclough's lack of enthusiasm in household matters but she believed that his disinterest was partly due to his preoccupation with the contents of the wine cellar.

"An academic lady came here to do some research on the Grange," stated Joyce emphatically in the hope of jockeying the butler into ascending the stairs to Prudence's attic suite.

Barraclough reluctantly buckled under from the pressure of Joyce's glares and her stern expression, coupled with a pleading look from Nancy.

"All right. I'll go and see her this afternoon."

"No, please go now because Nancy will need to collect the lunch tray soon and I don't want her subjected to another inquisition," announced Joyce with finality.

Barraclough conceded defeat and so he made his way up the Havercoyne Grange staircase to the summit.

"Come in," invited Prudence after Barraclough had knocked loudly on her door.

"Well?"

"I understand you're enquiring about a visitor to the Grange, madam."

Prudence remained silent yet expectant with a slight nod of her head.

"Our information is that an academic lady called to see Mister Damian."

"Yes. And what did she want to know? And why did she enter the house?"

"I don't have the details, madam."

"Useless man. Then send Damian to me immediately."

"Yes, madam."

Barraclough withdrew with relief. Having given Pru a minimal amount of information, Barraclough now simply had to inform Damian of Prudence's request before he could return to the sanctuary and comfort of his private pantry.

Barraclough entered Damian's office and explained the old tyrant's wishes to Damian.

"OK. I'll go and see her this afternoon. Thank you, Barraclough."

Damian groaned aloud after Barraclough had left his office but he procrastinated over his journey towards the upper reaches of the house.

Nancy eventually returned to collect Prudence's tray, safe in the knowledge that it was no longer her responsibility to report back to Prudence. But she was mistaken in this assumption.

"Well, have you found out who called on Damian yesterday? And why?" demanded Prudence even more vociferously than she had enquired previously.

Nancy looked flustered but summoned the courage to reply bravely.

"Mr Barraclough has asked Damian to visit you, madam."

"Well, where is the boy then?"

"I don't know, madam. But he should be here shortly."

"You don't seem to know much, do you, child?"

Nancy merely grimaced in reply but she quickly snatched the tray and she made her escape before the old lady could continue her offensive. Nancy recounted her confrontation with Prudence to Joyce who gave Barraclough another dose of stern encouragement in the hope that he could resolve the matter.

Barraclough felt that his life would be made worse if he did not go along with Joyce's wishes because the cook was almost as bad as old Pru. Barraclough thus reluctantly returned to Damian's office where he reported on the fact that Prudence had been continuing to pester and upset the servants. So Damian switched off his computer unenthusiastically and then he climbed the stairs. He banged open aunt Prudence's door without knocking.

"I gather you're being nosey again! You want to know who was visiting me yesterday, I gather?" was Damian's opening gambit.

"I couldn't care less who visits the museum but I object to having people traipsing about my house."

"It's not your house, Pru. And I'll entertain whoever I like here."

World war three was obviously threatening.

"Who was she and what did she want?" continued Prudence unabashed.

"If you must know, she's an academic who's doing some research into old estate houses and she wanted to talk to me, as curator of the museum, about Havercoyne Grange."

"Curator of the museum, indeed! You've always given yourself airs and graces."

"I'm the official curator of the museum and obviously I need to see important visitors."

"Then why did this woman need to come into my house?"

"For the last time, it's not your house!" yelled Damian.

"It is. I live here."

"No, it's not your house. You live here because Cuthbert is being kind to you. Though I can't think why. But if I owned the place you'd be out on your ear in a flash."

Prudence ignored Damian's inhospitable remark.

"I don't want you to bring people into my home without asking me first."

"Well, tough! Like I say, I'll entertain anyone I choose and when I choose. And I didn't bring my guest into your quarters. So I don't know what you're complaining about."

"I still don't want you to bring people into my home."

Damian exploded in exasperation.

"I'll do as I please," he screamed, "and, for the last time, it's not your house and never will be!"

Even the servants could hear this last proclamation from Damian.

"Temper, temper! Control yourself, Damian."

"Why the hell don't you control yourself, you old witch?"

"How dare you speak to me like that!"

Damian realised, eventually, that he was never going to win this argument and that he would never get through to his aunt. Hence he left the room with a final invitation to Prudence.

"Go to hell and stay there and rot," was Damian's parting shot as he loudly slammed the door and shook the rafters of the house.

Prudence was unmoved by Damian's words but she was severely disappointed that so many members of the family were still behaving like unruly children who were a great disappointment to her.

Damian immediately went back to his office where he phoned through to Barraclough in order to report his lack of progress with Prudence. But, at least, the matter had been settled and lifted from Nancy's shoulders.

"Could I tempt you to a glass of sherry, sir?" asked Barraclough solicitously, even though he was depriving himself of a tipple in the process.

"Make it a whiskey without too much soda, please, Barraclough."

Barraclough obeyed and he brought the whiskey into Damian's office. Damian downed the whiskey at lightning speed, thereby breaking all world records for the rapidity of its consumption. Damian replaced the empty glass on the tray as he left his office abruptly.

Barraclough returned to the servants hall with the empty glass but there was fortunately still some whiskey left in the decanter which the butler was pleased to note. Joyce skilfully managed to extract the latest gossip from Barraclough about the Prudence-versus-Damian encounter but apparently there was not much more to tell. The servants again collectively lamented the demise of the household's equilibrium as a result of the old boa constrictor resident in the attic rooms above their heads.

Then another fracas was heard in the distance above the servant's hall. The door of Cuthbert's office crashed open and Damian exploded into the room.

"That fucking woman has got to go, Cuthie!"

Ingrid, who had been taking dictation from Cuthbert, averted her eyes. Cuthbert nodded at her as an indication that she should leave the room.

"I do know how you feel. But there's very little I can do about her, Damian. I'd tried talking to her but it really doesn't work."

Damian sank into the chair which Ingrid had just vacated and he clasped his head in his hands in desperation.

"She was asking me about Florence Vanburgh's visit. Wanted to know who she was and why I was showing her the house. What business is it of hers, I ask you?"

"I know Damian. I do understand. I know it's no business of hers but there's obviously no stopping her."

"Is there nothing you can do to shut her bloody gob? I swear I'll hit her one of these days."

"Well, I'll see what I can do. Of course, I will. But I don't hold out much hope," Cuthbert said finally but with little confidence in his own success.

Ingrid now quietly tiptoed down the stairs having heard the best part of the conversation between Cuthbert and Damian after she had closed Cuthbert's office door.

When Damian returned to his room, moreover, Cuthbert was lost in thought. But he did think that there would be a permanent solution to the dilemma, even though he elected not to impart this information to Damian himself. And his resolve to rid the household of the pestilential infection which blighted the entire household was certainly strengthened by Damian's distress. It, furthermore, added fuel to his own discontentment with the woman. But he knew that a lasting resolution to the problem was, in essence, within his grasp.

## BYRON'S PROPOSITION

Byron was getting itchy. He had beheld three delectable females recently and he wanted to get his hands on at least one of them pretty soon. Well, I'd better take some action then. Who's first? Byron hence contemplated his options.

The delightful academic, Dr Katherina Vanburgh, was the top of his hit list but he simply had to wait for her to ring him. He had casually asked Damian whether he knew where she was staying but Damian seemed clueless on this subject. Byron had learned, however, that Katherina was married. This would not normally have been a deterrent to Byron but he guessed that it might be an impediment for Katherina.

Next Byron considered Ingrid. She worked in the administrative office on her own and so she might be a useful starting choice. Slim, good-looking and fit. I'll try her first!

Byron accordingly wandered across to the house one morning and peeked into Ingrid's office. Ingrid sat at her computer obviously engrossed in typing some of Cuthbert's correspondence. The phone was also ringing which served to overload Ingrid with things to do. Hence Byron took a seat while he waited for this surfeit of secretarial responsibilities to subside for Ingrid which eventually it did. Byron beamed with relief.

"Morning Ingrid," Byron began heartily.

Ingrid gave a polite smile but looked somewhat flurried with overwork and distraction. And she contributed nothing to the conversation which Byron had hoped they would soon strike up.

"What can I do for you?" asked Ingrid testily at last.

What an opportunity! I can think of several things, darling. But I don't think I can be that blunt.

"I came because I wanted to see how you're getting on."

Ingrid said nothing.

"I also wondered whether you enjoyed the party the other night and whether you got home all right?" continued Byron as a means of hoping to kill the silence and Ingrid's lack of response.

Ingrid still remained unmoved and distracted but she knew where this line of questioning was going.

"And, of course, I was still wondering whether you'd like to come out for a drink and perhaps dinner with me? We could perhaps . . ."

Ingrid, however, was saved by an interruption when the door opened and the brittle Elizabeth Garrick appeared. Byron cursed inwardly. Damn that bloody woman. She needs a good seeing to but I shall not be volunteering.

"Morning, Ingrid," stated the housekeeper as she waltzed into the room and she approached Ingrid's desk with purpose.

Byron despaired somewhat. Yeah, that was my opener. Blasted woman!

Ingrid now, at last, came alive. Well, well.

"I'm sorry Byron but I have a meeting now with Elizabeth. We're making the final arrangements for Cuthbert's forthcoming business conference," announced Ingrid who could see Byron visibly collapse at this newsflash.

Next Joyce arrived with a similar good-morning-type greeting and a sheaf of menus in her hand. She was obviously part of this vitally important conference. The cosmos was conspiring heartlessly against Byron.

Byron conceded defeat in the face of the opposition forces and so he left the office with a shrug of his shoulders. Byron wondered what he could do to compensate for Ingrid's frostiness and her lack of availability. And then he had a brilliant idea. I can kill two birds with one stone now.

As Joyce was now safely out of the way at the meeting in Ingrid's office, Byron entered the kitchen in which Nancy was again stacking the dishwasher after breakfast for the troops.

"I was looking for Barraclough," Byron lied, "Is he around, do you know?"

"Gone into the village to restock up on wines."

He's probably drunk most of the last consignment himself. Drunken swine.

"Is Joyce about then?" asked Byron for want of something to say which would engage Nancy in conversation.

"No. She's involved in a meeting with Ingrid and Elizabeth."

"Oh, well, I shall just have to talk to you then."

Nancy now started to peel the vegetables and to assemble the catering equipment on the kitchen table in readiness for lunch. But she did not reply to Byron's tentative approach. Byron felt that he would have to try harder. Why are all these females acting as if the cat's got their tongue?

"Any chance of a coffee?"

"Sure," replied Nancy who nodded in the direction of the kettle and the kitchen cupboard in which the instant coffee was kept.

"Would you like one?"

"No thanks. Just had one."

Byron was not a fan of instant coffee but he conceded that he would need to play the game if his quest were to succeed. He made himself a coffee and he helped himself to a rock cake. Byron then took a seat where he could be in full view of Nancy's bosom. The estate manager, of course, imagined what she might look like without her maid's uniform. How he could help her take it off. And what would happen once she had disrobed.

Nancy still remained silent while she industriously continued preparing the vegetables.

"What's for lunch then?"

"Mutton casserole."

"Wonderful! My favourite," enthused Byron.

Nancy still made no comment in reply.

Byron sighed gently. This is really going to be hard work. Why don't women want to talk to me? Perhaps I'd better come straight to the point?

"Well, I just wanted to ask you to come and have a drink with me one night soon," he said as breezily as he could.

Byron decided that suggesting dinner, as he had done with Ingrid, might not be the right approach with Nancy.

Nancy still did not answer. *What is it with women that they always give me the silent treatment?*

Nancy, however, began to consider Byron's proposal together with his persistence and she decided that a drink with the estate manager would not go amiss. She had, after all, probably got all the information which she needed from Ned but maybe Byron could add to the picture.

"Well, I shall be free tomorrow night at around 8.00 am. I always work late, of course," stated Nancy as she continued to peel the carrots and to wash the broccoli.

*Gawd! My luck's changed at last.* Byron nearly choked on his rock cake.

"That would be great, Nancy! Shall I pick you up from here?" asked Byron throwing discretion to the wind.

"No, let's meet at the pub."

"Good idea. Don't want to start any wagging tongues, do we?" laughed Byron. "The Hunting Horn then?"

"Okay. About 8.30 pm say?"

"Certainly. I look forward to it very much, Nancy," concluded Byron with a wicked grin.

Nancy proffered a seductive smile which did not go unnoticed by the desperate Byron. *Splendid! But I'll save Ingrid for another time.* Byron now took his leave and then returned to the estate office. Nancy noticed that he had left his half-empty coffee cup in the sink for her to attend to rather than putting it in the dishwasher. *I suppose he regards me as a servant. Well what did I expect?*

Delia noticed the contented and expectant look on Byron's face when he re-entered the estate office and she secretly wondered what mischief he had been scheming.

Byron soon made an excuse to himself to leave the office and to go for a trot around the estate so that he could contemplate the change in his fortunes. As he wandered through the orchard and the kitchen garden, Byron dreamed of nights of bliss with Nancy. And then his imagination stretched figuratively in order to include Ingrid and Katherina in his fantasy as well. Eventually his vision ended up in a threesome with all the delectable triumvirate of ladies romping in the hayloft with him. Byron was in seventh heaven. But Byron soon pulled himself back to reality. He decided that he had better check on the horses and the farm animals in order to see if any disasters had occurred while he was out gallivanting.

## CUTHBERT'S TEMPTATION

The phone on Cuthbert's desk did not seem to stop ringing next morning. All his calls were, of course, filtered by Ingrid but he still seemed to be a very popular fellow that morning.

"Peter Elliott for you, Cuthbert," announced Ingrid.

"Peter Elliott?"

"Your stockbroker."

"Oh, yes. Put him through please, Isabel, no, er . . . Ingrid."

Ingrid was by now beginning to think that she should change her name by deed poll to "er . . . Ingrid" in order to ensure that Cuthbert got it right at least some of the time.

When Peter's voice came on the line Cuthbert was glad to hear from him because, when studying the *Financial Times* that morning, he had wondered about the fall in the share price of a computer company in which he had invested.

"Cuthbert, good morning. I trust that you're well. I'm ringing because I think it advisable for you to sell some of your shares in Smart Face Technologies."

"Yes, I agree. I noticed that they've dropped two days running."

"Hm, the company's got a bit unstuck with launching their new product for online videoconferencing. Too many bugs in the software apparently."

Cuthbert, as an old fossil, was not good on the IT jargon and so he just murmured in the hope that Peter would believe that he had been understood.

"I wouldn't advise you to sell the lot because they may make a comeback but, at least, let's drop about two-thirds. You'd still have made a gain over the last three years, of course."

"Thank you for bringing it to my attention. Very grateful, old boy."

"I always have your interests at heart. But your oil and wind farm shares are doing really well."

"Yes, I read that too. Glad for the tip to invest in the fuel sector."

Cuthbert then went through the necessary procedure on the phone so that he could shed the appropriate number of shares in Smart Face Technologies.

Cuthbert's next call was from Florence Bankover.

"You had dinner with her and her brother Aubrey the other night," Ingrid reminded her employer.

"Oh, yes. Remember her well," lied Cuthbert, although the fog in his mind was beginning to clear as he recalled managing to avoid sitting next to his wife at dinner in the Old Foundry.

"Cuthbert, it's Florence," announced his former host.

"Splendid dinner the other night, Florence. I think Agatha wrote to thank you. Splendid. Simply splendid."

"Thank you. But I rang about another matter."

"Oh, yes?"

Cuthbert waited patiently for information.

"I've had contact with a journalist from the *Horse Breeders Gazette*."

"Oh yes, I take it regularly here."

"I thought you probably would. The journalist is writing an article about racehorse owners and I've agreed to be interviewed myself."

"Splendid idea."

"And Gina Wilcox-Ryan, the journalist, was wondering if she could come to you too."

"Certainly. Never too proud for publicity, you know," Cuthbert chuckled. "Do you have her number?"

"Oh, I'll get her to call you, Cuthbert."

"Would you? Most kind. Most kind," blustered Cuthbert as the call concluded.

Cuthbert rang through to Ingrid with the news that he was selling some shares and he asked her to file the accompanying papers when they came through by email. Ingrid thought that Cuthbert was being unusually efficient that morning because he normally simply left her to discover such information for herself when correspondence arrived either by electronic means or by snail mail.

When Gina Wilcox rang, however, Ingrid was reluctant to put the call through to Cuthbert because she had not been informed about this intended call. Cuthbert's efficiency in this quarter was obviously patchy. Ingrid was, consequently, forced to verify that Cuthbert was, in fact, expecting her call.

"Journalist from the *Horse Breeders Gazette*. Yes, yes. Put her through immediately. I'm expecting her call," proclaimed Cuthbert.

"Yes, of course."

Ingrid sighed. Her employer could be efficient in informing her of events on some occasions but obviously not on others which were slightly more important.

"What did you say her name was?"

Ingrid repeated the journalist's name which encouraged Cuthbert to write it down before he forgot it but, unfortunately, he couldn't find a writing implement.

"Lord Gansville-Stubbs? Good morning. I'm Gina Wilcox-Ryan from the *Horse Breeders Gazette*. Florence Bankover gave me your number. Is it convenient to talk just now?"

"Yes, certainly. Certainly," replied Cuthbert while still ferreting around for a pen.

"I wondered if I could come and interview you for an article I'm writing about racehorse owners? I know you're a very eminent member of the owner's clan," announced Gina who was determined to get her request across without delay.

Cuthbert's ego expanded considerably at this overt flattery. Cuthbert began to visualise his name in the headlines of the prestigious *Horse Breeders Gazette* and to imagine becoming a household name in the right circles. An appointment was thus swiftly made for the following day.

When Ingrid showed Gina Wilcox-Ryan into Cuthbert's office the next day, the peer brightened visibly. Cuthbert longed to see his name in print, to be feted by his associates and to be admired at racecourses across the globe.

But his spirits were uplifted for a very different reason as well. The journalist was also a good-looker and her presence did not fail to make an impression on the lord of the manor. Cuthbert instantly drew up a chair for Gina in front of his desk where he had a good view of the object of his interest. Cuthbert had hitherto thought that his philandering days were over. But Gina opened a door in Cuthbert's mind which had been locked and barred for years. This rejuvenation process continued to swell in a manner which took Cuthbert quite by surprise but the feeling was not at all unpleasant or unwanted.

"Good day, Miss . . . er."

"Oh, do call me Gina."

Again Cuthbert looked around for a pen in order to write down her name before he forgot it but, regretfully, he still could not find either a pen or a pencil. But somehow he managed to remember the name which savoured on his lips.

"Sherry, Gina? Or a cocktail?"

"No, coffee will do. Thank you."

Cuthbert, of course, was slightly disappointed that he did not have a legitimate excuse for a tipple himself but he resigned himself to ordering coffee via Ingrid who would ask the kitchen staff to accommodate the newcomer.

"Oh, and do call me Cuthbert, Gina."

He had remembered her name as if, when it was important, he could do so.

Nancy soon arrived with her silver salver and the requested refreshments.

"So tell me what you have in your stables, Cuthbert?" began Gina who also discreetly started the recording app on her phone.

"Well, there's Morning Mist, of course. He's done very well at Epson and Newbury. A very good investment in stud. And then Gathering Thunder won Epsom last year on the flat. And also another steeplechaser, Balleytree, who may start next year or, at least, we hope so. They all train at the nearby Braxwood Yard in Grayling Wood with Ian Manningbury, you know."

Cuthbert had to pause for breath not only because of his long rigmarole but also because he was so taken with his guest's undeniable appeal. Gina wore a very becoming pin-striped suit which gave her a masculine aura but her blouse had a plunge neckline which did not evade the peer's notice. Cuthbert, in truth, had difficulty in keeping his eyes directly on Gina's enchanting face.

"Can you tell me more about the horses then please? How you acquired them, their racing and stud history and which are your favourites, that is."

Cuthbert continued to burble on about his horses and he waxed lyrical about their progress to date and his hopes for the future. Gina, of course, noted that it was obvious that horses where probably the most important members of the family in Cuthbert's eyes. Gina then asked about the Gansville-Stubbs household and the stabling staff. Cuthbert accordingly outlined who lived on the premises but only in a scanty fashion which Gina had expected.

"Perhaps you'd like to see the livestock for yourself?" suggested Cuthbert who was eager to return to his favourite topic.

Gina agreed with alacrity and so the pair made their way out to the stables. Gina dutifully admired Morning Mist, Gathering Thunder and Balleytree.

"Allow me to introduce my sister, Carlotta. Gina, this is Carlotta. Carlotta, this is Gina who's writing an article about our horses for the *Horse Breeders Gazette.*"

"Pleased to meet you," declared Carlotta with a welcoming smile.

"Likewise," replied Gina who was patting the horses as her means of showing enthusiasm for what was important in the eyes of the Gansville-Stubbs siblings.

Gina's gesture of interest in the horses was naturally appreciated by those for whom it was intended. And Gina was delighted to observe that her intentions had been successfully realised. It was also clear to the observant Gina that Carlotta was more interested in horses than in people but that, while this fact could generally be applied to Cuthbert, he had not failed to notice that part of her anatomy which was currently exposed to the elements.

"I would like, if I may, to bring a photographer here so that we can feature Morning Mist, at least, in my article.

"Certainly. That can be easily arranged," responded Carlotta.

"And Gathering Thunder and Balleytree also photograph very well," supplemented Cuthbert.

Gina consented to this request and a date was soon fixed for her to return later in the week complete with photographer. Hearty handshakes and farewells accompanied the departure of Gina Wilcox-Ryan. And Cuthbert bid her farewell with a wistful air of expectancy and longing.

## PRUDENCE'S COMEUPPANCE

Cuthbert looked forward so much to the day when the lovely Gina would be returning to the Grange.

On the morning in question, he selected his vestments very carefully in order to present himself in his best possible light. He believed that some smart-casual trousers and a swishy hunting jacket were appropriate for the occasion. Cuthbert also secretly hoped that he could appear in most of the photographs which Gina would require and so he gave his unruly moustache a quick trim. And a bit of aftershave also featured in the equation.

Carlotta and Cuthbert assembled in Cuthbert's office in order to await Gina's arrival. They both decided that Gina could be shown some existing photographs of their beloved racehorses, both past and present, in order to provide some inspiration for her photographer. The siblings were determined to gain as much publicity as possible for their enterprise.

Gina was shortly announced together with Bertie the snapper and his elaborate gear. Flashbulbs, prime lenses, tripod, extra lighting batteries and computerised storage facilities were in abundance.

"Allow me to introduce you both to Bertie, our photographer," began Gina, even though the nature of Bertie's profession was obvious.

Bertie shook hands with Carlotta and Cuthbert but, as it happened, he turned out to be a man of few words.

Cuthbert eagerly showed Gina and Bertie the existing collection of shots of the horses and the stable yard as well as some of the house in former times. Gina endured all and feigned interest with a sense of calm which did not normally inhabit her psyche. Sometimes one must make a sacrifice.

The party next decanted to the stables where Bertie came to life. The taciturn Bertie then earned his stripes once he was in action by taking numerous shots of the horses, the stable, the farmyard and some distant views from the house. Because Carlotta and Cuthbert were keen to be included in the pictures, they featured prominently by sitting astride Morning Mist, fondling Gathering Thunder and mounting Balleytree in a variety of poses drenched in smiles. Again Gina realised how necessary it was to make the sacrifice. Carlotta even suggested that the photographer might like to take some indoor shots in the house, which Bertie tentatively agreed to do, together with some snaps of the extensive grounds. Gina, however, sought to decline this offer on Bertie's behalf before events overtook her.

"I think we have a fine collection of photographs for my article now, Carlotta. And Bertie can show you what he's taken."

Bertie then showed the Gansville-Stubbs siblings the product of his labours to an accompaniment of "ooh" and "aah" from the viewers. Gina also began to wonder whether Cuthbert's interest was more focused on himself than on his horses when looking at the shots. This activity, however, diverted the siblings attention away from asking Bertie to take pictures of the house and grounds and so the distraction had served some purpose.

Cuthbert now broached the subject of sherry or cocktails before lunch, although he hesitated to invite his guests to lunch because of the impending threat of attack from the mad woman in the attic.

Barraclough, however, arrived to change the climate.

"What time would you and your guests like lunch please, your Lordship?"

"Oh. Er . . ."

"Most kind. Thank you," interjected Gina before she was actually asked. "Although Bertie will have to be excused. He's needed on another urgent assignment very shortly."

Bertie mumbled his apologies and then made his much-sought-after getaway.

"I think twelve o'clock as usual, Barraclough, please."

And then a brilliant idea struck Cuthbert.

"And could we sit in the small dining room behind the kitchen please?"

"Certainly, your Lordship," said Barraclough.

"And ask Damian if he'd like to join us?"

"Indeed, your Lordship," replied the butler as he withdrew contemplating what wine could be offered at the table.

The small and informal dining room behind the kitchen was an ideal place for an intimate meal because it was a territory into which Prudence seldom ventured. Cuthbert, in fact, often wondered whether his aunt actually knew of the room's existence. And so he lulled himself into a false sense of security. Poor sod!

When Barraclough returned, he brought the news that Damian would be able to join the party but that he might be a bit late in arriving.

Gina, Carlotta and Cuthbert were given rainbow trout with celeriac mash and salad. Gina offered compliments to the household's cook which were passed back to Joyce via Barraclough when he returned to the kitchen. Cuthbert was especially pleased that Gina was impressed by the quality of his staff. As the meal progressed and the muscadet flowed, Carlotta and Cuthbert began to relax in the mistaken belief that their idyll was safe from invasion. How wrong can you be?

"Cuthbert!" came a thunderous voice from outside the door.

Carlotta and Cuthbert quaked with terror as they recognised the sibilant tones of the old sorceress. Cuthbert nearly swallowed a fishbone and Carlotta choked on her wine. Carlotta, however, was the first to take the initiative. She rose from the table and speedily stormed out of the room. Gina and Cuthbert, however, could hear the rumpus clearly outside the door, despite the fact that Cuthbert had raised his voice in order to distract the journalist.

"Get back to your room, you nosey old bitch. You've come to snoop on our guests again, haven't you? How many times do I have to tell you to mind your own business?"

Gina was smiling politely as Cuthbert could obviously no longer distract her from the events which were taking place outside the room. And so he politely excused himself by claiming that they were having trouble with one of the servants. Cuthbert them marched out of the small dining room and into the small hallway which led to the main entrance hall.

"I'll deal with this!" announced Cuthbert who indicated by a nod of his head that Carlotta should return to the lunch table.

Cuthbert then forcibly took Prudence by the arm and literally shoved her out of the vestibule and into the main entrance hall.

"Get back to your room right now or I'll have you forcibly evicted from this house!"

Cuthbert steered Prudence through the hall and frogmarched her up the stairs to her quarters. Cuthbert now displayed a degree of determination which he had never hitherto exhibited. Prudence made little in the way of protest because she was in shock. And so Prudence simply had to return to her attic room in order to bewail her demise and again to sorrow over the atrocious behaviour of her family. There were several lace hankies ready for washing and ironing from Prudence by the end of that day.

Cuthbert returned to the dining room where he found to his relief that Carlotta and Gina were chatting amiably. But, by this time, Cuthbert had come to a decision which would ensure that the old witch would not for much longer continue to be the bane of all their lives.

Damian soon arrived full of cheer and greetings for Gina.

"Sorry I'm a bit late for lunch. Have I missed anything?"

Carlotta and Cuthbert exchanged knowing looks and grimaced. Gina smirked but she attempted not to show her feelings publicly.

Barraclough entered promptly with Damian's trout and some more muscadet. Barraclough made a valiant attempt to disguise his feelings but he was definitely on the verge of collapsing with laughter over Prudence's demise.

So we leave the luncheon party with Prudence wallowing in self-pity in her room, Cuthbert congratulating himself on his triumph over Prudence, Carlotta feeling confident that Cuthbert would soon join her team and Damian looking somewhat confused. And Gina insatiably interested in the events which had taken place at Havercoyne Grange.

Prudence, of course, had to have her lunch brought up to her attic suite but she had very little appetite that day.

In the servant's hall, meanwhile, Barraclough was downing the remains of the muscadet and becoming hysterical with laugher while Joyce and Nancy nattered excitedly like a pair of chattering monkeys in the kitchen.

Gina, of course, left feeling that her work for the day was more than accomplished. And that she had enough information for a Gansville-Stubbs encyclopaedia, let alone a mere magazine article.

*You can't complain about the sea if you suffer shipwreck for the second time.*
**Icelandic proverb**

# PART 2
# LIGHTNING STRIKES



*Everyone knows where to squeeze the shoe.*
**Spanish proverb**

## ROUSEL'S EXPLORATION

"I yam from zee French toureest board, madame. May I pleez speak with Mees Jessie Braithwaite?" asked the man with a strong French accent while consulting an important-looking document on his clipboard.

"That's my sister but she's out shopping at the moment. She usually goes down to the butcher's at this time of the day."

"Zen you must be Mees Elsie? Am I right, cher madame?

"That's correct. Won't you come in Mr . . . er . . ."

"I am pleez to introduce myself as Monsieur Rousel Bergère from the French toureest board in London, madame," announced the stranger with an exaggerated bow.

Elsie had always been told by her sister Jessie never to answer the door to strangers but she, Elsie, felt that this man was so polite and charming that it would be quite safe on this occasion. And, in any case, Jessie won't be back for some time yet.

"Would you like some tea, Monsieur Bergère?" asked Elsie who was trying hard to simulate a French accent for the occasion, although she was not coming across as that convincing.

The stranger was shown into the small lounge in the cottage.

"Zank you, kind lady," replied her guest.

Tea and biscuits were soon fetched on a doily-adorned tray with milk in a milk jug and sugar lumps in a sugar bowl. Blimey!

"I have come to talk to you about Betsy Drury who work at zee Grange in Havercoyne Stanley and she work zer wiz you and your seester, I believe. You see, she woz reported missing and zee last time she was seen was in France."

"Oh," proclaimed a dismayed Elsie.

Elsie remembered Betsy Drury very well from her time at Havercoyne Grange and she had often wondered about Betsy's untimely overnight disappearance. She knew that Betsy had become quite friendly with the young Lord Cuthbert Gansville-Stubbs then but she was still surprised when the stable girl had vanished unexpectedly. Had Betsy been warned off or paid off by that old aunt Prudence?

Elsie also recollected that Cuthbert had withdrawn into himself when Betsy had done her vanishing act and that he seemed never to have recovered from the loss of this member of his staff. Perhaps he was really smitten with the girl and he was pining her loss? It was certainly a mystery. And much talked about by the staff. Elsie had listened to all the gossip and speculation which was flying around on the estate at that time but no conclusions had ever been reached.

"Do you remember Betsy Drury by any chance, madame?" asked Rousel whose French accent was beginning to slip slightly.

"I do indeed," remarked Elsie who was looking forward to sharing her knowledge with her enchanting visitor.

"Can you tell me about 'er becoz, we are urgently trying to discover 'er? Dee family would like to know where she haz been," invited Rousel who pulled himself back on track as far as his accent was concerned.

Elsie didn't need any more prompting and so she proudly related what she knew.

"Well, she worked in the stables at Havercoyne Grange. My sister Jessie was head cook there then and I worked as part of the housekeeping staff. I remember Betsy quite well because we often met her in the kitchen for afternoon tea at that time. A lot of people believed that she and His Lordship were very good friends, you know."

Rousel knew all right. And because Elsie had averted her eyes, Rousel knew exactly what she meant by this insinuation. But he remained silent – largely because his mouth was full of biscuit. They were quite tasty even though they came out of a packet. But beggars can't be choosers.

"I know it was only talk but I think the rumour was true, because Betsy was very chirpy and obviously in love with someone. Also I heard from some of the stable lads that the hayloft was well used about that time, if you know what I mean. And His Lordship would often ride in those days."

Again Elsie exhibited embarrassment while Rousel kept munching with comprehension at every juncture.

"I know it was just a rumour but I believed it myself, you see. His Lordship was certainly a wild one in those days – and even after he had married Lady Gansville-Stubbs."

Elsie's embarrassment was beginning to disappear rapidly following her confessions and she smiled at the remembrance. Rousel decided that he had struck oil and so he simply sat back, swigged the tea and munched at the biscuits until they were finished without any further remarks. He, of course, hoped that Elsie would offer some more biscuits shortly, particularly if she intended to continue her scandalous narrative for very much longer.

"Some people said that they were going to run away together but I didn't believe that for a moment."

Rousel nodded and murmured more encouragement. He had now polished off all the available biscuits and he had scooped up the remaining crumbs and so he had nothing else left to do but to make a pretence of listening attentively.

"I expect Betsy felt that something would come of the affair but, of course, she was too young to realise that His Lordship wouldn't be free to make a permanent relationship with her, you see."

"And then she left her employment, ees zat right?" contributed Rousel.

"Yes and quite suddenly, you know."

"Why was zat, cher madame?"

"Well, personally," continued Elsie conspiratorially, "I think she got in the family way and had to leave before the evidence was obvious, you see."

"Really?"

"Yes, I was convinced of it but Jessie was less certain. But I was on the housekeeping team and so you get to know about things."

"Why were you so certain zat the girl was 'aving a bébé, cher madame?"

"Well, there are tell-tale signs, you know. She had definitely missed a . . . well, you know."

Elsie was obviously adept in expecting people to know things, you see, and Rousel felt that he had got the gist of what she was implying. Elsie wondered momentarily whether she had imparted too much information at this point but her unfinished sentence was not lost on her biscuit-chomping caller.

"Hm. Yez, madame."

Elsie, however, continued for some time talking about life at Havercoyne Grange, Cuthbert's exploits and Betsy's predicament. Rousel realised that he was gathering quite a substantial body of knowledge during this interlude but, of course, he appreciated that all the so-called evidence was only hearsay.

"When woz you and your seester at Havercoyne Grange zen, madame?"

Elsie supplied the appropriate dates most efficiently which Rousel noted equally proficiently on his notepad-and-clipboard prop.

"And when woz Betsy employed there then?"

More accurate dates were supplied, all clothed in more tasty gossip and wild speculation about the reasons for Betsy's moonlight flit.

"Did anyone try to contact Betsy after she 'as left, madame?" asked Rousel.

"No, well, I think . . ."

Elsie's narrative was about to restart when the front door was heard to open and Elsie rose apprehensively to her feet in order to inform her sister of the existence of the French visitor. Rousel could hear a brief exchange between the sisters. Jessie then hastily dumped her shopping in the hall and she stormed into the lounge like a tigress on heat.

"And who are you and what are your credentials?" demanded Jessie.

Rousel noticed that Elsie was much better company than her belligerent elder sister. I don't supposed Cuthbert ever thought of pursuing you, darling! Rousel hastily and obsequiously explained who he was and about the information which he was seeking. Jessie was not amused.

"I must ask you to leave now, sir, because we have no information for you and we don't know who you are?"

Rousel attempted to fish a business card from his jacket but Jessie was not interested in seeing evidence of any sort.

"Please leave now, sir. Immediately! Or I shall call the police."

Rousel felt that he should obey this edict. Elsie lamely protested at her sister's attitude but she was shouted down by the irascible and self-important Jessie who only reproached her sister for even considering allowing a stranger into the house. Rousel could still hear the fag-end of the tirade as he walked down the garden path.

"I've told you before not to let anyone into this house while I'm away. You never know who it might be," scolded Jessie vociferously.

"Well, he seemed such a nice man. So polite."

"But we know nothing about him. He could be a criminal!"

Even as he walked away from the house, Rousel could still hear the hapless Elsie being severely reproached by her domineering sister. He felt the anguish which she must have been feeling. But the conversation was soon out of earshot.

Rousel thus left ignominiously but not with any regrets. He had, after all, consumed loads of biscuits and he had obtained quite a lot of fruity information into the bargain. And the whole dialogue was recorded on a neat little device.

The Frenchman then called an associate in order to report on his conversation with Elsie but to state that her sister Jessie was not so accommodating. Rousel's research had thus borne fruit and he knew that his patience would be handsomely rewarded in ready cash quite soon.

Rousel then sloughed off his exaggerated French accent and he made his way to the local pub as his way of washing down the excess of carbohydrate which he had consumed for free that morning.

# BYRON'S ESCAPADE

"A half and an orange juice coming up, sir," repeated barmaid Nellie at the Hunting Horn.

"That's right. I think she'd notice if I slipped a vodka into it, don't you?"

Landlord Dave sniggered in the background but he made no comment to the new arrival as Nellie poured the drinks. Nellie, however, did not really appreciate the jest.

Nancy was sitting by the fire again in the place which she had chosen when she had last frequented the pub with Ned. She was obviously going to make a habit of sitting here when men were trying to get her drunk with a view to seducing her. Dave noted the fact that the kitchen maid was a magnet for some of the staff from Havercoyne Grange and he approved of their choice. He could see that this new girl would obviously have caused a stir and, of course, Byron would certainly be at the head of the queue. But, hey, it was good for business.

"Thank you," proffered Nancy as Byron handed her the fruit juice.

"So how long have you worked on the estate?" began Nancy.

"Over ten years now. Most of my working life, that is."

Nancy did a quick calculation in order to estimate Byron's age and she concluded that he had worn quite well.

"What was the place like back in those days?" she enquired.

"Much as it is now."

"So we're in a time warp then?"

"Well, I suppose so."

"Who worked there back then?"

Byron considered the question for a moment.

"I came here just before Cuthbert took over the estate. Carlotta was still travelling in Europe at that time but she soon joined the firm. And Damian had already laid claim to the museum as he calls it."

"And who else was here then?"

"Barraclough. He's been there for donkey's years. He had originally worked for George, Cuthbert's brother, and Cuthbert had simply inherited it from him. William, George's son, died before taking over."

"I see," commented Nancy.

"But the rest of the staff were quite different then. A different cook and kitchen staff, for instance. But Elizabeth joined quite soon after me."

Byron recalled the parade of ladies who had entered and left the establishment. His trip down memory lane had also reminded him of the conquests which he had made along the way. Byron's recollection of a former housekeeper brought a wry smile to his cheeks. But he then returned to his present project with determination.

"But what about the stable staff?" asked Nancy as she interrupted Byron's reminiscences.

"The only one who's been around from the old days is Ned in the stables. Do you know him?" asked Byron diplomatically wanting to test the temperature of the suspected rival.

"I do," stated Nancy blandly. I wonder how much he knows about Ned's designs on me?

There was now a slight hiatus in the discussion while Nancy considered her next question and Byron wondered how he might encourage Nancy to talk about herself.

"But what were the house and grounds like then?" Nancy continued.

"The house has been modernised quite a bit, of course."

"In what way?"

"The museum was created and the lower-ground café was installed so that the punters could have lunch and spend more money in the place."

"But the rest of the house has not really been updated much, I suppose?"

"You suppose right. They're all clinging to the past."

"But some of the outbuildings look new surely?"

"Yes, several of the barns have had to be replaced because they'd rusted or become too dilapidated for storing anything properly. Routine maintenance really," stated Byron.

Nancy was now beginning to get the picture but she still needed more detail.

"The grain store looks quite new," she observed, "and the main stable block with the hayloft."

Byron was pleased that Nancy had broached the subject of the hayloft in the hope that it would get her thinking along the right lines.

"Yes, all that's new. It was replaced, oh, some ten years ago now. Just after I joined and was a new broom."

This piece of information was what Nancy had been searching for and so she probed further.

"New building and flooring, I would imagine. A total refit."

"Certainly the former structure was sold off for scrap metal and in its place was one of these non-rust plastic DIY kits which provides stabling for the racehorses, a hayloft, a make-shift kitchen, a shower room and some living quarters."

"I was surprised to find a floor in the stable block because most farm buildings – and especially where animals, such as horses, are housed – don't usually have floors," she volunteered.

"No, I agree. But Cuthbert insisted that the staff should be accommodated in some degree of comfort."

Nancy merely murmured at this snippet of information as she contemplated her next move. Cuthbert's not that considerate surely?

"So what was the place like previously then?"

"Well, it was closed to the elements, of course, but still very primitive. Staff still lived there but the accommodation was very spartan by today's standards. The hayloft was more comfortable than some of the staff quarters," Byron contributed with a laugh.

So, thought Nancy, the hayloft was comfortable, the living quarters primitive and the floor non-existent. But Cuthbert had insisted on installing a floor where previously there had been none. Thus he could have buried Betsy Drury under the stables and then given it a makeover in order to cover his tracks. What a thought!

Byron, by this time, was getting even more itchy as he could see the object of his interest before his eyes but he could observe no evidence of her turning her attention in his direction.

"But let's not talk shop. Tell me about yourself?" asked Byron who could think of nothing more original to say in order to turn the tide in the conversation.

Nancy then proceeded to explain briefly that she had previously worked in London with a few small hotels and in another couple of estate houses further up country but that she had chosen to come down to the west country where the weather was a bit better. And, of course, to work for the landed gentry which would look good in her career history.

"We've a bit of a micro climate here in this corner of the country," remarked Byron who still did not feel that things were going in the path of his choice. "So you left your last job in order to get better weather?"

Nancy made no comment in response to this non sequitur because she was beginning to think she was at an interview.

"Well, I bet you left a series of broken hearts in your wake?" suggested Byron.

Again Nancy failed to comment. Byron tried again.

"Do you have a boyfriend currently, Nancy?" asked Byron who was pretty sure that he was on safe ground.

"No," responded Nancy with an air of vagueness about her.

"Well, I'd like to apply for the job," stated an emboldened Byron.

Nancy again failed to respond. Byron felt deflated and he was on the point of giving up. But this defeatist attitude is really not like me! Byron hence gave himself a good reprimand and then decided to make a more concerted effort.

"Would you have dinner with me one evening? Or at the weekend, if you'd prefer? We could get well away from the Grange."

Nancy considered for a moment and then she gave Byron a seriously seductive look. Byron was now putty in her hands under this promising gaze.

"When where you thinking of?" she drawled.

"How about this weekend? Sunday, say?"

"It might work for me," she reported.

Keep trying Byron.

"Anywhere in particular you'd like to go? Away from Havercoyne Stanley and Grayling Wood, of course. Further afield perhaps? You just say. Anywhere take your fancy?"

Don't try too hard Byron. Careful!

A silence ensued but Byron was determined not to fill the gap with more urgent entreaties to Nancy. He waited until, at last, she broke the silence.

"You choose."

Byron was triumphant. I've really had to work hard for this one and so I hope she'll be worth the effort.

Dave noticed that the couple were getting along better than Nancy's previous admirer. And he was even more delighted to note that Byron soon returned to the bar for more drinks.

"Same again?" enquired Nellie as Byron approached the bar, "I'll bring them over."

Byron and Nancy now finalised the details of their date scheduled for the coming Sunday. Byron felt proud that his persistence had succeeded in principle. And it has only cost me two orange juices this evening. But I'll need to invest some more cash in my quarry before I reach the target. Nancy, at the same time, looked forward to extracting as much information as possible from the randy estate manager.

Nellie was glad that the customers were ordering more drinks as it gave her something to do. And Dave was grateful that more money was passing in the right direction across the bar. I wonder how many other men will be wishing to entertain this kitchen girl?


## AGATHA'S PERFORMANCE

Lady Agatha Gansville-Stubbs was in her element as Helen Lancaster in the production of *Waters of the Moon* presented by the Havercoyne Stanley

Players. And she hoped that everyone in the world would behold her magnificent performance.

The players had been rehearsing for about three months and the date of the first night was fast looming. The director was, consequently, having a few tantrums, the cast were getting nervous and the backstage crew were cursing the limited facilities in the Havercoyne Stanley Village Hall as usual. But Agatha, conversely, was prancing around expecting first-night flowers, an adoring public and a series of scintillating press accolades which would put her name on the map for centuries to come.

Agatha was, moreover, delighted that Professor Lyall Vanburgh had obtained a ticket for her opening night and this knowledge spurred her on to persuade others to attend. So she hastened to recruit more candidates who could witness her triumph. Cuthbert, Carlotta and Damian had reluctantly agreed to come on the last night, mainly because Agatha would have made life so unpleasant for them all if they had refused. It was easier to just submit and suffer. Prudence, however, was not invited to witness the spectacle.

The servants had been pressured to attend, although Cuthbert had agreed to foot the bill for their tickets out of his own pocket and the kindness of his heart. Elizabeth, Ingrid, Barraclough, Joyce and Nancy, therefore, felt compelled to accompany the family on the last night. Byron was, however, determined to be the party-pooper but when he discovered that Nancy would be watching the performance in the back row, he managed to wangle a last-minute ticket for himself in order to sit next to her.

*Waters of the Moon* is a play set in a remote country house hotel which is inhabited by a sad collection of personalities who have fallen on hard times and who now wish to spend their remaining days in long-suffering yet gentile poverty. The action of the play takes place immediately after Christmas when a ridiculously wealthy family get stranded in the snow and they have no recourse but to invade and to disrupt the quiet ambience of the establishment. The fur-coated and bejewelled Helen Lancaster then proceeds to make a thorough nuisance of herself in the eyes of the hotel's guests and staff who will never quite recover from the experience. Agatha was obviously admirably suited to playing the part of the affluent yet exasperating Mrs Lancaster.

On the opening night, Agatha hastened to the theatre in order to claim her dressing room and to adorn her temporary dwelling will trinkets, mascots and good-luck charms. She had also recruited Nancy to come along early in the evening before the performance in order to help her to dress. Agatha and her dresser arrived in style in the Bentley, even though the village hall was only a stone's throw away from Havercoyne Grange and it would have taken them barely ten minutes to walk.

Nancy was first detailed to press Agatha's costumes and to spray the dressing room with fragrant lavender incense in order to relax the star. Agatha, meanwhile, busied herself with admiring her collection of cuddly toys, a silver horseshoe, a gold clover leaf and a China rabbit's foot. Nancy played the game by admiring the decorations and seeing that everything was organised to perfection in order to curry favour with the mistress of Havercoyne Grange as the stage-struck star.

Nancy also helped Agatha into her costume and assisted with her makeup. Agatha gave precise instructions to Nancy about highlighting her cheek bones, accentuating her eyebrows and outlining her cherubic lips as well as adding an artificial mole to her chin. Nancy tried her best and she hoped that Lady Agatha Gansville-Stubbs would appreciate her efforts. Some hope! Nancy had actually trained as an actress in former times but she did not impart this salient piece of data either to the star of *Waters of the Moon* or to anyone else in the vicinity of Havercoyne Stanley for that matter.

At last the stage manager called for beginners and the house lights began to dim. Nancy returned to Havercoyne Grange as she did not see it as any part of her duty to watch all the performances. The last night would more than suffice.

As the play begins the mundanity of the hotel and the life of its residents is soon shattered by the arrival of Helen Lancaster and the first night proceeded with Agatha expecting to be admired by all who were privileged enough to witness her achievement. Agatha was also mindful of the fact that Professor Lyall would be the first to see her in all her glory and this knowledge gave an uplift to her performance.

Barrington sat about half way down the hall on a raised platform where he commanded a good view of the stage and he remembered to note which aspects of Agatha's debut could provide fodder for comment later after the final curtain. Barrington was, however, bored to tears with the production and he was nauseated by Agatha's histrionics and self-indulgent overacting.

Barrington had resigned himself to having to wait around after the show in order to congratulate Agatha on her outstanding presentation. Agatha, as expected, found herself surrounded by admirers from the village who knew that their livelihood depended on keeping the residents of Havercoyne Grange sweet. In this arena of adoring fans, Barrington made his entry.

"Oh, Agatha, I do congratulate you heartily on your performance. I enjoyed it so much."

Agatha feigned humility rather unconvincingly. She was not that good an actress.

"Ah, Lyall, how nice of you to come. And where is your lady wife this evening then?" asked Agatha who was disappointed to observe that Katherina Vanburgh had not been there to watch her success in action attentively.

"She had a prior engagement, I'm afraid. But she hopes to attend later in the week."

Agatha was relieved by this news. She also introduced the professor to some other members of the cast and the production crew of the Havercoyne Stanley Players. Barrington made the right noises in the right places accordingly.

"Can I tempt you to a drink in the bar?" enquired Barrington who was keen to pursue his mission and eventually to make his escape.

Agatha agreed with magnanimity. Even though she was now off stage, she was still playing the theatrical miracle on legs.

"Champagne, I think? Don't you?" suggested Barrington.

Agatha was overcome by this suggestion from the professor and so the two of them sailed into the bar in order to toast her dramatic success. The rest of Agatha's followers took the heaven-sent opportunity to make themselves scarce and to return to their homes with relief.

Agatha and Barrington then proceeded to dissect the details of the star's achievement but very little else. Barrington felt that he had not concentrated sufficiently to be able to contribute much to the post-show analysis but fortunately Agatha did most of the talking. Barrington thus simply contributed a number of observations, such as "You're extremely talented. Have you ever considered taking it up professionally?" and "The Havercoyne Stanley Players must be delighted that you're willing to perform for them so regularly."

Agatha swelled with pride at Lyall's observations and Barrington hoped that he had not overdone it. But Agatha did not appear to see through his transparent insincerity.

"I'm sure you must be tired after your triumph but would you do me the honour of having dinner with me and Katherina one evening next week? As a way of celebrating your success further?"

Agatha was so flattered that she could not stop herself from accepting this kind invitation from such an eminent academic.

"How kind. Yes, certainly. Do give me a ring and we'll certainly arrange something for next week."

"But I must take my leave of you now, Agatha, because I need to get back to Katherina who's expecting me shortly. And I'm sure you'll be tired."

"Of course," replied Agatha, "And thank you again for coming."

"My pleasure."

"And I hope that Katherina will enjoy my performance too," stated the actress. "But I must get home myself and get some rest in readiness for tomorrow night."

Barrington took his leave as Agatha looked about expectantly for more of her fans to come flocking to her side. Barrington left, however, in the hope that this occasion would be instantly and permanently wiped from his memory because he longed to return to his beloved Calendula.

Agatha, in fact, did not feel a bit tired but she wanted to give the impression of a dedicated professional. Agatha fervently expected that she would go down in the annals of history as the epitome of thespian victory. Agatha then made her way home in the absence of any more of her adoring public and she swept up the staircase to bed with a hot chocolate and a warm feeling inside.

"Any luck with the mark?" asked Calendula once her beloved had returned from his theatrical outing.

"I asked her to dinner with us but I doubt whether she'll be able to tell us anything interesting. She's far too wrapped up in herself."

"Oh, you never know."

"Doubt it. She's too much of a narcissist."

"We'll soon wheedle something out of her and complete the picture, I'm sure," stated a confident Calendula.

"Anyway, how was the play?"

"Bloody boring. I had trouble not falling asleep."

"Talking of sleep, shall be go to bed?"

"I'm all up for that," said Barrington who came to life as he swept her into his arm and carried her romantically into the ensuite shower room.


## CUTHBERT'S WINDFALL

Ian Manningbury decided to pay a call on Cuthbert one morning and so he made arrangements with Ingrid for a meeting after the morning gallops.

"Ian, old boy, nice to see you. Good morning!" announced a chirpy Cuthbert, "Come in and take a seat. Delighted to see you."

Actually Cuthbert was pleased to see his horse-trainer because it would give him an excuse for an early morning tipple which he knew Ian would not refuse.

"Good to see you too, Cuthbert."

"Whiskey?"

"Draft question. What do you think? A cup of cocoa?" quipped Ian.

Cuthbert tittered at the joke but he poured two large whiskeys with aplomb and gratitude. Ian was always up for a snifter and the two of them had been drinking buddies for many years now. Cuthbert had no trouble in remembering Ian's name. But then he was not just a minion. He was a real person who enjoyed a drink.

"Well, how are the horses doing then?" asked Cuthbert once the mellow liquid was descending his gullet.

"Yes, very well. Very well. That's what I want to talk to you about."

Cuthbert grinned as his favourite subject was broached.

"I think we should enter Morning Mist and Gathering Thunder at Gantry Downs again this year. And we could also tentatively try Balleytree there too just to see how he does in one of the yearling races. How he copes with the journey and the noise of the screaming hordes at the course and all that."

"Are you sure about Balleytree? Very young colt you know."

"Oh, this would only just be a trial run to see how he takes to the crowds."

"All right. Just as you think."

"No hope of winning, of course."

"I realise that."

The two horse enthusiasts then discussed the pros and cons of which races to select and they then fixed a date for all three horses to be transported to the racecourse.

Gantry Downs Racecourse was a small circuit in the north of England where most of the up-and-coming young horses earned their stripes in order to get into the swing at the beginning of their racing history prior to performing up to speed at more serious venues. It was also ideal for those racers who were well-heeled but who needed to be reminded of their mission in life for their owners and trainers quite early in the season.

Morning Mist and Gathering Thunder were always given this annual induction for their first race of the season while Balleytree was to be initiated into steeplechasing as his debut. All the horses were fulfilling their destiny as primitive animals who were genetically programmed to get to the head of the herd but they often needed a little encouragement from some humans. The humans were spurred on by the thrill of the chase and the money which they might make to boot.

The Gansville-Stubbs tribe hence came out in force for the occasion. Cuthbert and Carlotta had been counting the days until the race date arrived.

The stable staff were, of course, obliged to attend in order to tend the horses, to ride in the horseboxes and to look after their charges. Ned especially enjoyed these jaunts because he was frequently given free drinks while on duty. And he always found favour with his employers by joining the race party.

At the Gantry Downs Racecourse the owners and punters did what they usually did on such occasions. The siblings inspected the horses in the saddling enclosure before each race and they became hopeful stand-in horse whisperers immediately before the flag and whistle signalled the off. Carlotta and Cuthbert wished all the jockeys good luck before each race and they gave each rider the benefit of their supposedly good advice which most of the jockeys often studiously ignored with contempt.

Carlotta and Cuthbert then inhabited their private box where they could get a good view of the course and where they could swear loudly when their horses were running. They ate copious quantities of smoked salmon and caviar and they drank several bottles of champagne.

The siblings, of course, studied the form books and they discussed the odds for all races. Carlotta reviewed the second-by-second race card and race guide app on her phone and she relayed the information back to Cuthbert who was glad that she was taking charge of the technology for the event. And then the bets were placed with a degree of confidence, despite the fact that the outcome of the race was in the lap of the gods. Carlotta and Cuthbert diplomatically placed bets on their own horses and they made a point of letting Ian know this fact.

If one of their horses won, Cuthbert was obliged to buy drinks for everyone else. If one of the stallions lost, however, he and Carlotta secretly hoped that someone else would foot the huge bill for the drinks with which to drown their sorrows as they tore up their betting slips. But generally a good time was had by all because losses and gains seemed to magically even themselves out for most punters.

Morning Mist, a steeplechaser, won his two races while Gathering Thunder, a flat-racer, won one race and came second in another. Balleytree, as expected, had not given a particularly good account of himself as a novice steeplechaser but, at least, he had finished the course without too much disgrace.

By the end of the day Cuthbert had actually netted a relatively small gain because he had judiciously bet on some real favourites while diplomatically backing his own horses. But he and his sister were still drunk as a result of the champagne and the frivolity of the occasion. But, all in all, Cuthbert was pleased with the performance of his horses and he felt that their early-season introduction augured well for the future.

Ian Manningbury sighed with relief at the results of the races and he heartedly congratulated all the stallions in consequence. Cuthbert bought him a few drinks by way of appreciation and Ian felt that this reward was well deserved. Ian had attended the race meeting as a vital part of his work commitment in order to keep his customers satisfied while he had left some of his underlings in charge of the rest of his stables.

Byron Travers, who usually came along for the ride, was sorry to be away from home because he was denied access to the delicious Nancy. After a few glasses of champers, however, Byron soon forgot his troubles. Elizabeth Garrick was now notionally in charge of running the estate but she was content to do so while the family were out at the race meeting.

Agatha had rootled around for an excuse not to attend as always and fortunately one of her charities was conducting a major fundraising auction to which she felt she would need to give priority. Agatha, consequently, simply when off to her fundraising auction with not a further thought about who was at home and who was away.

Damian, who really had little interest in horses, remained close to his heart-throb Vanessa and his beloved museum in the hope that Dr Vanburgh might return in order to shower him with further compliments. But he was content to leave the estate business to others in the absence of Carlotta and Cuthbert.

The kitchen staff back at Havercoyne Grange began to relax because their duties were reduced while some of the family were away. Joyce and Nancy rather liked having their load lightened. All they had to do was cook for Agatha, Damian, Prudence, the household staff and the farmworkers.

Prudence was virtually unaware that the family were away and she was certainly unconcerned about where they had gone. So she kept to her room.

Delia took advantage of Byron's absence to take some time off in order to visit her parents because she believed that, if the farmworkers and the remaining stabling staff needed any assistance, then the officious housekeeper or the efficient Ingrid would willingly take charge. After all, anyone could pick up the phone to call the vet for god's sake. And Albert would come running with his swelling bank balance looming before his very eyes.

Ingrid amused herself in Cuthbert's absence by catching up on filing, restocking the stationery supplies and inspecting Cuthbert's office still further now that she had a feel for the way in which the business was run. Ingrid's snooping was all adding grist to the mill of her scrutiny of Cuthbert's activities.

## Ingrid's Progress

Ingrid was already becoming part of the furniture at Havercoyne Grange but she liked her work colleagues and so this factor made her dreary work venture more palatable. After a few payslips, moreover, Ingrid had managed to get herself a new second-hand car. Her ancient mini was thus consigned to the scrap heap but the automobile was resigned to its fate and so accepted old age and death gracefully.

Lunch with Delia Perkins became a regular feature of Ingrid's employment at Havercoyne Grange as the two both needed an escape from the rough and tumble of work. After a couple of lunchtime meetings, Ingrid soon realised that Delia had Byron's measure. He was good at his job as manager of the estate but he was an unremitting philanderer. But Ingrid had realised that fact long ago, although she had decided to keep Byron on a string for a while because he might be a useful source of information in future. Delia, furthermore, spoke of all those occasions when she had been obliged to cover up for Byron's absences when he was out chasing skirt.

"Why don't you just simply let him get caught?" asked Ingrid.

"If he got caught by Cuthbert or anyone else, I don't think much fuss would be made. They know that Byron's valuable as an estate manager. I just cover up for him out of habit, I suppose."

"I see. And as long as no one complains, then Byron can carry on? Is that it?" suggested Ingrid.

"Right. But I don't think anyone would even care enough to reprimand him. After all, some of the male members of the family are not exactly beyond reproach."

"Like Cuthbert, you mean? Cuthbert reputedly has been an old roué in his time, I gather."

"Yes, Cuthbert has been a bit of a devil in the past and his son and heir is not much better. Lives with a woman in Spain," confirmed Delia.

"So I've heard. What a family?" mused Ingrid.

Delia apparently had done some occasional secretarial work for the big boss when Louise had been away sick during the early stages of her pregnancy. Delia hence learned a bit more about Nathan and the way in which Cuthbert forked out the readies quite frequently. Ingrid made a mental note to check Cuthbert's accounts in order to verify this statement of fact. Ingrid now decided that she would keep up her regular lunch dates with Delia for the foreseeable future because Byron's secretary was a very useful source of data.

Ingrid had settled into her nearby bedsit which was within walking distance of the Grange. Mrs Jones was the chatty type and the two of them often met for a natter particularly when the landlady was in need of company. One evening when Ingrid and Mrs Jones were having a cup of tea, Ingrid discovered that she could find out more about the Havercoyne Stanley estate when she was offsite than when she was hard at work.

"How's your job working out then, Ingrid? Are you settling in nicely then, dear?" began Mrs Jones.

"Oh, yes, the work is quite pleasant and not too exhausting."

"Good. Glad you're settling in nicely then."

Ingrid did not want to leave the subject at that and so she probed further before her landlady's butterfly mind moved on to shopping or the weather for this time of the year.

"I like the people I'm working with very much. But Lord Gansville-Stubbs is a bit eccentric, shall we say."

With this brief invitation, Mrs Jones zoomed off.

"He's been that way for some time now. Well, actually, there were a lot of rumours about him and a local stable girl some time ago and he's never been the same since she disappeared."

"Yes, I heard something of that. Betsy, wasn't it? She vanished overnight, I understand."

"Yes, dear. Betsy Drury, she was. And there was several rumours about her and Lord Gansville-Stubbs then, you know."

Ingrid did know but she wanted to glean more information about this juicy topic.

"What kind of rumours?" she enquired.

"She and him were friendly then, you know."

"Really. Betsy and old Cuthbert? He's a dark horse."

"And there's some as say that they was sweet on each other then. And wanted to run away together."

"Is that true?"

"Well, I heard it from several people. Jessie Braithwaite who was cook there and her sister Elsie who was on housekeeping then. Very upset they were when Betsy left, they were."

"Was it a rumour? Or just speculation?"

"Definitely true," returned Mrs Jones with several nods of her head.

"But Betsy left very suddenly. Why was that?"

"Well, I got it from Elsie as she was in the family way then, see."

"Tell me more. It's helpful if I know something about the family I'm working for," asked Ingrid while simultaneously hoping that she did not sound too inquisitive about her employer.

Ingrid then decided to remain silent and to just let her landlady burble on. She felt that this stance would be the best policy. Ingrid hence learned more detail from the loquacious Mrs Jones about the romps in the hayloft, Betsy's pregnancy, Betsy's sudden disappearance and the effect which this event had had on Cuthbert who had withdrawn into himself following the departure of his mistress. Ingrid now realised that the information which she was receiving from her landlady was very valuable but she was naturally still curious to know more in order to pad out the story.

"And where did Betsy go?" asked Ingrid who had emerged from her cocoon of silence.

"No one knows. That's the mystery then. She vanished without trace."

"What d'you think happened to her?" probed the secretary.

"Probably went to London to get rid of it."

"Her baby?"

"Yes, dear."

"Or returned to her parents, perhaps?" Ingrid suggested.

"No, dear. Betsy never went home cos there was a letter sent to her from her mother a while ago then. She lives in Newcastle somewhere. The housekeeper opened the letter and returned it to Betsy's mother saying as she'd left and no one knew where she'd gone then."

"I see. So no one's heard from Betsy since she left?"

"No. It's a mystery. She left and never came back. That's a fact."

"And no one's ever heard from her since."

"No."

"Very mysterious," concluded Ingrid conspiratorially which concurred with her landlady's sentiments.

But no further information was forthcoming from Mrs Jones and so Ingrid made an excuse to retire to her room for the night. Ingrid was now in a quandary with much food for thought in her mind. She had learned that Cuthbert was a bit of a lad back in the day but that he had withdrawn into himself when Betsy Drury had suddenly left Havercoyne Grange. Did this mean that he was pining for his lost love? Or had her disappearance suddenly sobered him up? Did Cuthbert worry that Agatha had discovered his infidelity and forced him to put on the brakes? Had Cuthbert developed a guilty conscience? What am I missing in this equation?

Ingrid continued to mull over the facts which she had learned from Delia and Mrs Jones but she decided that the story was incomplete even though all the pieces of the jigsaw were ostensibly assembled. Perhaps I should go and play with the Overland Shuttle in order to receive some insight from a divine source?

## AGATHA'S INDULGENCE

"Do you think we should both go?" asked Barrington.

"I've been thinking about that question myself," replied his lover.

"And what have you decided, lambkins?"

"Not sure, sunny bunny."

"Well, we need to take a decision sometime soon, turtle dove."

"Why don't we both go? She's not up for the seduction routine and so the two of us asking probing questions would probably have the desired effect," decided Calendula.

The decision was thus made for a double act. Calendula and Barrington made themselves ready for their dinner date with Lady Agatha Gansville-Stubbs. Calendula wore a slinky pale blue-grey dress and jacket while Barrington adopted a similarly semi-formal attire of flannel trousers and sober sporting jacket. The only exception to Barrington's conservative appearance was a bizarre-patterned tie in garish colours.

"I don't want anyone to think I'm boring," he declared when Calendula's eyebrows lifted at the sight of his neckwear.

"Really?"

Barrington drove their car through the gates of the Havercoyne Grange estate in order to collect Agatha from her door. Might as well do the thing in style. We're entertaining the landed gentry, after all.

The door was opened by Barraclough who greeted Agatha's guests with suitably obsequious formality. Calendula and Barrington were then invited to wait in the parlour for Agatha to make her entrance. Agatha, however, decided not to make her guests wait for any length of time because she precipitously appeared at the top of the stairs in order to make her dramatic entrance like the Queen Mary on her maiden voyage, complete with broken champagne bottle.

"Good evening, my good friends," proclaimed the superstar as she descended the stairs like a prima donna at an international film festival. The only omission was an avid camera crew and a truculent artistic director on the film set.

"How appropriate," whispered Barrington before Calendula made a signal for him to keep his comments to himself for now.

As Agatha swept down the stairs Calendula and Barrington thus both endeavoured to look appropriately spellbound.

Barraclough immediately withdrew with a slight smirk on his face which instantly turned to a grimace of disgust once he had returned to his quarters and he was well out of eyeshot of the diners.

"They've gone," announced Barraclough as he passed through the kitchen on his way to the butler's pantry.

"So we only have the rest of the family to worry about for dinner this evening then," stated Joyce who was glad that she now just had to cater for Carlotta, Cuthbert and Damian in the main dining room and the old mad woman up in the attic that evening. The rest of the resident estate contingent, moreover, ate in Joyce's kitchen but they were seldom any trouble on the catering front for Joyce and Nancy.

"I thought we'd go out of town, Agatha," suggested Barrington as he drove out of the gates of the estate.

Agatha gave a gratified smile. She had spent the day planning and organising a fundraising function on behalf of a dog-rescue charity of which she was the president. This task had involved several meetings with the committee members of the charity after which she had simply left others to do the grunt work while she took the credit for organising the event. A garden fete was to be held at Havercoyne Grange and Agatha could thus instruct everyone else to attend to the detail while she simply waltzed around as lady bountiful.

"I'm so sorry I missed your performance, Agatha. Barrington told me how good you were. But I had to be away on business a lot that week," apologised Katherina.

Agatha was indeed sorry that Dr Katherina Vanburgh had been called away while she was on stage. Agatha did not want anyone to be absent from witnessing her triumph but she did appreciate that not everyone in the world could attend.

"How kind everyone has been. Your compliments are so gratifying, Katherina. I really try my best, you know. And I'm so glad when my paltry efforts are appreciated."

Hypocrite! But Calendula and Barrington remained impassive.

The chosen restaurant was situated some twenty kilometres beyond Grayling Wood. The journey, consequently, took some time, especially as many country roads needed to be navigated carefully. Eventually the party arrived at a small yet plush hotel for their evening repast. Agatha approved of the splendour to which she had been escorted and she viewed it as a fitting tribute to her status and her accomplishment as a thespian.

The restaurant was a mixture of old and modern décor. Oak panelled walls and a central candelabra jostled with metal ceiling lights suspended over each table. White table linen, crystal glass and silver cutlery, in addition, mingled with designer seating and floor-to-ceiling filigree drapes. The party had been allocated a table near the log fire and, had the spring daylight lasted into the evening, they could also have enjoyed a view of the hotel grounds. But you can't have everything.

The table d'hôte menu seemed to be the obvious option because Agatha was more used to basic cooking than posh nosh. The choice was essentially oxtail soup or pheasant paté for the starter course followed by either roast lamb shank, baked seabass or devilled kidneys. Calendula and Agatha opted for the oxtail soup and the seabass while Barrington chose the paté. Barrington then dithered about trying to decide between the lamb shank and the devilled kidneys and his indecision was beginning to get embarrassing. Just before the impasse started to get really difficult, however, Calendula kicked him under the table and then she ordered the lamb shank on Barrington's behalf.

"Yes, lamb shank would be nice," agreed Barrington with a nod to the waiter.

"You know that lamb is your favourite," explained Calendula.

The conversation now turned to Agatha's favourite subject – herself.

"So what else do you have planned at the Havercoyne Stanley Players? When will your next production be?" enquired Calendula.

"Our next production will be in July. But I'm not sure what we'll be doing. We have a committee meeting next week at which we'll have to decide between *The Importance of Being Earnest* and *The Cherry Orchard*."

"Unfortunately, we shall not be around then. Our work may well be completed before the summer comes," explained Barrington who desperately wanted to nip this flower in the bud.

Agatha looked disappointed but she took the opportunity to turn the conversation towards her charity fete.

"Pity. But perhaps you'll both be able to come to the Walkies Dog Rescue fete next month. It's being held at the Grange and should attract a large and influential crowd."

"Certainly," replied Barrington who groaned inwardly at the prospect of a village fete and more of Agatha's histrionics.

"I'll let you know when the details have been finalised," asserted Agatha.

"Perhaps coming to the Grange for a fete would also help with my research on Havercoyne Grange," suggested Calendula expansively, hoping that Agatha would take the bait.

"Possibly."

"I'm, of course, keen to know more about the house and those who were in residence when you arrived. I've had a long talk with Damian about the history already."

Agatha did not seem to warm to this topic because she was left out of the equation.

"I don't think I can tell you very much," stated Agatha dismissively.

Calendula and Barrington now realised that they would have to stick to their mission and just keep on at Agatha until she gave them something to chew on. The starters, unfortunately, arrived as a slight interruption to the proceedings but Calendula ploughed on with determination.

"I gather that there was an upheaval some years ago when one of your stable staff disappeared recently," she continued.

"We're trying to trace her because she might be able to tell us what the estate was like back in those days," added Barrington.

"Betsy Drury. Do you remember her by any chance?" asked Calendula.

Agatha blanched. She remembered bloody Betsy all right because of Cuthbert's association with the girl.

"I do remember vaguely but I really have no details of any consequence," replied Agatha.

"I gather there were some nasty rumours about her association with your husband," stated Barrington who poured some more wine for Agatha in the hope that the alcohol would loosen her tongue.

"There are always rumours flying around at Havercoyne Grange and Cuthbert is a particular target, I'm afraid," replied Agatha laconically.

"So it's not true then that Cuthbert was in a liaison with Betsy then?" asked Barrington.

"I neither know nor care," stated Agatha wearily in the hope of concluding the conversation on this topic.

Calendula and Barrington exchanged knowing looks but they collectively decided that the well had run dry.

"Do you think your aunt Prudence would be able to tell us more about the history of the house and its inhabitants?" suggested Barrington.

"She's a bit gaga these days. Hardly knows what day of the week it is," said Agatha in an attempt to change the subject.

"I didn't get an opportunity to meet her when I came to see Damian."

Agatha made no comment.

Calendula and Barrington now reluctantly concluded that Agatha would not be a good source of information and so they simply let the evening take its natural course. The topic of conversation hence returned to Agatha, the Havercoyne Stanley Players, Agatha's dramatic accomplishments, the dog rescue fete and her activities at the local women's institute. The members of the Medici Squadron were, therefore, very relieved when the meal was over and they were able to take their guest home.

"Well, that was a waste of time and the price of a meal," stated Barrington.

"Not that wasted," said Calendula enigmatically.

"Yeah, I supposed she did, at least, sort of confirm Cuthbert's involvement with Betsy by her silence."

"Indeed. Very useful snippet of info."

"Well, perhaps the evening was not that unfruitful after all," concluded Barrington.

## CARLOTTA'S CANTER

Carlotta was no stranger to living it up. She had, in the past, done the rounds of the nightclubs and the high spots around the globe. She had seen a few sights and she had ravished a few men in the process. But she thought that she had left all that behind her and she had put it down to experience – never to open that box again.

Funny thing the universal instinct for procreation – it keeps us interested in sexual partners and in pursuing any possible new partners for all our pubescent years and most of our adult life. Oxytocin (the love hormone, to you) can be relied on to make us attractive to others and it will be sure to attract others to us, even though we might know for certain that the prospect and the experience will decidedly not be a good idea.

Carlotta was, consequently, in a quandary. She was attracted to Aubrey Bankover very much. Well, actually, she fancied the pants of him if she were truly honest with herself but she did not want to be distracted from her mission of looking after the Havercoyne Grange stables and of training a winning racehorse or two one day. Fate, unfortunately for Carlotta, had other ideas. And so the stable manager waited patiently and expectantly for Aubrey to arrive that morning for the training routine after which they would go for a canter together.

Carlotta looked out at the shimmering dawn which heralded a fine spring day. It was rather cold that morning but there was a promise of warmth in the air and she knew that it would only be a matter of time before some exercise would warm up her blood. And the sight of Aubrey would have a similar effect. What is it about Aubrey that I find so scintillating? He's handsome? Yes. He's intelligent? Yes. And he's interested in horses? Of course. It must be a recipe for a successful union, surely? Yes. But I don't want to get into any more of those messy relationships. Really? No, I'll be strong. Definitely? Maybe?

Aubrey strode up to stand beside Carlotta and all her resolve melted as the morning dew might do under the heat of a blazing sun. He smiled and looked into her eyes. Fatal! He parted his slips slightly. Terrible! And he gave her a warm hug and a platonic kiss on the cheek. Devastating! Carlotta was lost for words and, even if she had known what to say, the dryness in her mouth would undoubtedly have prevented anything other than a groan being emitted from her larynx.

Carlotta could not keep her mind on watching the horses go through their paces on the track and the jumps. She and Aubrey had decided not to participate in the exercise with their own horses that morning because they did not want to tire the animals out before their own rendezvous. And so they just watched the other jockeys who could handle the bloodstock more skilfully than either of them. Jonquil and Honey Nectar would have their turn after the official exercise programme had been completed and the string of racehorses were being refreshed prior to their saunter back along the lanes to the Grange or the Old Foundry.

Carlotta and Aubrey then set off once they were assured that the racehorses in training were well cared for by the stable grooms who would escort them back to headquarters. Few words were spoken as the couple cantered across the nearby hills in order to allow themselves and their horses to get some feeling for the day, the weather and the romance in the air.

Carlotta and Aubrey rode together and they toyed with the idea of a gallop. Carlotta was not keen to ask too much of Jonquil and so Aubrey did a bit of showing off for the lady on Honey Nectar before coming back to continue riding with her at a more leisurely pace.

He's a very impressive horseman, thought Carlotta. She watched him glide over a couple of hedges during his exhibition of masculine talent. And a jumper too! Oh, Aubrey. I'm so glad I've met you.

"Shall we stop for a rest and a snack?" invited Aubrey on his return.

"A rest certainly. But a snack?"

As good as his promise, Aubrey then flourished a hipflask of wine and some stilton and fruit which he took from his saddlebag. Aubrey also produced a waterproof ground sheet – like a rabbit from a hat on – which Carlotta could sit on for their refreshment interlude. Carlotta was enchanted. How considerate he is? He's not like other men. He's thought of everything for my comfort. He's just what I've been looking for all these years. All right, Carlotta, don't overdo it! He's just a bloke.

Carlotta and Aubrey then consumed the goodies like a couple of naughty children who had just raided the larder while matron was not looking. They laid back on the ground sheet dangerously close to each other, warmed by their exercise with each mutually uplifted in the company of the other.

"It's good to rest," remarked Aubrey.

"You've earned it more than I have," contributed Carlotta.

"Well, it's wise not to overtax Jonquil. Particularly after her recent lameness."

He remembered. He's so considerate. Oh, Aubrey.

The pair then discussed the performance and progress of their horses on the gallops that morning and their hopes for the future.

"Did I hear you entered a couple of yours at Gantry Downs recently?"

"Yes and they did really well. Morning Mist won two races while Gathering Thunder won one race and came second in another."

"And it's only the start of the season. Well done," proclaimed Aubrey.

"Thank you. We're all very pleased," replied a reticent Carlotta who had transformed herself from a rough horsey woman into a simpering violet under the gaze of her heart's desire.

Jonquil and Honey Nectar were tethered to a tree while their owners went through a love quadrille. The two horses gave each other knowing looks while munching at their own mid-morning snacks of nuts and oats.

"Funny lot, these humans," remarked Jonquil.

"Yeah," agreed Honey Nectar.

"What are they doing?"

"It's called flirting. Humans do it a lot."

"Why?" asked the filly.

"Well, they take their time before they get down to the mating bit, you know," replied the all-knowledgeable stallion.

"Why's that?" asked a curious Jonquil.

"Don't know. Cos they're stupid, I think."

"I see."

"I don't suppose you fancy a bit of . . . "

"Not just now, Honey. I'm busy eating."

"Some other time, perhaps?"

"Perhaps when the weather's a bit better."

Honey Nectar neighed with anticipation but he continued to munch his treat until the idea of enjoying Jonquil had passed.


## NANCY'S SUSPICION

"Oh, Nancy, is that the dinner tray for aunt Prudence?"

"Yes, your Lordship."

"Well, I'm going up to see her now. Shall I take it up for you?"

"I don't mind climbing the stairs, sir. Really."

"Well, it'll save you a job. I'm sure you've lots to do in the kitchen, er . . . Nancy, yes."

Cuthbert was no better at remembering Nancy's name than Ingrid's. It was, therefore, nothing personal.

"Very well, sir," agreed Nancy as she handed the tray to Cuthbert.

"Thank you."

"I'll come up to collect the tray in about half an hour as usual."

"Of course. Thank you."

Cuthbert's being exceptionally considerate today, thought Nancy. Perhaps he's had a win on the horses? Or a killing on the stock market?

Cuthbert climbed the stairs to the attic suite while Nancy wondered why the heck Cuthbert would want to see Prudence. I thought he avoided the old bitch like the plague as the rest of the family seem to do. Oh, well. Saved me a trip up those bloody stairs anyway.

Cuthbert did not bother to knock on aunt Pru's door – he simply walked in and placed the tray unceremoniously on the table.

"Your evening meal," he announced unnecessarily.

Prudence gave a barely audible grunt as her acknowledgement of the fact that Cuthbert had acted as waiter. Thanks were not normally in Pru's repertoire of remarks.

Cuthbert promptly left aunt Prudence's room in favour of entering his own sanctuary wherein he could play with the Overland Shuttle in some peace and quiet and where he could be alone with his thoughts and his hipflask. Cuthbert mused on the topic at the forefront of his mind as the train chugged around the track.

When the train reached the church, Cuthbert had an attack of conscience. Is what we're doing right? Is it wicked? Will she suffer at the end? Well, actually, I'm sure the gods would want us to rid the world of someone who makes all our lives a misery. Carlotta and Damian have been driven to distraction and I certainly don't want the lovely Gina to be frightened off.

The signal box demonstrated that the train could pass unrestrained and so Cuthbert took this as a further sign that the plan was necessary and that it definitely should go ahead. As the Overland Shuttle passed under the railway bridge, Cuthbert envisaged a new life for himself and his family and so he concluded that he was justified in his endeavour.

When the train stopped at the Homeland Village station, moreover, Cuthbert had by now convinced himself that he was actually making a magnificent sacrifice for the good of the whole household – including the long-suffering servants. Nancy, for instance, would not be upset when Pru cross-questioned her about the family's activities and Barraclough, who was not getting any younger, would not have to climb the steep staircase in order to attempt to sort things out. Yes, I'm definitely on the right track.

On a second snaking of the train around the circuit, the Overland Shuttle passed the farm, the factory and the town and these features seemed to agree with Cuthbert's thoughts about the situation. The sound and the momentum of the train appeared to be in keeping with Cuthbert's conclusion.

Eventually the train entered the dark tunnel and slithered into the siding in order to repose overnight. Cuthbert thus felt that he could now rest in peace because he was rendering a great service to the world by exterminating the old harridan who was a prickly thorn in the flesh and blood of Havercoyne Grange. My ancestors would be proud of me. Contented with his contemplation, Cuthbert eventually retired for the night and hence he had pleasant dreams of a happy future.

Nancy, meanwhile, was interested that Cuthbert should be so considerate. I wouldn't have thought old Cuthbert would have that much imagination. He's hardly spoken to me since I arrived. I wonder what he's up to?

"You must have got up those stairs pretty quick," remarked Joyce when Nancy returned to the kitchen.

"Cuthbert offered to take the tray up."

"And you let him?"

"He insisted."

"My god. That's a turn up for the book."

Joyce's last remark fuelled Nancy's suspicions even more. But Nancy, without further comment, began her usual toil of stacking the dishwasher after the evening meal had been cleared from the dining room and she thought no more on this out-of-character occurrence that evening.

About a week later, however, Nancy was again surprised to be accosted by Carlotta this time who made a similar request.

"I'll take up aunt Pru's tray, Nancy. I've to go up myself anyway."

Nancy made the usual gesture of refusal but Carlotta simply ignored her protests and almost snatched the tray from her hands. Nancy stood for a moment watching Carlotta climb the stairs but she still saw Carlotta's actions as no coincidence.

"Carlotta took the tray up this evening," announced Nancy before Joyce had a chance to make any comment.

"My goodness. Perhaps the roles will soon be reversed in the Grange. Cuthbert and Carlotta will shortly be slaving away in the kitchen while we prance around on horses without a care in the world."

Nancy believed that the Gansville-Stubbs family were not exactly without any cares but she neglected to mention this self-evident fact. She merely laughed politely at Joyce's observation. But Nancy continued to wonder about this unusual turn of events.

And then a pattern started to emerge. Both Carlotta and Cuthbert seemed to be continually relieving Nancy of her duty of taking old Pru's tray up to the attic suite. And, on a few occasions, Barraclough was even helped out when drinks were needed by Prudence late at night. Damian, moreover, became a somewhat regular messenger for taking old Pru's bedtime drink to her.

Prudence, however, saw it as her privilege to be waited on by all and sundry in the household. She hardly noticed the servants in any case. And when the family arrived to deliver her food and her beverages, she only took note but failed to comment. She thought that perhaps the family were now trying to show some contrition by making an effort for her but she soon dismissed the thought as her right of passage. Prudence certainly regarded her domain as a pantheon temple to which all would be expected to make an obligatory pilgrimage and so she continued to live undisturbed by this new practice.

One day when Nancy was actually permitted to take Prudence her early morning tea, she noticed that the old lady looked a bit peeky. She was still in bed and not quite awake which was quite unusual for the old biddy.

"Are you all right, madam?" asked Nancy.

"I'm feeling a bit out of sorts. I think I'll skip breakfast today."

"Very well, madam. Can I get you anything else?"

"No. Well, perhaps bring up some water, child."

"Certainly, madam."

Nancy scurried down the stairs and organised a carafe of water with a glass for Prudence.

"She's not well this morning."

"What's wrong with her," asked Joyce unsympathetically.

"Don't know. But she looks a bit off colour. She doesn't want any breakfast."

"No breakfast? How unusual. She usually eats like a horse."

Actually Pru was a horse – wild and unbroken.

"But, at least, that'll save us a job," added Joyce.

There was obviously no love lost on Pru as far as Joyce was concerned.

"Yes," commented a relieved Nancy.

"We'd better ask Barraclough to see about a doctor then," decided Joyce, even though she knew that Barraclough was unlikely to be stirring just yet. Last night's wine was probably still having its effect.

"Will, he be up yet?" enquired Nancy tentatively.

"Probably not. Go and get Elizabeth to wake him."

"OK," stated Nancy as she left the room in the direction of the housekeeper's office.

"Aunt Prudence is ill and Joyce was wondering if you could get Barraclough to make some enquiries. Perhaps she might need the doctor," began Nancy when she reached the housekeeper's office.

"Of course," replied Elizabeth who delighted in any crisis of which she could take charge.

Barraclough's room was below stairs and Elizabeth hastened to wake the butler whom she knew would probably be sleeping off the effects of last night's claret. Because there was no immediate reply, Elizabeth crashed into Barraclough's room and shook him vigorously when he failed to respond.

"Get up and bloody quick, Barraclough. The old lady's not well and we need to inform the family. And possibly call a doctor."

Barraclough told Elizabeth where to get off in rather impolite terms and he promptly turned over and went back to his slumbers. Elizabeth despaired of her mission with Barraclough and so she took it upon herself to make the announcement.

"Your Lordship, I'm sorry to disturb you but I think you should enquire after Prudence who seems unwell this morning," proclaimed Elizabeth.

"She'll be making a fuss as usual. Just ignore her. Histrionics, no doubt," said Cuthbert derisively.

"She's not got up yet and she's refused breakfast. I think a doctor should perhaps be called."

Cuthbert realised that the glyphosate and paraquat (weedkiller, to you) could, at last, be having its effect.

"All right. I'll see to it."

"Thank you, your Lordship."

When Cuthbert arrived in Prudence's bedroom, he at once realised that something was actually wrong. Prudence looked a bit vague and confused and she reported a headache.

"Shall I get the doctor, aunt Pru?"

"No. I'll be all right in a minute," proclaimed the obdurate Prudence who was used to maintaining the stiff upper lip.

"As you wish, aunt Pru."

"I'm aunt Prudence, if you please, Cuthbert."

"Whatever, you old bitch!" he murmured in reply under his breath as he left the room.

Cuthbert feverishly consulted with Carlotta in order to report on the fact that the old witch was, at long last, responding to the treatment. Grigori Rasputin would probably have been easier to kill off. Perhaps our version of cyanide cakes were having the same effect on Pru?

"She's refused the doctor, did you say?"

"Yes."

"Just as well. We'll see how she is in a couple of days. Things are obviously going according to plan now, Cuthie."

"Indeed," smiled her brother.

The two siblings chucked wickedly with little in the way of a guilty conscience or any compunction about their clandestine activities.

Nancy, meanwhile, was still curious to know what was going on and she continued to wait, to watch and to observe with interest.

# AGATHA'S EXTRAVAGANZA

Agatha decided that the front lawn would be the ideal spot for the Walkies Dog Rescue Charity garden fete. If the fundraiser was held near the entrance to Havercoyne Grange then the household and the estate workers would not be disrupted too much. And parking, for those who were travelling in from outside the village, could be provided along the sweeping horseshoe front drive and the rear car park.

The household was obviously press-ganged into service by Agatha and the necessary facilities were commandeered.

Joyce was detailed to make some pasties, quiches, pizzas and cakes. And the cake stall was then manned by Joyce and Nancy. Ned had been asked to provide a power cable in order to serve the microwave which would heat Joyce's produce. He also set up the tea urn so that water could be provided for hot drinks.

Byron was reluctantly put in charge of running the auction of prizes which had been contributed by benefactors who were either in sympathy with rescuing dogs or who had agreed to sponsor some prizes in order to avoid being nagged to much by Agatha. Byron made a creditable auctioneer, even though he was not that interested in rescuing unhappy dogs from their former cruel owners. Ex-wife Matilda, with his children Leone and Constantine, put in an appearance out of some misguided sense of loyalty to Byron. Leone and Constantine were clearly there under sufferance and, when he realised this truth, Byron regretted even more the fact that he had, in a moment of madness and lack of concentration, agreed to help out as the auctioneer.

Cuthbert and Damian were shamed into attending but they both drew the line at making any significant contribution. Cuthbert merely circulated among the attendees and he looked every inch the peer of the realm. Damian, on the other hand, ate a lot of Joyce's cakes but he avoided paying for any of them.

Ingrid and Delia had been paid overtime as an inducement to organising the craft stall which sold some very expensive items. These articles had been donated by local crafts men and women with a charitable inclination and/or the need to curry favour with Agatha. The craft stall in question displayed knitwear items, crochet shawls, hand-painted pictures, wood carvings and handmade jewellery. The event gave Ingrid and Delia a chance to catch up on gossip about the antics of the family and the estate personnel – so there was some compensation for the loss of free time.

Elizabeth was an eager participant and, consequently, she marshalled her team of housekeeping staff into organising the tombola, the lucky dip and the guess-the-weight-of-the-giant-panda competition.

Ned and a few of the other stable grooms took charge of the dog shows. The poodle parade proved to be the most popular but the hound dog and husky competitions ran a close second in terms of attracting entrants and keen observers. Ned felt very important when he was given a loudhailer from which to make his announcements. He felt that he had been elevated in the world to a position of clout and authority and he confidently expected – but never, in fact, received – much in the way of thanks from Lady Agatha Gansville-Stubbs.

Other members of the committee of the Walkies Dog Rescue Charity organised the remainder of the stalls and the bazaar activities at the fete. Visitors could, for instance, win a goldfish, have their photograph taken in an Elizabethan costume, have their faces painted in non-toxic acrylic materials by a local make-up artist and have their fortune told by a Madame Arcati who read the tarot and looked into her crystal ball. There was also a burger and hotdog stand, a second-hand bookstall, a cheese and wine table and an information point.

The Walkies information point encouraged visitors to become members of the charity in order to receive regular copies of the *Walkies News* and to be notified in advance of future events. Those fete attendees who were not in their first flush of youth were also discreetly encouraged to leave the charity some money in their last will and testament.

Damian, who had left Joyce's cake stall in favour of the cheese and wine table, was delighted to be greeted by Katherina who had returned to the Grange especially for the occasion.

"I didn't realise you were coming, Katherina?" announced Damian who felt that the degree of boredom which he felt could be instantly alleviated by the return of his academic acquaintance.

"Yes, Agatha sent us a flyer and we decided to come and join in the fun. We came with Florence and Aubrey Bankover," explained Barrington.

"Have some cheese and wine," invited Damian whose generosity did not extend to paying for the produce which Katherina and Lyall had ordered obediently.

Calendula initially asked a few more questions about the architecture of the Grange and the way in which it had been refurbished over the centuries but she then turned to a topic which was of slightly greater interest.

"I gather that some of the outbuildings have been refitted in living memory. The stabling quarters, for instance?"

"Yes, Katherina, the stable block has been updated. Cuthbert insisted on this several years ago because he felt that the place needed to be a bit more comfortable for the staff."

"A floor has been laid. Is that correct?"

"Yes. Quite correct."

"Why was the stable block refitted? Was it very dilapidated?" interjected Barrington.

"I believe so, Lyall," replied Damian, "but that's not the side of the estate I get involved in at all."

"What did the refurb consist of?" enquired an eager Calendula.

"Oh, Cuthbert wanted to provide better accommodation for the horses and the living quarters for the grooming staff in one location. More space was needed for his racing team."

"I see."

Calendula made a mental note of what had been done to the stable block and she decided that it accorded with the information which she had already received.

"Were any other changes made at that time?" asked Barrington.

"The barn was enlarged when it was replaced at about the same time."

"And why was it replaced then?" asked Calendula.

"Because it was falling to bits, I gather."

Damian then invited the two academics to view the refurbished outbuildings, mainly because it gave him an excuse to get away from the hubbub of festive activity. Damian thus shepherded Calendula and

Barrington over to the stables and the barn so that they could see for themselves the scope of the improvements and the size of the enterprise.

Byron had noticed the presence of the beautiful Katherina at the fete and obviously he now sincerely regretted being stuck in the auctioneer's tent.

Another attendee at the fete, however, delighted Cuthbert even more than Damian's appreciation of his chance to renew his acquaintance with Katherina. Cuthbert noticed the journalist Gina Wilcox-Ryan make an entrance and suddenly his presence at the fete became worthwhile. Cuthbert, therefore, intercepted her as she approached the tombola.

"Gina, how nice of you to come. Nice to see you again," Cuthbert stated by way of greeting his former guest.

"Well, I felt I ought to put in an appearance as my way of thanking you for your contribution to my article. And for your hospitality."

Cuthbert acknowledged Gina's compliments but he hoped that she had forgotten about the contretemps with old Aunt Pru during lunch. Cuthbert and Gina then wandered around the grounds and looked unenthusiastically at the stalls which were run by over-enthusiastic devotees of the cause.

"Can I interest you in some cheese and wine perhaps? Or a hotdog if you'd prefer?" enquired Cuthbert.

"Some cheese and wine would be nice," remarked Gina who gladly accepted Cuthbert's invitation to sit down and to ignore the rest of the world.

Gina and Cuthbert then made their way to the cheese and wine stall where the peer of the realm magnanimously ordered a bottle of sparkling wine. Barraclough was obviously managing the wine stocks and he was pleased that his employer would be giving him an excuse to open yet another bottle legitimately.

"And have one yourself, Barraclough," said Cuthbert in an expansive mood.

Barraclough hardly needed to be told but he thanked his employer all the same.

Gina partook of a microwaved cheese and tomato quiche with a baked potato and a side salad garnish as her lunchtime repast which she found surprisingly tasty and she remarked on the fact.

"Yes, Joyce, our cook, has made most of the food for the fete," explained Cuthbert.

"No wonder it's so nice. Just like the lunch she kindly provided when I last visited."

Cuthbert now took up his cue.

"Well, I was wondering whether I could tempt you to dinner one night?" he asked bravely, "I know of a nice little place out of town where it's quiet and the food is superb."

"How very kind," remarked Gina with a cherubic smile.

"If you would do me the honour, I would like to repay you for your interest in me and my racehorses."

A date was duly selected and placed in Gina's electronic diary and in Cuthbert's memory for the following week. Cuthbert felt like a spring lamb who had just seen his first daisy.

Florence and Aubrey Bankover made a point of catching up with Carlotta at the event. Florence soon realised that she should make herself scarce, after greeting Carlotta hospitably, while Aubrey continued his chat-up formula with the daughter of the house.

Ian Manningbury and Albert Fotheringay were both sensible enough to find an excuse for staying away from the fete completely – apparently claiming something about pressure of work as a justification. The two men had defiantly decided to remain impervious to Agatha's entreaties. And the scheme worked so well that they went out together and had a drink and a laugh about their successful escape while everyone else was suffering from their sense of duty and obeisance to Agatha. One or two people suspected the plot hatched between Ian and Albert but they merely applauded them for their courage and wished that they could have found their own pretext for being absent.

Aunt Prudence, fortunately for most, did not attend the fete because she felt a bit jaded that day. She decided that the exertion would be too much for her. And so she merely sulked in her room as a party-pooper. Several people envied her courage in being adamant about not attending the function and being able to please herself about her activities at the Grange. Agatha and Cuthbert were, of course, slightly relieved that Pru was in a huff that day up in the attic. Prudence's suite was at the back of the house where, fortunately for all, she could not observe and pronounce judgement on the activities in the front drive.

## CUTHBERT'S CONFERENCE

The great day for Cuthbert's business conference arrived, although he felt a mixture of pride and tedium at the prospect of the event. Cuthbert, on the one hand, was keen to show some eminent people his domain, to exhibit his prowess as a businessman and to discuss some potentially lucrative plans for the expansion of his empire. Cuthbert, however, did not look forward to a tiring day, pressure to take decisions and the need to stay sober for some length of time. Along with the rest of the household, Cuthbert, wondered, furthermore, to what extent aunt Pru would disrupt proceedings and perhaps tarnish his image.

The dining room was being used as a conference centre and so Ingrid was busy setting out the meeting papers for each of the delegates. Elizabeth and Nancy were organising beverages and mineral water for the influx of meeting participants while Joyce was hard at work in the kitchen baking little cakes and biscuits for the mid-morning break.

Barraclough had not yet emerged from his bed because of a hangover, despite several inducements from Elizabeth who had threatened to chuck a bucket of cold water over him if he did not arise from the sack within minutes. While Elizabeth was ensuring that all was well in the dining room, therefore, she was also intent on putting her plans with regard to the recalcitrant butler into swift action at the first opportunity. Hence Elizabeth left the dining room on a mission as soon as she could. The cold water tap even turned itself on automatically. And the rest is history.

"What the bloody hell are you doing you sodding woman?"

Barraclough was sober enough and awake enough to realise that Elizabeth was his attacker.

"Get up you drunken, lazy swine!"

"I'll get you for this, Miss High-and-Mighty Housekeeper. Get the fucking hell out of here before I hit you."

Elizabeth left the room unfazed by the insult but Barraclough now had no option but to get up, get dried, get dressed and put in an appearance downstairs. Joyce and Nancy suppressed a smile at Barraclough's rude awakening into the morning air when the butler at last materialised in the kitchen. Barraclough ignored the reactions of the kitchen staff as he made his way into the pantry in search of the hair of last night's dog.

In the absence of Barraclough on door-opening duty, Ingrid showed the delegates into the dining room to be welcomed by the lord of the manor as they arrived.

The first contingent to appear was a party from London who were in the property development business. John Mackintosh, Philip Grainger and June Siddington arrived from Property Magnum plc in a Mercedes which outshone all the cars parked at the Grange. John, who had originally made contact with Cuthbert some years ago, introduced his two colleagues to the peer of the realm. Cuthbert put on his most welcoming smile and he gave both June and Philip a hearty handshake before cordially inviting them to join him in the dining-cum-conference room.

The next arrival was Anthony Huffington and Manfred Jutland who represented Bryant Collective Holdings – a company which was, like Cuthbert, considering investment in the property deal to be presented by Property Magnum.

The party was completed by the entrance finally of Justin Pryor who was acting as Cuthbert's financial advisor.

Ingrid served all the newcomers with tea and coffee before ushering the parties to their seats around the dining table and then taking her place next to Cuthbert because she had been instructed to act as the minute secretary for the day.

Cuthbert kicked off the proceedings by inviting each conference delegate to introduce himself or herself to the rest of the room. Ingrid sensibly had also produced name tags for each invitee – particularly in view of the fact that Cuthbert's memory might fail him when addressing or referring to anyone present.

John Mackintosh from the Property Magnum crew outlined the nature of their organisation's work, their company's track record and their collective expertise in land and property development. He also mentioned several of the company's more impressive portfolio projects as his contribution to the name-dropping exercise. June and Philip also handed around some brochures which supported John's claims. John was the Chief Executive of the conglomerate while Philip and June were both responsible for acquiring and co-ordinating the development of land, estates and property. All three were involved in the current deal under discussion.

The team from Bryant Collective Holdings then undertook a similar introductory exercise when Anthony Huffington explained that he and Manfred Jutland were keen to invest in lucrative and viable projects such as the one which was being proposed today.

Justin Pryor finally announced that he was representing Cuthbert's interests and that he would be advising him accordingly before any decision was finally taken.

Philip Grainger then took to the floor and flamboyantly presented a number of slides which outlined the project under discussion. Philip declared expansively that for investors this would be a heaven-sent opportunity which could turn all sponsors into multi-millionaires overnight because it cannot fail. Really?

Apparently Cuthbert, along with Bryant Collective Holdings, was being asked to put some money into Seabird Cliffs – a large-scale development project on the south coast which would comprise a holiday village, a shopping complex and much in the realm of entertainment facilities. Philip's outline plans illustrated accommodation for those who wished to live onsite as well as holiday homes for rental and a marina for those who wished to sample the delights of the sea. This venture would be enhanced by a colossal fun-for-all-the-family-type complex which would attract both residents and day-trippers from far and wide. Disneyland eat your heart out.

A flood of questions seemed to be hovering on many a potential investor's lips but June staved off this deluge by requesting a comfort-break with her most feminine guile. John had previously initiated this tactic with June as his way of avoiding talk of dosh for as long as possible. John obviously wanted the dust to settle on the glamour tactics before talking turkey.

Cuthbert, who was suffering from information-overload, however, was pleased to accept John's suggestion that it was an ideal time for a break. Nancy thus, on request from Ingrid, brought beverage replenishments, cakes and biscuits accordingly. Cuthbert, however, felt that he needed something stronger than tea, coffee or bloody mineral water after being bombarded with so much detailed information. So he quickly nipped up to his office in order to satisfy this whim. Keep a cool head Cuthbert! Just one swig will suffice. But he took three instead – much against his better judgement.

When the assembly resumed, John continue to extol the virtues of investing in Seabird Cliffs by outlining the appeal of the sea birds, the impressive and limitless vistas across the briny together with the virtues of a venue on the sunny south coast.

Questions were then posed from the floor about such technicalities as planning permission, market research, construction timescales and the likelihood of other investors. Justin seemed particularly concerned to enquire about costs and whether the deal would be floated on the stock market. John had hoped that he could delay talk of money until after lunch but it seemed that his ploy did not find favour with the rest of the meeting. Once the ugly topic of the readies had been broached, the meeting was now well into the nitty-gritty stuff.

June had been elected to present the facts and figures which she did with aplomb. Cuthbert seemed impressed, although Justin was wary of this well-known strategy of asking a female to be the bearer of bad news. The sums in question were obviously over-inflated and they would almost certainly spiral upwards as the project progressed. Everyone in the room, of course, was aware of this fact with the exception of Cuthbert who did not really inhabit the real world.

Anthony and Manfred were certainly sceptical while Justin insisted on hearing more about the investment proposition in order to be able to advise his client knowledgeably. This additional and lengthy discussion was the cue for lunch which Cuthbert had been waiting for avidly and so he sent Ingrid to make enquiries in the kitchen.

When Barraclough arrived to announce that lunch was ready, therefore, the meeting participants collectively breathed a sigh of relief for a number of varied reasons. The Property Magnum team wanted to circumvent any further talk of money, the Bryant Collective Holdings gang wanted to think hard, Justin wanted to halt proceedings, Ingrid wanted to lie down and Cuthbert wanted to have another go at his hipflask.

Joyce surpassed herself by providing what passed for coq au vin for the delegates accompanied by baked potatoes and fresh farm vegetables which brought forth handsome compliments from Cuthbert's guests.

Barraclough, however, was sorry that a good wine had gone to waste on someone else's lunch.

The afternoon session finally had to discuss the embarrassing topic of finance in more depth. Cuthbert's eyes glazed over, Anthony and Manfred listened attentively to June's proposal while Justin kept his antennae fully functioning. The final figures which were asked of the moneyed members of the party were shocking and show-stopping.

The discussion then adopted the stance of a merry-go-round similar to the one proposed for the Seabird Cliffs project. John reiterated details of the envisaged project, a breakdown of expenditure, projected timescales and, of course, the expected return on investment. All this stuff went over Cuthbert's head and he longed for the meeting to conclude so that he could dream of a vast accrued income which would set him up for life while burying his head in the sand at Seabird Cliffs.

Finally Justin took the initiative and drew the meeting to a close in order to consider the proposition. His suggestion that the investors would need time to consider the proposal was heartily supported by the moneybags delegates around the table and it was accepted by the hopefuls as inevitable. John advocated that a further meeting date could be nailed while all delegates had their diaries handy but Justin managed to deflect this suggestion which was backed by Anthony and Manfred.

Once all the delegates had finally been waved farewell, Cuthbert slinked off to his office in order to replenish his supply of mind-numbing alcohol while Ingrid longed for an early night.

## FOXY'S PRURIENCE

"Hello. You a stranger round here then?" asked old Harry.

"Well, I am now. But I used to live here many years ago."

"Oh, really. Whereabouts?"

"Grayling Wood. Near the Old Foundry."

"I know it."

"Used to work on a few farms round 'ere doing casual labouring."

"So why did you come back to Havercoyne?"

"Well, I been travelling for a while and wanted to visit one of me old haunts. Had a girlfriend here and I's wondering if she were still 'ere."

"Who was that then? Anyone I know?"

"Used to work at the big house in Havercoyne. The Grange. You know it?"

"Worked there meself, I did," proclaimed old Harry, "but it was way back."

"This would 'a been about ten years ago perhaps. Were you around then?"

"Yeah. And I worked at the Grange around then."

"You may know her then. Betsy she was. Betsy Drury."

"Course I know 'her. Good looking she was. Caused quite a stir."

"She was, yeah. We went out for a while and then she got interested in someone else and I couldn't compete."

"Well," whispered old Harry, "heard as she took the fancy of one of them gentry."

"Cuthbert, he was called."

"Cuthbert Gansville-Stubbs. Owns the big house, yer know!"

"The bastard pinched her from under me nose. He turned her head," announced the stranger bitterly.

Old Harry commiserated with his new friend as he had fancied Betsy a bit himself.

"What became of her then?" continued the new arrival to the Hunting Horn.

"Well," hesitated old Harry while Foxy interpreted his reluctance to speak as being due to a dry throat.

"Fancy another?" asked Foxy.

"Veerry kind. Thank you. Er, Mister . . .".

"Bob's the name. What'll it be?"

"Whiskey and soda, please. Thanks. I'm Harry, by the way."

Foxy went across to the bar in order to replenish the drinks while old Harry wondered how much information he should impart to this here Bob. Harry finally decided that he could tell all he knew because Bob seemed a nice chap and he'd been badly treated by that Betsy woman. And, of course, he wanted to complain further about that stuck up Cuthbert nob.

"She's left here now. Just upped and left one day," stated Harry when his new friend had returned and the conversation had resumed.

"What just like that? But where's she now?"

"Dunno. No one knows. It's a mystery. She vanished into fin air."

"And no one knows why?" mused Foxy.

"Nah."

"What do you think 'appened to her then?" Foxy asked persuasively.

"Well, if you ask me, 'e done away with 'er."

"Blimey! What Cuthbert? Why d'you think that then?"

"Well, used to have a few rows. They made good use of the hayloft at night to do the business, if you knows what I mean. And then afterwards they used to row."

"What about?"

"I heard as she wanted them to run away together. And she threatened to tell 'is wife if he didn't agree."

"Gawd."

"And I think, between you and me that 'e done away with her and buried her under the stable," stated old Harry decisively – giving his opinion as if being the voice of providence from the cosmos.

"What makes yer fink that?" replied Foxy feigning incredulity.

"Well, you see, shortly after Betsy left, Cuthbert had the stable block re-done. All poshed up like. New floors and posh accommodation for the stable lads and all that."

"Yeah?"

"There was a lot of digging too. The floor had been disturbed just before the builders moved in, you know."

"Really?"

"Yeah, and I reckons as 'e done 'er in. Buried 'er there under the floor. And then 'ad the place fixed up. He had the money after all."

Foxy soon felt that he had been bombarded with information which was speculative but, nevertheless, quite interesting.

"And old Lord C then went very silent. Sort of went into hisself, yer know, after that," continued the irrepressible Harry.

"You mean, he withdrew from life generally? Gone to a monastery like?"

"Nah, he still runs the estate and all that but he wasn't the same after she'd gawn. Changed man, you know."

The two men then went on reminiscing and drinking for some while. Foxy concluded that it was very likely that Betsy had been murdered and then buried beneath the stables prior to its refit. But how could my theory be proved either way? It seems likely, even though it's old Harry's pure speculation. But I need to find out more. And I think I know how I could do it.

As soon as he had left the Hunting Horn, Foxy punched a speed-dial number into his mobile telephone in order to prepare the ground for the next stage of his investigation.

"Miss Fortescue-Bligh? Foxy here."

"Dear Foxy. Great to hear from you. Any news?"

Foxy, alias Bob, then proceeded to relate his discoveries and his suspicions to his employer. Calendula nodded in agreement to what she heard from Foxy as this information had confirmed her own suspicions.

"Foxy, I think we can sort that problem out quite easily," stated Calendula as she beckoned her lover over so that he could join in the discussion.

Once Foxy had spilled the beans, a plan was hatched in Calendula's mind. Calendula concluded the conversation with Foxy by promising to remunerate him for his work so far, agreeing to meet up soon and suggesting that he stay around in the area because his services might be required further in the near future.

"I 'ave to get back to London for a couple of days, Miss Calendula, but I'll then contact you 'gain to see if you need ol' Foxy 'ere again."

"Good plan," interjected Barrington, "I'll fix things up at this end. Shouldn't be a problem."

Foxy was most content with the praise which he had received from his employer as well as the dosh which would soon be winging its way into his bank account.

Arrangements were duly made for the next lap of the operation. Barrington now grabbed his mobile phone in order to summon assistance from the appropriate quarter. Barrington made a call to North Africa where he knew that his contact there would either solve their dilemma or would know a fellow who could. Things were certainly moving forward for the Medici Squadron.

Calendula and Barrington had now finally had their suspicions about the skulduggery at Havercoyne Grange more or less confirmed. After their visit to the refurbished stable block at the Grange accompanied by the attentive Damian during Agatha's garden fete, they had both felt that the premises should be investigated below ground level. And, following Barrington's overseas call, they now had found the solution to the way in which their mission could be accomplished and the necessary evidence collected.

Calendula and Barrington, therefore, decided to celebrate the fact that the fog had now cleared somewhat and that it would only be a matter of time before the key to the whole mystery was uncovered. To this end a slap-up meal in their hotel was followed by a protracted session in the ensuite shower during which the couple sampled the delights of the flesh and the exhilaration of uninterrupted bliss fuelled by expectations for the future.

Meanwhile, across the high seas, a whizz-kid marshalled his resources and he picked up his laptop computer in order to purchase a cut-price thermal-imaging camera. He then booked himself on to the next flight to Bristol airport and kissed goodbye to his flatmate who felt bereft by his departure and the certain knowledge that he would be alone for a considerable while.

The Medici Squadron's agent in Morocco was uplifted at the prospect of another trip to the UK and a chance to tickle his brain cells with the challenge of providing the necessary evidence which would clinch the sad fate of Cuthbert Gansville-Stubbs and his associates.

# CUTHBERT'S CONSENT

Cuthbert felt that he had kept his sexually adventurous inclinations in a box for far too long now. He had regrettably abstained from sizing up the female employees on the farm and he had not romped in the hayloft with any of the stable girls for many years. This took an enormous effort on Cuthbert's part but he was helped in his endeavour by the shock of Betsy Drury's abrupt departure many moons ago.

But the appearance of Gina in his life had finally awakened the dormant tiger and so Cuthbert had shaken himself out of his torpor at the thought of some fun with her. It was, therefore, with great anticipation that the lord of the manor drove southward to a quiet country hotel in order to meet the object of his desire. On the journey Cuthbert reviewed his options. Gina was certainly attractive and, as far as he knew, not in a relationship with anyone else. She was, unfortunately, a bit younger than Cuthbert and, while he did not see this as any obstacle at all on his part, he wondered whether Gina would regard his advancing years as an impediment. But hey ho! Let's wait and see.

The White Horse Hotel was a sober establishment which catered for all outlandish culinary tastes yet still maintained its typically British persona. The hotel had moved with the times as far as the fashion in cuisine was concerned but it had, nevertheless, not forgotten its traditional roots.

Cuthbert believed hence that his gastronomic preferences and that of his guest would be adequately catered for sufficiently. Cuthbert's palette had obviously not been taken to great heights by Joyce's cooking. And he had seldom ventured into uncharted territory in the local restaurants. But he approved of the name of the hotel and so this was his preference for a dining experience on such a special occasion. He would, in fact, love to have owned a live white horse himself but it would undoubtedly be an expensive luxury and it would not necessary win the grand national.

Gina was waiting in the bar when Cuthbert arrived and, although he saw this as a good omen, he apologised profusely for keeping his female guest waiting. Gina was, of course, unperturbed by having to wait unescorted in a hotel bar – she was a girl about town after all. Cuthbert ordered himself a drink from the hotel bar before joining Gina while she finished the wine which she was consuming. Cuthbert felt further embarrassed about the fact that Gina had purchased her own drink but he remained silent on this score.

After nattering about the weather, what a nice place the establishment was, the vagaries of the journey to the White Horse and the health of both parties, it was time for the duo to transfer to the restaurant. A waitress showed Gina and Cuthbert to an inconspicuous table and then flourished a menu and a wine list for her customers. Cuthbert with largesse promptly ordered champagne as his means of impressing his female guest.

"Could I also have some still mineral water please, Cuthbert?"

"Certainly, my dear," replied Cuthbert.

Gina, with her adventurous palette, ordered a starter of baked camembert with a truffle and wild garlic relish while Cuthbert predictably stuck to what passed for a prawn cocktail in today's catering trade. Cuthbert then selected a peppered steak which he felt was an adventurous departure from his usual practice while Gina showed him up by ordering a roasted game cassoulet cooked with a Mexican herdez salsa-style sauce. Cuthbert couldn't even pronounce the name of the sauce, let alone understand what she was requesting or how to eat it.

Then the conversation proper commenced. This is always the moment when both parties are unsure whether they will find enough to talk about for the entire evening. And, perhaps, whether they have enough in common which would constitute a viable friendship or even courtship.

"Cuthbert, I wanted to ask you another favour, if I may?" began Gina.

"Ask away, my dear," replied Cuthbert magnanimously.

"Well, my editor wants more on the racehorse angle. That is, what makes a good racehorse. And I was wondering if another of our photographers could come to your stables in order to take some more shots of the horses with a special camera which will show the bone-structure and musculature of the animals? You see, racehorses have certain quality assets and we want to discover what they are for your bloodstock."

"Er – a special camera, you say?" enquired a cautionary lover of the beasts.

"I don't understand the technicalities myself but, it seems, that the new photographic technology can do wonderful things. Like photograph bones and things."

"But is it safe?"

While Cuthbert was keen to oblige the lady, he did naturally want to ensure that his beloved racing team would not be upset or injured in any way.

"Oh, it's quite safe, I can assure you. They won't be harmed in any way, I am certain of that. Just a couple of quick shots, you know. Won't take up any time," pronounced Gina who hastened to reassure her host about the integrity of her request.

"Well, yes, of course," answered the obliging, mollified and enamoured peer of the realm.

Gina smiled as a date was duly arranged for her return visit to the Grange with her photographer. Cuthbert decided that he would risk inviting her to lunch at the Grange again when she returned but he decided to leave the invitation until later in the evening when, hopefully, his designs on the lady had progressed satisfactorily.

When the starters arrived, Cuthbert took a quick peak at Gina's camembert and instantly was relieved that he had opted for a more conventional starter. His quasi prawn cocktail, however, bore little resemblance to what he had been used to by convention.

The diners talked a lot about winning racehorses and Cuthbert reported his recent successes at Gantry Downs early in the season. Gina made all the appropriate complimentary remarks as Cuthbert was extolling the virtues of his champions. Gina thus learned of Morning Mist's two wins and Gathering Thunder's success in gaining first and second place in his two races. Cuthbert also praised Balleytree's induction into the sport. Cuthbert's face was a picture of pride and self-congratulation as he related the victories of his stable.

Once this topic had been somewhat exhausted, if not overworked, Cuthbert wondered how to get Gina rather more interested in the owner than his horses. Even though Cuthbert was, in truth, more interested in horses than women generally, he wanted to make an exception this evening by way of tempting her into a dangerous liaison.

Conversation during the main course brought forth some more intimate details about Gina. She was unattached. Good. She lived alone. Very good. She was often free in the daytime. Even better. And she liked dining out.

Great. She played a lot of tennis. Not so good but never mind. Cuthbert's days for running about with agility on tennis courts were decidedly over. Cuthbert felt, however, that he was backing a winner here, especially as her smile became more seductive with every mouthful of that disgusting Mexican stuff which she was consuming. It looked ghastly to Cuthbert's eye but she was obviously enjoying her meal.

"Have some more champagne, my dear?" requested Cuthbert as he proceeded to pour more of the stuff into Gina's glass without actually gaining her consent. Cuthbert now simply had to wait for that smile to become more seductive. His resolve to behave himself had now, of course, vanished completely into thin air. The mishap with Betsy Drury was merely a distant memory which was eager to be suppressed.

Cuthbert noticed, with regret, however, that Gina was not drinking much of the champers which he had ordered with such hope. Candy's dandy but liquor's slicker was an adage which obviously didn't obtain in this case. Gina studiously resisted any more attempts on Cuthbert's part to ply her with drink for his own wicked purposes.

Cuthbert wondered what his next move should be. Shall I reach for her hand? Should I say that I intend to enquire about staying the night here? And would she like to join me? No, maybe too forward of me. Should I attempt to kiss her at the end of the evening? But perhaps I should behave like a gentleman with this one. The stable girls were certainly more obliging and didn't need any of this preliminary seduction stuff. Oh, what a bore some women can be. But I suppose it will be worth all the effort and expense if I can get her in the sack. Here would be an ideal place because then no one would know. But maybe not.

The old fossil was obviously out of practice because by the end of the evening no further progress had been made and so Cuthbert decided that a quick peck on the cheek would have to suffice for now. Cuthbert did, at least, know that he would be seeing her again and so he consoled himself with this knowledge. He fervently hoped, of course, that their next date would deliver the goods as he expected. On a second date surely I can be more direct and adventurous? But he could not, in fact, tell whether his intended victim would be willing or not. Perhaps Cuthbert's previously well-honed antenna was rusting slightly with age and a lack of recent experience. He had forgotten how to read the signs obviously. Cuthbert – you're really out of practice!

The two then went their separate ways both with mixed feelings about the evening's entertainment. Cuthbert was unsure of his ultimate success while Gina could see what his intentions were but she decided that, for the time being, she would not give him too much encouragement. But, at least, another visit to Havercoyne Grange was on the cards.


## PRUDENCE'S DECLINE

Nancy had been allowed to resume her duties with regard to taking Prudence's breakfast tray up to her room for some days now. She thus climbed the stairs as usual and knocked on the door while she was still breathless. But she received neither an invitation to enter nor an enquiry about who was knocking. And so Nancy entered Prudence's room without further ado.

"Your breakfast, madam," Nancy announced as she placed the tray on the table.

Still no response was forthcoming from the old lady.

"Madam?" enquired Nancy again in the hope of raising the dormant figure.

Still nothing from Prudence. Nancy began to get worried as she could detect no movement. Nancy's quandary, however, was alleviated by a groan from Prudence. So Nancy drew back the curtains and tried yet again.

"Are you all right, madam? I've brought your breakfast."

Prudence's only reply was yet another groan but no words spilled forth.

Nancy then retreated back down to the kitchen in order to report on the state of play.

"She's not very lively this morning. Just groaned. Should I tell someone?"

"We'll get Elizabeth to check. Go and tell her. Just to be on the safe side."

When Nancy located the housekeeper, Elizabeth agreed to climb the stairs in order to check on the state of Prudence's health and her frame of mind. When Elizabeth entered the attic suite, she was instantly alarmed because Prudence was not responding to enquiries about her health that morning. And so she decided to attack Barraclough again.

"Get up you lazy swine and call the doctor for old Pru."

At the sound of Elizabeth's not-so-dulcet tones, Barraclough hasten to wake himself out of his slumbers for fear of another dowsing with icy water. Well, at least, he did not have a hangover this morning and so he was able to respond appropriately. But he was still reluctant to stir.

"Pru's just making a fuss as usual. That's all, woman," proclaimed the butler in an effort to remain in bed for five more minutes, "bugger off and leave me in peace."

"Get up and go and see for yourself then."

"You call the doctor if you must. What's she got to do with me?"

"You need to alert the family. This could be serious."

"Bah," replied the defiant butler who remained beneath the sheets and attempted to turn over so that he did not have to face his adversary.

An exasperated Elizabeth left Barraclough's room. But Barraclough conceded defeat in that he felt that no further sleep would be forthcoming that morning. So he reluctantly decided to get up. Perhaps that bloody housekeeper's going to get another bucket of water. But if she does, I'll chuck it back at her this time! And throttle her too!

Because Elizabeth regarded Barraclough as less than useless, she resolved to consult Cuthbert directly herself. Cuthbert then returned with Elizabeth to Prudence's room. Action stations were immediately initiated as Cuthbert instructed Elizabeth to call Dr Fenwick immediately. Dr Fenwick was the family doctor who had visited Prudence on several occasions over the years and he despaired of her ever being taken off his register of patients. Henry VIII made a similar request to be rid of Anne of Cleves – probably the only woman in the world whom Henry did not want to shag. Lucky Anne!

Ralph Fenwick was not actually keen on visiting the old harridan because he invariable received a mouthful of abuse from her together with nothing in the way of thanks for his efforts to appease her. And so he hoped in vain that this time his visit would be short-lived and uneventful. But, on entering Prudence's attic room on this occasion, Ralph became somewhat alarmed when he noticed a positive lack of response from the old lady.

Although Dr Fenwick could see that Prudence was in a bad way, he attempted to save her and his neck at the same time. Ralph hence grabbed his mobile phone and he called an ambulance as much to get himself off the hook as concern for his patient. Prudence, it seemed, was barely conscious and so Fenwick wanted the situation to be dealt with by someone else before he was accused of negligence. The ambulance took some time to arrive and the family and household showed the appropriate concern for aunt Pru's welfare while waiting for the vehicle of hope.

Nancy cleared the breakfast tray from Prudence's room, Elizabeth was relieved that she had acted wisely, Barraclough contemplated returning to bed but decided against it and Joyce hoped that Pru would be in hospital for some time in order to spare the household any further disruption.

Carlotta and Cuthbert cosseted themselves in Cuthbert's office in order to review the situation in hushed tones.

"Do you think this is it?" asked Cuthbert.

"I hope so," replied his heartless sister.

"But only time will tell?"

"Do you think that if she goes to hospital, they will be able to detect the weedkiller?"

"Don't know."

Both siblings looked dismal at the prospect of their discovery but they were both secretly pleased that their machinations were having the desired effect.

Prudence was eventually carted off in the ambulance and Ralph confidently informed the family that she would be in safe hands in hospital. Carlotta and Cuthbert had decided that one of the family should attend the hospital and Damian was elected as the family representative. Damian, however, refused point blank to pander to the old bitch. And so eventually Carlotta drew the short straw and she went in the ambulance with her aunt instead.

The news spread like wildfire around the estate. Byron put in an appearance in the house in order to receive the gossip directly from Joyce in the kitchen. Ned called in to see if he could discover anything from Nancy – straight from the horse's mouth so to speak.

Damian, who had been trying to chat up the reluctant Vanessa again, wandered back to the museum relieved that he had not been forced to take on the role of nursemaid to Pru. Damian was not at all concerned for the health of aunt Prudence and so he made no further enquiries after her departure.

After this initial flurry of activity and excitement, the household then lapsed into its usual routine and the subdued atmosphere quickly subsided. Breakfast turned into preparations for lunch, Byron did his rounds of the estate, Ingrid made a date for lunch with Delia in order to exchange gossip, Elizabeth organised the housekeeping staff and Barraclough got drunk in the pantry. Situation normal.

When Carlotta returned from the hospital, she reported that aunt Prudence was being kept in overnight for observation but that she was expected to be discharged in a day or two.

Prudence, in fact, returned from hospital within two days without any further bulletin from the hospital. The hospital staff could find nothing wrong with her other than the fact that she was old and that she needed to rest. Carlotta and Cuthbert, of course, breathed a sigh of relief at this news.

Prudence, however, had her own agenda and she obligingly died in her sleep the following night. Ralph Fenwick explained away her demise simply as old age and he speedily signed her death certificate with relief. The household rejoiced when the corpse was promptly removed by the undertakers with an impressive degree of speed and efficiency.

Freedom, at last, reigned at Havercoyne Grange.

Carlotta and Cuthbert smirked at the success of their mission. Damian was delighted that he was, at last, rid of the tyrant. Agatha was hardly aware of the upheaval which Prudence's death had occasioned because she was solely concerned with her own good health rather than the welfare of others.

Barraclough felt that he might be able to get more time in bed especially when nursing a hangover now that the major irritation in the household was absent. Joyce regarded Prudence's departure as one less to peel potatoes for and Nancy cheered because she did not have to climb the stairs in order to deliver meals any more while Byron couldn't care less either way as his main field of operation was outside the house.

# Jules' jamboree

Despite the disruption at Havercoyne Grange occasioned by the demise of aunt Prudence, Cuthbert was determined that the photo-shoot with the lovely Gina would still go ahead as planned. Ingrid had been super-efficient in contacting the undertakers who acted promptly in removing the unwanted baggage from the premises and, in consequence, there was nothing which could prevent Cuthbert from seeing Gina again.

All that remained, as far as Prudence was concerned, was to arrange a funeral date and then to attend the event. Prudence, after all, had caused enough trouble when she was alive and so Cuthbert was hellishly determined that she would not cause any more havoc now that she had perished.

Once the corpse had been taken away by the undertakers, therefore, Cuthbert made ready to see the woman who was uppermost in his thoughts these days. Cuthbert accordingly spruced himself up and awaited Gina's imminent arrival. She drifted into the hall like a dream come true in Cuthbert's eyes with her photographer in tow. Gina greeted Cuthbert with a kiss on the cheek which sent his pulse racing and his heart beating a staccato pitter-pat. Her new photographer, however, seemed reticent to engage in conversation with Cuthbert when they were formally introduced but this situation suited the randy lord perfectly.

"Will you have a drink first?" enquired Cuthbert who was himself gasping for an early-morning tipple.

"A quick coffee, perhaps, while Norman is taking the shots. That would seem sensible, don't you think?"

Cuthbert, although sorry to miss a quick snifter, agreed to Gina's request. Ingrid, who had met the party on arrival, was, therefore, asked to arrange coffee for Cuthbert and his guests.

Gina then suggested that Norman was best left alone to do his work and, as it happened, this too suited Cuthbert admirably. Gina explained that, in fact, Norman had his own beverage supply and that he could drink while he worked.

"About how long will it take, do you think?"

"Probably only about half an hour. That's right, isn't it, Norman?"

Norman nodded his agreement.

The trio then made their way to the stable block where Morning Mist, Gathering Thunder and Balleytree were awaiting their fate. Gina made appreciative noises about the horses and she diplomatically patted each in turn. Cuthbert billowed with joy at the sight of Gina showing so much affection for his much-loved racing stock. There was obviously some global warming going on inside the core of Cuthbert.

Cuthbert told the stable staff that they could take a break while the photographer was there and both staff and photographer were glad of this space in time. Carlotta was not around and so she did not need to be dismissed. The staff scurried off to annoy Joyce and Nancy in the kitchen while Gina and Cuthbert withdrew to the parlour in order to enjoy their morning coffee. Norman now proceeded to carry out his mission without interruption. Norman's own beverage, however, turned out to be a shot of brandy rather than coffee.

Jules had not encountered any trouble in getting his thermal-imaging camera through customs at Bristol airport. He had then made haste to his west country hotel in order to inspect the goods and to discover the way in which it could detect things usually hidden from the naked eye. Jules had not had time to unpack the camera prior to his departure from Morocco but now it had been assembled and it was ready for impressive action.

Jules set to work by photographing the stable block with his thermal-imaging equipment with speed and efficiency – uninterrupted by any observers and safe in the knowledge that he would have the place to himself for a while. The telescopic attachment to the infrared spectrometer soon got busy while a computerised device recorded and analysed the data as only high-tech equipment can do. Jules, for the sake of appearances, took a few quick shots of the horses but, in reality, he concentrated his efforts on the stable block itself and, in particular, the floor on which the bloodstock stood.

Jules then sent a text to Gina which read "*mission accomplished*," and he was then invited back to the house. When he entered the parlour, he gave Gina, unseen by Cuthbert, a knowing wink and she smiled inwardly at this news.

Cuthbert had spent his time productively in chatting up the alluring Gina while they were alone and he had invited her to lunch that day. Cuthbert beamed when he discovered that he and Gina would have the run of the house now that the old martinet had been carted off in a box.

"Very kind of you to invite me to lunch, Cuthbert. Thank you," declared Gina, "although Norman must be on his way pretty soon."

How convenient, thought Cuthbert.

Joyce was thus informed of the lunch arrangements, about which she had been previously warned, and Cuthbert offered Gina a pre-lunch sherry which she gladly accepted. When Barraclough brought in the drinks Cuthbert was, at last, able to imbibe his whiskey which he felt would set him up for a congenial and intimate lunch with the object of his desire. Cuthbert proposed to ask Gina for another date in due season as the lunch progressed. And so, all in all, he felt chirpy and uplifted.

The sensitive topic of the funeral was soon raised and Gina offered her condolences in generous terms. Both diners, however, quietly remembered the occasion when Prudence had interrupted their previous lunch party and an embarrassed silence ensued until it was broken by the arrival of Barraclough who replenished the wine glasses. Cuthbert was relieved by Barraclough's entrance and he felt that now would be a convenient time to steer the subject away from aunt Prudence – a topic never to be mentioned in the house ever again.

"Did you get home all right the other night?" asked Cuthbert politely, concerned that he had not been personally able to escort Gina back to her residence himself.

"Yes, no trouble at all. I really enjoyed our evening. Thank you again."

This was Cuthbert's cue.

"Could we make another date, perhaps?"

"Yes," replied Gina getting out her electronic diary.

"Would you like another meal somewhere else? Or perhaps a trip to the theatre? Or the races?" ventured Cuthbert.

Oh, glory be. Not the bloody races! Gina racked her brains for an alternative suggestion in order to avoid this form of torture.

"I'm very keen on the theatre. Could we do a London show perhaps?"

Cuthbert did not relish the thought of going all the way up to the metropolis but he conceded that he would have to make a few sacrifices in order to conqueror this filly. He, consequently, agreed to find out what was on and to report back to Gina. But a provisional date was put in their respective diaries for the following week.

Jules, meanwhile, had packed up his equipment and he was leaving the premises forthwith. Before he was even out of the gates, however, he made a quick call in order to report on progress.

"I've got some pretty good shots of the stable block," he proclaimed, "and I'm sure there's evidence enough there of the kind you need."

"Brilliant. When can we meet?"

"Well, I need some time to process the film and to examine the evidence but tomorrow all should be ready."

"Let's have lunch at your hotel then, Jules" decided Barrington.

"Right," replied Jules, alias Norman, the photographer.

When Calendula learned that, at last, some tangible evidence had been procured she jumped for joy. Calendula then suggested that she and Barrington take a shower and have an early night in order to celebrate their progress which was leaping forward towards its natural and satisfactory conclusion.


## PRUDENCE'S EXODUS

The funeral cortège slowly made its way to St Mary's church in Havercoyne Stanley where Prudence was despatched into the family vault in order to lie with her husband George and her son William together with her sister-in-law Wilhelmina and her brother-in-law Quincey.

Carlotta, Cuthbert and Damian earnestly endeavoured to look the part of distressed mourners but secretly they were all delighted to be attending such a joyous event.

Carlotta was sorry to have missed the training runs on the downs that morning and, of course, she was dismayed not to have met up with Aubrey again while doing so. Carlotta felt no sorrow at the old lady's passing and she only regretted that Pru had not gone to meet her maker much sooner.

But Carlotta had no qualms whatsoever about her role in the demise of the deceased.

Cuthbert was delighted that the old termagant had finally got out of his hair for good but he now lived in dread of a knock on the front door over his part in her passing. Carlotta and Cuthbert had wanted to have Prudence cremated in order to avoid any question of exhumation if enquiries were ever made into her death. But a break with tradition might, in itself, have aroused suspicion and so Prudence was consigned to the family vault in St Mary's church in the village. Fortunately Ralph Fenwick had signed her death certificate without demur because of her advanced age and as a result of her recent visit to the hospital where nothing had been found to be wrong with her. Carlotta had thus reassured Cuthbert that Prudence's death had been officially ascribed to natural causes but this factor regretfully did not stop Cuthbert from some degree of worry.

Damian was also relieved that his aunt could now become a distant, albeit distasteful, memory and it was a recollection which he was determined to forget instantly. He wondered briefly whether his brother and sister had assisted Pru to an early grave but he turned a blind eye to any further speculation. As long as they can get away with it, why should I care?

Agatha came along to the funeral not because she mourned the passing of the irritating Prudence but because she relished the drama and spectacle of a grim scenario in which Pru's ashes were interred in the family grave. The occasion gave Agatha an excuse for dressing up in her severest funereal black costume and thereby acting the part.

Elizabeth and Barraclough felt obliged to attend the memorial service as representatives of the household who had served the family faithfully for many years. Because the funeral took place in the early morning, Elizabeth gave Barraclough the usual ultimatum about what would happen to him if he failed to rise early enough for the event. The previous shot across Barraclough's bows had been enough, of course, to ensure that the butler rose at the appointed hour, was fully dressed for the occasion and was ready to depart with the family.

Byron had been put in charge of the estate in the absence of the mourners and he was thankful to have been spared any coffin-side duty. Byron instead did the rounds of the house and the grounds as his means of showing how important he was in the absence of the family. Byron knew that Prudence was a thorn in most people's flesh and so he was glad that she was being shipped off, even though he was not actually there to witness the event. He would, of course, join the drinks reception afterwards.

Joyce and Nancy got an exemption with regard to attending the service on the grounds that they were preparing the funeral baked meats in readiness for the return of the mourners. The kitchen staff had their work cut out for them in the scullery preparing for the aftermath of Pru's exit from the globe because they realised that there would be many people present to enjoy the fruits of their labours.

Ingrid and Delia too were left in charge of the offices in order to keep the pot boiling but, in any case, they really had no desire to attend the funeral of someone whom they hardly knew.

Vanessa Maunders had been granted a day off because, out of respect for the late Prudence Gansville-Stubbs, the museum was closed for the day. Damian, of course, hoped that Vanessa would stand by his side at the funeral. But think again sonny boy! Vanessa showed no interest whatsoever in the doings of the family and so attending Prudence's send-off seemed hardly important. Vanessa, indeed, had only met aunt Pru once or twice and the old harridan had not made a favourable impression even then. Prudence had only arrived at the museum occasionally in order to sneer at Damian's role as its curator.

Ian Manningbury managed to avoid the funeral by making his usual convenient claim of pressure of work which was readily accepted by the family because their precious racehorses were in his care.

Dr Ralph Fenwick and the veterinary practitioner Albert Fotheringay were similarly absent with the lame excuse of overwork but no family member questioned these assertions. Who cares about who comes to her funeral anyway?

Most of Prudence's friends had undergone a similar fate some time ago and, those who were still alive, were, in fact, too infirm to attend or too demented to remember who Prudence was anyway. A collection of wreaths were, consequently, delivered either to the Grange or to St Mary's church by people, either attendees or escapologists, who felt obliged to make a gesture for the sake of appearances.

And so the funeral procession was a meagre and poorly attended affair — just the immediate family, a couple of faithful retainers and a few others from the village who felt it diplomatic to put in an appearance.

Back at the Grange, the funeral cortège was augmented by the household staff who partook of Joyce's fayre and Barraclough's wine cellar. The post-ceremonial wake afterwards was, in fact, better attended than the funeral itself because of the supply of free food and drink. Nancy had laid out a spread of the usual stuff which was now all too familiar to the inhabitants of Havercoyne Grange. Sausage rolls, sandwiches and cheese straws were the order of the day but the wines were flowing abundantly in order to send Aunt Pru off in lavish style – Barraclough had seen to that side of things, of course.

Byron regarded the occasion as yet another opportunity to chat up the females in whom he was interested. As Ingrid seemed to be fully engaged in talking to Delia, he sidled across the room to Nancy. Their dinner date on the previous Sunday had been shelved following Prudence's demise but Byron was anxious to ensure that a new date could be secured speedily. He was concerned that Nancy's agreement to have dinner with him might be slipping through his fingers like sawdust and so he made haste to be by her side.

"Are we still going to have dinner one evening, Nancy?" asked Byron in a stage-whisper.

"Maybe."

Byron was downhearted. He had made tremendous progress during their recent outing to the Hunting Horn but was this dame now going to play hard to get after all his efforts?

"Only maybe?"

"Maybe?"

"Have you changed your mind then? I'll take you anywhere you want."

Nancy made a show of considering Byron's proposition and, in order to prolong his agony, she began handing out some more plates of food to the assembled company.

Come on Byron. Get on with it!

Byron stepped forth, arrested the plate from Nancy's grasp and said with feeling, "I'll meet you in the Hunting Horn on Sunday for a drink before dinner – 8.00 pm, OK? And no arguments."

"OK," replied Nancy who promptly picked up another plate of grub and began to circulate among the guests before swiftly disappearing into the kitchen.

Byron thus had to be content with a vague response in the affirmative. But he put all his money on the fact that she would be there on Sunday evening as requested. He then helped himself to a sausage roll before replacing the food platter, which he had snatched from Nancy's delicate hand, on the table.

Nancy proceeded to make ready for the family's lunch and she hoped that she would not be further disturbed by the prowling rake. Joyce was also there to protect her notionally but Nancy now had another reason for wanting to extract information from Byron and she was not about to play it cool this time. And so she earmarked 8 pm on Sunday in the diary of her mind.

The drinks and eats were soon cleared away as the hangers-on began to disperse and life at the Grange started to return to normal. Prudence, it seemed, was the kind of woman who would not actually linger in anyone's thoughts fondly for any length of time.

Damian went back to the museum and he noted how deserted it felt without Vanessa. Carlotta went to the stables to visit her cherished horses and she chuckled as she did so. Cuthbert asked Ingrid if anything had occurred in his absence and he was relieved to learn that nothing required his urgent attention.

Delia and Ingrid returned to their respective offices – where both were aware of the overtures which Byron had made towards Nancy during the wake and they each decided to keep abreast of developments in that department.

Barraclough took the remains of the wine back to his pantry while Joyce put the finishing touches to lunch and she then asked the butler to announce its readiness. Lunch was not the sober affair one would have expected after a funeral but, in fact, the household felt the relief of never again having to contend with the antics of the late Prudence Gansville-Stubbs.

A breath of respite hence spread through the Grange with each of its inhabitants feeling that the sword of Damocles had been banished so that it was not likely to fall on anyone's head ever again. It would be interesting to speculate who was the most relieved by the new peace in the atmosphere. All bets accepted with favourable odds.

*A crisis is an opportunity riding the dangerous wind.*
**Chinese proverb**

# PART 3
## STORM IN A TEACUP

*Don't go to another monastery with your own rules.*
**Russian proverb**

## FOXY'S INFILTRATION

While the family were paying homage in various ways to aunt Prudence at her funeral, the running of the household and Cuthbert's business affairs had to continue. There was much activity in the house and grounds but Ingrid had some time to herself undisturbed by old Cuthbert's petty demands and forgetfulness. And so she made very good use of her limited free time.

"*Any time you like now,*" said Ingrid's text message.

"*Right, gal,*" came the reply followed within minutes by a light tap on her window which Ingrid hastened to answer by opening the front door while simultaneously putting her fingers to her lips in order to request silence from her visitor. The caller obliged with a similar fingers-to-lips gesture and an understanding wink. Ingrid's visitor was clad in a business suit and he carried a briefcase but his wink when he saw Ingrid belied his image. The secretary and her guest then quietly tiptoed up the stairs to Cuthbert's office.

"Cor, them stairs could do you in easy!" proclaimed Ingrid's guest with a slight wheeze when they reached the top.

Ingrid waved her hand in order to encourage his silence. Foxy saluted in acknowledgement of Ingrid's request. Once inside Cuthbert's dishevelled place of work, Foxy set about his ingenious safe-cracking task at the coffer hidden behind one of the miserable pictures which adorned the walls of the office.

"I'll keep watch outside," counselled Ingrid.

"Shan't be more than a tick-tock, gal," replied Foxy Ferguson as his expert fingers and his state-of-the-art equipment discovered the combination of the safe within minutes.

Harry (known as Foxy) Ferguson lived up to the name by which he was generally known. His nickname had also been known to the police in bygone days when they had nabbed him for safe-cracking which had obliged Foxy to be retained at her majesty's pleasure. The law now deemed Foxy to have become a reformed man and, as long as he only worked for a selected few, such as the Medici Squadron, he had managed to stay out of jail for a couple of decades by now.

Ingrid waited with bated breath for Foxy's announcement that he had been successful and, when she received the thumbs-up sign, she briefly inspected the contents of his discovery and she then indicated which documents needed to be photographed. Ingrid resumed her post as sentinel on the landing outside Cuthbert's office while Foxy did the business. There was no one about fortunately and so Ingrid's sentry duties were principally concerned with keeping alert in the face of boredom.

Not only did Foxy photograph the contents of the safe but he also made copies of a few tasty nuggets which resided in Cuthbert's desk and on a side table. The crack-smith had also been detailed to plant a bug under Cuthbert's desk and a microdot camera on one of the other pictures in order to ensure that no stone remained unturned. Foxy's friend, a high tech mastermind, had furnished him with a supply of bugging devices which could be used for recording clandestine conversations in private closets.

"Mission accomplished," said Ingrid's visitor as he peeked his head outside the door in order to impart the news of his success so far.

Next the pair crept stealthily up to the top floor of the building where Cuthbert's sanctuary underwent a similar treatment both in terms of Foxy's document inspection and his bug-planting activity. The Overland Shuttle looked up briefly but then went back to sleep – relieved that Cuthbert would not be making him work overtime. The train, of course, was largely ignored by the duo because it held no fascination for Ingrid. And Foxy had naturally seen everything in his travels.

"I see 'e likes to play with his trainset then," remarked Foxy in passing.

"Sssh!"

Another thumbs-up sign was soon emitted from Foxy who could understand Ingrid's concern. Ingrid was naturally relieved that aunt Prudence could not possibly be nosing around anymore in order to enquire about their mission. And, if her ghost were to appear, then she wouldn't be able to tell on them anyway. So there, aunt Pru!

Finally Fox reported that his work for the day was complete and the pair then checked through the photographs in order to ensure that all eventualities has been covered. Both Ingrid and Foxy were satisfied with a good morning's work.

Ingrid walked with Foxy back to his car as her means of ensuring that he did not get lost when leaving the estate and in order to give her guest some credence if anyone had noticed his arrival. Her cover-story was that Foxy was a photocopier salesmen whom she had agreed to see on Cuthbert's behalf. The two finally shook hands formally in the car park and Foxy gave Ingrid another wicked wink.

"See you tonight," he whispered.

At the High Woodfield Hotel in Grayling Wood, a table was set for four guests who had booked the best seats in the house for the evening sitting.

Calendula and Barrington were the first to arrive and the pair were enjoying a drink in the cocktail bar. Calendula was consuming a refreshing Mint Julep while Barrington had acquired a taste the Whiskey Sazerac cocktail with absinthe, Peychaud's bitters, Angostura bitters and a citrus zest as the hotel's speciality. Once sampled, Barrington asserted, never to be neglected again. Barrington was contemplating a second Sazerac when Foxy arrived.

Foxy had now ditched the business suit disguise but he still wore smart casuals in deference to visiting a hotel and being entertained by his esteemed hosts. Calendula greeted Foxy with a kiss on both cheeks while man-hugs were in order from Barrington.

The final member of the party arrived in splendour for the occasion. And Ingrid too received her fair share of hugs and kisses from Calendula, Barrington and Foxy.

Some more cocktails were dispensed for the occasion. Ingrid was tempted by a Kentucky Kiss because she loved strawberries while Foxy, on

Barrington's recommendation, went for the Whiskey Sazerac. Barrington, of course, was also glad of the excuse to imbibe a second Sazerac before dinner. Steady Barrington!

In the restaurant the party were shown to their table so that their celebration could continue. Foxy proudly displayed his wares to Calendula and Barrington to the accompaniment of a chorus of appreciative comments and joyful utterances. As Foxy flicked through the goodies, Calendula was contemplating the next move of the Medici Squadron while Barrington was planning the way in which he could launch this fodder on the unsuspecting press and thereby gain maximum bucks from the experience.

"You've excelled yourself this time, Foxy," exclaimed Barrington.

"Really useful stuff," added Calendula.

"Well, thank you, Miss Calendula. Very kind. I always aims to please, does ol' Foxy."

"We got the timing just right, too. While the family were away at the funeral," interposed Ingrid.

Calendula silently thought that she and her partner in crime and passion should investigate the matter of Prudence's expiration further.

"Yes. I gather she made a rapid exit from the world, did old Pru?" enquired Calendula.

"Well, rumour has it that she was helped out of this world a bit!" announced Ingrid conspiratorially.

Calendula conceded that she had heard the gossip from her side of the fence too.

The party then continued to talk about the documentation which Foxy had recorded and the scandal which attached to Aunt Prudence's demise. It seemed that a picture was rapidly emerging and both Calendula and Barrington felt the bubbling excitement of their project almost reaching fruition. More discussion ensued between Calendula and Barrington after the dinner guests had left the hotel. Calendula was beaming with intrigue and so Barrington raised an eyebrow of enquiry to which Calendula dutifully responded.

"Well, now that we have a goodly amount of evidence about Betsy. I think it's time to start on Pru's exit from this planet."

"Hm?" asked Barrington with a yet higher eyebrow lift in the hope of encouraging Calendula to expand on her thoughts.

Barrington could tell that his beloved was hatching one of her ingenious plans which would add spice to the adventure. Calendula was the planner while he specialised in being the fixer and the organiser.

"I've worked it all out and I have a job for you."

"Really? Any sex involved?" enquired a cautionary Barrington who did not relish the thought of having to go back to doing the seduction routine as he had done so often in the past.

Recently the Medici Squadron leaders had taken a committee decision to leave all the seduction stuff to other members of the team. Barrington had claimed that he was too old for all that nonsense and Calendula had seen the sense of just remaining at the helm without having to endure the sea spray. She too was rather fed up with having to sleep with a collection of uninteresting people for the sake of the empire. Her days of needing to extract money from rich French aristocrats, which she had been forced to do when she was struggling to make ends meet while living in Paris, were now decidedly over. Calendula was thankful for small mercies and she knew that the Medici Squadron could achieve their aim now without soiling the bedclothes.

"No sex involved whatsoever. But I have a sneaky plan to tie this one up."

"Tell me more."

And so Calendula set out her scheme as the two of them were wrestling around in the shower before bed where a more interesting tussle was on the agenda. Despite his over-indulgence in Whiskey Sazerac, Barrington was still on great form for his nightly exploits with his beloved.


## BYRON'S CONQUEST

Byron met Nancy as arranged at the Hunting Horn on Sunday night. Dave and Nellie were both fascinated to note that Nancy had agreed to a second date.

"Mr Travers seems to be making some headway with the kitchen maid," remarked Nellie with a twinkle.

But Dave only smirked because he did not want to admit that he too had noticed.

"I'll have a dry white wine, please," stated Nancy in reply to Byron's offer to buy her a drink.

Byron's hopes rose as he realised that she had not opted for the stay-sober orange juice again. This fact did not escape Dave or Nellie's notice either.

"Would you like a meal later? I'm famished. Didn't get much of a lunch today because some of the cattle seemed reluctant to come out of the fields at milking time. The combine-harvester broke down. And Balleytree was off his food and I had to coax him to eat."

"That would be nice," replied Nancy.

"Shall we move on somewhere else or shall we stay here?"

"Well, I like it here. Let's eat here."

So Byron reserved a quiet table at the computerised till, Nellie prepared a table in the restaurant and Dave handed out two leather-bound menus. Nellie and Dave exchanged glances at this new development. Dave smiled because was glad to be earning some more money as a result of the advent of the new kitchen maid.

"How d'you think the funeral went off?" asked Nancy when Byron returned with the drinks.

"I think it went OK. Though, of course, I wasn't at the church myself."

"Not sure she'll be much missed, though," began Nancy who was trailing her coat.

"Don't suppose she'll be missed at all. Quite the reverse," replied Byron who was not about to pull any punches on this topic.

"Hm. She certainly created quite a stir in the house often enough."

"Oh, she was a bloody nuisance most of the time!"

Byron was obviously going to be quite upfront about the deceased and Nancy regarded his adopted stance as a compliment to her. And so she went for the whole hog.

"I think the family hated her," continued Nancy, "particularly Carlotta for some reason."

"Carlotta had her wings clipped a few times by the old witch, certainly."

"What d'you mean?"

Byron proceeded to fill Nancy in on the gen about Carlotta's ex-lovers who had been regularly bought off. Byron put the finishing touches to the story by telling all about the way in which the old lady had vetted any new admirers and then had swiftly despatched them.

Nellie appeared briefly to inform the couple that their table was awaiting.

"Awful! I'd have killed her if I were Carlotta."

"Shall we go through to the restaurant now?"

Nancy agreed but she noted the abrupt change of subject with great interest.

Byron tucked into his steak with French fries while Nancy partook of a cod mornay with green salad. Byron also consumed a sherry trifle while Nancy contented herself with a lemon sorbet. The meal was certainly a cut above Joyce's farmhouse fayre to which both Hunting Horn patrons had now become more than accustomed. But, although their meal filled a gap, it was still no great gastronomic delight.

During the repast Nancy decided that she would take up the cudgels of their previous conversation with a shot across Byron's bows while he was still eager to oblige her before she obliged him.

"I find it curious, you know, that old Pru died so suddenly."

"Hm, yes," replied Byron rather guardedly.

"And there were rumours in the kitchen that she was poisoned by the family," persisted Byron's would-be lover.

Byron stopped chewing his medium-rare steak for an instant as his attention was captured and his curiosity intensified.

"Really?"

"Can't say I blame them from what I gather," continued Nancy who had noticed Byron's attentiveness.

The glacier hence melted as Byron himself became interested in the scandal.

"Well, who d'you think snuffed her out in then?" he asked in a pathetic attempt to appear nonchalant.

"I thought you'd know more than me."

"How would I know? I don't actually work in the house, remember."

"But you must hear all the gossip?"

A slight pause ensued before Byron's insatiable inquisitiveness got the better of him and he threw caution to the wind when he suspected that Nancy might know something more than he did.

"Well, who do you reckon done it, then? And how d'you think they did it?"

Nancy then explained the tray-transportation ritual which had started in recent weeks and Byron's fascination strengthened visibly before Nancy's eyes. Hm. Now we're getting somewhere.

"So they all three must've been in on it!" declared Byron whose eyes were popping out with excitement at this bit of evil rumour.

"Seems so. They all took the tray from me at some point. Carlotta and Cuthbert more often than Damian, I admit."

"And what d'you think they put in her grub then? Sleeping tablets, crushed glass, arsenic?" continued Byron avidly.

"Don't know. But Ned mentioned that Carlotta went into the potting shed quite regularly and that some of the weedkiller had been . . . well . . . tampered with recently, shall we say."

Well, that was a conversation-stopper for starters. For a moment Byron even forgot about his mission for the evening. Byron abandoned his steak at this news and he resolved to check up on this story as soon as he could. This bulletin disturbed him greatly. He cared not a jot whether aunt Prudence might have been bumped off but he did worry about the implications of any investigation.

Byron considered the situation. How will this scandal affect me? Will I be implicated? I can easily check on the supplies of weedkiller tomorrow. I wonder who actually planned it? Was it Carlotta or Cuthbert or both? Could it have been Damian? It must have been one of the family because if Prudence had made anyone else's life such a misery they would simply have walked out and found another job. So it must have been one of them. But which one? Or all three probably. All in cahoots together. One mixed the weedkilling arsenic into her food and they all took turns in taking it to her. That was probably it.

Nancy noted that Byron's mind was working overtime with some degree of amusement, although she earnestly suppressed her snigger. How shall I play it now? Shall I tell him that I regard it all as a joke? Shall I suggest talking to the police? Can I get him to investigate further? What will his reaction be if he discovers the truth? Will he convey this information to me? Is he in a position to provide any more evidence?

After several moments of silence during which both minds were preoccupied with the demise of Prudence, the conversation resumed on more mundane matters.

"Would you like a coffee or something else as a nightcap?" suggested Byron.

"Not yet a while," responded Nancy with a seductive implication which Byron did not fail to observe.

"Would you like to come back to the Lodge for a nightcap perhaps?"

"Perhaps."

Byron's hopes escalated and all thoughts of whether Prudence might have been murdered in or who had killed her vanished like the morning mist on a summer's day. Byron felt that he should be compensated for all his efforts in Nancy's direction and Nancy felt that Byron should be rewarded for any information which he could impart about the situation at Havercoyne Grange, the fate of Betsy Drury and the demise of old aunt Prudence.

As the pair strolled back to Byron's residence at Havercoyne Lodge, Byron tested the water by taking hold of Nancy's hand. When she did not resist, Byron felt as if he were walking on air. Well, this is what I've been waiting for now for far too long. All that needs to happen now is for Ingrid and that Katherina woman to come across and then I can die a happy man.

Havercoyne Lodge was a cosy little dwelling, albeit a tad masculine and untidy. Byron had, however, managed to secure the services of a cleaner from Elizabeth's housekeeping team and so he was not too embarrassed by the Lodge's dishevelled appearance because, at least, it was clean.

The downstairs consisted of a lounge, a kitchen-diner, an outhouse-type utility room and a downstairs loo. Upstairs three bedrooms and a bathroom were the order of the day. The décor was country-style and olde-worlde which Nancy considered to be in keeping with the gatehouse residence of Havercoyne Grange.

The nightcap became a bottle of wine which was transported up to the main bedroom of Havercoyne Lodge for consumption before and after the principal event of the evening.

Byron felt the satisfaction of fulfilling his genetic purpose by spilling his seed and thereby obtaining a full belly and an empty sack that evening. He was a man for whom the pleasures of the flesh were far more important to him than boring budgets, ailing farm animals, abundant income and even murder. The satisfaction which Byron received from his romp under the duvet with Nancy surpassed all thoughts, furthermore, of work, worry and other women. She was something else – a dynamite woman! Nancy had now taken Byron above and beyond the stratosphere where even jet planes travel with caution.

Nancy too felt that she had earned her keep that evening as she contemplated the way in which she could extract the maximum amount of information from her lover with the least possible effort and commitment on her part. As Nancy stole back to her servant's quarters in the early hours of the morning, therefore, she felt that significant progress had been made on contributing to the rumour-mill.

## AUBREY'S FLOTATION

Well, this is, at least, original, thought Carlotta. Although she was well able to row a boat with the strength of a weak man, she was equally wise enough to allow Aubrey to show off his masculinity yet again. She also accepted his hand as he helped her into the rowing boat. And then she sat demurely on the passenger seat trying to look beguiling.

Aubrey clambered into the boat, took up the oars valiantly and started to row as if he had been a sailor all his life and he had formerly rowed for Oxbridge. The effect was not lost on Carlotta who only wished that they were in Venice on a gondola instead of on this minor tributary of the River Thames. But, hey, he's the only man who's taken an interest in me for years and so beggars can't be choosers. Shut up and enjoy the treat.

The usual topic of the funeral again reared its ugly head which Carlotta endeavoured to brush aside at the speed of light.

"I shall miss her like a hole in the head," she announced.

"Yes, but she was your aunt."

"Perhaps. But she was a meddling old cow. You saw that for yourself, surely?"

Aubrey did not comment immediately and his silence spoke louder than words.

"But did she do you any actual harm, though?" enquired Aubrey after a moment's reflection, not wanting to drop the subject entirely.

"Well, she got rid of my friends faster than you can say the word. And she bought off a couple of ex-lovers in no time at all."

Aubrey appreciated that the same fate would not now befall him.

"Well, she'll not have a chance to buy me off. And I'm hoping we can really get to know each other. What d'you reckon?"

Carlotta blushed – not like a comely maiden but as a woman of the world. Carlotta has lost her virginity on her world travels but, once she had settled in the Grange, any further action was somewhat curtailed by bloody Prudence. But she was now lost for words at Aubrey's forthright assertion.

Another lull in the conversation, however, was again broken by Aubrey.

"How did she die, by the way? I wasn't aware she was sick at all."

"No. Just old."

"Well, we've all got to go sometime, I suppose. Pity. I didn't think she was that bad."

"You didn't know her."

"Maybe but I always think it's a shame when people die. Poor old thing."

"I won't shed a tear," persisted Carlotta who did not like Aubrey's sentimental approach to the death of her late aunt Pru.

When Aubrey started to look a bit jaded and the conversation seemed to be getting somewhat heavy, he suggested that they stop for lunch at a riverside pub. The Ferry Boat Inn had its own mooring and so Aubrey rowed ashore, tied up the pleasure craft and assisted Carlotta gallantly out of the boat.

Lunch was not a gastronomic delight but it was tasty and it filled a gap inside two hungry stomachs. The Ferry Boat Inn's fayre consisted mainly or burgers, pizza and fish fingers together with curry and kebabs for the more adventurous palate. Nothing on the menu delighted Aubrey but he settled for fish and chips while Carlotta, rather more schooled in mundane cuisine, chose a cheese burger and was glad of it.

Next a stroll along the riverbank was called for – at which point Aubrey slipped his arm around Carlotta's shoulders and rested his head against hers. She did not, of course, object but she wished they were somewhere more private for further intimacy. But she lived in hope that something more interesting would happen later in the day.

When the pair returned to the boat, again Aubrey flexed his muscles for some more river exploration and the return trip. They talked mostly of horses for the rest of the day and this seemed a safer topic of conversation than discussing the merits or demerits of Prudence's expiry.

Carlotta was hoping to extend the outing to dinner that evening but her prospects were shattered when Aubrey calmly announced that he had an unspecified engagement that evening with Florence. Carlotta's face fell to the ground at this news. But Aubrey redeemed the disaster when he suggested that they go away for a couple of days. Carlotta visibly came to life again. A date for the following week was arranged and Aubrey volunteered to make a booking for a midweek break with three overnight stays.

The finishing touches to this burgeoning romance were put together when Aubrey kissed Carlotta fondly on the lips which held the promise of more passion in store before returning her to Havercoyne Grange. Carlotta could hardly contain her excitement at the prospect of a dirty away-day or three with Aubrey as she staggered up the steps of Havercoyne Grange – having gone weak at the knees when Aubrey had kissed her goodbye some moments before they had reached the house.

Carlotta then decided that she would take Jonquil for a light canter in order to clear her head and to escape any questions or innuendo from the family who were, as yet, ignorant of her association with Aubrey.

Aubrey returned to the Old Foundry where Florence was preparing an evening meal.

"How did it go?" asked Florence.

"Yeah. She's certainly interested. And I've arranged for us to go away next week."

"Good. Well done."

Aubrey then pounced on his laptop. He proceeded to find a suitably quiet hotel and to book a room for two. Aubrey found a reasonably priced midweek special which footed the bill in terms of time, location and price and he instantly made the booking.

Aubrey then sent a confirmatory text message to Carlotta whose heart was still fluttering from his kiss. Now all that had to happen was for the prospective lovers to wait for the day of the event to arrive. Carlotta did so by counting the hours with anticipation while Aubrey simply went about his daily routine with hardly a thought for Carlotta. He did, however, give some consideration to the way in which he would broach the delicate subject of Prudence's passing again but he didn't lose much sleep over this problem either because he knew that the inspiration would come to him when the time was right.

Carlotta looked forward to the morning gallops the next day in the hope of catching sight of the object of her passion but she was disappointed not to see him prior to their forthcoming excursion. Florence greeted Carlotta the next morning with the news that Aubrey had needed to go to London on urgent business but that he had sent his apologies and his warmest regards.

"He asked me to tell you," announced Florence, "that he's really sorry to be missing you. But he wants to complete his urgent business before your midweek break together next week."

Carlotta was very disappointed but she understood the position and she sympathised. So I shan't be seeing him until next week? Oh, hell. How shall I survive? But it will soon come around. I realise he has his work to do and so I'll have to be content. It'll be worth waiting for, I'm sure.

"Thank you for telling me. I realise he's very busy, I know. But I do appreciate your message," stated Carlotta who was surprised that Aubrey had not imparted this news himself either in person or by phone. Without him it seemed as if there was a gap in the ozone layer. But, optimistic as ever, Carlotta contented herself with the temporary absence of her would-be lover by consoling herself with Florence's company.

"Aubrey said he would contact you immediately on his return," added Florence giving the crestfallen Carlotta her warmest and most encouraging smile.

"Thank you," came the sad reply from Carlotta.

Florence then took pity on Carlotta.

"Aubrey's really looking forward to your mini-holiday. He's very excited that you have agreed to come. I'm so glad for you both," concluded Florence for which Carlotta again thanked her with a demure blush.

Carlotta and Florence watched the horses being put through their paces together. Florence made several complimentary remarks about the performances of Morning Mist, Gathering Thunder and Balleytree as well as giving her a report on the progress of Pink Dust and Magic Fury.

"We really do think that Pink Dust has come on by leaps and bounds – just like your Morning Mist and Gathering Thunder who I hear did great things at Gantry Downs recently. You must be very proud."

"Oh, we are," replied Carlotta whose mind was really on other things for a change.

Florence continued her narrative about the horses from both sets of stables but Carlotta's replies were merely polite and perfunctory because she was obviously pining for her lost love. Florence, however, noted Carlotta's reactions as she could see that Aubrey had really made an impression. Florence smiled kindly at Carlotta, therefore, as she finally took her leave of the aging lovelorn maiden from Havercoyne Grange.

## BARRINGTON'S ESPIONAGE

Byron and Nancy decided to have an evening meal in the Black Grape wine bar and bistro in Grayling Wood in order to secure a change of scene. They were also celebrating their newly consummated union.

Byron was feeling so contented that he seldom gave a second thought to either Ingrid or Katherina these days. Nancy now occupied most of the room in Byron's thoughts during the day in addition to entertaining him in grand style a few nights a week. Byron was bewitched by Nancy and he began to imagine that his relationship with her could keep him out of mischief for some time to come. And, as far as he knew, the gossip had not yet hit the streets. Well, as far as he could tell.

After a litre or two of wine, Nancy ordered a scampi Provençale while Byron stuck to plain old burger and chips. Nancy was getting a bit adventurous in the culinary department obviously yet Byron was too brainwashed by Joyce's homely cuisine. The wine was definitely having a mellowing effect and Byron was looking forward to the night which lay ahead when Nancy would get laid. With this in mind, he studied her features with dreamy concentration and much appreciation.

"So have you checked up on the weedkiller in the potting shed, Byron?" enquired Nancy casually as a portion of scampi coated in tomato and garlic sauce danced in mid-air before it reached her inviting lips.

Nancy did not want to leave the topic of aunt Pru's demise and she was determined to extract as much information as she could from the obliging estate manager who could creep into the locked potting shed to which she did not have access. Byron was jolted out of his reverie. He didn't really want to think about anything else apart from Nancy but the subject of aunt Pru's death had occupied some portion of his mind recently because he feared that he might be implicated in some way if foul play were discovered.

"Er . . . well, yes, it seems that quite a bit of weedkiller has unaccountably gone missing recently. And I noticed from the accounts that this year we've had to order more than last. Not that it would take that much to kill off old aunt Prudence, I wouldn't have thought."

Nancy was interested that Byron had felt moved enough to check up both on stocks and in the accounts. So he believes the theory then? And he's curious enough to know more.

"So she might have been done in, then? And what d'you think we should do about it? Should we report it to the police, d'you think?" asked Nancy.

"We can't do anything. We can hardly contact the police just because a bit of weedkiller's gone missing and an old dear's died. That's not evidence," protested Byron.

"Only gossip, I suppose."

"Nothing really to go on, you see."

"Apart from the fact that Cuthbert, Carlotta and Damian starting taking her meal trays up to her room regularly. I know it relieved me of a job but it's suspicious, don't you think?"

"Yes, but it's still only speculation."

"So there's nothing that can be done?" concluded Nancy who was really not happy with the situation as it stood.

"No. Not really," agreed Byron, "we might have our suspicions, or even know it for a fact, but I don't think the fuzz would be at all interested."

"Well, s'ppose not. But it's not right."

"I agree but there it is."

"But she went to hospital, so there must be something on record," Nancy continued.

"Well, as I understand it, they found nothing wrong with her when she was in hospital. Put everything down to old age."

"But isn't weedkiller something you can't detect?"

"Don't know. Never poisoned anyone personally."

"And I might be implicated," persisted Nancy, "because I work in the kitchen. And you might even be implicated if the police started to investigate. I'm worried about keeping silent. If we know something, we have a right to report it."

"How can I be involved?" protested the estate manager with vehemence, even though he was actually worried about this possibility himself too.

"I don't know," admitted Nancy, "but I'm just worried about what might happen if it all came out and we'd kept quiet."

Byron, it seemed, was more concerned for himself than for Nancy obviously. Byron, now realising his omission, sought to rectify the situation.

"And what possible reason could you have for killing her off? I ask you."

"Well, I've no reason at all but, if I keep silent, it might look fishy."

"No, there's nothing we can do," affirmed Byron by way of bringing the topic to a close.

"I suppose not," Nancy concluded.

"Let's forget it for now," urged Byron.

Both bistro diners frowned at the hopelessness of the situation. They couldn't speak up and yet, if they remained silent, would there be a backlash? And so an impasse of dissatisfaction and anxiety remained at the table with no satisfactory conclusion reached – except a decision not to take any further action despite the consequences.

Nancy looked despondent about the situation while Byron's thoughts turned to the night of fun ahead. And so whatever had caused aunt Pru's expiration was largely ignored as a hopeless case. Lack of evidence. Nothing concrete to chew on. No further action required. No one's guilty. No one knows anything. Case closed.

A man, however, who was sitting at a table nearby was curious. He had heard every word and he had recorded the conversation for posterity. This gave him food for contemplation as he consumed his mushroom risotto. He knew the Grange reasonably well because he had done the guided tour there with the robotic Vanessa. He recognised Byron who was well known in the district as the estate manager for the Havercoyne premises. And his dinner-date partner obviously worked at the house and in the kitchen moreover. The two were lovers undoubtedly by the way Byron was looking at his companion with such relish and with his mind on things to come later in the evening. The stranger, of course, knew that Byron Travers had a reputation with the ladies.

Thus the man who had done his earwigging on the conversation at the next table considered the facts which had been imparted by the couple as he tried to put the pieces of the jigsaw puzzle together. So that old Prudence Gansville-Stubbs may have been poisoned by her family, eh? Poisoned with weedkiller which was put in her food over a period of time. I did know that the old lady had been in hospital recently. But these two are not going to report their suspicions to the police. I think some action should be taken, however, if only to allay these rumours. Could it all be speculation or could there be some substance here? That was an interesting piece of evidence about the family members taking the old lady's meal trays up to her room. And the stocks of weedkiller have diminished. All very interesting stuff.

Eventually Nancy and Byron left the wine bar and the man returned homeward himself. Nancy and Byron then became preoccupied with the night ahead while the eavesdropper was now on a mission to take matters further in the interests of justice and so he reported his discoveries to his partner when he finally reached home.


## DAMIAN'S INCREDULITY

The next morning brought spring sunshine which heralded the prospect of the forthcoming summer and lightened everyone's spirits. The daily toil at Havercoyne Grange continued commenced as usual. The family, the household staff and the estate workers thus went about their business.

Byron inspected his domain while Delia carried out her usual secretarial function.

Ingrid tried to decipher Cuthbert's handwriting in order to type a few letters and to make some telephone calls.

Nancy was busy stacking the dishwasher and scrubbing the pine table while Joyce got stuck into preparing lunch.

Ned and the other lads in the stables were ensuring that the horses were fed and watered and that they were recovering from their morning exercise. And the farmworkers were sowing some of the crops and waiting for harvest time.

Cuthbert went up to his office, Carlotta visited the horses and Damian sauntered off to the museum. Damian's telephone was urgently ringing when he reached his office and, when he answered it, he was delighted to hear Katherina's voice.

"Good morning, Katherina. Great to hear from you."

"Good morning. And it's a lovely one indeed."

After these initial pleasantries, Katherina stated the purpose of her call without further ado.

"I wanted to have another quick word with you, if that's possible. Could I call round for a brief chat sometime soon?"

This request brightened Damian's morning up even more than the sunshine when he learned that the learned academic wanted to consult him yet again.

"How about this afternoon? Any good?"

"You state a time and I'll be there."

Damian felt that Katherina's request for a further meeting augured well for his ambition to become a household name and for his museum to be the hottest topic on social media. Mid-afternoon, therefore, Katherina was greeted by an eager-faced Damian.

"Shall we go down to the café for some refreshment?" offered Damian in his most hospital vein.

"Could we perhaps go somewhere more private?" suggested Calendula who instantly dampened Damian enthusiasm.

"Oh, well, we could go to my office, if you'd prefer."

"As long as we won't be overhead."

Damian readily agreed to Katherina's request and he hastened to assure her that they would not be disturbed as he led the way to his office. Damian had assumed that Dr Vanburgh wanted to take advantage of his special expertise about the Grange. But he was also a little curious about the reason for Katherina's appeal for privacy. Did she not want to see more of the house or the museum?

"Of course not. This way, please. Shall I arrange for some tea to be brought in?"

"No, thank you. I've just had a cup. And I shan't be staying long."

Damian didn't like the sound of Katherina's last statement. He had hoped that their meeting would be a long session and that she might be tempted to have afternoon tea with him – and perhaps with Vanessa present. Some hope, chum! You should be so lucky.

"So what can I do for you?" asked Damian who was still eager to please.

"Well, it's about a rumour I've heard. It may affect my research article."

Damian was all ears and all smiles.

"My husband accidentally overheard a conversation between two of your staff in a local wine bar last night. The Black Grape wine bar that is. In Grayling Wood. And I find this information disturbing."

Damian knew the Black Grape well but he was a little disconcerted by Katherina's enigmatic statement and so he urged her to reveal her knowledge.

"You see, the staff in question believe that the late Prudence Gansville-Stubbs was poisoned by the family," stated Calendula in lowered tones.

Damian instantly went a whiter shade of pale and he was lost for words.

"And, of course," laughed Calendula, "I wanted to consult you to make certain that it's simply a malicious rumour. I don't believe it myself, of course. Not for a moment. But I just wanted your assurance that you'd scotch the rumour and put an end to any further speculation so that I can continue to write up and publish my research. And, of course, I felt that you might want to reprimand the staff concerned."

Damian remained tongue-tied while Calendula continued.

"I think the conversation was between your estate manager – I met him the other day, if you remember – and one of the kitchen or household staff, I believe. Something about the family taking meal-trays up to aunt Prudence regularly before she died. And something else about the stocks of weedkiller diminishing. I know this can't be true but I thought you ought to know about the gossip."

Damian stared straight through Katherina with his mind full of scorpions in a whirl and his brain addled with shock. Calendula, of course, noted the effect which her words had engendered.

Damian wondered whether he was going to faint. He also felt that fainting might extricate him from this dodgy inquisition which might not be a bad thing. He remembered the fact that Carlotta and Cuthbert had persuaded him to take some of Pru's evening meal trays up to her room once or twice just before her death on the pretext of helping out the servants. At the time Damian had thought this to be a strange request but he had complied without much thought – mainly because he never gave much thought to anything. The suspicions which Damian had, in fact, harboured had, of course, been supressed. Cuthbert often had strange ideas, you see, about how to run the place and Damian assumed that maybe this was just another of his hare-brained schemes. Self-deception is a dangerous commodity.

Then miraculously Damian found his voice again.

"I'm sure it's only a rumour, Katherina. It's certainly not reached my ears."

"I thought so," reassured Calendula, "but I just wanted to check. Thank you. And you didn't personally take any trays up to aunt Prudence then?"

"I might have done. But I can't remember," lied Damian who was shaking in his shoes behind his desk with his heart in his mouth and, all the while, hoping that his guest had not noticed.

Calendula stood up in readiness to depart and Damian, for once, was relieved that she wanted to leave. Calendula looked as if she was satisfied with Damian's lame denial of her assertion. He thus escorted her to the front door and closed it with relief behind her. Now Damian really had some thinking to do. No sleep for you tonight, sonny Jim.

Damian returned to his office and sat down – still trembling and feeling faint. A thunderstruck Damian flopped into his chair and felt as if he were glued to the seat with shockwaves. The impact of this revelation still hadn't really hit the younger son in the Gansville-Stubbs family.

Can I believe what Katherina has just said? That Byron thinks that we murdered old Pru? Can I really believe that? Do I actually believe it myself? Would Carlotta and Cuth be capable of such a thing? Who would have thought out the scheme? Carlotta, surely? Cuth wouldn't have the sense or the guts. And they both sought to involve me – the bastards! I can't believe it. It's just a malicious rumour, isn't it? Please gawd let it just be a rumour.

And who was Byron with? One of the staff. I know he's a bit of a philanderer. I'd think it's probably that new girl Nancy in the kitchen. Couldn't be either Delia or Ingrid. They're not really household staff. And Joyce and Elizabeth are out of the question. God, what a situation. And what a scandal! And my bloody brother and sister at the bottom of all this! I'll have to act now. And they've tried to involve me! I need to know the truth.

The steam began to exude from Damian's nostrils as he realised the implication of what he had heard and, try as he might, he could not convince himself that it was simply a rumour.

# CUTHBERT'S GULLIBILITY

Cuthbert had just put the phone down after a conversation with his financial adviser, Justin Pryor, about the Seabird Cliffs proposal. Cuthbert had of late been dreaming of a permanent solution to all his financial worries by investing in this promising venture. He had been most impressed by John Mackintosh of Property Magnum who had outlined the nature of the investment during the recent meeting at Havercoyne Grange. And information about the project had haunted Cuthbert's sweet dreams ever since.

Justin, however, had strongly cautioned Cuthbert against investing any money in the development because there were too many imponderables and unanswered questions. But Cuthbert was convinced that it would be a good deal and that any investment in Seabird Cliffs would pay handsome dividends. After a verbal scuffle, therefore, Cuthbert instructed Justin to tell John Mackintosh that he would be prepared to advance a sizeable sum. Justin, however, declined to agree to Cuthbert's request.

"I think you'll find, Cuthbert, that Property Magnum are a fly-by-night outfit and I would strongly advise you not trust them."

"On what grounds do you make that assertion?"

"I've been checking up on the organisation. And, as far as I can see, they don't have a good track record. Several disastrous failures have lost vast sums for the investors."

"That doesn't necessarily mean that this project is not a lucrative one."

"Property Magnum may, as far as I can tell, have also been involved in a number of, shall we say, questionable deals in the past and they have emerged from some with egg on their face more than once," persevered Justin in an endeavour to finally get through to his client.

"Can you be more specific? Have they broken the law?"

"No, I'm just quoting the word on the street."

"But that's not concrete evidence, Justin. It's only speculation. I'd need more details if I were to change my mind at this stage. I'd like to invest in this very worthwhile project," asserted Cuthbert who seemed to have found his voice of authority as he spoke with confidence.

"Then I can no longer act for you, Cuthbert, in these circumstances. And I'll put my decision in writing today."

"As you wish, Justin. I'll go elsewhere for advice in future then."

Tough! Whatever! There are plenty of others out there who will be honoured to work for me as a financial advisor and they will, no doubt, give me better advice. I'll get my secretary, er . . . what's-her-name, to fix it.

The relationship between Cuthbert and his financial advisor hence disintegrated completely. Justin officially resigned his position and he washed his hands of any further involvement as the conversation came to an abrupt conclusion.

But Cuthbert, in a belligerent frame of mind, elected to contact Property Magnum directly. Cuthbert, still fuming from his contretemps with the obstructive Justin Pryor, then tried desperately to remember Ingrid's name before he lifted the phone but his action was rudely interrupted before he had a chance to cudgel his memory. The office door crashed open with a resounding clatter and a purple-faced Damian stormed into the room demanding Cuthbert's immediate and undivided attention by banging on the desk.

"We need to talk and now!" snarled the incandescent Damian.

"What, right now?"

"Yes, this won't keep for a second."

"OK, what's it all about then? I'm trying to sort out our finances. Can it be more urgent than that?" sighed Cuthbert.

Cuthbert could not believe that Damian had anything important to say because aunt Prudence was, these days, merely an element of bygone memory. So what did he have to storm and rave about now?

"And we'll need Carlotta here too," demanded Damian, "I've just heard a devasting bleeding rumour which could kill us all."

"What rumour?"

"I've just had a meeting with Katherina Vanburgh."

"Who's she?" replied a foggy-brained Cuthbert whose memory for names was abysmal at the best of times as Damian well knew.

Damian explained who Katherina was and Cuthbert's memory was suitably jogged. Damian then went on to give a blow-by-blow account of the substance of his meeting with Katherina. His elder brother turned a peculiar shade of grey in the process which blended with Damian's purple complexion.

"I'll ring my secretary and get her to fetch Carlotta," said Cuthbert as he reached for the phone on his desk.

"Oh, er . . . "

"Ingrid," supplied Damian obligingly.

"Yes, er . . . Ingrid. Could you get Carlotta out of the stables and ask her to come to my office immediately?"

Cuthbert hardly waited for Ingrid's reply before he put the handset down. He felt that his word would be good enough after all. Carlotta, as it transpired, was fortunately available and, at Ingrid's urgent request, she mounted the stairs to Cuthbert's office.

"What's so urgent, Cuthie?" enquired Carlotta tetchily as she entered the room.

She had barely had a chance to brush the stable dust from her clothing and she certainly had not had enough time to wash her hands. But she felt that she ought to oblige her brother in order to see what he wanted this time.

Carlotta was soon apprised of the situation from Damian's angry lips and she too changed her skin colour to a blush. So Cuthbert had turned grey, Carlotta pink and Damian purple – quite a colour palette for the siblings. Cuthbert, of course, had started to panic because he feared exposure and its consequences. Damian was showing signs of exploding before the assembled company. Carlotta, however, made a point of calling for calm but her mission pointedly did not succeed.

"Let's go up to the top floor. The servants can't hear when we're up there," suggested Carlotta as she realised that a heated discussion was just about to erupt.

Cuthbert and Damian agreed with their sister's wise suggestion and they all stomped up to the top floor. In the attic room Cuthbert had the advantage of having his hip flask to hand which had now taken up permanent residence there since aunt Pru's untimely exit from the establishment. He took a swig or two but, unfortunately, it did not have the desired effect.

"So what was all that nonsense about taking the meal trays up to Pru in order to help out the servants? That was a load of old bollocks then, wasn't it? You were slowly poisoning the old dear, weren't you? Admit it, the pair of you. And you were using me in the process!" began Damian again once the party were ensconced in the vicinity of the Overland Shuttle.

"Well, you didn't like her any more than we did," exclaimed Carlotta.

"I hated the fucking bitch but not enough to kill her and go to jail for it!" screamed Damian who was just about to burst a blood vessel.

"Keep your voice down, you idiot," counselled Carlotta with a placatory wave of her hand, "the servants might hear you if you shout – even up here."

Now that Damian had extracted something of a confession from his sister and brother, the triumvirate were obliged to discuss the dilemma with a degree of pragmatism, albeit underpinned by insipient anxiety, worry, indignation and wariness. Carlotta, nevertheless, remained the voice of rationality throughout the discussion. Hers was the cool head which had wreaked this havoc on the family but now her task was to steer her two numbskull brothers through any troubled waters ahead in order to ensure that no icebergs were struck.

"Now let's think this out sensibly. It's only a rumour after all," cautioned Carlotta.

"But this Katherina claims that her husband overhead a conversation between two of our staff. And I think one might have been Byron," asserted Damian.

"And the other?" asked Cuthbert.

"Don't know. One of the household staff. And mention was made of taking trays up to Pru's room. So it might have been one of the kitchen staff."

"That Nancy, no doubt. Byron would probably go for her," observed Carlotta.

"Well, I'll sack them both," concluded Cuthbert.

"Don't be a bloody fool, Cuth. That would only make things worse," snapped Damian.

"And they would then be free to spread more gossip," added Carlotta with her common sense approach to life.

The conversation now sifted through all the possibilities for future action and a series of suggestions were proffered into the equation.

Should we have a word with Byron and tell him it's all lies?

Can we explain that taking up trays of food was our means of helping out the servants and to show our appreciation for all their hard work over the years?

Could someone have a stiff word with that Nancy and put her straight?

Could we bribe Byron to keep his mouth shut and silence Nancy?

Could we threaten them both with the sack if they continue to spread malicious, unfounded gossip?

The conclusion which was reluctantly reached was that Cuthbert should approach Byron, tell him that taking trays up to Pru was a way of relieving the servants of their interminable burden of work. And then offer him a sweetener, if necessary. Although this did not seem like a satisfactory solution, it was the only one which all three of the party could agree on and so Cuthbert was left holding the baby in order to do the dirty work. But Carlotta decided to be present when the deed was done in order to ensure that Cuthbert did not screw it up. Damian, however, stated emphatically that he preferred to distance himself from this meeting with Byron because, he protested, he was only an unwilling participant in the whole scheme of his siblings.

Cuthbert returned to his office a changed man. But after all this much ado, he did actually remember to ask Ingrid, whose name he had now written down on his jotter after another quick reminder from Damian, to contact John Mackintosh about the Seabird Cliffs development.

The household were unaware of the nature the discussion in the attic room but a tiny device was put to good use in recording the damning evidence of the conversations both in Cuthbert's office and in the attic room.

The Overland Shuttle was naturally bored by the whole affair but, in any case, the train would not have been able to bear witness to the exchanges between the Gansville-Stubbs siblings in any court of law on this planet.


## TONY'S INVOLVEMENT

Detective Inspector Tony Croonacre and Detective Sergeant Dimity Myers had been a team to be reckoned with for some years now. They had between them cracked many celebrated cases which had earned them accolades both from their colleagues and their superiors. They were now definitely on the promotion ladder and on the map as movers and shakers in the police force.

But with some cases they had actually had a bit of divine assistance. Inspector Croonacre and his detective sergeant had, for instance, prized open a drugs racket which was run by certain unscrupulous members of the now-disgraced and disbanded pop group Vendetta Ice. The deadly duo had also unearthed the nefarious dealings of Lucinda Ketterworth who had organised a prostitution racket for her guests at the health spa once known as Squirrels Bank.

"I think I have received another one of those anonymous tip-offs, Tony," proclaimed Dimity with glee.

"Well, the last two were reliable and fruitful. So let's hear it then," replied her superior eagerly.

The team had recently begun to believe that the criminals on their patch had taken a permanent holiday and so Tony was keen to redress the balance with a bit of excitement.

Dimity read out the content of her text message.

*"Cuthbert Gansville-Stubbs of Havercoyne Grange could be a double murderer. And we have recorded and documentary evidence, of course. Worth a look? Want to see it? It will be delivered by messenger to your office later today. And we'll have more soon!"*

"Fuck!" exclaimed Tony.

"And before you ask, the mobile phone cannot be traced. But I think it's a press tip-off like on the last couple of occasions."

"It's probably either a burner or a bum job mobile which would be destroyed before it was even registered."

"Or run off someone else's network," added Dimity.

"That's life."

"They want to remain incognito obviously. But, if this stuff delivers the goods, then who cares about the identity of the mobile's owner."

"But let's hope it's copper-bottomed."

Barrington, in fact, had become an expert at acquiring mobile phones, using them and then disposing of them rapidly so that the police could not possibly trace him. Barrington had learned his craft from that renown high-tech expert Jules Axminster with whom he had lunched recently. Jules had been an excellent teacher and Barrington a star pupil.

A mysterious parcel soon arrived as promised by special messenger and Tony and Dimity opened it with much exhilaration and anticipation. Christmas had come early this year for the detective team. The courier outfit, on investigation, claimed that the sender was a shoe manufacturer in China which, on further enquiry, did not actually exist. Well, what did you expect?

The two detectives spent some time looking through photocopies of a series of love-letters which Cuthbert Gansville-Stubbs and Betsy Drury had exchanged.

"Can we check on this Betsy Drury then?" demanded Tony.

"Done it. She was reported missing about a decade ago. Not sure yet who reported her missing. But I'm having it checked as we speak."

Further researches confirmed the fact that Betsy had worked for the Havercoyne Stanley estate but that she had without warning suddenly vanished overnight.

"Any relatives?"

"Parents living in Newcastle."

"Check up on her can you then, Dim?"

"Yeah," responded Tony's sergeant while reaching for the phone.

Dimity rang Mrs Drury in Newcastle who was much surprised that yet another person was enquiring about her long-lost daughter.

"Well, as I said to the gentleman who rang a couple of weeks ago, I haven't seen or heard from her for years, you know. I reported her missing, of course, just so as the police could trace her for me. But she was never found."

Dimity raised an eyebrow when she learned about the enquiry from another quarter and Tony, who was listening in on the speaker phone, also murmured his curiosity at the news.

"And you reported her missing at your local police station in Newcastle. Is that right?" continued Dimity.

"Yes, that's right enough. I live in Newcastle and so I just went down to the station here and a policeman on the desk took all the particulars down. But I never heard nothing more about her."

Mrs Drury was beginning to sound tearful and despondent at this recollection.

"Sorry we couldn't trace her for you, Mrs Drury. Nationwide enquiries are always made for missing persons but often the person missing goes abroad and then we can't then find them unless they commit a crime," stated a sympathetic Dimity.

"I see. Well, she's such an honest girl. She'd never commit no crime, you know."

Dimity decided to change tack and pick up on one of Mrs Drury's former statements by way of deflecting her mounting sorrow as well as gleaning some more information about the mysterious yet anonymous informer.

"And who was the other person who rang you about her recently?"

"Said he was from London. The consensus office or something. Nice kind gentleman, he was."

Obviously a scam, thought the astute Dimity. Tony grimaced his agreement with Dimity's assumption and sniggered at Mrs Drury malapropism.

"Do you remember his name?"

"No. I can't say as I do. I don't think he said his name actually."

Dimity frowned at Mrs Drury's commentary. This stranger also wanted to remain anonymous, obviously.

"And when did you last hear from Betsy, Mrs Drury?"

"Well, I tried to contact her, you know, when she worked down south for some gent who owned a big place down there. She loved horses and worked in the stables, you know."

"Havercoyne Grange, the estate of Lord Cuthbert Gansville-Stubbs?" enquired Detective Sergeant Dimity knowledgeably.

"Oh, don't rightly remember the name. But it could be. He was a lord or something, he was."

Mrs Drury next revealed that she had reported her daughter missing after trying to contact her at Havercoyne Grange and after she had learned that Betsy had left and that no one knew where she'd gone. Mrs Drury, however, could provide Dimity with little additional information other than the fact her husband was now ga-ga. And so the conversation concluded with Mrs Drury feeling tearful and Dimity compassionately promising to bring further news if she could find Betsy.

A call to the Newcastle police station confirmed Mrs Drury's assertion that she had indeed reported her daughter missing but the call shed no further light on the subject.

"But it seems that the household staff might know something according to this recorded message," announced Tony who had discovered another important treasure in the goody-bag.

"Who's speaking?"

"Don't know. Sounds like a couple of servants. But if we went down to Havercoyne, we could probably identify the staff who've been gossiping."

"And maybe we could discover who worked there when Betsy went missing and interview them."

And then, as if by magic, another text message arrive which revealed the information which Dimity and Tony were seeking.

"Wait a minute, what's this?" asked Dimity.

Another text invited the two detectives to make enquiries of Jessie and Elsie Braithwaite who lived in Ivy Cottage in Grayling Wood and old Harry who frequented the Hunting Horn.

"These people are obviously mind-readers as well as useful informants," concluded Tony.

A trip to Havercoyne Stanley was hence planned for the following day and a car was ordered by Dimity for the occasion. The pair of detectives first visited Ivy Cottage in Grayling Wood in search of the Braithwaite sisters.

Jessie did most of the talking while Elsie looked afraid to speak in the presence of her dictatorial elder sister.

"We both worked at the Grange. I was head cook there while Elsie was only part of the housekeeping staff," announced Jessie Braithwaite who apparently felt that she was superior to her sister in more ways than one.

"And we understand that you were there when Betsy Drury disappeared. Can you confirm this?" began Dimity.

"Yes, we were both there at the time of Betsy's disappearance. But we hardly knew the girl. She worked in the stables."

Doubtless Jessie regarded stable lasses as lower order servants as well as housekeeping staff.

"We gather that she left rather abruptly but that she may have had an association with Cuthbert Gansville-Stubbs at about the same time," said Tony somewhat testing the water.

"We know nothing of that," replied Jessie tetchily, "and we certainly don't listen to rumours."

Elise shook her head in agreement with her sister's assertion.

"Can you shed any light on where Betsy might have gone then?" persisted Dimity.

But again Dimity drew a blank when questioning Jessie who simply stated that she and her sister knew nothing and that they didn't listen to tittle-tattle. Elsie, however, came to life momentarily and gave Dimity and Tony a sweet snippet of information by stating that a French gentleman had called from the French Tourist Board making enquiries about Betsy's disappearance.

"I sent him away. We didn't know him. And I always tell Elsie not to answer the door to strangers," reprimanded Jessie.

But, essentially, no further information was forthcoming from this particular quarter. Once outside Ivy Cottage, Dimity and Tony felt that their enquiry had not acquired anything new other than the fact that a Frenchman had called on the sisters which did offer a basis for curiosity.

The interview with old Harry at the Hunting Horn was similarly unsuccessful in that Tony and his detective sergeant could discover nothing new which would add any kindling to the fire. Harry, of course, consumed a goodly amount of alcohol in the process but Tony's investment was fruitless.

"So doing the spadework tells us nothing," declared Tony.

"Perhaps we need another sweetmeat from our anonymous source just to clinch the deal?" replied Dimity with a rhetorical question.

## CARLOTTA'S ADMISSION

The day of the midweek break for which Carlotta has been pining for days had at last arrived. The occasion was marred slightly, however, with the knowledge that rumours had been flying around about the demise of aunt Prudence and this had temporarily put a damper on Carlotta's longing to see and to sample Aubrey in the flesh. Although she was, of course, beside herself with excitement there was, consequently, a weft of anxiety running through the thread of anticipation.

Aubrey collected Carlotta promptly at 10.00 am and the duo set off for their country house hotel. The journey was leisurely and the weather complemented the anticipation which was keenly felt by both protagonists. The Stag Retreat did not disappoint. It was tucked away in a quiet spot surrounded by lakes and woodlands through which the couple could stroll in order to obtain fresh air, exercise and privacy.

The embryonic lovers arrived in time for lunch and they celebrated the start of their three-night break with sparkling wine followed by a dip in the pool, a spell in the jacuzzi and an afternoon between silken sheets because waiting until official bedtime proved to be too much of a challenge for the eager couple. Aubrey turned out to be a passionate lover and Carlotta was taken to dizzy heights of ecstasy and paradise. What a pity her conscience was troubling her because the troublesome underlying strand could not even be obliterated by her exciting transportation up to heaven. But maybe she was destined for another place?

The first morning called for a stroll to the nearby small village for a spot of browsing in the shops, a walk through the local country parkland and a morning coffee break. The twosome then returned to the Stag Retreat for lunch and yet another round of passion in the afternoon.

The next morning called for breakfast in bed and, as Aubrey was consuming a croissant with apricot jam, he felt that it was time to get down to business.

"You troubled about something, dearest?" Aubrey asked with his mouth full.

Carlotta looked up in surprise. Had he noticed? He's so attentive. I think I'm in love with him. In fact, I'm sure I am.

"It seems as if our time together has been marred by your troubles. Are you worried about the horses?"

"No, it's not that," replied Carlotta somewhat letting the cat out of the bag by confessing that she was concerned about something.

"Money worries? Surely not?"

"No."

Try again Aubrey.

"Do you want to talk about it?"

"Not really."

Having finished his croissant, Aubrey now got up and announced casually that he was going for a swim. Carlotta was chagrined. Because I don't want to talk about things, he's going to leave me here alone. A streak of desperation coursed through Carlotta's veins and a deep-seated anxiety began to grip her heart. But I can't tell him about the aunt Pru stuff. I can't, I just can't. Can I?

"I'll come with you then," pleaded a distraught Carlotta who instantly jumped out of bed in order to follow her lover hurriedly to the pool like a lovelorn puppy.

Aubrey made no comment as he strode off rapidly leaving Carlotta desperately trailing behind. The conversation between the two erstwhile lovers promptly dried up. The atmosphere thus became strained to its limits for Carlotta.

Carlotta did some more panic thinking. He's cooling off because I won't talk about my troubles. I might lose him if I don't make some comment. What could I tell him I'm worried about? Could I tell him I'm worried about cashflow? Or Cuthbert's drinking? Or Jonquil's health? No, he won't buy any of that. Could I say that some repairs are needed to the stables and the budget can't accommodate them? Or some staffing problems? Or what? No, none of these things will wash either. My troubles go deep. And I've already said that it's not money or the horses that's troubling me anyway. Nothing mundane will explain the reason for feeling as I do. But I don't want to lose him. I can't lose him. Why should I worry about it anyway? Why should my conscience be troubling me? I thought we could easily get away with it – that's why.

The afternoon love-and-sex session just didn't happen which made Carlotta even more fretful. He's withdrawing from me. But then I've confessed to keeping secrets from him, so what do I expect? At last, Carlotta, devastated by the fact that she might be losing the love of her life, finally broke her silence.

"Well, I am worried about something," she confessed over dinner.

Aubrey looked up in mock surprise from his chateaubriand and frowned. That's a good sign. She's coming round.

"You see, I'm troubled about some rumours which seem to be blighting the Grange," admitted a fraught Carlotta at last.

Carlotta had little appetite that evening and so she was not obliged to speak with her mouthful. Aubrey smiled encouragingly as he took hold of Carlotta's hand. Carlotta decided to abandon her Dover sole meunière and to make an effort to get back into Aubrey's favour at any price because the thought of losing him completely was unthinkable. She had been neglected by the opposite sex for far too long and, now that she had found someone who she could love to distraction, she was not about to jeopardise her last chance of happiness because of what had happened to aunt Pru. And she was certainly not going to let aunt Pru get her revenge from beyond the grave.

"You see," Carlotta continued, "some of the servants think that we poisoned aunt Prudence and I'm worried that some people might believe this silly story."

Aubrey said nothing which hence forced Carlotta to continue her narrative. Aubrey simply frowned some more by way of asking for further information while stroking her hand.

"You see, your friend Katherina, who's doing her research on the Grange, told Damian that someone had overheard a conversation between two of our staff."

"But it's all nonsense, of course, sweet love," replied Aubrey emphatically.

"Of course," contributed an eager-to-please Carlotta.

"Well, why can't you just reprimand the staff concerned, if you know who they are, and leave it at that. It's surely not worth worrying about, my pet."

"But that may make things worse. If we deny it, I mean."

"Why didn't you tell me sooner? Shall I have a word with Katherina for you and tell her that she's out of order? How dare she start such a rumour!"

"No, don't do that. That too might make things worse."

"And what evidence do these people have anyway?" continued Aubrey with a smattering of curiosity.

"Well," continued Carlotta tentatively, "Cuthbert came up with the idea of taking some meal trays up to Prudence in order to help out the servants and . . ."

"And now everyone thinks you poisoned her food. Well, that's absurd. You must scotch this rumour and warn your staff that if they continued to make this claim, then they'll be dismissed without a reference."

"But, you see, to an extent they're right . . . "

"I can't believe that," protested Aubrey.

"Well, we did all hate her."

"Maybe, but that doesn't mean you actually killed her. Does it?"

There was no retreating now for Carlotta and so after lunch and another round of passion, she confessed all to Aubrey who seemed to love her all the more for it. Carlotta was in seventh heaven. I've told him everything and he still loves me.

The rest of the mini-break continued on a high. Carlotta was transported to seventh heaven and beyond all the while she was beside Aubrey. Carlotta also felt the relief of unburdening her soul to her inamorato who obviously did not judge her and probably did not believe that she was guilty anyway. But don't kid yourself sister!

Aubrey too found the holiday a very fruitful one. He'd quite enjoyed a bit of rumpy-pumpy here and there and, moreover, he'd accumulated a mass of damning evidence – all of which was cleverly recorded on an ingenious little bugging device which he had put to good use. Mission accomplished. I can ditch the silly bitch now!


## NANCY'S CONVICTION

Nancy and Byron lay cheek by jowl in bed after a night of utter bliss for Byron and sheer boredom for Nancy. Nancy, who had once been an actress, however, was well qualified to simulate excitement which would convince the easily swayed estate manager. Byron, in appreciation of Nancy's nocturnal performance, had brought his mistress breakfast in bed as a reward for his pleasure and his gesture was genuinely appreciated by the kitchen maid.

As Nancy dipped her toast into a soft boiled egg and she munched contentedly, Byron's lover felt that some more probing about the main topic under discussion was in order.

"So if the family killed off old Pru, then it's quite likely that Cuthbert also did the same for that Betsy what's-her-name," said Nancy in pensive mood.

"That might be going a bit far. And we know nothing for sure."

"Yeah, but it's possible, isn't it? And there were rumours back then, I heard."

"Yet again they were only rumours," maintained Byron stoically.

"But there's no smoke without fire. And she did disappear suddenly without trace."

"Well, steady on," cautioned Byron in an attempt to stem the tide of speculation.

While Byron was pretty certain that Cuthbert was likely to be a murderer, he was not willing to be the one to spread malicious gossip worldwide and then to get it in the neck as a result. He was, in fact, becoming increasingly convinced that Carlotta, Cuthbert and possibly Damian had assisted aunt Pru into an early grave but he did not want to start conjecturing about Cuthbert being a mass murderer. It was not so much that he wanted to spare Cuthbert but he didn't want to be the one to be accused of being the muck-spreader. Byron had also, of course, pocketed a heft bribe from Carlotta and Cuthbert in order to keep his mouth shut about aunt Pru and the circulating rumours.

"You see, if the three of them plotted and schemed to poison Pru then it would be no hardship for Cuthbert to get rid of Betsy and bury her under the patio," continued Nancy in a dreamy and contemplative vein.

"Hm."

"And the outbuildings were refurbished at about the time she disappeared, weren't they?"

"Well, yes. But that proves nothing."

"And Cuthbert started to behave strangely after she'd disappeared, I gather. I think that proves everything. I'm convinced that old Cuthbert killed Betsy as well as Prudence. It's as if Cuthbert had the experience with Betsy and then, when it came to Pru, he was already a wrong'un," asserted Nancy decisively.

Byron began to mull over their discussions. He actually agreed with Nancy about Betsy and Prudence but he was more concerned for his own safety than for the guilt of the family. But if the Gansville-Stubbs lot were all found to be guilty then how will it affect me? And, if I reveal my suspicions, will I be out of a job if it all proves to be mere dust? If I conceal my knowledge, however, then will I cop it from the cops?

"I really don't know what to do. I think I agree with you in principle but I don't see that we've enough evidence to take it further, as I've already said," Byron concluded.

But Nancy jumped out of bed in a determined mood which surprised her partner.

"I'm going down to the police station right now. It's my morning off," she announced.

"Hold on. Not so fast."

"Are you coming with me or shall I go by myself?"

Byron was stultified. He now had to make a decision. If Nancy reported her suspicions to the police, what would the reaction be? Will they dismiss her statement as speculative nonsense? Or will they come knocking at my door?

Nancy walked out of the room purposefully and she left Byron to his quandary. Nancy, having showered and dressed hastily, left the lodge with hardly a word to Byron while the estate manager remained with his thoughts about what action to take, although he jumped with surprise when he heard the front door slam shut. Nancy hesitated only slightly about contacting the law but she felt that it was her duty. And, after all, she had some evidence because she had recorded her conversation with Byron that morning.

Byron's contemplation and anxiety kept him preoccupied for the entire day. The estate manager neglected the accounts, ignored Delia's requests for a review of farm stock, failed to answer his phone and did not undertake his daily inspection of the farm and grounds – an activity which usually distracted Byron in times of crisis. Byron was evidently a seriously worried man. Byron did, however, seek refuge in the company of his surrogate mother Joyce who soothed him with tea and scones.

"Anything troubling you, my dear," invited Joyce who placed a tender hand on Byron's drooping shoulders.

"No, nothing really."

"You're not yourself, I can see that," remarked the observant mother-figure.

Byron, head in hands, opened the floodgates and revealed all to Joyce. His affair with Nancy came into the open, Nancy's suspicions about Prudence's demise and her justifiable convictions about Betsy Drury. Tears flowed on to the scrubbed kitchen table which Joyce did not bother to mop up in her eagerness to comfort Byron. Now the cat was really out of the bag and there was no going back for Byron.

While Joyce was consoling her dearest Byron she was also shocked by the news which he had imparted because, in essence, it made so much sense. She had heard that Betsy had been pregnant when she had disappeared and she had guessed that Cuthbert may well have been the baby's father. Joyce could also see the logic in the family wanting to poison aunt Prudence and, indeed, she felt that she could not blame them. But murder is wrong and, therefore, something should be done about it.

"I think we should go to the police with these suspicions, just to be on the safe side," advised Joyce.

"Well, Nancy told me that she was going there this morning," replied Byron.

"Oh," replied Joyce who was now becoming worried herself.

"What shall we do?" asked Byron.

"Let's just wait and see what happens with Nancy, shall we?"

Constable Dougall at the Havercoyne Stanley village police station, meanwhile, was pleased to see such a ray of sunshine enter the premises and he greeted her with an appreciative smile and a polite "Good morning, Miss."

Nancy began to explain that she worked at the Grange and that she wanted to report a murder or two.

"Yes, Miss," replied the constable whose smile of appreciation now turned to that of incredulity and indulgence in the presence of this obviously insane woman.

Nancy proceeded to voice her suspicions about Betsy and Prudence at a pace with which Constable Dougall could hardly keep up, even though Nancy realised that the policeman was not taking her report too seriously.

"This is a very serious accusation you are making, Miss," cautioned the sergeant, "I'll have to consult with my superiors."

Dougall then proceeded to take the scullery maid's contact details and he made a brief note of what she was claiming. He then escorted her from the building with a promise to be in contact in due course if he needed any further information. Nancy flounced out of the police station in disgust. She had done her duty but she had been received with contempt and even

                    *Landed Gentry*

pity. However, thought Nancy, I still have some evidence in my pocket which I shall deposit with a more welcoming taker.

Really, thought Constable Dougall, I would have thought that the big house would have employed more intelligent staff – even below stairs. To accuse the Gansville-Stubbs collectively of murder is unthinkable. The Gansville-Stubbs family have been around for centuries. They are well thought of and respectable members of the community and how dare this little kitchen maid make such outlandish accusations? She's obviously insane. But insanity is no crime for which she could be charged – except for wasting police time perhaps!

And really what a time to choose, mused Dougall. I have so much to do at the moment. I have Miss Ridley's cat to find and those boys to reprimand for breaking a few greenhouse windows. And there's that dispute between two neighbours about what colour to paint a boundary fence. So I'll have no time to waste on the rantings of a servant – however pretty she may be.

Constable Dougall, consequently, made a brief note of Nancy's visit and filed it away somewhere deep in his filing system with a shake of his head and a sigh which indicated that no further action would be taken.

Nancy, meanwhile, decided that she no longer wanted to work in a household in which murderers haunted the established and so, on returning to the Grange, she promptly told Joyce that she would be leaving at the end of her current shift. Joyce, of course, didn't know whether to be sadden or relieved.


## ANDREW'S ENLIGHTENMENT

"Could I speak to Dr Katherina Vanburgh please?" requested the caller.

Damian had decided that he would ring Katherina and try to put her off the scent. Damian planned to say that he had spoken to the staff concerned and that they had been reprimanded for spreading malicious and unfounded gossip. Damian wanted to be assured that the academic would not believe what her husband Lyall had overheard. By this means Damian was confident that he could gently defuse the potential volcanic eruption. Damian's explanation would be that the household staff often played games with their employers being the butt of their jokes.

"I'm sorry, sir, but Dr Vanburgh checked out of the hotel yesterday," came the reply from the receptionist at the High Woodfield Hotel in Grayling Wood.

"Checked out?" repeated a stunned Damian.

Damian's query was confirmed in the affirmative and so the telephone conversation abruptly ended. Damian thus saw his family in the soup and his fame and fortune via academic accolades crumbling before his eyes. And he remained reeling from the shock for most of the day.

Calendula and Barrington had decided to withdraw from the scene smartly in order to let the caldron simmer in their absence.

"I think we've done as much damage as we can here, don't you, honey pie?" asked Calendula.

"Yes, sweet pea, let's go home now. I'm longing for our love-nest in Grove Naxton. We can conclude the operation from there very easily."

"I agree. Let's go now," said Calendula eagerly packing her things and, by implication, suggesting to Barrington that he should do the same.

The journey back to Grove Naxton Cross was, consequently, a joyous one with both the travellers looking forward to restoring their life to a degree of normality.

Once home, Calendula made a beeline for her art studio where she wallowed in oils and acrylics to her heart's content. She did not actually have an outstanding commission to fulfil at present but she liked to be back at her easel and to smell the paint. Calendula was working on a meadowland scene in oil pastels and gouache on canvas using pointillist textures and impressionist techniques which were something of a calling card for the artist. Calendula had achieved an international reputation for her work under the umbrella of Two City Designs which maintained an office with studio both in London and in Paris. This lucrative enterprise was a good cover story for the Medici Squadron's extramural activity and, fortunately, the bulk of the work at the two studios was undertaken by managers in both locations. Two City Designs was, furthermore, run in order to keep the taxman happy.

Barrington similarly busied himself with unpacking a delivery of groceries and provisions from the local farm as his means of restoring the house to a working enterprise. After this activity Byron was out in his garden at the first opportunity and he set about tidying, weeding, pruning and planting. He also harvested some new potatoes, carrots and courgettes for lunch which he always prepared lovingly for his lady-love. A late lunch of stir-fried vegetables with lamb chops crowned Barrington's labours for that day. And the repast was served in style on the patio at the couple's home in Grove Naxton Cross.

A stroll in the garden was called for after Barrington's delightful lunch.

"I think we should start the ball rolling now," concluded Barrington who was waving his mobile phone in order to signify his intentions.

A meeting in London was hence arranged between the Medici Squadron and Andrew Ormerod and his colleague John Fanshawe of *The Times* for the end of the week.

"No sooner are we home but we must go the London," mused Calendula wistfully as she retired to the swing which Barrington had erected for her in the garden as a special treat and as a token of his undying love.

Barrington, who began raking over one of his vegetable patches, agreed but he did emphasize that haste at this juncture could be crucial for their current assignment.

"We need to get Andrew on red alert and get the wheels in motion," he affirmed.

Andrew Ormerod was the editor responsible for the 'News in Parliament Today' page of *The Times* while his colleague, John Fanshawe, was more concerned with general gossip about celebrities whose lives were lived in the public domain.

Andrew, with the Medici's Squadron's assistance, had, for instance, been instrumental in exposing the corrupt politicians James Fetherington and Gregory Tranter who had manufactured a scam with the Elisian Federal government some years ago. Fetherington and Tranter, of course, were now well and truly on the scrap heap. Andrew had, moreover, acted on information received from Barrington about the activities of Reginald Trevelyan of the Benefice Charity Trust who had engaged in unsavoury financial dealings and who was now in jail for the privilege. John had also helped bring down Lucinda Ketterworth who had exploited her staff at the former Squirrels Bank Hall health retreat.

Both journalists, therefore, were delighted to be meeting up with Calendula and Barrington because this augured well for what might transpire from the notorious couple who were experts at unearthing the rats in the forest.

The four conspirators met at the Braided Duck in Tooley Street in London. This was a favourite haunt of Andrew's because he was a fitness freak who relished the opportunity to run to the pub-restaurant from his office. John, on the other hand, took a taxi as did Calendula and Barrington. An upstairs room had been reserved for the quadrumvirate by Andrew who greeted his guests once the taxi passengers had caught up with him. Whiskey and wine were ordered for the troop together with a posh ploughman's working lunch – although no ploughman would ever have recognised such luxury. The perpetually health conscious Andrew, however, restricted himself to orange juice. Poor sod!

"So what have you got for us this time?" began Andrew, even though he knew perfectly well that Barrington would tantalize him mercilessly before giving him even a hint of the cards in his hand.

"What makes you think I've anything for you, old boy?" teased Barrington.

Andrew decided to play it cool and to wait while all the time shuffling his feet under the table in anticipation. Andrew, therefore, tucked into a piece of hot smoked venison breast with a fig preserve while regarding the gruyere, brie, black cherries and grapes which would undoubtedly follow. To hell with the healthy diet for once.

John reminisced with Calendula about the way in which they had clipped the wings of Lucinda Ketterworth which seemed a more practical solution for steering the conversation towards the object of the meeting.

"You see," announced Calendula, "we've uncovered some shady dealings at Havercoyne Grange."

"Oh, Lord Cuthbert Gansville-Stubbs' pile in Havercoyne Stanley," remarked the knowledgeable John who seemed to have tabs on all the gentry and he certainly had an impressive computer-driven memory system.

John retrieved his mobile phone from his top pocket and he proceeded to apprise the gathering of the location of Havercoyne Grange and its inhabitants. But Calendula and Barrington had something important to add to the news which John had imparted.

"We think that some skulduggery is afoot there, you see," explained Calendula.

The journalists' eyes were now focused on the female in the room and their ears were flapping in keen anticipation of learning more from the Medici Squadron.

Barrington then woke up and joined in the conversation by outlining the documentation and the recordings which he held in connection with Betsy Drury's disappearance. Barrington, however, only intimated that there could have been another person who took an early exit from the planet with the help of the family.

Calendula and Barrington had, in fact, not, as yet, decided whether they would prosecute their mission for the details of aunt Prudence's untimely demise because they were rather in sympathy with shifting her out of the way. Calendula had claimed that she was a meddling old cow and Barrington had agreed. The two were undecided, therefore, whether they actually wanted to expose Carlotta, Cuthbert and Damian over this affair. But they flagged it up on the agenda at this meeting as an unspecified possibility without revealing any details – other than indicating that there could be more gossip to come.

Another date was then arranged for the handover of the relevant information which the journalists could utilise in connection with Betsy's murder.

"But what about this other matter of someone else being shifted offstage?" asked a persistent Andrew in the hope of obtaining some more newsworthy fodder.

"We're not sure of our facts yet," responded Barrington dismissively as he stood up in order to indicate the conclusion of today's meeting.

Barrington knew perfectly well that if he revealed anything at all to Andrew and John the world's press would probably arrived on the doorstep of Havercoyne Grange within seconds.

"But leave it with us and we'll report at our next meeting," Calendula assured the journalists with a radiant and disarming smile with which the two men were unable to argue.

Don't press the point, thought Andrew. Softly, softly. Don't rock the boat, thought John. We will get to the truth eventually.


## WINSTON'S WONDERMENT

Winston Blakefield and Kyle Ebury of the scandalmongering magazine *Public Enquiry* were overjoyed to receive an invitation to lunch from Calendula Fortescue-Bligh and Barrington Flint.

Winston had already benefited enormously from tip-offs received from the Medici Squadron previously and his career had been assured as a result. Winston and Kyle had recently been involved in exposing Lucinda Ketterworth as a peddler of prostitutes and, prior to that adventure, the duo had taken part in uncovering the scandal against the now-disbanded pop group Vendetta Ice – some members of which had been clandestine drug-dealers. These two scoops had elevated Winston and Kyle to eminence within their profession and their work had earned them the respect of their colleagues, superiors and fellow-journalists as a force with which to be reckoned.

The investigative team from *Public Enquiry*, therefore, arrived at the Fish Supper Brasserie in Soho for their lunchtime meeting with the Medici Squadron with both ravenous stomachs and hungry minds. Kyle especially looked forward to seeing the lovely Calendula yet again as he certainly had an appreciative eye for the ladies. Winston, however, had warned Kyle before the lunchtime meeting that if he made any improper suggestions to his hostess he, Kyle, would be on the dole by the end of the day. Kyle heeded the warning and concluded that he could look but he'd better not touch. Pity!

Drinks were ordered before lunch so that the party could collectively unwind from the pressures of work and the ordeal of travelling through the London traffic. The Fish Supper Brasserie was renowned for its upmarket haute cuisine as a fashionable place to be eating fish any day of the week. The lobster and the Coffin Bay oysters were the talk of the West End certainly. Lobster indeed was the most popular with the diners who elected to share two whole lobsters with a thermidor-style white wine sauce accompanied by spring vegetables, crushed lentils and a creamy mash as a tasty accompaniment. Winston wondered briefly why Calendula and Barrington were entertaining them in such style but the reasons were soon revealed by Barrington who kicked off the business of the day.

"We've an interesting parcel which we'd like you to deliver to Detective Inspector Tony Croonacre for us," began Barrington mysteriously.

Both Winston and Kyle knew the detectives Tony Croonacre and Dimity Myers from their previous dealings with Calendula and Barrington.

"So we're to play postman for you," responded the joker Kyle in a light-hearted mood.

"And will we know the contents of the package?" enquired the more pragmatic Winston.

"Certainly," said Calendula, "that's the whole idea."

Barrington then proceeded to explain that he had previously tipped off Tony and Dimity with a juicy carrot which had already been dangled about Betsy Drury's disappearance from Havercoyne Grange. But they now needed to provide some more reliable evidence which could be presented to the investigative team so that Tony and Dimity could use in their endeavour to nail Cuthbert Gansville-Stubbs and some of his kin. Barrington, at length, explained what had been going on at Havercoyne Grange and he itemised the evidence which the Medici Squadron had accumulated to date. The evidence consisted of recorded audio-visual conversations from vital witnesses, photographed documentation and, most precious of all, a thermal imaging video.

"Wow, I can well see why you need a special messenger to ship this little lot out of port," remarked Kyle.

"But there is, of course, a price tag?" enquired Winston.

"Of course," replied Calendula with an endearing smile while simultaneously avoiding to name her price.

Calendula and Barrington between them then elaborated further on the disappearance of stable lassie Betsy Drury in the light of the evidence which they had collected. But they were reluctant to mention the untimely demise of old aunt Prudence because, in essence, they did not really regard this as a crime.

"And we may also have another piece of gossip for you about old Cuthbert but we are still gathering info about this," added Barrington as his way of keeping his options open about whether to reveal his knowledge of aunt Prudence's annihilation from the earth.

The price-tag was next mooted. Winston winced when he heard what his magazine would need to pay for the low-down but he decided that the price would be worth the investment and that, if he did not pay what was being demanded, one of his competitors would.

The conversation now turned to aunt Prudence.

"It could also be," announced Calendula enigmatically, "that the recently diseased Prudence Granville-Stubbs may also have been helped on her way but we're still looking into this one."

This statement then clinched the deal. Winston agreed to pay the price. Arrangements were then made to pay the money and for the consignment of evidence to be shipped, in the first instance, to the offices of *Public Enquiry*.

The party thus dissolved with Winston and Kyle returning to their office while Calendula and Barrington went home to their riverside apartment in Vauxhall.

Winston and Kyle felt that this project would be further evidence of their prowess as investigative journalists and they both jointly and severally looked forward keenly to the trophies which would soon come their way in due season.

Calendula and Barrington visited the Lagunita Spa Leisure Complex which was a shared residents-only facility within a few minutes' walk across the quadrangle from their penthouse flat. Calendula indulged in a short, leisurely swim before retiring to the jacuzzi. Barrington swam more vigorously and for a longer period of time before joining his lady-love in the jacuzzi.

"Shall we decant to the sauna? I notice it's empty just now," invited Calendula.

Barrington indicated his assent by a nod of his head as he climbed out of the jacuzzi. Once installed in the sauna the pair continued their discussion about aunt Pru.

"You see we could sell the evidence we have but it'll not necessarily result in a conviction," remarked Barrington who was always interested in maximising profits.

"Well, I've been thinking," announced his partner in love and crime. "I think we should tell all – or almost all – we know about Pru so that the culprits could be let off the hook if they're lucky."

"You mean peddle the scandal but not put sealing wax and string round it."

"Precisely!"

The Medici Squadron meeting then went on to discuss the way in which they could create a furore over aunt Pru's death but not actually provide that much by way of silver-plated evidence about how she had been helped out of the world. So agreement had been reached and a decision had been taken. And thus the meeting of the Medici Squadron concluded successfully.

Once back at the flat, Barrington made a quick telephone call to *Public Enquiry* in order to inform Winston that more scandal about aunt Prudence was on its way. Winston was elated and he imparted the additional tidings to his colleague with all due speed. Winston also made arrangements to get some more dosh out of the bank.

Barrington then contacted Andrew Ormerod with the news that he had some further information about the demise of aunt Pru and this good news was similarly received by Andrew with acclaim. Andrew too readily agreed both to pass the information on to his colleague John Fanshawe and to get some more money out of the bank in readiness for the handover.

Andrew invited Calendula and Barrington to dinner at his London residence for the handover ceremony. Barrington, however, engineered the situation so that he would meet Andrew for a quick lunchtime bite rather than a dinner date which would include Calendula and Andrew's wife Maureen. Although they were old friends and he and Calendula had often dined with Maureen and Andrew, Barrington could not face the thought of Maureen's cooking coupled with her acute embarrassment over her shortcomings in that department for a whole evening.

Barrington then began to prepare supper himself and he excelled as the head chef by producing a chicken and vegetable soup with toasted cheese croutons and a warm salad as a fitting follow-up to their large and splendid lunch. The rest of the evening took its usual course and it ended with a shower before bed for the couple, complete with a rose-scented spray in order to enhance the pleasure of the union.

## TONY'S INVASION

Byron was a lost soul now that his beloved Nancy had left the Grange. The last time he had seen her was after they had spent an unforgettably night together but she had left in the direction of the local police station with hardly a parting word. Byron had later learned from Joyce that Nancy had left her job that day but she, Joyce, had no notion of her former kitchen maid's current whereabouts. Byron was, consequently, devasted by the loss of his mistress and, for a day or two at least, he could not consider a replacement.

Byron, unfortunately, did not have a mobile number for Nancy and neither did Joyce. He learned from Joyce that Nancy had not left any number or a forwarding address with anyone. And so he could not contact her in order to continue their whirlwind affair. She was, after all, only a kitchen helper who lived onsite and so contact details were not relevant to her employment. Byron had then wondered whether to ask Ingrid if she, by any chance, knew Nancy's number but he decided against this course action because it might raise a few questions in the secretary's mind which he did not really want to have to answer.

Byron was further disturbed by the fact that Nancy had actually reported her suspicions about the not-altogether-unexpected death of Prudence – and possibly the disappearance of Betsy Drury – to the police. Byron shook at the thought that he might be questioned as to why he had not acted on any knowledge in his possession and thus he dreaded the proverbial knock either on his office door or on that of Havercoyne Lodge. As Byron's thoughts were jangling around in his head, however, activity from a different quarter was rumbling like distant thunder.

Tony Croonacre and Dimity Myers had received yet another consignment of evidence from one of the members of the press and they assumed that there was more from whence that came. A bundle of photographic documentation, recorded evidence and, most important of all, a thermal imaging video had arrived by courier preceded by a phone call from Winston Blakefield of the *Public Enquiry* magazine. Winston, of course, steadfastly failed to reveal his source by stating that he was merely acting as a go-between for one of his trusted yet unidentified informants. Tony then concluded that Winston's source was the anonymous benefactor who had helped him and Dimity to unravel some celebrated cases previously by procuring juicy nuggets of damning evidence. And so the unspecified nark was both trustworthy and reliable to a fault.

Hence Tony and Dimity and a few underlings headed for Havercoyne Grange.

A loud knock on the front door of the Grange, together with several cars and voices in the drive, raised Ingrid early one morning. She promptly answered the insistent call.

"I'm Detective Inspector Tony Croonacre and this is Detective Sergeant Dimity Myers and we'd like to speak to Lord Cuthbert Gansville-Stubbs, please," proclaimed Tony to an open-mouthed Ingrid.

Ingrid, who was normally calm and efficient, was nonplussed by this statement and she merely replied by opening the door wider while closing her mouth slowly.

"We'd also like to speak to Lady Agatha, Miss Carlotta Gansville-Stubbs and Mr Damian Gansville-Stubbs and all members of staff at Havercoyne Grange," added Tony, "and would you be able to arrange for this, please?"

"And may I ask your name please, madam?" enquired Dimity.

"I'm Ingrid Durbine, Lord Cuthbert's secretary. But he's not in at present," protested Ingrid.

"Oh, where is he then?" persisted Tony before Ingrid had even had a chance to elaborate.

"He's at a board meeting in London."

"Can you supply details of the name of the company and its address then please, madam? And where Lord Cuthbert's attending this meeting?"

Ingrid led Dimity into her office where she fished out the address of Play It Again Toys plc where Cuthbert's meeting was being held that day. Ingrid had noted the sense of urgency in Tony's voice and so she felt inclined to co-operate fully with the police.

"Lady Agatha's actually away at the moment on a short rest-cure. But I'll summon Carlotta and Damian," stated Ingrid obligingly. As good as her word, Ingrid picked up the phone in order to summon Carlotta from the stables and Damian from the museum. Carlotta, she learned, had not yet returned from the training gallops but Damian was able to answer the call.

When a disconcerted Damian arrived, Tony accompanied him back to his office for an interview.

Dimity, seizing the opportunity, decided that now would be an excellent time in which to interview Ingrid.

"Could I take a statement from you now please, Miss Durbine?"

"Look, what's this all about?" demanded Ingrid at last finding her voice as her equilibrium was returning in the heat of the fray.

"We've reason to believe that Lord Cuthbert has information which may help us to trace the whereabouts of one of his former employees," replied a cautious Dimity.

"Well, I've only been here a couple of months. I'm covering maternity leave for Lord Cuthbert's usual secretary. But she's due to return at the end of next week when I'll be leaving. She may be able to help you."

"What's the name of the permanent secretary please, Miss Durbine," continued Dimity who began feverishly taking notes.

"She's Louise Fulham-Price," answered Ingrid who then supplied contact details for the new mother of baby Harrison.

Dimity soon realised that Ingrid would not herself be able to supply any enlightening facts about Betsy Drury but that she would be a good source of reference for the employees resident at the Grange. She, therefore, asked for a list of current staff and she asked Ingrid to arrange a series of interviews. Dimity also requested that Ingrid supply a forwarding address to the police when her own employment was terminated.

The first to be interviewed by Dimity was, in fact, Byron Travers. The detective sergeant was escorted over to the estate office by Ingrid. Byron was initially enchanted to see Ingrid at his office door but his smile soon faded once he had learned the identity of her companion. Delia returned with Ingrid to her office in the house and both secretaries then guardedly discussed the issue in hushed and conspiratorial tones.

Byron admitted that he had been around when Betsy had disappeared but he was eager to state that he did not listen to household gossip. The estate manager also confirmed that the barn and the stables had been refurbished shortly after Betsy's disappearance but he endeavoured to imply that no suspicion should be attached to this occurrence.

"I know all the estate workers normally but I cannot say that I remember Betsy Drury all that well," Byron lied, "I don't really have much to do with the day-to-day stabling staff as Carlotta's in charge of the stables. She'll be back shortly if you want a word with her. She normally goes with the horses for training at this time in the morning."

Byron was trying every trick in the book to get Dimity out of his office – not because he did not find her rather attractive as a woman but because he did not welcome her prying questions. He didn't like the implied air of authority.

"And what was the feeling at the time of Betsy's disappearance," asked Dimity wanting to see if Byron had heard any gossip or whether he would admit to anything unsubstantiated.

"Can't really remember," replied Byron evasively.

Dimity realised that this witness would be a hard nut to crack. Dimity and Tony had listened to the various recorded conversations which had been made by an unspecified person of Byron's various discourses with Nancy. But Byron was obviously not going to share this knowledge with Dimity as his interrogator. Dimity felt that Byron was just trying to save his own skin in order to avoid any personal repercussions by not submitting any hearsay evidence. But Dimity still believed that Byron had more to tell. Perhaps this will emerge in time?

Dimity then spoke briefly to Byron's secretary, Delia, who had very little to offer, even though she looked as if she would be willing to assist if at all possible.

Dimity undertook a similar exercise with Joyce Glemtree but again she came up against a brick wall of resistance. Joyce had heard various snippets of gossip but she had ignored them all as groundless. When pressed, however, Joyce did admit that she had heard that Betsy was pregnant and that this might explain her rapid departure. But she would not be drawn on who the father might have been. And, when Dimity suggested that the father might have been Cuthbert, the ever-faithful Joyce reared up in horror in his defence.

Dimity next sought Barraclough as a potential witness but he proved too drunk to be of any use. Dimity realised that the butler might be a mine of information and so she made a note to interview him at a later date when he was likely to be sober.

Elizabeth Garrick was similarly a useless font of information as her mission in life seemed to be to safeguard her employer. While she was around at the time of Betsy's disappearance, she was not about to speculate or to confirm any rumours which had been cruising around back in the day.

Dimity, however, had made copious notes of her conversation with Ingrid, Byron, Joyce, Barraclough and Elizabeth which would form the basis for deeper discussion with Tony when he emerged from his interview with Damian. Dimity had, nevertheless, discovered a new angle for the investigation because she had encountered a brick wall of loyalty and resistance which, in itself, was a telling testimony. Dimity had thus found some evidence by omission.

The stable lads and Carlotta were still on the agenda to be interviewed but time had run out for the investigators. Dimity decided that she and Tony could return at a later date in order to attack Lady Agatha, Carlotta and the stable staff. The farmworkers could probably be interviewed by the local police if she or Tony could not find the time or the inclination.

## Damian's ordeal

Damian, accompanied by Detective Inspector Tony Croonacre, returned to Damian's office – all the while dreading the fact that he might be forced into confessing to his crimes in the presence of the steely inspector.

"Would you like a cup of coffee, Inspector Croonacre?" asked Damian as his way of deflecting the inevitable consequences of the meeting.

Tony declined as he was aware of Damian's tactic and he wanted to get down to serious business. And I don't want to appear too friendly, even though I could do with a cuppa right now.

"I wanted to ask what you knew of Betsy Drury, sir," stated Tony.

Damian thought it wise to remain silent and with an aura of feigned recollection on his face.

"Betsy Drury. She worked here as a stable hand some years ago but she left suddenly," prompted Tony.

Damian was rather taken aback by this question. What had Betsy Drury got to do with anything? What had she got to do with aunt Prudence's disappearance, for example? He hesitated again and with a renewed puzzled expression on his brow.

"Er . . . "

"Betsy Drury disappeared without trace. And we're trying to locate her," repeated Tony, "and we wondered if you could tell us anything about her?"

Damian realised that now he had better find his voice.

"Well, I do remember vaguely who you mean but I really didn't know her at all."

"But I gather your brother Cuthbert did," provoked Tony in severe tones.

Damian hardly remembered the girl but he certainly did recall the scandal. He knew that Cuthbert had been screwing some lassie in the hayloft and that she might have had a proverbial bun in the oven. Damian also knew that she had left abruptly and that Cuthbert was devastated when he learned of her departure. He suspected that Cuthbert had truly in love the girl but that his sense of loyalty to the family had prevented him from doing anything decisive about it. And Agatha and aunt Pru may well have put pressure on him to end the affair, particularly when they discovered that the girl was pregnant. Damian, however, did not want to impart these facts to the menacing inspector.

"Cuthbert has more to do with the stabling staff than I do. I'm only responsible for running the museum. I don't have the same interest in horses as the rest of the family."

"By that you mean Cuthbert and his sister Carlotta presumably?"

"Yes."

Keep trying Tony.

"We believe that Betsy and Cuthbert were having an affair and that the girl was pregnant and Cuthbert was the father."

"What?"

"And we suspect that her disappearance was not accidental."

Tony had now decided that he would put pressure on Damian by telling a few fibs in the hope of jockeying his interviewee out of his complacency.

"Not accidental! What does that mean?"

Tony ignored the question.

Damian began to think hard about his next move. This policeman seemed to know a lot but presumably he cannot prove it. It may well be that someone helped Betsy on her way and I suppose it could have been Cuthbert. I do know that Betsy was trying to blackmail him into running away with her. And then an ingenious idea struck the usually dim-witted Damian.

"Well, our aunt Prudence was often in the habit of paying off troublesome employees," he blurted out.

And then Damian stopped dead in his tracks. He really did not want the topic of Prudence to come to the surface because that might open yet another more lethal can of worms.

"Yes, I may want to speak to you about your aunt Prudence later but, for now, can we concentrate on what you know of Betsy Drury please, sir."

Now Damian was seriously rattled.

There was then a knock on the door which Tony got up to answer. Tony disappeared outside for a brief discussion and then returned with Dimity Myers.

"This is Dimity Myers, sir, my detective sergeant."

Damian nodded while shaking in his shoes at the prospect of now being interrogated by two detectives – neither of whom he had even a remote chance of outwitting. Damian realised that the detectives must know more than Tony had already revealed in that they knew some intimate details of Betsy's disappearance and possibly of Prudence's untimely demise.

"And we understand that the stables were refurbished shortly after Betsy disappeared," continued Tony, "and we regard this fact as suspicious."

Damian went white. His limited brain remembered this fact and it suddenly occurred to him that Cuthbert may actually have been responsible for doing away with Betsy and burying her under the stable floor. Cuthbert, after all, had proved that he was not adverse to despatching Prudence and so he may have had some previous experience of being a murderer. Damian remembered that Cuthbert had insisted on laying a floor in the stables which was unusual because most stable floors are merely left bare because of the insanitary habits of the horses. But, at the time, Damian had assumed that Cuthbert was just being precious about his beloved horses.

Tony and Dimity watched the circumlocutions of Damian's mind and they felt that they were on to something as a result.

"So I wonder, sir, whether you can shed any light on this situation?" interposed Dimity.

"You see we believe that your brother Cuthbert may have been involved in her disappearance in some way and we find it suspicious that she has now disappeared without trace," added the senior officer.

Damian, now a desperate man, replied that he knew nothing about anything.

"Could you please show us the stables then, sir?" asked Dimity.

Damian hesitated.

"We can, of course, get a search warrant, if necessary."

"Well, you had better do just that then," remarked Damian who felt that he ought to take a more aggressive stance, although, unfortunately, his ploy failed.

"We will," announced Tony who nodded to Dimity as an indication that she should action the procedure.

"Thank you, sir," concluded Dimity.

Both detectives then rose and walked in the direction of the door.

"One moment," said Damian in his endeavour to detain the police contingent, "I can show you the stables if you're really interested, though I can't see what good it will do."

"Thank you, sir."

Damian felt that a quick look at the stables would satisfy the pair as there was really nothing to see. He did not, of course, want to be the one to bring the search warrant on to the premises for fear of what it might actually reveal. Damian thus silently led Tony and Dimity out to the stable block. The detectives gave the stables a cursory inspection but they did not question any of the available staff who were tending the horses.

"Thank you, sir," said Tony again, "that will be all for now."

Damian returned to his office as a very shaken man in order to contemplate his next move. He decided to ring through to Ingrid in order to be able to contact Cuthbert and to warn him that the police were about to descend on his head. Ingrid supplied Damian with Cuthbert's contact details, which she had also given to Dimity, but she held out no hope whatsoever that Damian would be able to get to Cuthbert before his interrogators did.

"I just wanted to warn Cuthbert that we have had some unwelcomed visitors here this morning," explained Damian.

Ingrid had worked out that fact for herself but she did not feel the need to enlighten the curator of the museum. Predictably Damian did not manage to track down his brother at his board meeting.

Once off the premises, Tony and Dimity discussed the case on their journey home.

"All those I spoke to are being highly evasive," began Dimity who then listed those whom she had interviewed.

"Out of loyalty to the family name?"

"They know something all right. I'm convinced of that. But it may only be hearsay evidence rather than fact."

"And we've still to interview Carlotta and Cuthbert. But I think we certainly have a case to investigate."

"Not forgetting Lady Agatha and the other estate workers. We've still to see them, of course. Or we could get some of the local constabulary to see to that for us, if necessary?"

"Hm," replied Tony, "but I think our next step is to apply for a search warrant.

"Well, we'd better see Cuthbert first."

"Yeah, let's do that right now."

"And I'll get that search warrant lined up."

*The devil's favourite piece of furniture is the long bench.*
**German proverb**

# PART 4
# FAIR WEATHER FRIENDS

*Better to be alone than accompanied badly.*
**French proverb**

## CUTHBERT'S INTERROGATION

Cuthbert sat in the meeting of the board of directors of Play It Again Toys plc with a slightly bored expression on his face. He was well paid for having his name on the company's headed stationery and for attending stodgy board meetings such as this one. But he contributed very little to the proceedings because his knowledge of business, in general, and the enterprise of Play It Again Toys plc, in particular, was scanty to say the least.

The directors had first discussed the company's financial imperatives, such as the staffing arrangements and the advertising budget, which had gone straight over Cuthbert's head. The board members then turned their attention to forward planning and the launch of their new product range. Protypes of new board games, computer games and construction toys, which reminded Cuthbert of the Overland Shuttle, were self-importantly displayed. And, finally, the pièce de résistance was presented as the ingenious Robbie Rabbit. At a voice command from his proud owner, Robbie Rabbit could tweak his nose, flap his ears, wag his powder puff, hop about and squeak like a mouse. Cuthbert was fascinated to see these exhibits but his interest was only transient as he was itching for a whiskey or two and a lavish buffet lunch which was normally provided gratis in the boardroom by a more-than-competent catering staff.

When the discussion around the boardroom table resumed, Cuthbert took the opportunity to dream about his latest investment scheme in the Seabird Cliffs project and to imagine himself as a seriously wealthy man who would no longer need to attend any rotten board meetings in order to flesh out his income. Cuthbert had contacted John Mackintosh of Property Magnum plc and he had agreed to the deal. He had also made arrangements for a vast sum of money to be forwarded to Property Magnum once his solicitor, Colin de Winter, had vetted the contract.

The chairman of the board stood up with a view to delivering a slide presentation to his fellow directors about the forthcoming product launch. His first slide showed photographs of the games and toys which the delegates had already inspected while his subsequent slides gave a detailed product specification. The next set of slides got more involved in the financial side of things but the chairman, remote slide changer-cum-pointer gadget in hand, was interrupted by an insistent crash as the door swung open followed by the abrupt entrance of Tony Croonacre and Dimity Myers. The dangerous duo were accompanied by an apologetic secretary who was about to say something which, in fact, got lost in the maelstrom.

"I'm Detective Inspector Tony Croonacre and this is Detective Sergeant Dimity Myers," began the policeman with his usual opening gambit.

"What is this unprecedented and untimely interruption all about? This is a meeting of the board of directors," protested the chairman.

"Sorry to disturbed you, sir," replied Tony, "but we need to speak urgently to Lord Cuthbert Gansville-Stubbs in connection with the disappearance of one of his staff."

Cuthbert shuddered when he heard his name and more so when he realised that the policeman might be referring to Betsy rather than to aunt Pru. So who has let the cat out of the bag then? It cannot be Carlotta surely? Maybe one of the stable staff? Are there any grooms still hanging around from back then? But why would they speak up now after all these years? And this interruption seems to look serious. Or perhaps it's that kitchen maid girl who used to work with Joyce. Forget her name, though. That's who it must be. But why all this urgency?

"Could you come with us please, sir?" requested Tony.

Cuthbert reluctantly obeyed the inspector's command as he allowed himself to be led from the board room. The rest of the members of the board meeting looked rather mystified but after a shrug of their shoulders they carried on with the business of the day. They still had his name on the headed stationery – so what the heck?

"We wish to question you about Betsy Drury," announced Dimity whom Cuthbert had hardly noticed.

Dimity offered Cuthbert a chair in a nearby meeting room and the peer of the realm meekly sat down with his mind in a whirl. And he looked as if he needed to sit down in the eyes of the onlookers.

"Betsy who?" he blustered in the hope of deflecting any further questions and thus letting himself off the hook.

"Oh, come now, sir," sneered Tony, "surely you remember Betsy? She was one of your stable staff some years ago and you had an affair with her. Remember?"

"Yes, vaguely," returned Cuthbert who deduced that playing the innocent as a tactic was not going to bear fruit.

"Can you tell us more about your relationship with Betsy please, sir?" interjected Dimity.

"Well," Cuthbert admitted, "I met her a couple of times. She was a pretty girl."

"I think your relationship was a little more than that," proclaimed Tony with an air of frustration.

"We hear that it was a full on affair lasting almost a year and that you were the father of the child she was expecting," contributed Dimity.

This really threw Cuthbert. How had these people accumulated so much accurate detail? And how much else did they already know? What can I do now in the face of this onslaught? But Cuthbert still decided to dither.

"Can you answer the question please, sir?" ordered Tony.

Cuthbert looked like a scared rabbit but he still kept schtum.

Tony got to his feet.

"Would you like to come down to the station with us, sir? Or are you going to tell us what you know now?"

The flustered Cuthbert decided that going down to the police station would, at least, get him off the premises of Play It Again Toys and it would possibly save him any further embarrassment. But he certainly did not really want to leave under a police escort.

"Could we not just go to a café or somewhere like that?"

"No," replied Tony emphatically.

"But, if you accompany us down to the station voluntarily, then that will avoid our having to arrest you," added Dimity in the hope that the peer of the realm would play ball.

Cuthbert and the two detectives, consequently, left the premises with what Cuthbert hoped was a casual manner. He asked the secretary who was guarding the boardroom door to extend his apologies to the rest of the directors by explaining that an emergency had arisen because one of his staff had gone missing and so the police were now urgently trying to trace her. Cuthbert assured the secretary that he would return as soon as he could once the crisis had abated.

In the car, Cuthbert, quite naively, hoped that he would gain some thinking time and a bit of respite. But think again Cuthie!

Dimity was the first to restart the interrogation.

"We would advise you, sir, to tell us as much as you know about Betsy Drury's disappearance and to tell us about your affair with the girl."

"I can't tell you any more than you already know. I admit that we did have a brief liaison."

"More than a brief liaison, I think," remarked Dimity.

"Did your wife know?" interjected Tony.

"I don't know. Probably not."

"And what did you think when Betsy left you so abruptly? Did you have any further contact after she'd left?"

"I may have done. I really can't remember."

"And how did you take her departure."

"I was surprised, I think. I don't really know. Again, I can't really remember."

Tony and Dimity concluded that either Cuthbert was stalling for time or he actually did have a bad memory or both. Dimity believed that Cuthbert had a bad memory but that it was selective when he wanted it to be.

Back at the station, the two detectives continued their questioning with an increased degree of fervour and the questions flowed in an incessant barrage.

"So how serious was your affair with Betsy then?"

"Were you in love with her?"

"What did you think when she got pregnant?"

"Did you want her to get rid of the child?"

"Did your wife know about Betsy's pregnancy?"

"Did you want to keep in contact with Betsy after she'd left?

"Did you make any attempt to contact her after she'd left?"

"Did she tell you she was leaving?"

"Did you encourage her to leave?"

"Did you give her any money when she left?"

And so it went on for what seemed like half the day and night. Cuthbert seemed powerless to answer any questions coherently. Was he tongue-tied or just overwhelmed? Finally Tony asked the careworn Cuthbert if he would agree to a search of the Grange and the estate. Cuthbert, however, refused and he started muttering about calling his lawyer. It was as if the threat stirred him to make a stand. And by, this means, Cuthbert was attempting to field any further questions.

And then the tide turned.

"You can go now," announced Tony much to Cuthbert's astonishment, "but we'll be in touch again."

A weary and befuddled Cuthbert then made his way back home with a seriously troubled mind. Cuthbert did not even attempt to return to his board meeting which, undoubtedly, would have finished by now anyway. He did call his lawyer, however, who simply told him not to answer any more questions and a meeting was arranged for the two of them in order to discuss Cuthbert's dilemma on the following day.

Dimity, meanwhile, reported to her superior that the search warrant would be ready first thing in the morning.


## CARLOTTA'S INTERVENTION

Cuthbert was utterly exhausted when he arrived back at the Grange because of the long day and the impending threat to his liberty. He, therefore, slinked off to bed with a bottle of whiskey which was completely empty by the morning.

Carlotta came into his room the next day before Cuthbert had had time to open half an eye. She shook her brother vigorously in order to bring him to full waking consciousness before he was actually ready to stir. Carlotta had, by now, heard about the police invasion.

"Wake up, Cuthbert, for fuck's sake. We need to talk."

Cuthbert merely groaned and so Carlotta shook him some more.

"We need to talk urgently. The police have been here asking about Betsy."

"I know."

"Then wake up!"

Cuthbert conceded defeat and sat up in bed while groping for the empty whiskey bottle.

"And this won't help you, you idiot," she stated while snatching the empty bottle from the floor and waving it in front of Cuthbert's bleary eyes.

"We need to plan what we're going to tell the old bill when they return."

"I've already seen the police. But I told them nothing."

Carlotta nearly hit the roof with alarm and disappointment that her brother had told the police anything at all – and especially without a lawyer present.

"Put on your dressing gown and we'll go up to the attic," Carlotta commanded.

Carlotta's brother obeyed because he hadn't the strength for any argument or protest in the presence of his domineering sister. And nursing his hangover was obviously out of the question. Cuthbert, however, could appreciate the wisdom of a discussion far away from the ears of the servants.

Carlotta continued to question her brother about the information which he had imparted to the police already. Cuthbert felt that this interrogation from his sister was ten times as awful as the ordeal to which he had been subjected by Tony and Dimity on the previous day.

"Shall I get Damian in here too?" asked Cuthbert as a delaying tactic.

"I've already asked him to join us up here as soon as possible. We'll need to agree on our tactics so we can get our stories to tally."

Damian appeared shortly and it was obvious that he was a very worried man.

"So you've admitted that you had sex with Betsy?" continued Carlotta.

"Well, yes, probably but I didn't admit to being the father of her child."

"Did you admit to knowing she was pregnant?"

"I think so, but I really can't remember," replied Cuthbert meekly.

Carlotta sighed in exasperation at the bumbling incompetence of her elder brother.

"Did they ask you for a DNA swab?" she persisted.

"No. Why the hell would they do that?"

"In case they find the body."

"But how are they going to find the body?" asked Cuthbert who was getting a bit tired of the interrogation from his sister.

"If they dig up the stable floor, of course, you bloody idiot!"

Carlotta got up from her chair and paced the room in the hope of shifting some of her aggression and frustration.

"And what would make them dig up the stable floor, for god's sake? Eh? For the benefit of their health? They've no reason to dig up the floor," stated Cuthbert who also rose from his chair and began storming around the room.

Carlotta and Cuthbert continued to glare and snarl at each other as they prowled around the room.

Damian, as he listened to the conversation, at last had it confirmed that his siblings were a couple of murdering crooks. Not only had they despatched aunt Pru but now it transpired that Cuthbert had snuffed out Betsy Drury as well. Damian would win no prizes for brain of the century but this much he could work out for himself. And right now his siblings looked as if they could murder each other which might not be a bad thing!

So, into this caldron of venom, Damian put in his contribution which stopped both his sibling in their tracks.

"The police asked to see the stables."

The world ceased to spin on its own axis, the sun spontaneously combusted, the moon stopped revolving around the earth and hell froze over. The interval lasted for several seconds before Carlotta broke the silence.

"And did you show them the stables, Damian?"

"I had no choice. They were threatening to get a search warrant, for Christ's sake."

The silence continued unabated. Cuthbert neglected to fill the gap by saying that he had probably forced the detectives to obtain a search warrant because he had yesterday refused permission to allow them to search the premises.

"But they just looked and went away," reassured Damian.

"Did they ask about the new floor?" asked Cuthbert anxiously.

"I'm not sure," stated Damian.

"Shut up both of you and let me think!" commanded Carlotta and her brothers obeyed in the hope that their sister, as the brains of the family, would come up with a solution instantly.

"Let's get in touch with Colin de Winter," Carlotta decided at last.

"I've already rung him and he told me to say nothing. He's coming here this afternoon for a discussion."

"Why on earth didn't you say that before? You stupid old fossil. That whiskey's addled your brain obviously."

Cuthbert did not reply to his sister. Damian agreed with Carlotta but he was not about to take sides in a dispute between the two of them.

The meeting continued to discuss tactics with Carlotta grilling each of her brothers about what information they had already imparted to the police and then making copious mental notes about what the police actually knew. Carlotta's job, of course, was made quite difficult because Cuthbert had an unreliable memory and Damian was not that bright. Carlotta then instructed her brothers to say as little as possible in future and to speak only to Colin de Winter before opening their mouths during any police interview.

The party then disbanded.

Damian returned to his museum in despair. If his brother and sister were carted off the jail, he, in all likelihood, would probably follow. And then all hope of Vanessa coming around to his way of thinking would be permanently and irrevocably lost forever.

Cuthbert went back to his room and got into bed but he realised that sleep would evade him for many days and nights to come. Cuthbert took some pills in order to relieve his headache but he was not at all convinced that it would easily shift. Cuthbert pondered on what the police had made of his replies to their questions and he tried to work out whether they would actually accuse him of any crimes.

Carlotta despaired of ever getting through this fracas alive. She knew of the ineptitude and the stupidity of her brothers and she believed that whatever happened they would all be highly likely to go down. Carlotta, who had wisely had the foresight to take mental notes when interrogating her brothers, reviewed the jottings which she had subsequently made. She dismally concluded that, at best, she could only mount a damage-limitation exercise rather than get Cuthbert off the hook as far as Betsy Drury was concerned.

Carlotta next instructed both her brothers to relate the same story to the police and she schooled each of them in the script which they were required to adopt. Cuthbert was required to maintain that he had learned that several men had had sex with Betsy at about the time of her departure. Damian was detailed to assert that he knew nothing about Betsy and Cuthbert's liaison other than from hearing vague gossip.

As for aunt Pru's exit from the world, Carlotta believed that she would probably get away with this one if she kept her wits about her. And if she, Carlotta, could contain the damage to Betsy alone, then the police would not be interested in investigating anything else. It was, however, a wet sandcastle on which Carlotta was pinning her hopes.

So what do you think? Do you want to engage in a soupçon of speculation? Place a bet perhaps? Or just let things take their natural course? And do you feel any sympathy for any of the culprits? The mind-boggled Cuthbert? The lame-brained Damian? Or the bloody-minded horse-trader of the triumvirate?

# TONY'S BREAKTHROUGH

The search warrant arrived on Tony's desk first thing the next morning and Dimity appeared simultaneously with further news.

"It's an anonymous text this time," announced Dimity as she read the phone message aloud.

"*Don't forget to look under Cuthbert's desk and under the table with the Overland Shuttle. A few pictures on the walls might be inspected as well.*"

"What's the Overland Shuttle?"

"Don't know. A courier service? A businessman's toy perhaps? Maybe a toy trainset?" Bingo!

"Of course, that's probably it. Just the sort of thing a small mind would be amused by," remarked the cynical sleuth who had made a pretty good guess.

But they grabbed the search warrant and the pair headed for the hills.

Elizabeth, the housekeeper, answered the door of the Grange that morning because she happened to be in the hall while Ingrid was collecting documents from Cuthbert's office.

"Good morning, madam," stated Dimity who recognised the housekeeper from her fruitless interview the day before.

"We have a warrant to search these premises," stated Tony blandly as he beckoned to a full team of officers who had accompanied him in order to undertake the search.

Tornedo-like the search team swept through the house – ignoring Elizabeth's protests. She did not like her domain to be disturbed in any way and she wanted to ensure that nothing would be damaged or broken.

"Can I see your so-called search warrant please? And I want your assurance that nothing will be disturbed in the house?"

"They're usually very careful and respectful of property, madam," replied Dimity unconvincingly.

Dimity, nonetheless, tried to soothe the flustered Elizabeth but her reassurances were not believed.

"There are some highly valuable items in the Grange – not to mention the museum."

"We'll not need to enter the museum today," continued Dimity, "but we'll need to inspect the stables."

Elizabeth, of course, realised that she could not actually prevent the search team from ransacking the house but she couldn't care less what was done in the stables.

"I shall expect you to compensate the family for any damage or breakages," blustered Elizabeth, "although many items are priceless and irreplaceable."

"That goes without saying, madam," concluded Dimity who then turned away in order to avoid any further discourse and to accompany her immediate superior to the stables.

Elizabeth hastened to the attic room in order to warn Cuthbert of the invasion. Cuthbert was so absorbed in his thoughts as he watched the Overland Shuttle slinking around the track that he had not heard the commotion downstairs. But, once alerted to the danger, Cuthbert jumped up in alarm. Carlotta, whom Cuthbert usually ran to in times of crisis, was still out exercising the horses. And then a thought struck him. Where will they be searching?

"Are they just searching the house," enquired an anxious Cuthbert.

"Yes, sir. But I'm assured they will pay for any damage," reassured Elizabeth.

"Anywhere else?"

"Not the museum, I gather, but I believed they'll be searching the outbuildings."

Cuthbert left the Overland Shuttle to its own devices as he fled the room – more upheaval and the train would have been rerailed. He went straight out to the stables in order to inspect the state of play. Elizabeth was considerably startled by her employer's rapid exit from the attic room.

An officer was guarding the door to the stable block and he told Cuthbert that he could not enter until the search was complete.

"But what are they doing in there?" Cuthbert demanded in what he hoped would be his most authoritative upper class manner, although it cut no ice with the policeman.

"I'm sorry, sir, but you can't enter just now. Detective Inspector Croonacre's orders."

Cuthbert retreated as a crestfallen creature and he withdrew to a secluded corner of the estate in order to call Carlotta on her mobile phone. Carlotta then told Cuthbert not to panic in threatening tones. She also advised her stupid brother that she would return to the Grange as soon as possible. Despite the crisis, Carlotta still wanted to catch a glimpse of Aubrey if at all possible but, when she realised that he would not be attending that morning, she cantered Jonquil back home with a degree of hurriedness.

Once back on the estate, Carlotta found Cuthbert in the hall while the search was in progress.

"Have you seen the search warrant?" enquired Carlotta as she steered her brother outside and away from the house.

"Well, no, but, I think, Elizabeth has."

"So you don't know what it actually says and what is being searched?"

"Well, no."

"Fat lot of good you are."

"Shall we go and ask the police?"

"No, that might arouse suspicion," replied Carlotta who was trying to calculate her next move.

"But, I don't think they're doing the museum."

"I'd better see that search warrant."

Carlotta marched off in the direction of the stables and she demanded to see the search warrant which Dimity supplied. It clearly stated that the house and the stables would be searched but no mention was made of the museum. But would the museum be considered to be part of the house?

Talk of the devil and he always materialises. Damian approached to ask what the fuss was all about and Dimity informed him that a search of the museum would not be necessary at this stage.

"But I'd like to ask you a few questions, Miss Gansville-Stubbs," stated Tony turning to Carlotta, "as we didn't get a chance to speak to you yesterday."

"What are you doing in my stables," retorted Carlotta in her attempt to evade the issue.

"Just a preliminary search, madam. Perhaps we could use your younger brother's office for the purpose of brief talk?" asked Tony.

Damian felt that he had no option but to agree and so Tony, Carlotta and Damian returned to the house and headed in the direction of the museum.

"Might I ask what all this is about?" asked Carlotta in a casual manner.

Tony ignored the question as he escorted Carlotta into the museum and he opened the door of Damian's office. When Damian attempted to enter his office, Dimity put out a restraining hand.

"We shall not need you just now, sir," stated Dimity as she ushered Damian away from the door.

Damian was thus obliged to leave the house and to make his way towards Cuthbert who, still looking defeated and forlorn, was mooching about on the drive in front of the Grange.

As expected Carlotta remained the picture of calm innocence throughout her interview and no pressure tactics on Tony or Dimity's part could shake her resolve.

"Did you know Betsy Drury at all?"

"Betsy. Yes, I did meet her once or twice but, at the time, I had been travelling and I had not actually decided to join the team at that stage."

Carlotta felt that this statement would keep her soundly in the clear.

"But, according to our records, you had become the stable manager and were in residence at the time of Betsy's disappearance," proffered Dimity with an inscrutable smile.

"Possibly," admitted Carlotta.

"Certainly," countered Dimity who herself was not a woman with whom to trifle.

"I can only talk when my solicitor is present," Carlotta stated with finality, although Tony reminded her that she was not being formally interviewed under oath.

Carlotta said nothing further. She was subjected to the same set of questions with which her brothers had been bombarded but she steadfastly remained evasive and lacking in knowledge throughout her interview. Tony and Dimity thus concluded that interviews with the Gansville-Stubbs family were a bit of a non-starter.

Lady Agatha was not to be found that morning because she was still enjoying her rest-cure apparently and so the detectives felt somewhat as if failure were looming.

And then the tide turned in their favour. Tony had arranged for his version of Jules Axminster to come along with a thermal imaging camera for the search of the stables.

"Can you come to the stables please, sir?" asked a local constable who had been recruited to help with the search of the premises.

Tony and Dimity were then shown some evidence which tied in nicely with that which they had already received. Now the two detectives could claim that they had discovered the truth for themselves. But all they had to do now was to prove it.

Another local constable who was searching the house sure enough discovered the letters and the bugs in Cuthbert's office and in the attic room where the Overland Shuttle was viewing proceedings with little or no interest.

"Things are looking up," remarked Tony to Dimity with delight.

"Right," responded Dimity, "now we can really put the thumb screws on them."

Tony then proceeded to arrest Cuthbert and to take him into custody down at the local police station while Carlotta and Damian looked on in horror. It was a bit like watching an execution knowing that you would be the next in line.

Cuthbert was first asked to give a DNA sample and then he was ignominiously left to wait in a cold and uncomfortable room at the station for his interview. Cuthbert had demanded that Colin de Winter be present which meant that his wait was prolonged even more. During this fallow period Cuthbert thought feverishly about what he would say in his own defence and he tried to remember what Carlotta had told him should be the official party line.

When solicitor Colin de Winter arrived a brief discussion between the two ensued at which time Cuthbert admitted his guilt to his long-standing friend who attempted to ignore the comment which Cuthbert had made. Colin endeavoured to impress upon Cuthbert that he should only answer questions which he, Colin, had sanctioned during the police interrogation. Cuthbert seemed more confused than ever about what he should say and he was certainly terrified at the prospect of being tripped up by Tony and Dimity.

## Dimity's triumph

It was, of course, pretty plain sailing for Tony and Dimity from now on. They probably had enough evidence with which to convict the entire family but most of the evidence was questionable because it had been obtained by dubious means as far as a court of law was concerned. A confession, consequently, would be ideal.

Inevitably a posse of muscle-bound men arrived at the stables with picks and shovels alongside mechanical digging tools. The men worked in tee-shirts and exposed their bare arms even in early spring when the weather was inclined to be changeable because these specimens of masculinity were tough and they didn't feel the cold.

Tony shortly received word that a woman's body had been discovered beneath the stable floor on the Havercoyne Stanley estate and that the corpse was being taken to the nearest laboratory for inspection by a pathologist.

"Now let's start that interview with old Cuthbert," Tony instructed Dimity while savouring the thought of ultimate success.

"Should we also round up some of the others?" asked Dimity.

"Yes, bring in Carlotta, Damian, that estate manager, the housekeeper and the cook. Oh, and that drunkard of a butler."

"Barraclough."

"Yes. And get hold of Lady Agatha too."

Dimity instantly set the machinery for the round-up in motion.

Tony and Dimity, back in the interview room, again asked Cuthbert what he knew of Betsy's disappearance and about his relationship with the stable lass. But, this time, the interview was recorded and Cuthbert was reminded that, because he was under oath, he should answer truthfully this time. Cuthbert, of course, couldn't quite remember what he had admitted to in his last round of questioning and so he tripped himself up on several occasions. Cuthbert had also predictably forgotten the instructions from his sister about what to say to the police. Colin de Winter observed all with grave concern and he earnestly took a few notes – mostly as a reminder to Cuthbert later about what he had said during the interview.

"So you did know that Betsy was pregnant then?" asked Dimity who had taken the lead during the interrogation.

"Well, I'd heard that, yes. But it was only gossip, of course."

"But did she tell you herself?" interjected Tony.

"No."

"But in your interview yesterday you said that she'd told you and you'd rowed about it," proffered Dimity who felt that Cuthbert was beginning to show signs of wear and tear.

Cuthbert hesitated with confusion and loss of memory. Dimity read Cuthbert's exact words from her notes in order to jog his memory but this tactic only made the peer even more confused.

Tony and Dimity continued to ply Cuthbert with a fusillade of questions and the peer became more and more agitated and muddled-headed. He was now definitely showing signs of fatigue under the strain. As the clock ticked on Cuthbert visibly became more burdened with every second which passed. The tree was beginning to bend under the rage of the storm. Colin de Winter, consequently, requested that his client be given a breather for some refreshment.

When the interview resumed, Cuthbert was informed that his brother, sister, estate manager, housekeeper, cook and butler had all been brought in for questioning and that his wife was being called back from her rest-cure.

"What's my wife got to with this?" enquired an outraged Cuthbert while Colin perched a restraining hand on his arm.

Silence enshrouded the room for some moments while Cuthbert felt intimidated more by the lapse in the conversation than by the questioning routine.

"You see we have just found a body under the stable floor which you had installed about the time of Betsy's disappearance and we believe it to be the body of Betsy Drury," announced Dimity slowly and distinctly in a moment of quiet.

Cuthbert went white and green at the same time and his heart took the elevator to the top floor of his mouth.

"I shall be questioning your wife, your siblings and your household staff carefully about what they know. So I'd advise you to stop lying to us, Cuthbert, and own up to the truth of your involvement in Betsy Drury's death," added Tony.

"We also have your letters to Betsy," stated Dimity.

The search team had found the bundle of letters which Cuthbert and Betsy had exchanged with a little help from Ingrid who had fished them out of his desk drawer and put them on the top of his desk where any idiot would have found them at first glance. These were the originals of those previously received by Tony and Dimity from *Public Enquiry*.

"Letters?" asked Cuthbert lamely.

Dimity realised that she was on swampy ground here but she could see that the peer of the realm was about to crack. Cuthbert went into a brown study of shock. How the hell did my letters to Betsy get discovered?

"What letters? I never wrote any letters to Betsy," he repeated.

"A number of letters were found in your office. Correspondence between you and Betsy," replied Dimity pressing home her advantage.

Colin interposed by asking whether he could see the evidence for himself so that he could then consult with his client. But Colin had attempted to take charge of a situation which was rapidly spiralling out of his control.

"Are you intending to charge Lord Gansville-Stubbs with anything? Because, if not, I think His Lordship has been subjected to enough questioning for one day," demanded Colin.

There then came an urgent knock on the door of the interrogation chamber and Tony suspended the interview while Dimity responded to the call.

"We have just heard some very interesting information which throws light on the murder of Betsy Drury. Your brother has confessed to his knowledge of your involvement in Betsy's death," proclaimed Dimity proudly on her return.

Before Tony had a chance to formally charge Cuthbert, the landed gent put his head in his hands and wept. And then he blurted out, "It was an accident. I didn't mean to kill her. I loved her dearly."

After a short break for a consultation with his solicitor, Cuthbert made a full confession and signed it. Betsy had apparently wanted them to elope but Cuthbert found it impossible to accede to her wishes. When Betsy had announced that she was pregnant, Cuthbert had offered to bring up the baby at the Grange provided that she married one of the stable lads or a village boy. The couple had then rowed violently and Cuthbert had struck Betsy who was knocked to the ground. But she hit her head as she fell. Cuthbert had next buried her where she had recently been found.

Cuthbert was detained in custody pending further enquiry – having been charged with the murder of Betsy Drury. A formal identification had, of course, yet to be made of the body but, it seemed, that dental records might oblige in this respect. Mrs Drury would naturally need to be alerted by the local police in Newcastle but Tony hoped that she could be spared the ordeal of identifying the body which was not really in a fit state to be beheld.

"Well done, Dim. You're a star," said Tony giving Dimity a congratulatory hug after Cuthbert had been trussed up.

Tony then decided to interview Damian so that he could make his confession as an accessory after the fact. But Dimity also made her own confession.

"Damian hasn't actually been interviewed yet," she confessed.

"What? Dimity! What are you saying?"

"I lied. But . . . we got a result," she protested.

"Well, yes. But for fuck's sake never do that again!" said an exasperated but happy Tony.

"But my claim wasn't being recorded. You hadn't turned the recording equipment back on yet before I spoke."

Tony was relieved to be reminded of this fact but he was still a tad cross with Dimity despite the success of her ruse.

"Then let's put the thumb screws on Damian and Carlotta quick. Damian should crack easily, I think. He's probably even more stupid than his brother. But that Carlotta is a woman of steel."

"But we'll get her in the end."


## Vanessa's tendresse

As Tony had predicted, Damian was a pushover.

"We have just received a confession from your brother Cuthbert that he was responsible for the death of Betsy Drury. He's been formally charged with murder and he'll remain in police custody until further notice," began Tony who was anxious to kick off the proceedings.

"Well, I did realise that – but only recently. And I knew nothing about aunt Pru, I can assure you," protested Damian.

The room went silent for several seconds while Tony and Dimity – and Colin de Winter – took in this astounding revelation.

"So when did you discover that Cuthbert had murdered Betsy Drury?" continued Tony, ignoring the aunt Prudence question for now.

Damian confessed that he had gleaned this snippet of information during the discussion which he, Carlotta and Cuthbert had conducted in the attic room only days before. He was obviously keen to protest his innocence in the equation.

What a pity we can't interview the Overland Shuttle, thought Dimity.

The recording of the conversation in the attic room was hence played back to Damian who confirmed that his siblings were speaking.

"But this was the first time I knew anything about it. Please believe me," he pleaded.

"And why didn't you report it at the time to the police?"

"I was shit scared, that's why," continued Damian with conviction – the sentiment of which the police detectives could believe even though they did not agree with his inaction.

Dimity could certainly see the logic of the interviewee's claim while Tony reckoned that Damian's vulnerability could actually be exploited to their advantage. The questioning continued carefully, consequently, until Damian had confessed all he had heard about Betsy's demise. But he was still charged with obstructing the police enquiry and he was taken down to the cells pending a trial. Damian consulted further with Colin de Winter when he realised that what he had said to the police would almost certainly incriminate him as well as his wicked brother and sister.

After Damian had spent a night in the police cells, it seemed logical to begin the interrogation all over again but, on this occasion, the topic under discussion was a different one. This time, however, the detectives wondered what mayhem Colin's appearance would cause during the interview.

"So what do you know about the death of your aunt Prudence?" began Tony gingerly who suspected that Damian may now wish to retract his former statement.

But again Damian was a putty in the hands of his inquisitors and he generously imparted all he knew. Damian spoke about taking the meal trays up to aunt Pru but he maintained that he believed all the while that this was Cuthbert's ploy to help out the servants. Colin de Winter was powerless to stop the flow from Damian's larynx and, by now, he totally despaired of the entire Gansville-Stubbs family in general. Was anyone in the family not a bloody criminal?

"Cuthbert often had crazy ideas like that and so I just went along with it a couple of times. But Cuthbert and Carlotta took most of the trays up to Pru."

It was not, of course, until the now-famous attic room discussion that Damian had realised that his brother and his sister were both a couple of merciless fiends. But Damian did his best to mitigate the impact of the crime as far as it affected him. Self-protection is a powerful motivator and so the detective duo exploited this human weakness to the hilt by telling their interrogee that his position would be favourably considered in court if he co-operated fully. Damian obliged. Poor sod! Colin de Winter then conceded defeat for his client and he concluded that speaking up would be the best option at this juncture.

While Colin de Winter made a valiant attempt to get bail granted for Cuthbert at which task he failed miserably, he did manage to get Damian out of custody until his trial. The judge realised that Damian would be of little harm to the public as he was such a twit. At worst, Damian had just been an impediment to the enquiry. And so Damian returned to the Grange with his tail between his legs and a self-pitying expression on his face.

Vanessa appeared in his office on Damian's return and the sight of her reduced Damian to tears. Vanessa, however, rested a comforting hand on Damian's shoulders which did wonders for restoring his equilibrium.

"I think we'd better close the museum for now," suggested Damian.

"I've already done it. I sent the staff home and closed the office – even though we'd probably get some novelty value from keeping it open but the press could be too oppressive."

Vanessa then asked Damian about his ordeal down at the local police station and the culprit was forced to retell his story. Vanessa, however, gave her employer a sympathetic ear and a kindly smile which restored Damian somewhat to his former self. Damian was keen to assure Vanessa that he was not a criminal but merely a victim of circumstances and at the mercy of his evil siblings.

The pair continued talking while Damian contemplated yet another proposal to the love of his life but, for now, at least, he decided against it. Damian took a different tack, however, in the – probably erroneous – belief that formal courting might work the magic.

"Would you have dinner with me tonight, Vanessa? I really don't want to dine alone."

"Of course."

Damian left Vanessa in his office and headed to the kitchen in the hope that Joyce would not throw a saucepan at him. Joyce greeted Damian with a worried look yet with a welcome-home aura about her person.

"How are things?" Joyce asked cautiously.

"It seems my brother has been charged and detained but I may have to go for trial as a witness," Damian replied airily not wanting to flesh out any details and thereby deflect any further enquiry. He also did not want to style himself as an accomplice as his means of protesting his own innocence.

"But you're quite safe?"

"Yes, thank you, Joyce. But, as I've had a hard day, would it be possible for you to serve dinner for me and Vanessa in the dining room this evening?"

"Our course, Damian. It should be ready at about 7.00 pm," stated Joyce obligingly who knew of Damian's partiality for the tour guide.

Joyce prepared roast beef with all the accoutrements as a special treat for the diners. Barraclough too was pleased to have a legitimate opportunity for opening another bottle of wine. He accordingly selected a rich red burgundy as it was one of his favourites and he hoped sincerely that the customers would not consume the lot.

Vanessa was flattered to be eating in the dining room that evening and she found herself looking around the room trying to assess the value of the property. Who knows, it might be sold and Damian may come into some money? I wonder what will happen when Cuthbert and perhaps his sister go down? Will son Nathan inherit or might it pass to Damian? Perhaps a union with the exasperating Damian would have its compensations after all? Vanessa thus smiled encouragingly at Damian as she consumed her tasty roast beef, roasted parsnips and savoy cabbage and she drank a goodly portion of Barraclough's bunce.

## TONY'S PERSISTENCE

Tony and Dimity realised that they would need to gather some supporting testimony for the Betsy Drury case from the staff of the Havercoyne Stanley estate and so they set about the arduous task of formally interviewing all and sundry. And they still had to open up the question of aunt Prudence more fully.

Byron was the first to receive the treatment in the hope that he might crack with both the detectives grilling him. Byron had not revealed very much when Dimity had interviewed him in his office.

"And we believe that you had a conversation with one of the kitchen staff about his situation?"

Tony and Dimity had easily recognised Byron's voice on the recording which they had received from the anonymous source.

"I did speak to Nancy, the kitchen assistant, but she went to the police and then resigned her job."

Byron then confirmed the gossip to which he had been party and the fact that he had checked up on the weedkiller supplies. But, as Byron had been handsomely bribed by Cuthbert in order to keep his mouth tight shut, he tried to be evasive when answering questions.

"And you didn't think to contact the police yourself?"

Byron was beginning to get worried about the fact that he had not come forward sooner. And the fact that he had maintained no further contact with Nancy seemed to throw suspicion in his direction.

"Well, I felt it was only idle gossip," protested Byron who was desperately trying to remember his conversation with Nancy so that he could get his own story straight.

"And d'you know where Nancy is now?" put in Dimity.

"No idea. She left no forwarding details."

"You were obviously having an affair with her so why didn't you keep in touch?"

"It wasn't really an affair more like a brief fling. I wanted to see Nancy again, of course, but she disappeared off the face of the earth once she'd left the Grange. And she didn't ever contact me again."

"Can you give me her full name please, sir? So that we can trace her." asked Dimity.

"Nancy Emery," supplied Byron.

Dimity wrote down the name.

"But someone at the Grange may know," added Byron without any degree of conviction that the police enquiries would be any more successful than his own.

Tony continued to question Byron about what he knew of Betsy's disappearance, her liaison with Cuthbert and her pregnancy but nothing new emerged. Dimity took the lead in asking further questions about Nancy's departure and her whereabouts but she acquired no additional information from the estate manager.

"You don't think that Nancy was done away with too?" asked a concerned Dimity once Byron had departed.

"Well, as far as we know, she was not involved with Cuthbert and she wasn't pregnant. I think she just fled out of fright."

"I'll check at the police station where she reported the incident," stated Dimity who proceeded to contact the local constabulary.

It took desk Constable Dougall some time to unearth Nancy's statement which he had dismissed as the rantings of a mad woman. And he was reprimanded accordingly. But Nancy had only given her address as Havercoyne Grange and this snippet of data was less than useless as far as the investigation was concerned. Nancy had simply told Dougall that she thought she was living with a lorry load of murderers but no hard facts were actually provided.

Joyce was next for the interview routine. Joyce confessed that she had strongly suspected that Betsy was pregnant when she had disappeared.

"And did you think the father was Cuthbert Gansville-Stubbs?" asked Dimity gently.

"Well, I really couldn't say. A lot of men at the Grange had a roving eye at that time and that goes for the men from the village too. It could have been anyone," Joyce proclaimed cautiously – all the time hoping that Byron was not one of the happy stage army.

Joyce then admitted that she had heard gossip from Byron about aunt Prudence's death but again she maintained that this was only speculative chatter. Joyce, however, elected to relate what Nancy had told her in the hope that it would deflect attention away from her dearest Byron. But once more this was only hearsay evidence. And, when Dimity consulted her notes again about what Joyce had told her previously, she realised that nothing new had transpired.

Barraclough, sober for once because Joyce had nagged him to death about copping out of the situation, was called to account. Tony asked him what he knew of Betsy Drury and her affair with Cuthbert.

"They may well have been having an affair because my employer was a bit of a lad," admitted the butler with a grin, "but whether he was having a fling with Betsy, god only knows."

Probably too drunk to really know anything about the doings at the Grange, thought Tony.

"And what did you think when she disappeared suddenly?" asked Dimity.

"Didn't think anything of it."

"You didn't think anything had happened to her? You weren't suspicious at all?"

"Why should I be?"

"And what did you think when the stables were refurbished?" tried Tony again.

"I wasn't involved with any of that. Not my department."

Tony and Dimity hence concluded that Barraclough's brain was obviously too sodden with drink for him to really think anything worthwhile, except what wine to have with dinner perhaps. And so the formal interview with Barraclough was concluded as a sheer waste of time.

Elizabeth Garrick proved to be as tight-lipped as ever until Dimity came up with an inspiring idea.

"I gather from some of the other staff that you had discovered that Betsy had missed several periods."

Elizabeth replied that this may have been the case but that it proved nothing.

"And we have reason to believe that Cuthbert Gansville-Stubbs was the father," persisted Dimity.

"I know nothing about that. Just malicious gossip, I expect. Cuthbert was respectably married to Lady Agatha," maintained the stodgy housekeeper who was obviously implacable.

She's not going to budge, thought Dimity, as she surveyed the housekeeper's stiff upper lip. And Dimity was right.

Lady Agatha entered the interview as if she were coming on stage to receive a standing ovation from her adoring fans.

"You wanted to see me," she proclaimed in dulcet tones.

Tony and Dimity then questioned Agatha about her knowledge of Betsy Drury in the hope that she would reveal something new about the situation.

"A stable girl, you said?" enquired Agatha languorously.

"Yes."

"Well, I really have nothing at all to do with estate staff. And horses are not my thing either."

"But your husband has been charged with her murder," protested Dimity.

"Really? Well, if you say so."

Dimity and Tony were astonished by Agatha's lack of concern for her husband and they were left somewhat open-mouthed by her attitude. Perhaps old Cuthbert was justified in finding some distraction in the shape of a comely stable wench.

"But you can provide us with no information about your husband's liaison with this girl?" asked Tony.

"No. My husband has always had something of a roving eye. But I really take no notice."

"It doesn't concern you at all?"

"Not really. Boys will be boys, you know."

"But we gather you asked him to end the affair when the girl got pregnant?" interjected Dimity.

"Did I? Well, I would have done, I suppose."

"Were you pressurised by Prudence Gansville-Stubbs, for instance, to ask your husband to end the fair?" asked Dimity with a flash of genius.

"I may have been but Prudence usually issued her own reprimands rather than getting others to do it on her behalf," replied Agatha calmly.

Dimity and Tony thus despaired over using Agatha as a witness and so the formal interview was terminated with both detectives left with a feeling that the landed gentry were all on another planet which they personally could not even envisage.

## DIMITY'S INITIATIVE

"Why don't we get an exhumation order for Prudence?" asked Dimity.

"On what grounds?"

"We have more or less got a confession from Damian about Prudence Gansville-Stubbs and, if we had some more tangible evidence, we could then nail Cuthbert and his sister over that one too."

Tony thus decided to apply for the exhumation order mainly on the premise that one confession of murder might presuppose that there were other murders in the offing. Once Prudence had been disinterred, the pathologist, sure enough, found traces of weedkiller still lingering in her system in larger than normal quantities.

"Right, let's get that bitch Carlotta in here again and put the heat on," declared Tony.

Carlotta was brought to the local police station where Tony had secured some space for his investigation. Carlotta was asked to wait in the reception area while she waited for Colin de Winter to arrive. She had informed the police that she would answer none of their questions without her solicitor present and Tony and Dimity had been obliged to comply with this edict.

While in the reception area, Carlotta mused on her situation. Carlotta intended to range herself against Cuthbert and Damian and to play the innocent victim. Carlotta believed that her brothers were expendable while she was invaluable. She reckoned that this stance would protect her and thus she relaxed in the comfort of this knowledge.

Carlotta also knew, of course, that Aubrey would always love her and that her future with him would be assured. Aubrey had, after all, listened to her confession and he was still willing to love her even if she were guilty. Carlotta was, consequently, smug when Colin arrived because she supposed that somehow he would soon loosen the noose around her neck.

Carlotta and Colin were duly wheeled in to the interview room where Dimity and Tony were patiently waiting but Carlotta looked implacable as she entered the torture chamber much to the consternation of the detectives who were out to get her.

"We shall be interviewing you, Miss Gansville-Stubbs, under caution and we will be recording your interview," announced Dimity as her opening patter.

Carlotta was more fazed by being addressed as a single woman than by being worried about what might transpire during questioning. But *perhaps I won't be single for long when my darling Aubrey rescues me.*

"Your brother has been charged with the murder of Betsy Drury who used to work at the Grange."

Carlotta made no comment in reply because she was doing what Colin de Winter had advised.

"Do you have anything to say?"

"No."

"Then let's turn to the death of your aunt Prudence. We have evidence from the exhumed body that your aunt was poisoned," continued Dimity.

Again Carlotta showed little in the way of reaction. She was more concerned that the family grave had been disturbed and left untidy than she was by the fact that Prudence's body had been probed by an inquisitive pathologist.

"We also have reason to believe that you were instrumental in causing her death by poisoning," added Tony.

"Really? I would have thought that my elder brother was obviously the culprit. If he murdered this Betsy woman as you say then he would be ideally placed to kill Prudence."

Tony and Dimity noted that, on this occasion, Carlotta had responded rather than taking the no-comment stance.

"But we have statements from various members of your staff and your younger brother which indicate that you were the prime mover in the murder of your aunt."

"There's no evidence to support that and the staff are obviously lying, although I can't think why," maintained Carlotta adamantly.

It seemed obvious to Dimity and Tony now that they would need to put pressure on Cuthbert in order to ensure that Carlotta cracked. The interview was, therefore, suspended by Tony.

Carlotta was left to kick her heels in the reception area yet again. Colin guided his client to a private corner where he questioned her further about her knowledge of Cuthbert's dealings with Betsy and her involvement in Prudence's poisoning. Carlotta, of course, maintained her innocence even in the presence of the trusted Colin by claiming that she was only involved unwittingly in Prudence's death which was principally masterminded by Cuthbert. Colin, however, noted that Carlotta showed no regret over the demise of her aunt and he doubted whether Cuthbert had the wherewithal to supervise Prudence's murder.

Tony and Dimity recalled Cuthbert in order to question him about his sister. Cuthbert, who was by now very amenable to persuasion. He admitted that Prudence's death had been Carlotta's idea but that he had gone along with it. Cuthbert felt that he might as well be hung for a sheep as a lamb but he was damned if he would let his bloody sister get away scot-free. Cuthbert also admitted that Damian had been roped in by his sister but that his younger brother had participated without knowing what he was doing at all. Further signed statements were taken from Cuthbert and his interview was recorded for posterity.

Dimity and Tony hence returned to their interrogation of Carlotta with a degree of enthusiasm.

"We now have an admission of guilt from Cuthbert over Prudence Gansville-Stubbs murder. And he has detailed your involvement in the crime."

"Then he's lying too. He wants to let himself off the hook, obviously," sneered Carlotta who was undaunted by this revelation.

Colin looked somewhat worried as he felt that the net was closing in on Carlotta. And Colin and his client appeared to be suffocating under the strain.

Often the universe works against us but, on some occasions, a lucky break can be granted to the chosen ones. An urgent knock was thus heard on the interview room door. Dimity rose to answer the call and she briefly left the room. Tony spoke to the recording device in order to announce Dimity's temporary absence. Dimity then called her superior officer to the door for a brief consultation. When the two detectives returned, they both looked triumphant.

Tony then made a proclamation in a voice which sounded as if he were announcing the winner of the lottery at fifty million pounds.

"We have just received a signed statement from Mr Aubrey Bankover, a licensed private detective, who has informed us that you were responsible for planning and executing the crime which resulted in the death of your aunt Prudence Gansville-Stubbs.

'What?" cried Carlotta who rapidly rose from her seat while her hopes instantly deflated.

Colin, of course, intervened appropriately with a demand to read the statement which this Aubrey Bankover – whoever he was – had given to the cops. The interview was thus suspended pending the perusal of this new evidence and the party disbanded.

Tony, Dimity and Colin left the room so that the solicitor could be shown the signed statement. Dimity sought to question Aubrey further in order to see if there was anything which he could add to his statement but the private detective had nothing further to say.

Carlotta was left alone in the interview room with her shattered dreams, albeit guarded by Constable Dougall. Carlotta's troubling thoughts naturally plagued her massively. She felt as if a ton of bricks had fallen on her head and that her world had caved him. Everyone is against me. Aubrey has taken me for a chump. And he doesn't love me anymore. He never has! He's let me down. I'm so alone. No one cares for me.

Colin returned to the interview room where he dismissed Constable Dougall so that he could be alone with his client. A nod from Dimity conveyed to Dougall that he could leave the two dispirited individuals alone in order to chat without a witness. Once Dougall and Dimity had left the room, Carlotta's self-pity speedily subsided. It is normally only the province of rabid dogs, women who live in the attic and hungry tigers who display uncontrollable and unsociable anger. But we can now add Carlotta to that list.

"That bloody brother of mine is a traitor," screamed Carlotta, "and so is that fucking Aubrey!"

Colin warned Carlotta to keep her voice down and he wished she was in a padded cell. Dimity and Tony, nevertheless, had heard the commotion because they had been listening outside the door in the hope that Carlotta would blow.

Carlotta continued to rant for some minutes while Colin tried desperately to pacify her. But the detectives listened with glee outside the door. Colin, of course, now advised his client to plead guilty as her way of avoiding a protracted trial and a punitive prison sentence.

"Let's get back in there," decided Tony at the appropriate moment and Dimity was keen to obey.

Carlotta had now lost it completely and she had been reduced to a snivelling wreck. Colin then indicated that his client would be willing to make a confession. The interview continued with the two detectives on a high while Carlotta had become a broken woman who was ready to spill the beans. Colin, in these circumstances, hoped that his fee would be paid.

Aubrey Bankover returned to his office in order to prepare an invoice for his client. Well, at least, I got a shag or two out of it, although she wasn't that rewarding.

## CUTHBERT'S CATHARSIS

Cuthbert was taken to a prison some distance away from Havercoyne Grange. He was grateful that the Havercoyne Stanley locals were not at all near at hand as he languished in his cell.

Cuthbert found prison life very confusing. His fellow inmates talked of strange things to do with crime and women and what they would do when they got out. Cuthbert's main regret, of course, was not seeing his horses. And while he did not experience any remorse over aunt Prudence's demise, he was devastated by his loss of Betsy and his involvement in her death. When he thought of Carlotta, herself in prison somewhere, he shuddered that he had been so foolish as to be emotionally blackmailed by her into taking part in Prudence's assassination.

Very few people visited the peer of the realm other than in the early days. Agatha did not put in an appearance at all and she made no further contact with her husband. The only contact which concerned Agatha was a letter from Colin de Winter in order to inform him that his wife intended to file for a divorce and that she would be demanding large a sum of money in her financial settlement.

A rather embarrassed Barraclough visited Cuthbert soon after the peer's incarceration but his visit was essentially intended to ask about the household functioning and, of course, the supplies of wine. Cuthbert gave a vague answer because he really couldn't care less what happened to the wine cellar now.

"Speak to Damian if you want to know anything," Cuthbert stated without enthusiasm.

"Very well, sir," the butler replied.

Cuthbert was pleased that, at least, he did not have to run the estate now and that fortuitously it was no longer his responsibility.

Damian had also visited Cuthbert soon after his arrival but their conversation had been heavily monitored. Their interaction had been officially recorded by one of the warders in case the brothers were endeavouring to collude in order to get their stories to match up. After this initial visit, therefore, Damian saw no point in returning to see his evil brother, especially as he was not certain whether he himself would soon be joining Cuthbert in clink.

Cuthbert had informed his brother that he, Damian, was now in charge of running the estate and so Damian had Cuthbert's formal blessing to get on with it. Damian, however, was not actually interested in what happened to the estate and so, on returning to the Grange, he merely handed the job in its entirety over to Byron and he washed his hands of any further involvement.

Byron was quite glad to be soldiering on with regard to managing the estate without anyone, such as Damian, who might interfere with his work or in the decisions which he made.

Louise, together with baby Harrison in a carry-cot, returned to her employment. She had not read the latest news and, consequently, she was astounded to be told that her employer was in prison. Ingrid related the story to a dumfounded Louise and she provided the details as best she knew them. Louise toyed with the idea of going back home but, when she learned that Ingrid was leaving forthwith, she felt obliged to stay at least for the time being and to be on hand when any news broke.

Louise then helped out Byron occasionally in a secretarial capacity while she also kept the pot boiling on Cuthbert's affairs as best she could. Byron was now less obsessed with his budgets and more inclined to spend money recklessly. Joyce kept him fed and Elizabeth continued to run the house efficiently. Byron still had the problem of where to find his next bedfellow but he felt that his notoriety in working for a serial killer would soon rectify that shortcoming. And when he observed the press at the main gates, Byron also felt that he could further promote his fame and fortune in the fullness of time and the idea appealed enormously. But he decided to keep the notion on ice for the time being.

Cuthbert had been in chokey for some months while awaiting his trial date and the nights were beginning to draw in as the summer was fading fast. Colin de Winter came occasionally to report on progress – or rather the lack of it – but his visits were purely functional and businesslike. Poor old Cuthbert! The peer hence resigned himself to a life in clink which was devoid of excitement or interest and he sank down deeply into a dim state of depression as a result.

But there was a ray of sunshine of the Cuthbert's horizon when he was called from his cell one day in order to meet a visitor. Cuthbert had not even bothered to shower that morning because of his mental malaise but he regretted this oversight when he clapped eyes on the lovely Gina. The journalist would have greeted Cuthbert with a kiss on the cheek, had a prison guard not called a halt to her attempt. Cuthbert was overcome by embarrassment at being found in such reduced circumstances but Gina seemed to ignore his distress and to bring great joy into his humble existence.

"I am so sorry not to have been able to come sooner but pressure of work has prevented me. But I'm here now and delighted to see you looking so well in the circumstances. I do hope that justice will be done and you'll be set free quite soon," proclaimed Gina.

Cuthbert visibly brightened at this prospect even though he knew in his heart that his was a hopeless case. Gina repeatedly assured him that she wholeheartedly believed in his innocence and Cuthbert was delighted to hear her view, despite the fact that he knew that she was deluded. But lies can sometimes be music to one's ears.

"Why don't you tell me your story in writing so that I can get it published by some of the nationals?" enquired Gina. "If we put your story across to the press, then maybe your actions would be understood by the public who are distressed that you should have been accused so unjustly."

"Oh, I don't think so," replied Cuthbert who was doubtful about the possibility of protesting his innocence.

"Well, if you write it all down in a series of letters, I can get them published easily. And you would be paid a handsome fortune for your trouble, Cuthbert. We could publish all after the trial, of course. It's the least I can do for you, Cuthbert," Gina declared.

Gina was obviously used to ploughing through the furrows and she was as determined as a rat when attacking a weasel. Cuthbert took the details of Gina's office address – which she seemed to be pressing on him – but he was still very lukewarm about unfurling his innermost thoughts formally in writing. The likelihood of a meeting or two with Gina was, however, a great incentive for Cuthbert, particularly when Gina assured him that she would visit frequently.

Back in his cell, Cuthbert was again beset by doom and gloom and, because he hardly spoke to his cellmates or any other inmates, there was no one with whom to discuss his dilemma. After a day to two, however, Cuthbert did start to write down his account of events, even though he had no intention of sending the stuff to the journalist. A couple more sleepless nights and a hunger for Gina's company, of course, soon changed his mind – together with the prospect of some ready cash when he was eventually freed. But maybe never, old boy?

Cuthbert's financial problems had, in fact, escalated since his imprisonment because he had heard of the distress of the Seabird Cliffs project into which he had poured most of his reserves. Justin Pryor – even though he no longer represented the peer in financial matters – had written to Cuthbert in order to bring the sad tidings about the foundering of the project. Perhaps on the I-told-you-so basis? Cuthbert had scowled a bit but essentially he felt that he was powerless to control external events from his dreary prison cell.

Colin de Winter, on one of his infrequent visits on official business, had reported that extra capital would be needed in order for the project to succeed. Cuthbert realised that he could no longer continue to invest in the enterprise and that his initial investment would, in consequence, be lost given his current financial state. And then, of course, there was that matter of settling Agatha's financial demands which were exorbitant. So, all in all, Cuthbert had a pressing need to get some money into his coffers damn quick and Gina was dangling the carrot before his very eyes and his mouth was watering correspondingly.

The expectation of some incoming cash, therefore, was a great temptation for the peer of the realm. And so Cuthbert made it his mission in life to pour out his feelings, thoughts, reasoning, hopes, fears and dreams to the appreciative Gina. Strangely enough Cuthbert felt the benefit of this activity which seemed to give him a new lease of life and so he did not stint on sharing his story with the world.

Gina received the first letter from Cuthbert about a month after her visit and she eagerly wrote back to say that she would visit again. Gina was excited to keep the pot boiling for some time yet, all the while that Cuthbert was willing to commit his inner thoughts to prison writing paper. Gina had tried to encourage Cuthbert to type his rantings and to send the stuff to her via email but Cuthbert cited techno-phobia as his excuse for not doing so. He claimed, moreover, that he was too old to learn. Gina was actually quite glad that Cuthbert could not even turn on one of the prison computers because she felt that Cuthbert's handwritten testimony was probably more financially valuable than mere soft copy anyway.

And so a pattern was established in that whenever Cuthbert sent Gina a letter, she instantly materialised. Cuthbert liked the game because it brought some gladness into his bleak existence and so he strung his story out for as long as possible. Cuthbert's opus magnum hence became the most protracted confession in the history of humankind.

## NATHAN'S PREDICAMENT

"Natty," said Luciana while simultaneously nudging her common-law partner firmly in the ribs.

Nathan groaned. He had just finished a long and late shift at the bar in Malaga where he worked and he desperately needed his sleep.

"Not now, pet, I'm too tired."

"But you must read this. There's an article in the English press about your family."

"Couldn't care less," grumbled Nathan who promptly fell asleep.

"But your father has committed a crime," Luciana said in a raised voice as she shook Nathan.

"Still couldn't care less," replied Nathan who was really not at all interested in what his family got up to – legally or otherwise.

"He's killed your aunt Prudence!" Luciana this time spoke so loudly that the whole village would have heard her and, at last, Nathan opened his eyes.

"The old bastard's not capable of killing a mouse," drooled Nathan but, by now, he was curious enough to rouse himself in order to read the news.

The headlines of various articles read "Cuthbert the Serial Killer", "Gansville-Stubbs Exclusive," "Cuthbert's Sex Killing," and "Gansville-Stubbs Murders – The Inside Story."

Nathan initially perused the short first article by Kyle Ebury in *Public Enquiry* which captured his attention utterly and provided Nathan's mind with a mishmash of facts which he then had to piece together like a giant jigsaw puzzle in the light of his knowledge of the family.

---

### *Cuthbert the Serial Killer*

*The police – who last week charged Lord Cuthbert Gansville-Stubbs with the murder or his former lover, Betsy Drury, who worked in his stables – have now also charged the peer of the realm with assisting in the murder of his aunt Prudence Gansville-Stubbs.*

*Sources close to the investigation have also indicated that Lord Cuthbert was in cahoots with his sister, Carlotta Gansville-Stubbs, and his brother, Damian Gansville-Stubbs, with regard to the demise of their aunt but this information has yet to be confirmed. Carlotta and Damian are helping the police with their enquiries into her death.*

*We understand that Cuthbert confessed to his role in the death of both Betsy Drury and Prudence Gansville-Stubbs and that the case will shortly go to court. Cuthbert, meanwhile, has been detained in custody because his lawyer, Colin de Winter, has been unable to obtain bail for his client.*

Kyle Ebury
*Public Affairs Correspondent*

---

Another article from the editor of *Public Enquiry* gave further details of the Gansville-Stubbs family and their nefarious activities.

---

### Gansville-Stubbs Exclusive

*Public Enquiry can now confirm that Carlotta Gansville-Stubbs has been implicated for her role in the death of her aunt Prudence Gansville-Stubbs at Havercoyne Grange in the small village of Havercoyne Stanley in the west country.*

*It is believed that Carlotta was the mastermind behind the poisoning of her aunt and that she cajoled her two brothers into assisting her to administer weedkiller which Prudence Gansville-Stubbs consumed in meals taken to her room in the attic of Havercoyne Grange.*

*Miss Gansville-Stubbs is currently being questioned by the authorities but we understand that an announcement of a formal charge may shortly follow. Carlotta has been detained in police custody pending enquiries into the case.*

*Public Enquiry will bring its readers up-to-date news immediately information has been released to the press with regard to the murders of Prudence Gansville-Stubbs and Betsy Drury.*

Winston Blakefield
*Editor-in-Chief*

---

Nathan was now wide awake. He was enraptured by what he read and, of course, he was hungry for more.

---

### Cuthbert's Sex Killing

*Cuthbert Gansville-Stubbs, who is currently in prison for the murder of his former lover, Miss Betsy Drury, has confessed to burying her body beneath the floor of the stable block at Havercoyne Grange in the west country village of Havercoyne Stanley.*

*An official press statement has revealed that the police were obliged to dig up the stable floor in order to complete their investigation into Betsy Drury's death. Betsy Drury disappeared suddenly about a decade ago and, since then, no one has been able to trace her whereabouts.*

*Lord Cuthbert apparently commissioned a refurbishment of the stable block on the Havercoyne Stanley estate at the time of Betsy Drury's disappearance and when this was carried out, Lord Cuthbert insisted on a floor being laid in the stables – not an action normally undertaken by stable-owners. But this event, in itself, did not arouse suspicion at the time.*

*A tip-off from the press galvanised Detective Inspector Anthony Croonacre and his deputy, Dimity Myers, into action. When asked why the detective team had not originally investigated Betsy's disappearance, Inspector Croonacre replied that she had been registered by her mother in Newcastle as a missing person but the police authorities had been unable, as yet, to trace her.*

*A police guard has been placed in Newcastle around the home of Mr Edward Drury and Mrs Emily Drury, parents of the deceased stable assistant, in order to protect them from distressful intrusion.*

Kyle Ebury
*Public Affairs Correspondent*

---

Finally, Nathan read the most recent article in *The Times* before his eyes became too tired to function competently.

---

### Gansville-Stubbs Murders – The Inside Story

*We can now reveal that Miss Carlotta Gansville-Stubbs, of Havercoyne Grange on the Havercoyne Stanley estate, has been formally charged with the murder of her aunt Prudence.*

*It appears that Carlotta Gansville-Stubbs was the evil Lady Macbeth behind the scheme which involved poisoning her aunt and she coerced her two brothers into administering poison. Her brother Cuthbert has already admitted to his involvement in the crime but Damian Gansville-Stubbs, Carlotta's younger brother, claims that he was an unwitting participant in delivering meals to his aunt Prudence without any knowledge of the poisoning scheme.*

*Previously Lord Cuthbert confessed to and was charged with the murder of his ex-mistress, Betsy Drury, but it now seems that he was also party to the killing of his aunt under the direction of his dictatorial younger sister.*

John Fanshaw
*Current Affairs*

---

The article by John Fanshawe went on to spell out the career history of Cuthbert, Carlotta and Damian as well as the activities of stabling staff, such as Betsy Drury, but Nathan was too jinxed to read any further. He had some serious thinking to do. Early the next morning Nathan trawled the internet in order to gain the full story. Luciana, by this time, had lost interest and she was fast sleep.

After apprising himself of the facts, Nathan decided to go for a walk by the sea in order to clear his mind and to organise his thoughts. What if they are convicted? What will happen to that pile of bricks? Where does this leave me? Who could I contact at the Grange for more information? Barraclough will be too drunk to know much. Byron might be cagey. Joyce may well be shattered. Elizabeth too loyal. But I do know what I had better do now, at least.

When he returned to their flat, Nathan was now the one to awaken Luciana with a degree of urgency because he had come to a momentous decision.

"Get up, pet. We need to get married quick!"

## LUCIANA'S SURPRISE

Luciana clad herself in a new dress of handmade Spanish lace sewn lovingly by some of her friends and family. Although her dress was a becoming shade of pale rose, she still looked every inch the demure virgin bride. It was only the presence of their son Sebastian at the wedding which gave the lie to Luciana's appearance.

Luciana and Nathan were hence married in Malaga at the local civil registry office for births, deaths and marriages. The reception was held in the wine bar in Malaga in which Nathan worked because, with a discount, the cost was, at least, within Nathan's budget for the occasion. But, once married, Nathan resigned his job at the wine bar in order to go on his travels with his new wife.

Luciana's extensive family were all in attendance at the wedding and certainly the female members of the clan were relieved that Nathan had, at last, made an honest women of Luciana. The neighbours had taken exception to the couple cohabiting but Luciana's mother was defiantly determined that she would still continue to ignore those people in her village who had shunned her as result of her daughter's unseemly conduct. Luciana's mother was somewhat dismayed that her daughter was not being married in a church but, even so, she still wept throughout the whole of the short marriage ceremony.

The couple partied for most of the night with a group of their fun-loving friends. The family also joined in the celebrations until they were too exhausted to walk home. Various cabs were hence hired. Nathan woke with a bit of a hangover but Luciana had been more abstemious because she still needed to attend to her son.

The next day saw the couple board a flight to Bristol and then head for Havercoyne Grange. They arrived unannounced in order to surprise those members of the family and the household staff who had decided to remain in situ.

Joyce had remained as the cook because she wanted to see what would happen to Cuthbert and Carlotta and she did not want to walk out of her job if her employers were acquitted of their crimes. While Joyce was pretty sure of their guilt, she did value her residence at the Grange and she felt reluctant to apply for another job because telling the world that she had previously worked for a commune of murderers might not sound too impressive at an interview.

Barraclough decided to stay because the wine cellar was too big a box-office draw for him to abandon it without a very good reason and working for a load of crooks was not a viable enough pretext for his departure. The butler, however, did little in the way of work. He stayed in bed for most of the day, got up when Joyce had cooked his meals and padlocked his bedroom door against any further attack from the vicious tyrant housekeeper.

Elizabeth herself kept an avid eye on the news and she decided that the best option would be for her to remain at the Grange in the hope of obtaining a reasonable redundancy package when her employers were sent down. While she maintained a loyal front to the outside world, she was not really too surprised by the deeds of others. Elizabeth, of course, had known that Betsy was pregnant because she had missed several periods and it had been reported at the time that the stable lass was in a liaison with Cuthbert. When her employers were in residence, therefore, Elizabeth maintained her staunch loyalty to the Gansville-Stubbs family unit but, in her heart, she knew the truth and she decided that she would act on her instincts only when absolutely necessary.

Byron remained mainly because his residence in Havercoyne Lodge was surrounded by reporters from the national and international press as well as television crews from across the globe. He also liked his generous salary and the comforts which Joyce brought into his life. And, of course, he didn't want anyone to know of the sweetener – designed to keep his mouth firmly shut – which he had received from Cuthbert.

Ian Manningbury continued to exercise the horses essentially because he had obtained his fees in advance for their training. When he learned that there was trouble down at the Grange, however, he decided to offer Ned a job in his stables which the dejected employee of Havercoyne Grange gladly accepted. Not only was Ned able to be near more horses and to receive a better wage but he also had access to more female staff who took his eye and showed signs of being more promising as seduction fodder than that Nancy had been.

Albert Fotheringay still, of course, managed to earn his fees by tending to the horses either at the Grange itself or at Ian Manningbury's stables – particularly as the two men had become allies in sponging off the Gansville-Stubbs estate.

Delia had been considering leaving the estate office for some time because she had become tired of her manager's philandering. Once the news had broken of the family's criminal misconduct, Delia decided that this rumpus was her cue to exit. Accordingly Delia found herself employment on another estate some distance away from the troubles of Havercoyne Grange. Louise, who had been helping out in the estate office intermittently, was easily able to step into Delia's secretarial shoes.

Ingrid's term of office had by now come to an end but, in the circumstances, she was not given the splendid send-off which Louise had received when she went on maternity leave. Ingrid finally made her way back to her newly acquired second-hand automobile in the staff car park and she prepared to bid farewell to the Grange for the last time. As she approached her car, Byron came out of the estate office and cordially greeted her.

"I understand from Louise that you'll be leaving us?" asked the estate manager with a degree of agitation.

"Yes," replied Ingrid in a bland voice.

"Can't say I blame you in the circumstances, of course. Pity though. I'll miss you."

"It's time for me to move on now that Louise is back."

"I say, would you care for a farewell drink? We never quite got round to having that drink and perhaps a meal."

Ingrid considered that Byron had no information to impart which would be of any use to her now and so she once again politely but firmly declined his offer.

Lady Agatha floated about the house and the village undaunted by the fuss created by her husband and her sister-in-law. She still attended meetings of the Havercoyne Stanley Players, gatherings of the local women's institute and events run by her charity organisations. She was delighted to learn at the last meeting of the Walkies Dog Rescue Charity, for instance, that her efforts at the fete had secured a whacking profit and Agatha was personally thanked by the chairwoman and other members of the committee for her participation and that of Havercoyne Grange. Agatha accepted this accolade with her usual theatrical humility.

When Nathan, Luciana and Sebastian arrived, of course, the house was under siege from the press who had swarmed all over the village and some of the grounds before being shushed away by the local constabulary who were trying to keep the intrusion to a minimum.

Luciana was overawed by the grandeur of the house, despite the fact that much of the furniture had seen better days, the household staff looked like a load of fossils themselves and the place was unbearably cold and she could not acclimatise.

## AGATHA'S ORGANISATION

Agatha came into the hall in order to greet Nathan, his new wife and her grandson on their arrival with exaggerated pleasure. She had been sitting in the morning room when she had heard what she thought was Nathan's voice. Agatha had then discarded her cherry brandy and gone to investigate. Agatha's joy at the sight of her prodigal son was obvious and Nathan was glad to be received genially. Agatha, of course, was not as glad to see a strange Spanish woman with a child but she observed social niceties with the intention of finding out further information as soon as possible. Agatha hitherto had no cognisance of Luciana's existence – let alone the child. Nathan had calculated that the element of surprise would work in his favour.

"We weren't expecting you, darling. What a lovely, pleasant surprise," said Agatha showering her son with kisses.

"This is my wife, Luciana and our son Sebastian," announced Nathan who managed to render his mother speechless for several seconds.

"Come into the morning room," invited Agatha as her way of buying herself some thinking time.

Her son and daughter-in-law obediently followed Agatha into the morning room where she offered the newly-wedded couple drinks.

"I'll have a glass of red wine but Luciana prefers orange juice," proclaimed Nathan.

Agatha was flustered because the drinks cabinet had neither of these preferences.

"I'll get some drinks ordered," she announced, "and will you be staying to lunch?"

"Yes, we're here for some time yet."

Agatha left the room, noting that her new daughter-in-law had not yet spoken but that she had contributed a smile to the discourse so far.

Luciana and Nathan inspected the morning room and then decided that they would stay on at the Grange – mainly because they could not afford a decent hotel. But Nathan expected his impecunious situation to change imminently.

Agatha, meanwhile, decided to marshal the troops. She began by going into Louise's office and giving her instructions about organising Joyce into preparing lunch and getting it served in the dining room. Agatha also requested Louise to contact Elizabeth with regard to preparing a room for Nathan and his family.

When Joyce received the news of Nathan's return and the fact that he was now married with a child, she smiled wryly because she realised that Nathan was now about to become heir to the estate. No doubt, he was returning in order to claim his rightful inheritance. Joyce, therefore, decided to prepare a repast which would delight the senses of her new employer.

Elizabeth too was dumfounded when she heard the news of the new arrivals but she was galvanised into action as a result. She instructed some of her staff to prepare one of the nicest rooms in the house and to get out the best linen in order to clothe the beds. Elizabeth's next port of call was Barraclough's room. Obviously she could not enter unannounced because the butler had padlocked his door.

"Get up, you lazy swine, and look lively," urged Elizabeth, "the prodigal son has returned."

Elizabeth, of course, had to hammer insistently on the Barraclough's door until he deigned to answer it.

"What do you want now, you bloody noisy bitch?"

Barraclough had not been asleep but he had been enjoying a morning sherry, although it was too early in the day for him to be completely out of it.

"Nathan and his new wife have just arrived. And Agatha's instructed you to set up the dining room and get some wine for lunch."

Barraclough felt compelled to obey Elizabeth's instructions but he neglected even to acknowledge her presence outside the door. He simply brushed past the housekeeper and went down to the kitchen in order to secure the latest gossip from Joyce. Elizabeth followed Barraclough down the stairs while she ordered the butler to take the luggage up to Nathan's room. The housekeeper then went to the museum in order to pitchfork Damian out of his dreams of Vanessa.

"Get some red claret out for lunch and set the dining table for four people plus a baby," instructed Joyce who then proceeded to fill Barraclough in on the latest news about the advent of Nathan and his clan.

Barraclough was quite unconcerned about who had descended on the household while Joyce was agog with curiosity over the arrival of the absentee son and his family. Joyce resolved to have a peep at the baby and Nathan's new wife before long. Joyce then lovingly prepared a beef stew with a red wine gravy and a dessert of sherry trifle for the returning couple in the hope that it would be a welcome change from Spanish cuisine. Barraclough lamented the fact that a good red claret was commandeered for cooking. Why was wine used for cooking? It should be kept for drinking only. And sherry in the trifle is a travesty as well.

Back in the morning room, Luciana began to speak and Agatha was surprised to realised that Nathan's new wife spoke quite good English for a foreigner. Agatha also learned that Luciana had been a lawyer in Malaga before having to relinquish her career in order to become a full-time mother.

While making small talk of an inconsequential nature, Agatha was all the time planning the way in which she would play her next card. Agatha, of course, realised that, if Nathan took over the Grange and the estate, she would soon be obliged to live under her son's roof and she would need to be nice to him and his family in consequence. Agatha, therefore, shone her most radiant smile at Luciana and was suitably attentive to her grandson using all her considerable dramatic skill. Nathan and Luciana were in no way fooled but they were merely amused by the antics of this queen of stage and screen.

The subject of Agatha's murderous husband and Nathan's father was hardly mentioned. Nathan stated nonchalantly that he would be staying in the house until the trial so that he could be on hand in order to learn of the outcome.

Damian appeared just before lunch was announced and he was more than delighted to meet his nephew.

"Hello, Nathan. Wonderful to see you."

Damian was introduced to the new members of the family. Luciana and Damian seemed to hit it off instantly, perhaps because Damian had wedding bells very much on his mind at present. Damian had proposed to Vanessa several times recently and she was actually showing signs of wavering.

During lunch Agatha proceeded to fill Nathan in on her news.

"We held a fete for Walkies Dog Rescue here in the summer which was very successful. I was personally thanked by the chairman of the committee. And I starred in a play with the Havercoyne Stanley Players which was well attended and I got very good reviews. And at the Women's Institute . . ."

Nathan, at this point, decided that he had better get his mother off the subject of herself or she would continue all night.

"Mother, I shall need some cash while I'm here. How do I go about getting it?" interrupted Nathan.

"Oh, I don't know. You'd better ask Damian about that. Damian!"

Damian looked up from his intense conversation with Luciana while playing lovingly with the new infant.

"What?"

"Nathan wants some cash? Can you arrange this please?" asked Agatha.

Damian accordingly agreed to give Nathan access to the family bank account which hitherto the errant son had not been granted. Nathan thus felt that his trip home to the Grange had been a worthwhile gamble.

"Who's running the estate now?" enquired Nathan.

"Well, I am notionally but most of the work's done by Byron."

"But you may be taking over permanently soon, darling," added Agatha, "and, as you're here now, perhaps you could take things over immediately."

Nathan pretended to consider this option.

"Perhaps we could have a word with Colin de Winter. He may be able to fix something," contributed Damian who was actually keen to hand the estate over to Nathan officially.

And so the assembled company took the decision to contact their solicitor with a view to giving Nathan his inheritance early. At this point, of course, Agatha was forced to admit that she had initiated divorce proceedings against Cuthbert but she wondered, in fact, whether it might be advisable to withdraw her petition for the time being.

## NATHAN'S COUP

Colin de Winter arrived at the Grange as requested and he proceeded to outline his plans for Nathan's succession to the throne. Apparently Colin had found a loophole in the law whereby Nathan could inherent the estate provided that Cuthbert would officially abdicate and sign the necessary legal documentation in order to forfeit his share in the estate which would then pass legitimately to son Nathan.

"You see," began Colin, "Lord Gansville-Stubbs cannot in common law benefit from his inheritance as a convicted criminal but he can abdicate whereby it will be passed on to his successors in title."

"In English?" asked Nathan.

"Well, Cuthbert could sign the property over to you now – that is before he goes to trial. If he's convicted, the position will become quite difficult. But, of course, he has confessed to murder."

Colin was now quite convinced that Cuthbert would be convicted and so he saw this move on the part of the family as a wise one. Agatha, Nathan and Damian all agreed to this course of action and Agatha accordingly instructed Colin to wrap up the deal.

"If you cannot persuade him, Colin. I will visit Cuthbert and put some pressure on him myself," announced Agatha.

"That may not be necessary," assured Colin.

"Should I still proceed with the divorce?" she asked.

"I'm holding that in abeyance until after the trial. Then the divorce, if you still wish it, will go through speedily."

"Oh, yes, I still wish to proceed but I'll leave the timing and everything up to you."

When Colin next visited Cuthbert, he discovered that, indeed, the peer was more than willing to hand everything over to his son and heir. He keenly wanted to completely wash his hands of any involvement in the finances or the running of the estate.

This agreement was good news, therefore, to all concerned. Cuthbert was absolved of all his responsibilities which, in any case, he found tedious. Agatha felt glad that her beloved son would now come into his rightful inheritance and that his family would be raised under her roof. Damian felt that he could continue to run the museum as its curator and perhaps acquire a wife in the not-too-distant future.

A couple of weeks later, therefore, Nathan sat in Cuthbert's office as master of all he surveyed. He was now officially the new Lord Gansville-Stubbs but the title did nothing for his ego. Luciana had checked over Colin's documentation which she believed, to the best of her knowledge, to be in order. And the papers were now safely stashed away in the bank for safekeeping. Sebastian was adored by all the household and especially by Damian and the female staff.

But with his inheritance came responsibilities which Nathan had not bargained for when he had decided to return to his homeland. The finances of the estate were not as healthy as Nathan would have liked and the accountant had reported that some hefty losses may be in store. Nathan learned that Cuthbert had squandered most of the reserves on a property development project recently which may well be likely to collapse. Byron also reported that his budgets were tight and that the estate was in sore danger of bankruptcy.

Nathan contemplated returning to Spain and leaving it all behind because he could not milk the finances adequately for his needs. Nathan did, however, take an advantageous decision to sell the valuable racehorses because he felt that this would bring in some much-needed capital but regretfully this insightful move was only a stop-gap measure. But Luciana was still impressed by her husband's hitherto unknown business acumen. Had Nathan been hiding his light under a bushel?

And then the course of Nathan's life changed dramatically in just a few short weeks when he received a telephone call from John Mackintosh of Property Magnum plc.

"Hello, sir, my name is John Mackintosh of Property Magnum plc and I've had some dealings with your father previously."

"Oh, I see."

"And I'd like to visit the Grange again in order to discuss a proposition which you might be interested in."

"What proposition?"

"Well, I gather that your father may be in danger of losing money on a venture which, at present, looks rather bleak. But I may have the solution to this problem for you now that I understand you have taken over the estate."

Nathan was naturally interested but he needed to know more before he would grant this stranger an audience.

"So can you outline your plan in principle first?"

John proceeded to suggest an idea which seemed, on the surface certainly, to solve all Nathan's problems in one fell swoop. Nathan was, therefore, well and truly hooked.

John Mackintosh arrived a few days later in order to set out his plans. He explained that Cuthbert had already invested some money in the Seabird Cliffs project but that further investment was essential for the venture to be a financial success.

"But we can't afford further investment in any projects just now," protested Nathan emphatically.

"I realise that, of course, but if I could buy Havercoyne Grange and its estate, with a deduction for the further investment needed, of course, you would be able to benefit from the property development scheme and then have a considerable sum in hand."

Nathan began to salivate while John pressed home his obvious advantage.

"Most of your staff could remain in their present employment but you and your family would have enough money to relocate elsewhere. And your holding in the Seabird Cliffs project would pay out handsome dividends when the development is completed and sold."

Nathan could not believe his ears. But he, nevertheless, asked Luciana, with her lawyer's brain, to join the meeting as he realised that her input would be of value and that she could act as a reliable sounding board.

John continued to extol the virtues of his idea while Luciana and Nathan listened attentively.

"We shall have to take legal advice and we'll need time to consider your proposition, of course, John."

"Take your time, indeed, I'm just at the end of the phone when you have come to a decision, Nathan."

John then departed after leaving his calling card and a glossy brochure which extolled the prowess of Property Magnum.

"I don't see how the move could fail," declared Nathan.

"But, Natty, we shall need to see the documentation first before you sign. And I ought to check it over in principle, even though I'm not too well versed in English law."

"Colin de Winter and his team, of course, will need to inspect the papers."

Nathan thus picked up the phone in order to invite Colin back to the Grange yet again.

After Colin's visit the wheels were set in motion and the transaction was speedily completed.

Agatha and Damian were informed that they would need to move out of the Grange in due course but that they would both have enough money in order to purchase an impressive residence mortgage-free elsewhere.

Agatha felt that, together with her divorce settlement, she could live the high life without living in a draughty edifice and so she was well pleased. But she planned to remain in the village so that she could continue her charity work and to be the star performer at the Havercoyne Stanley Players.

Damian was even more delighted because he believed that he would now have enough money to be an eligible catch for Vanessa. And so he set off in the direction of the museum in order to find the lovely Vanessa and to propose to her once more. Damian reckoned that he and Vanessa would remain as curator and assistant curator of the museum but, if not, they could probably exist financially without working anyway. Vanessa definitely showed signs of succumbing to Damian's overtures now.

Once the deal had gone through, the household staff and the estate management staff were asked to remain in the employ of Property

Magnum who would eventually decide the fate of Havercoyne Grange.

Nathan and Luciana prepared to return to Spain. Nathan was delighted that money would no longer be a problem for the couple and Luciana was relieved to be returning to a warmer climate. She could now stop nagging Nathan in order to get him to install some more heating in their room which, of course, he could not afford.

## DAMIAN'S PROVIDENCE

The press had laid siege to Havercoyne Grange and the Havercoyne Stanley estate for several weeks after the announcement of Carlotta and Cuthbert's arrest but the paparazzi were really more of an inconvenience than a nuisance. The only entrance to the estate was via the main gates and a sturdy police guard ensured that the journalists and their crew remained outside. There was, in fact, a back entrance into the farm but it was virtually inaccessible by road – unless you owned a tank or a jet-propelled tractor – and the press contingent had not yet discovered its existence. And a helicopter would probably have been useless anyway.

Louise successfully fielded any irritating phone calls by blocking most of the unknown numbers.

Joyce and Barraclough ordered the house provisions by phone and the local retailers delivered the goods by braving the onslaught of the media at the main gates. Byron bought his farm supplies over the internet and these too were delivered by couriers who were used to difficult ingress and largely immune to it.

Ian Manningbury had by now taken the three racehorses into his care at the Grayling Wood stables in order to look after them before – and, perhaps, after – they were sold. The other horses, however, remained at the Havercoyne stables because it was not worth selling them. Jonquil and Angel Prancer, for instance, thus became part of the depleted stables on the Havercoyne Stanley estate.

Albert Fotheringay managed to visit the estate by using the back entrance to the farm which he reached by walking across the fields mostly in the early hours before the press gang had even got out of bed. When there was an emergency call-out Albert, of course, then had to brave the ambush. Albert was determined to tend to the remaining horses and the farm animals because the fees he charged constituted a large segment of his income.

Both Ian and Albert had met the new owners of Havercoyne Stanley estate and they wanted to milk the last drop out of Property Magnum before the house was converted into a theme park or something equally nauseating. As the farm was only just making a profit, it seemed sensible to be attentive until the farm too was turned into a pleasure park.

The trial of the Gansville-Stubbs siblings, when it eventually came to court, made world headlines and the attention of the press was diverted accordingly so that eventually Havercoyne Grange and its estate returned to normal. The trial, however, was a bit of a disappointment for the avid readers and viewers of news bulletins because the only thing to report was that Carlotta and Cuthbert had both pleaded guilty.

Calendula and Barrington realised, with some regret, that Carlotta and her brothers were going to have to take the rap for aunt Prudence's death. They had hoped that Cuthbert Gansville-Stubbs would be done for his involvement in Betsy Drury's demise but, in collecting evidence for this crime, it was inevitable that other worms would come out of the woodwork. And they did.

Cuthbert looked a pathetic figure in the dock because he was already resigned to his fate and he was probably only disappointed that hanging was not the penalty for murder these days. Cuthbert put up no defence and, in consequence, the judge was more sympathetic to his contrite manner. The prisoner was, therefore, sentenced to life imprisonment but with a recommendation that he need only serve twenty-five years.

Carlotta tried to play the insanity card but the jury did not buy it. Her barrister had charged her a princely sum for putting her case eloquently but she was still condemned to life imprisonment with a recommendation to serve a minimum of thirty years.

Carlotta found prison life fairly congenial once she had become accustomed to it but, of course, she had to undertake bereavement counselling because she missed Jonquil so much. The prisoner also seethed and raged about the way in which aunt Prudence had ruined her love-life and the old harridan had forced her into the arms of Aubrey. Carlotta regretted the loss of Aubrey whom she had regarded as the only true love of her life. But some more counselling enabled her to come to terms with the fact that her erstwhile lover had betrayed her unspeakably. Carlotta fulminated so much over Aunt Pru's meddling and Aubrey's deception that she shook the prison walls but they did not disintegrate so that she could escape. Get used to it Carlotta – this is your new home now!

Damian pleaded his innocence over his involvement in the murder of his aunt Prudence and, because he came across as so stupid and gullible, he was found not guilty by the jury. Vanessa, unexpectedly, appeared as a character witness for her employer which formed the major part of Damian's defence. And, in the absence of any really concrete evidence of Damian's guilt, the youngest sibling managed to escape conviction. The charges of hindering the enquiry, furthermore, had somehow got lost in the system.

Now that Damian was a free man with no stain on his character and, of course, a rich man, Vanessa finally succumbed to his proposal of marriage. An eligible bachelor can often turn a girl's head in the right direction. The couple set up home together far away from Havercoyne Grange and they were eventually married quietly some months later when the public furore had died down and the death of Betsy Drury and Aunt Prudence had become a distant memory in the eyes of the world.

Vanessa took an open university degree in history. She specialised in the Elizabethan period so that she could write historical novels. Damian took up philately and he constantly surfed the internet in order to expand his impressive collection of stamps which he invited national and international visitors to inspect for a modest fee.

The village gossips in Havercoyne Stanley and Grayling Wood all got on to the outcome of the trial but the verdicts left little room for manoeuvre or speculation. The chatterboxes were sharply divided into those who claimed that they had known all the time that the Gansville-Stubbs lot were an evil bunch while the remainder maintained that they had been set up by the old bill.

Elsie and Jessie Braithwaite were divided in their opinion about the outcome of the trial of the Gansville-Stubbs clan. Elsie believed wholeheartedly in the innocence of those convicted while her sister Jessie, traitor to the end, adopted a high-handed view that the family had brought disgrace on the locality.

Old Harry, who was a regular visitor to the Hunting Horn – and had unwittingly provided some of the evidence – was rather unconcerned with the outcome of the trial either way. Nellie and Dave, the proprietors of the Hunting Horn establishment, similarly thought little about the demise of the Gansville-Stubbs siblings. The publicans, however, welcomed the press contingent and other inquisitive visitors to the village in order to furnish these intruders into village life with food and drink. And, when there was a gossip-mill which needed to be fed, Nellie and Dave were then suddenly eager to make a contribution if it pleased the customers. Everyone's a prostitute at heart apparently.

As a consolation prize for the paparazzi, Cuthbert's testimonial, sent in dribs and drabs to Gina Wilcox-Ryan, was published in instalments by Winston Blakefield and Kyle Ebury of *Public Enquiry* and John Fanshaw of *The Times* who had parted with even more money for the privilege of obtaining the peer's telling indictment.

Ronald Turner, the Chief Editor for Political Affairs at the Guardian Media Group, which incorporated both *The Guardian* and *The Observer*, had also been willing to pay through the nose for the correspondence peddled by the Medici Squadron. Ronald, and his wife Dotty, were old friends of Calendula and Barrington but this did not prevent the journalist from doing business with the Medici Squadron when it suited his purpose.

Calendula and Barrington had also managed to sell selected passages from Cuthbert's letters to the gutter press so that their finances were more than healthy once the trial had concluded.

Ian Manningbury and Albert Fotheringay both gave interviews to the press in order to recoup some of their financial losses but they were both careful not to say very much which would incriminate them personally.

Agatha obtained her divorce on the nod and she eventually secured a hefty financial settlement from Cuthbert's estate. Agatha, when approached by the media contingent, delighted in being interviewed on television and she played the tragedy queen as the wronged wife whose life had been shattered by her ex-husband's unseemly conduct.

## JOHN'S RESHUFFLE

Once the trial was over and John Mackintosh from Property Magnum had collected his thoughts, he decided to take action.

Havercoyne Grange and Havercoyne Stanley estate was not, as universally predicted, turned into a theme park but instead the Grange was converted into a luxury hotel for the idle rich. The conversion ensured the structural integrity of the building and repaired some parts of the roof which had developed a leak or two. The attic quarters which had once housed the late, but not lamented, aunt Prudence and Cuthbert's Overland Shuttle had ironically sprung a leak just after Cuthbert had been carted off to jail. The builders also put in a powerful, and much needed, central heating system and they had clad the inside walls with thermal insulation.

Many intriguing historical features were lovingly restored and then given a brass plaque which detailed the exhibit from the former Gansville-Stubbs residence. Most of the furniture which had some sentimental appeal was tenderly restored by local craftsmen and/or reupholstered in order to render it in its best light yet without sacrificing any antique value. Any item of furniture or decorative item which was delicate or irreparable was kept as a sentimental relic of a bygone age for exhibition purposes only. The furniture wrecks which had liberally adorned Cuthbert's office were used for firewood in order to fuelled the gigantic wood burners which had been installed in all the inglenook fireplaces at the Grange.

The Overland Shuttle was provided with a glass cabinet in which it sat taking pride of place as the principal exhibit of the hotel. The Overland Shuttle graced the hotel's website, adorned the reception hall and was much admired by all guests on arrival.

The contents of the museum were sold off by a London auction house and these artefacts raised a pretty price for Property Magnum who laughed all the way to the bank.

A state-of-the-art swimming pool and health suite was installed in the erstwhile museum while the baronial hall, through which Vanessa had frequently escorted visitors, was turned into a concert hall. This move on the part of the Property Magnum gave the place a high degree of respectability and brought in more dosh because many visitors to the concert hall also stayed at the hotel.

The whole establishment was decorated in non-toxic eco-friendly paint which added a naturalistic look to the house and put the finishing touches to the restoration-conversion programme in readiness for the unveiling and grand opening of the Havercoyne Grange Hotel.

Agatha tried to negotiate a favourable rate for hiring the concert hall for the Havercoyne Stanley Players but she could not persuade the Chief Executive of Property Magnum to grant her any favours. She tried feminine guile and she attempted to appeal to John Mackintosh's better nature but, unfortunately for Agatha, the canny entrepreneur did not possess a weak spot. Despite this setback, Cuthbert's ex-wife continued much the same as before with her amateur dramatics, her charity work and her women's institute activities. And she gave not a spare thought to her former husband or the misdeeds which he had committed.

Elizabeth was elevated to the position of head housekeeper at the hotel. She was very pleased with this promotion and with her extended staff of cleaners and scrubbers.

A famous television chef was employed for the kitchen and Joyce was relegated to the rank of assistant cook. Joyce was not unhappy about this seeming demotion because she learned how to prepare food of a higher calibre than her own homely cooking style and this talent made her a more marketable commodity as a result. Joyce also received a salary increase and she was still permitted to live on the premises which suited her just fine. Some more kitchen staff were employed which meant that she no longer had to clear crockery, to stack the dishwasher or to scrub the kitchen table which had become her chore since Nancy had vacated the premises. Barraclough could not, at any price, be persuaded or bullied by Joyce into taking on the role of dishwasher stacker-and-emptier and he certainly was not up for scrubbing the pine table. Joyce's only regret in her new position was not being able to see and to mother Byron daily.

The three restaurants built in Havercoyne Grange Hotel were used not only for hotel guests but they were also opened to non-residents and these facilities were available, at vastly inflated prices, for weddings and other lordly banquets.

Barraclough was retained as the restaurant manager for a while but, because of his unsociable drinking habit, he was soon given a redundancy package on which he was able to retire in comfort and to drink himself to death if he wished.

Byron managed to negotiate a redundancy package which somewhat compensated for the loss of his residence at Havercoyne Lodge. And so he kissed goodbye to his surrogate mother, although he promised faithfully to keep in touch. Byron had contemplated selling his story to the press but his indecision had meant that he had missed his opportunity and so his conscience was clear.

Havercoyne Lodge was turned into a self-contained guest suite in its own right where guests could either go the self-catering route or else eat in one of the posh hotel restaurants while having the Lodge accommodation all to themselves. Those who could afford to hire Havercoyne Lodge often ate in one of the restaurants, of course, because they had enough money to afford the luxury of laziness when it came to preparing food and they had, furthermore, developed tastebuds which had become accustomed to rich food.

The Lodge was often used as a honeymoon residence by newly-married couples who had been wed at the hotel and who then wanted to retire for their first night of love without having to travel too far. The hotel premises, of course, managed to secure a marriage licence so that their wedding guests could tie the knot on the premises and the couples were then charged for this bonus facility.

Byron eventually found himself a job on another estate near the south coast and naturally he continued to search for desirable females with whom he could satisfy his sexual proclivities. He visited Havercoyne Stanley occasionally in order to see his children and his ex-wife but he did not venture anywhere near the Havercoyne Grange Hotel. When Byron saw his much-loved Joyce Glemtree, the pair customarily met elsewhere for their reunion.

The farming venture, of course, was given its marching orders because the hotel wanted to boast extensive grounds without the smell and inconvenience of straying farm animals. The stables were, however, retained in order to provide the hotel guests with horse-riding as an inducement to staying at the hotel. The remaining livestock, such as Jonquil, Angel Prancer and their friends, were used for this entertainment which proved quite a draw for the horsey types among the upper classes. One or two stable lads stayed on in order to supervise this activity but most went to work for Ian Manningbury or they simply moved on to other prospects.

Some ex-farmworkers were employed in the hotel as waiting staff. This meant that these employee could now toil in a well-heated establishment and get more money for the privilege. Those redundant farmworkers who preferred an outdoor life, and who could turn their hand to a bit of horticulture, however, were offered jobs as gardeners in order to tend the newly landscaped gardens. A softly undulating golf course was also provided for both residents and non-residents who could afford to pay high annual fees. Grass tennis courts, a bowling green and a croquet lawn had also been built which provided further work for the gardening staff who could maintain these crowd-pulling features to a manicured-lawn standard.

The village gossips on the whole approved of the new hotel because it brought a degree of respectability to Havercoyne Stanley. Nellie and Dave did not see the establishment as a rival because many guests came into the Hunting Horn in order to acquire a fascinating glimpse of local culture.

The Havercoyne Grange Hotel hence became an instant success with the well-oiled guests who came for the novelty value and the notoriety which its former owners had engendered.


## MEDICI'S CELEBRATION

A number of people were making ready for a short break in the south of France.

Maisie Clifton, for instance, was busy packing her suitcase. Maisie had previously assisted the Medici Squadron with the conviction of the former politician James Fetherington, certain members of the pop band Vendetta Ice and the prostitute peddler Lucinda Ketterworth. Maise and Barrington had once had a brief fling in the distant past but they were now the greatest of friends.

The last few months had been a great adventure for Maisie. She had worked as a kitchen assistant under the pseudonym of Nancy Emery on an investigative project for the Medici Squadron. Maisie had fortunately managed to disappear from the police investigation without stirring up any suspicion. She had made her statement to Constable Dougall and she had then exited from the scene.

But Maisie had, at last, come home to her East End apartment where she naturally resumed her inherent cockney accent once back in her own habitat. Maisie had spent some time acclimatising herself to her new environment after her rather fruitful assignment. Not only had Nancy been paid as a member of staff of Havercoyne Grange but she had also been remunerated for her fact-finding mission for the Medici Squadron. Maisie had obtained valuable evidence from Byron Travers by getting to know her mark intimately. She had also gained tasty snippets from the stable lad Ned by flirting outrageously. But now Maisie was making ready to travel to the south of France for a party.

The partnership team, which consisted of Vera Clough (formerly known as Florence Bankover) and Ivan Phelps (alias Aubrey Bankover), were similarly making ready for the journey to France for a short break. The couple had returned to their home in the Yorkshire Dales some while ago with a slightly healthier bank balance than before they had descended on the Old Foundry outside the village of Grayling Wood. Vera and Ivan had worked for the Medici Squadron previously when the corrupt lawyer Piers Wendell had been brought to heel over his unsavoury financial practices.

Vera and Ivan had followed the Gansville-Stubbs trial and were especially interested in the outcome for Carlotta but, now that all the fuss had died down, they could resume their normal life. Ivan, of course, acknowledged his part in Carlotta's downfall and he was pleased that she had got clobbered for being a cold-bloodied murderer.

Jules Axminster worked regularly for the Medici and he had assisted Calendula and Barrington on most of their projects not only because his computer skills were second to none but also because his knowledge of foreign languages, coupled with his ability to blend in with the natives, was extensive. Jules was thus prepared to kiss goodbye to Hakim yet again in order to go on his world travels.

Vivien Logan (who had once been known Ingrid Durbine) had returned to her house in Cumberland where she rejoiced in having been asked to become a member of the Medici Squadron and she had been handsomely rewarded for her efforts. Vivien had recently been recruited to the team when she had met Calendula in London one day and she had not regretted her decision to come aboard. Vivien looked forward to celebrating the success of her role in the latest project.

Felicity Howells (who had been masquerading as Gina Wilcox-Ryan for some time now) was also a member of the Medici Squadron clan and this was her first assignment. Felicity had been recommended to the Medici Squadron by Ronald Turner from the Guardian Media Group. Ronald had been impressed by Felicity's investigative journalistic skills and he had believed that the ex-journalist would prove to be an asset to the team. Felicity was glad to have been involved in the latest project of the Medici Squadron because it was both intellectually challenging and financially rewarding. She came home to her apartment in the London Docklands but she more or less instantly prepared to set off once again.

Maurice Moreau (known to Elsie and Jessie Braithwaite as Rousel Bergère) was now safely ensconced in his home in the west country from whence he had travelled only a short distance in order to wreak havoc on the lives of the Braithwaite sisters. But he had enjoyed some tea and a few biscuits in the process. And now there were more goodies in store.

Maurice had been instrumental in pumping Sandra Mullingar for information about the political scene when the Fetherington-Tranter political duo were run to ground. Maurice had also assisted Sandra to escape permanently from her boorish husband which was one of his good deeds during this encounter.

The safe-cracker Harry Ferguson (known usually as Foxy) was also an asset to the Medici Squadron because he was able to go places where no one else was able to tread. Foxy had assisted Calendula and Barrington on a number of occasions when documentation needed to be enticed into coming out of a coffer which had been proclaimed impenetrable to the rest of the world. Foxy looked forward greatly to the forthcoming festivities.

After each successful project mounted by the Medici Squadron, Calendula and Barrington celebrated by tradition with their friends and accomplices. And this year was no exception. A new mission was usually conducted annually and the party was normally held in the summer in the garden of their domain in the south of France. This year, however, the autumn weather persuaded the couple that an indoor event would be more appropriate.

Calendula and Barrington's pad in the south of France had been extended and refurbished recently and so the couple were able to use their own indoor accommodation for the occasion rather than having to hire a marquee for the garden. Two new rooms had been added to the couple's bijou residence and one of them was a spacious dining room in which a number of guests could be seated around a large and newly acquired dining table.

The usual complement of waiting staff, bar staff and kitchen helpers were commandeered from locals in the village who looked forward each year to the party held by that crazy British couple. The villagers, however, valued the presence of Calendula and Barrington as residents because they were quite free when spending money in the village and, when they had guests, these travellers were accommodated locally which brought in even more currency.

Barrington had prepared a sumptuous repast for the team which comprised the usual five courses in the upper crust French manner. The feast consisted of asparagus fritters, spicy parsnip soup, mutton cassoulet, green salad and a peach and black cherry fool together with a cheese board of local specialities.

Calendula had plied her considerable calligraphic skills to the task of giving each guest a table tent for when they sat down to eat in the dining room. She had also purchased a consignment of picturesque non-drip candles which adorned the dining table and the walls for the occasion. Calendula usually made some bunting which she hung in the marquee but this year she simply draped it over her own paintings. Calendula felt that it was somewhat sacrilegious to adorn her artwork in this way but then, she reflected, it was for a rather special event.

A good time was had by all at the celebration of the Medici Squadron and each member of the team related the fun which he or she had had when snaring the prey. Maisie reported her success with Ned and with the soft-touch Byron. Vivien and Foxy chuckled over their penetration into the inner sanctum of Cuthbert's office and the attic room. Jules reminisced about buying his imaging camera and sneaking it in to the stables with Felicity's help. Maurice entertained the entire company with his stories of the Braithwaite sisters. Vera and Ivan related their experiences with Carlotta and Cuthbert. And, course, Calendula and Barrington contributed tales of their antics with the Gansville-Stubbs family.

Finally the party retired for a good night's rest. Hugs and kisses all round were the order of the night as they all departed. The guests walked home to their respective hotels and guesthouses in high spirits and with an eagerness for their next assignment.

Calendula and Barrington eventually retired to their shower room as usual and spent a night of bliss in their love-nest in the French countryside. They felt that this year's project was worth celebrating in style.

"Are we going retire yet?" suggested Barrington.

"Oh hell, what would we do all day."

"Well, you could paint and I could garden and play the piano."

"We're not that ancient, surely?"

Enough said.

*Actions speak louder than words.*
**English proverb**

# THE HEEL OF ACHILLES

*The Heel of Achilles* is the first novel in the Medici Squadron series which traces the antics of Calendula Fortescue-Bligh and Barrington Flint of the Medici Squadron.

*The lascivious and mendacious politician James Fetherington believes that he can successfully keep his double-dealing securely under wraps when he teams up with Secretary of State Gregory Tranter. James, however, soon falls prey to the insidious and convoluted manoeuvres of Calendula Fortescue-Bligh and Barrington Flint of the Medici Squadron who mischievously worm their way into his psyche.*

.

# VENDETTA VICE

*Vendetta Vice* is the second novel in the Medici Squadron series which traces the antics of Calendula Fortescue-Bligh and Barrington Flint of the Medici Squadron.

*The talented pop-music band, Vendetta Ice, have effortlessly achieved worldwide fame largely due to their sensational lead singer, Rouchuka, but also as a result of the determination of guitarist, Rocker Blaize, and business manager, Gerry Paxton. Certain members of the company, however, undertake some nefarious behind-the-scenes activity which excites the interest of Calendula Fortescue-Bligh and Barrington Flint of the Medici Squadron.*

# SPARRING PARTNERS

*Sparring Partners* is the third novel in the Medici Squadron series which traces the antics of Calendula Fortescue-Bligh and Barrington Flint of the Medici Squadron.

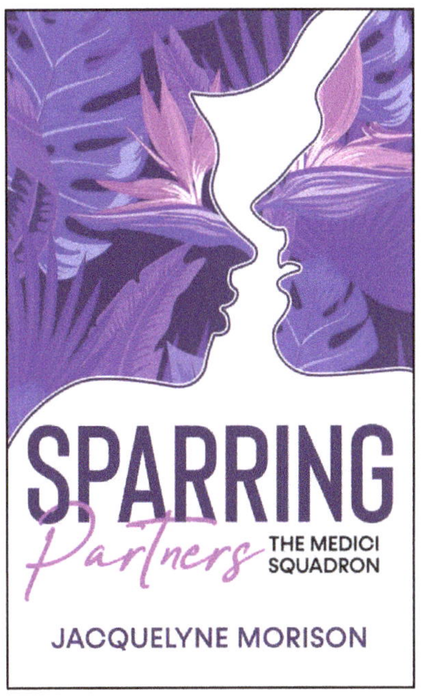


*Lucinda Ketterworth is a self-made entrepreneur who runs the hugely successful Squirrels Bank Hall, a health retreat, which attracts shoals of the idle rich. Lucy also offers an additional service for her guests in order to accommodate their needs fully. Members of the Medici Squadron, headed by Calendula Fortescue-Bligh and Barrington Flint, however, decide to unearth Lucy's salacious extramural activity with a view to exposing her duplicity.*